17

"As well written as its predecessor. . . . The mystery and intrigue feel more compelling, its characters are a bit more interesting, and it's got its share of action . . . it's what *Star Trek* could have been if it was conceived in 2016: dark and incredibly compelling. It would make a hell of a fantastic television series."

—*Lightspeed*

BREACH OF CONTAINMENT

BY ELIZABETH BONESTEEL

CENTRAL CORPS NOVELS

The Cold Between

Remnants of Trust

BREACH

OF

CONTAINMENT

‖‖‖

A CENTRAL CORPS NOVEL

ELIZABETH BONESTEEL

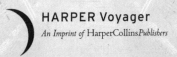

HARPER Voyager
An Imprint of HarperCollins Publishers

This is a work of fiction. Names, characters, places, and incidents are products of the author's imagination or are used fictitiously and are not to be construed as real. Any resemblance to actual events, locales, organizations, or persons, living or dead, is entirely coincidental.

HarperCollins books may be purchased for educational, business, or sales promotional use. For information, please email the Special Markets Department at SPsales@harpercollins.com.

Harper Voyager and design are trademarks of HarperCollins Publishers L.L.C.

FIRST EDITION

Designed by Paula Russell Szafranski

Title page and chapter opener art © medvedsky.k2/Shutterstock, Inc.

Library of Congress Cataloging-in-Publication Data has been applied for.

ISBN 978-0-06-241368-0

17 18 19 20 21   LSC   10 9 8 7 6 5 4 3 2 1

For the ones we carry

BREACH OF CONTAINMENT

PROLOGUE

T minus two days—Yakutsk

H ey, Dallas! Come have a look at this."

Dallas turned and squinted at Martine. On the nearly airless plains, the line between Lena's brightness and the stardusted black of open space was crisp and painful, and the backlighting always fucked with Dallas's eyes. Eye surgery might help, but that took money; and scavengers, even as experienced as Dallas, never made much money. The dealers made the money, and Dallas didn't understand why more didn't take their hoard and escape. After the failure of the Great Terraformer Experiment, they should have been leaving Yakutsk in droves.

Dallas wouldn't leave. Dallas preferred Yakutsk without diffuse sunshine, orbiting Lena with nothing but its thin atmosphere and meager gravity. Dallas had spent thirty years in the domes, and had childhood memories filled with jet-black days clomping across the dusty surface of the moon in weighted boots, finding discarded shipyard parts and the occasional trash—or wreckage—from passing freighters, starships, and even Syndicate raiders, and collecting it like gold. When the terraformers had been activated a year ago, Yakutsk had become alien, and any pleasure Dallas had felt scavenging the surface had dissolved. It seemed so wasteful, forcing a perfectly reasonable moon into a role it had not been born to play. Domes were efficient. Domes took nothing they did not need. Domes made sense.

So many people had been frightened and angry the month before when the terraformers had failed, and they'd had to move back into the old covered cities. The days had grown jet-black and familiar again, and Dallas had been relieved.

The object Martine was looking at was also silhouetted by the big gas giant, and getting close enough to see would require Dallas to drop a large, ungainly fragment of cargo hull. Freighter wreckage was almost always profitable, if mundane; Jamyung, the trader who paid them most promptly, always said he wanted the unusual, but Jamyung bought more standard parts than anything else. Dallas had built an entire career off of spotting the ordinary and scavenging quickly, bringing in three times the salvage of other scavengers and making twice the money. Breaking down this chunk was going to take time, and the afternoon was wearing on. Taking a few moments to placate Martine might cut the day's payoff by quite a bit.

Martine was new. Dallas remembered what it was like to be new, and the sting of realizing you really were in it on your own.

The fragment dropped back to the moon's surface, sinking gently in the low gravity to hit the dusty exterior with a quiet thump. Shuffling in weighted boots, Dallas crept up next to her to look at what she held in her hands.

It was cuboid, about fourteen by fourteen by three centimeters, and entirely unadorned. In the verdant light of the gas giant it was difficult to be clear on the color, but Dallas's unreliable eyes cast it as more or less gray. What kind of reaction was Martine expecting?

"It's a box," Dallas said.

Martine shook her head, disagreeing. Up close, Dallas could see the flash of excitement in her eyes. "It has no seams," she said. "None, Dallas. It's solid."

"Machined."

"Why would someone machine a random box? Besides, Dallas—feel it. It's *warm*."

"Can't feel anything through the suit." *And if it's warm, it's probably radioactive, you damn fool.* But Dallas ran a scan—no ionizing radiation, only thermal. And sure enough, the thing's surface temperature was nearly 37 degrees. *Body temperature.* Out here in the near-vacuum of Yakutsk's frigid, terraformless night. "Must be something inside."

Martine was grinning. "How much do you think he'll give me for it?"

"Jamyung?" Dallas scoffed. "Not fucking enough. He'll tell you it's shit, worth nothing."

"Then I'll keep it."

A vague uneasiness crept up Dallas's spine. "No, Martine. Get rid of it. Or just drop it. Leave it out here." That seemed wrong as well, but it felt important to get Martine away from the thing. Dallas clomped back to the hull fragment and wrenched a chunk of polished alloy off of it, extending it toward her. "Take this. He'll give you good money for this. It'll keep you in retsina for a week."

Of course she wasn't listening. She was tucking the box into her pocket. Dallas shrugged and took the fragment back. "Suit yourself." But Dallas fought a wave of amorphous dread, and no matter how superstitious it seemed, one thought persisted: *That thing shouldn't be coming back into the dome with us. It shouldn't be near people at all.*

A few hours later they took the surface crawler, heavy with the day's haul, back to the dome. Martine was chatty, talking about dinner and the game tournament starting at their pub this weekend. She seemed cheerful, almost manic, and Dallas couldn't stop feeling uneasy. She was herself, only . . . odd.

Jamyung will buy the box, Dallas thought determinedly. *We can go off and have dinner and tomorrow everything will be the same.*

But as it turned out, Dallas's first instinct had been right. "What the fuck is that?" Jamyung asked dismissively, and only Dallas saw the curiosity in the trader's eyes.

"Don't know," Martine said. Dallas had tried to teach her, but she was fucking awful at playing it cool.

"Fifty," Jamyung said.

Even Martine was outraged at that. "Come on! The thing's *hot*. It's got a power source, at least."

Jamyung picked up the box and turned it over in his hand. Dallas could see it better, here inside the dome: it was still that nondescript gray, but it had slightly rounded corners and edges, as if it were designed to be held. Something about the proportions gave it a strange sort of grace. Uncharmed, Jamyung tossed it back to Martine. "If it's a power source, it's a fucking weak one." He paused. "Fifty-five."

"Sixty," Martine said, just as Dallas said "Eighty."

Jamyung pinned Dallas with a look. "You guys unionizing on me?"

One for one. All the scavengers were taught that. You started teaming up, you lost all your business fast. But Dallas had to say something. "You know it's different."

"Different is useless." But then Jamyung sighed, and Dallas thought something in the trader might have softened a little. "All right. Seventy. But that's it, Martine. No more arguing, or you get shit."

Martine kept her hand outstretched as Jamyung counted out seventy in hard currency into her palm. She set the box back down on the trader's desk and waved at Dallas. "See you at the pub," she said, and ran off.

Jamyung had picked up the box again and was turning it over in his hands. He noticed Dallas almost as an afterthought. "You need to stop doing that," Jamyung said. "She's good enough without your help."

"You were ripping her off," Dallas pointed out.

Jamyung tossed the box on his desk and opened a drawer, pulling out Dallas's payment. "Sixty was a decent price."

"Eighty was better."

Jamyung snorted. "You're too smart to be a scavenger, Dallas. You should be on my end."

Dallas wouldn't have Jamyung's job for all the currency in that desk. "I like it out there."

Jamyung shook his head and handed over the money.

"Uninhabitable and freezing, except when we're facing the sun, and then your env suit will melt right into your skin unless you've got one of the fancy ones the military are hoarding."

"Maybe they'll get the terraformers working again."

Jamyung shot him a jaundiced look. "You think anybody's going through all that again, you're a damn fool. The surface is done. You should come in here and work for me."

It wasn't the first time Jamyung had offered, and it wouldn't be the last time Dallas would refuse. "Bird in the hand," Dallas said, and took the money.

"Suit yourself," Jamyung said. "Go beat Martine at whatever bullshit game she's hauled off the stream this week. And fuck, Dallas, stop telling her what her shit is worth. She learns on her own or she's no good to me."

"Okay." Dallas turned to the door, then stopped. "What are you going to do with it?"

Jamyung's eyebrows shot up. "What do you care?" And then his expression grew cunning. "You got a buyer?"

"Nope. Just curious." Dallas lifted a hand. "See you tomorrow."

But all the way to the pub, currency clanking and waiting to be spent, Dallas thought about that box lying on Jamyung's desk, and couldn't shake the feeling that, defunct terraformers or not, the days on Yakutsk were never going to be familiar again.

PART I

CHAPTER 1

BUDAPEST

Elena ran in patient circles around the perimeter of *Budapest*'s largest storage bay, the space around her filled with stacked crates towering like massive city blocks. The bay would be clear in a few hours, after they dropped off the seed stock and dried roots on Yakutsk, but even then there would be little room for exercise beyond running. A freighter, she had learned over the last year, wasn't like a starship. Starships were designed for sustaining large crews over long-term missions, and generally sported a fair number of human-centric spaces. Freighters were rarely out longer than six weeks, their crews rarely larger than ten people. Living space was not prioritized. All of *Budapest*'s crew quarters were small—if Bear Savosky, *Budapest*'s captain, operated with ten crew instead of six, she would have had to share—and there was no separate gym space.

Early on in *Budapest*'s venerable life, Bear had started packing cargo to leave a two-meter gap around the edges of the storage bay. Back when she had first met the freighter

captain, when she was just sixteen and awed by *any* inter-
stellar vehicle, even this inelegant, utilitarian cargo ship, she
had remarked on it. "It was either make space for running,"
he had told her, "or set the gravity to one-point-two so people can get some exercise walking across the kitchen. The
last thing you want after a long shipping run is to get home
and find out none of your clothes fit you anymore."

Elena had been young, her metabolism still half child, and
the statement had confused her. Now, at nearly thirty-five,
she was grateful for his practicality.

Arin lapped her for the third time, and she smiled. Bear
and Yuri's adopted son was nineteen. He was also taller
than she was, and so much more energetic; but he had no
patience for a marathon. She watched him disappear around
the corner, his heavy footfalls echoing around the cargo and
off the tall ceiling, and resisted the urge to catch up with
him. Controlling her natural competitiveness had been one
of her hardest lessons at the Academy, but she had learned
to pick a pace and stick with it, even if it was slow. The
sprints she always lost, but she had done well over long distances. She had even won a few endurance runs.

But when it came down to it, she preferred dance to running. Here on *Budapest,* where there was no room, she
missed it. With dance, time went more quickly; when there
was music, it was so much easier to let her mind drift. She
would be twelve weeks without dancing, out to Yakutsk and
back. Running was an efficient method of exercise, but it
left her restless and bored. She needed more than the mundane rhythm of her feet against the floor, and her heartbeat
in her ears. She needed more than *monotony.*

On top of that . . . running reminded her of *Galileo,* and of Greg. Always Greg. For so many years he had been the anchor of her routine, from breakfast to duty to the gym. She used to watch him run, kilometer after kilometer, sometimes more than twenty in a day. For years she had wondered what he was running from. She had eventually concluded that he wasn't trying to escape anything specific; he just felt the need to run. Movement. Forward. *Anywhere but here.*

A broken man. She had no good reason for missing him.

Arin came around again. "Slow old woman," he said to her as he passed, and she laughed, taking off after him. She caught up, and he ran faster; his long legs brought him past her again, but not as far as he might have wanted. When they reached the inner door, he dropped to a walk, breathing heavily. In sympathy, she stopped as well.

"'Slow'?" she objected.

"I beat you, didn't I?" He bent down to scratch the head of the sturdy orange tabby cat seated by the door. Mehitabel, *Budapest*'s standoffish and ubiquitous mascot, twitched her ears irritably and continued washing her face.

"Only because I stopped." Elena threw a towel at him.

"I'll make sure you catch up with me next time." He grinned at her, and blushed, and she didn't quite know what to make of it. She had never seen him flirt with anyone, regardless of sex. Even if she had—she was nearly old enough to be his mother. She knew he was fond of her, but it had never felt like a crush.

Although . . . She thought again of Greg. *Heaven knows I've never been particularly good at picking up on that sort of thing.*

She had not spoken with Greg in nearly a year. She had spent six months on the CCSS *Kovalevsky* after the Admiralty transferred her off of *Galileo,* and there they had talked frequently; but when she had decided to resign from the Corps, she had told him nothing in advance. Only Jessica Lockwood—Greg's second-in-command and Elena's friend—had known what Elena was going to do, and she had, after some pleading on Elena's part, kept it to herself.

"He's going to hit the ceiling," Jessica had warned.

"Then the Admiralty will know he had nothing to do with it."

In her most honest moments, Elena wasn't entirely sure that protectiveness was the only reason she hadn't wanted to tell Greg ahead of time. She had been increasingly careful in what she shared with him, sticking mostly with conveying any intelligence she had picked up from her crewmates on *Kovalevsky.* She would ask after *Galileo* and all of the people she loved. She would ask after him, and his father and his sister back on Earth, and tell him only good things about *Kovalevsky* and Captain Mirov.

Telling him the truth—that being in the Corps but not being on *Galileo* was like flaying her skin open every single day—would have led to a conversation she did not want to have. Returning to *Galileo* was not an option. In Greg's early career, he might have had the clout to swing it, but he'd lost any influence he had on the other side of a wormhole.

Becoming a civilian, she had reasoned, would give her different intelligence channels from the ones Greg and Jessica would find through the Corps. And it would be less of a daily reminder of having left behind everything and everyone, outside of her blood family, that had ever meant anything to her.

Elena kept her eyes on the cat. Mehitabel was still not reacting to Arin's ministrations, but Elena was certain she was beginning to hear the quiet rumble of a purr. Mehitabel did not care much for Elena—possibly, Elena had to admit, because most of their interactions involved Elena chasing the cat out of the engine room—but the animal was consistently and quietly affectionate with Arin, and Elena couldn't fault her for that. "Maybe next time," Elena remarked, "I won't let you get ahead in the first place."

Arin laughed, and Elena's comm chimed. She reached behind her ear to acknowledge. "Morning, Yuri," she said. "What's up?"

Yuri was *Budapest*'s comms officer, second-in-command, and head mechanic. He was also nominally Elena's superior officer; but *Budapest* had the reflexive informality of all civilian organizations, and she had learned—most of the time—to roll with it.

"You've got an incoming comm," Yuri said, and something in his voice made her ears perk up.

"Someone I know?"

"Don't know. A parts trader on Yakutsk, called Jamyung. Bear knows him, a little—we've dealt with him before, but not for a couple of years."

Elena frowned. She did know Jamyung—she knew most of the traders in the sector, having bought from nearly all of them when she was with the Corps. Like many salvage traders, he had some dubious ethical lines, but her dealings with him had always been straightforward. If he had what she needed, he charged a fair price, and she always got exactly what he'd represented. In return, she'd turned something of a blind eye to the less legal aspects of his business.

"Why does he want to talk to me?" she asked.

"He wouldn't tell me. He sounds a little . . . agitated." Yuri paused. "You want me to cut him off?"

It had been years since she had spoken with Jamyung. She couldn't imagine why he wanted to talk to her, never mind how he had tracked her down once he realized she wasn't in the Corps anymore. *At least it's not monotony,* she thought. "That's all right," she said. "Put him through."

She could picture the expression on Yuri's face, but he completed the connection.

"Is that you?"

She recognized Jamyung's voice: flatly accented Standard, his vowels clipped, his voice full and baritone despite the fact that in person he was slight, like most of the natives on Yakutsk. Yuri was right: he did sound agitated, and out of breath, as if he had been running before he commed her.

"Who else would it be?" she asked.

He huffed a breath in her ear. "Fuck me, Shaw, do you know how long it took me to find you? You left the fucking Corps, and nobody at that goddamned Admiralty of yours would tell me where you were. What the fuck?"

"If I'd known you were looking I'd have sent up a flare." There would have been no reason for the Admiralty to help him, even if they could have. She used to be certain her former commanders—or at least Shadow Ops, their secret intelligence division—had kept track of her location, even after she resigned. At this point, though, she was inclined to believe she didn't matter to them anymore. *None of which is his fault.* "Did you call me to yell, Jamyung?"

"No. No, no, no." Another huff. "Not yell. But I need a favor."

"Why me?"

"Because you're a straight shooter," he said. "These other Central motherfuckers, you can't trust them. And the freighter jocks—they haggle over shit like they're fucking royalty, like I don't know I'm the only one in six systems with that fucking field regulator they need to keep from blowing themselves to bits. Condescending assholes."

She unraveled that. "You're asking for a favor because you trust me."

"Yes. Yes. Because they'll just tell me I'm fucking nuts, and I need a fucking favor, Shaw." He was beginning to sound frightened. "You don't know. Lately, here, it's been—shit." *Huff.* "I am fucked, we are all fucked, and I need a favor, and I have to get rid of this thing."

"Calm down." She glanced at Arin, who had straightened, ignoring the cat, eyes on Elena. She gave him a reassuring smile, then stepped away, rounding the shipping cartons for some privacy. "Why are you fucked? What thing? Start from the beginning."

"Okay. Okay. Okay." *Huff.* "So you know it's been fucked here, dome-wise, since the Great Terraformer Experiment went to hell. Fucking politicians killing each other instead of fucking doing something to help people. Same old shit my whole fucking life, because those assholes are fucking bored or something, I don't know. Never made any fucking sense to me. And yeah, I make money off of it, usually, and why do I care if some lying dumbass governor loses some air?"

Jamyung was big on storytelling when he was trying to sell something, but he wasn't sounding like he had parts to move. "So it's fucked there . . . and you don't care?"

"Yes. *No.* Because it's not just the usual bullshit this time. This time people keep talking about nukes. Asking me if I can get them, then getting really fucking you-didn't-hear-us-ask when I tell them I can't."

Nukes. On a domed colony. *Shit.* "Is this a reliable rumor, or just the usual mine-is-bigger crap?"

"Reliable. Solid. They keep naming a Syndicate tribe: Ailmont. They're the real deal."

"I'm not Corps anymore," she told him. "I can't stop the Syndicates from selling their own cargo."

"Yeah, but now they've been fucking with me, and they keep coming back, and fuck it, Shaw, I can't give them this thing."

She parsed that. "Wait. You have something somebody is after?"

"Do you know what this fucking thing can do? I can't sell it to them!"

She closed her eyes. "From the beginning. What thing?"

Huff. "Okay. Okay. I have this scavenger. *Had* this scavenger. Few days back, she brings me this thing she found on the surface. No idea what it is, but it's warm, and it's not radiating fucking poison, so she thought it must be something useful. Next day—a pack of those assholes from Baikul fucking *vacates* her. A good fucking scout, too, and now she's a fucking frozen dessert."

Vacated. Local slang for exposing someone on the moon's airless surface. Elena gave an involuntary shiver. "Could be unrelated."

"And then," he went on, as if she'd said nothing, "I get an offer from some off-world trader I've never heard of to buy out my stock. A generous offer. A *stupid* generous offer, you know? Only it comes with a side order of *take it or we'll fucking kill you and take your shit anyway.*"

She frowned. "They were that explicit?"

"Of course not! But it was clear. And it's this thing, Shaw. This fucking thing. I know it is."

"Then why not just give it to them?"

"Here's the thing." *Huff.* "I sell shit. I've always sold shit. Your shit, their shit, I don't care. I have it, you need it, I'm taking your money, no questions asked. But . . . this *thing*, Shaw. I don't know what the fuck it is, but I don't want it in the hands of the *we'll fucking kill you anyway* crowd."

"Why not?" Ethics seemed entirely out of character for Jamyung. "What is it?"

"I just told you! I don't know what the fuck it is. But . . ." She heard him swallow. "It talked to me, Shaw. It got into my head and fucking talked to me and I'd nuke it if I could, but with my luck it's built to survive that."

"Hang on." She sorted through everything he'd said. If the conflict on Yakutsk was finally—after centuries of low-level squabbling—escalating into a nuclear conflict, he was right to be panicked. Nukes could destroy domes with alarming efficiency. Everything else sounded like unrelated events strung into some loosely related cause-and-effect chain generated by his anxiety.

Except the object.

"How did it talk to you? Does it have a comms interface?"

"It has *no* interface. It's a fucking *box*. Nothing on the surface, no lights, no connectors, no nothing. Only it's warm. Martine said it was warm when she found it, out on the surface in the fucking vacuum."

She had to ask. "What did it say?"

"It said *Get the fuck off Yakutsk, Jamyung.* Smartest fucking box I've ever found. I need airlift, Shaw. I need someone to get me off this fucking rock before they shove me outside as well. You're my last hope here."

There was the drop. The story of the object was likely a shaggy-dog tale couching his request . . . but she had known him a long time, and despite a business model that might have pushed him to do it, he had never lied to her.

She owed the truth to him in return . . . but she didn't think he'd want to hear it. Nukes on Yakutsk meant Bear would have to cancel the whole drop. *Budapest* was staffed with civilian freighter jocks who'd have no idea how to handle a nuclear zone, and she couldn't protect them all on her own.

"I can't tell you when we're going to get there," she said, with a pang of guilt at the prevarication. "But *Galileo* is close. Less than four hours, I think. Tell them we talked. They'll take you."

"After all this, you're shucking me off on the fucking Corps?"

"Best I can offer."

"Okay. Okay. Okay." He sounded calmer. "Four hours? Okay. But this thing, Shaw. Four hours, and they're after me, I know it."

"Hide it then," she told him.

"Where?"

"Do I know your workshop? Someplace nobody else knows about."

"There isn't—" He broke off. "Good. Yes. Good. Let them search. They won't find it. Thanks, Shaw. Four hours?"

"Four hours, Jamyung." She hoped *Galileo* would not be delayed. And that they'd be willing to offer help to a paranoid small-time parts trader.

Huff. "Thank you. Thank you. Four hours." He disconnected.

She leaned against a storage carton just as Arin crept hesitantly around the corner. He had picked up the cat, who blinked at Elena with bored green eyes. "Everything okay?" Arin asked.

No, she thought. She turned and gave him an absent smile. "For now," she said, not wanting to alarm him. "But I've got to talk to Bear."

Bear Savosky was an enormous man. Half again larger than anyone else Elena had ever met, he had broad shoulders, no neck to speak of, and a voice that carried even when he whispered. He had a severe jaw, shrewd eyes, and an entirely bald head covered in elaborate tattoos, nearly invisible against his night-dark skin. She had known him nearly nineteen years, and over all that time she had seen both his temper and his pragmatism. She had always found him to be consistent and fair.

But she had learned, after six weeks and more culture clashes than she could count, that there were things about him she was never going to understand.

The rest of the crew sat around her at the large common-area table, listening to her relate her conversation with Jamyung. She had expected a sensible response to the nuclear rumors, including a discussion about rescheduling the drop after the situation on Yakutsk had cooled down. Instead, when she finished, they all looked at Bear, awaiting his assessment. For Bear's part, he was watching Elena, his dark eyes narrowed thoughtfully.

"I've heard these rumors already," he told them.

She gaped at him. "Then why are we still headed there?"

"Because," he said, straightening, "nobody has actually seen any bombs. I spoke to one shop that ordered a few just to see what would show up, and they've had nothing but delays and excuses since then."

"So this is some governmental fear tactic." This came from Naina Chudasama, the ship's accountant, and the one Elena would have expected to be the most likely to want to leave the entire mission behind.

"That'd be my guess," Bear told her. "But Elena's right: we don't know, and if I'm guessing wrong, the downside is pretty big." He leaned back in his chair. "What do you all think?"

Good God, Elena thought, *he's letting them vote.* She fought to sit still, hands on her lap under the table, where nobody could see her fists clenching.

"I think we should go," Arin said.

Bear shot him a look. "Some of us will be staying in orbit," he said. "And that means you."

"But—"

"Not now, Arin," Bear said flatly.

Arin slumped back in his chair, glowering. Elena felt a wave of sympathy for him, but she was relieved. At least Bear had heeded her enough to protect some of them.

Naina glanced at Arin, then turned back to Bear. "Whoever goes," she said, "I agree. We need to complete this delivery. The contract only calls for us to have someone on Yakutsk accept the cargo on the record. Once we have that, the funds are released. What happens afterward makes no difference to us."

"It's a quick trip, then," said Yuri. "We make the drop, get some bureaucrat to stamp the paperwork, and we're gone."

"Which is fine," Elena put in, "until someone blows a big fucking hole in the dome."

Yuri, usually so sensible, gave her a resigned smile. "If we worried about eventualities," he told her, "we'd never deliver anything."

Eventualities. She opened her mouth, but Bear quelled her with a look. "Chi?"

Elena knew she would get no help from the supply officer. Chiedza, taciturn and standoffish, could usually be counted on for pragmatism, but Elena, who had been watching the woman throughout their trip, had come to believe Chiedza's background involved activities less aboveboard than cargo delivery. Chi wasn't going to turn down a sale for what Bear apparently considered an imaginary risk.

"This is rumor," Chi said dismissively. "We can't call a delivery over a rumor."

Bear was silent for a moment, and Elena beamed desperate thoughts in his direction. *You're the captain of this ship.*

Civilian freighter or no, you're in charge here. Overrule them. Tell them no. Why the fuck did you ask them to begin with? "Nai," he asked, "how much could we get on the secondary market if we skipped this drop? Theoretically."

Naina was frowning in concentration. Elena, who was no slouch with numbers, was continually amazed at how quickly Nai could do calculations in her head. "We couldn't make it up with what we're carrying now," she said. "We could resell some of it, but not enough." She looked at Bear. "Eighteen thousand decs, three weeks minimum, and that's if we find a buyer for the surplus right away."

Elena could tell from everyone's posture, even Arin's, that her argument was lost.

She did, in the end, get a compromise from Bear: only three of them would head down to the moon's surface. Elena and Chiedza would each pilot a cargo shuttle, and Bear would accompany them to deal with the financial validations. "The paper pushers will keep us there for a while," he said, "but it shouldn't be more than a couple of hours. Then we can get out of there, and they can buy nukes from whoever the fuck they want."

They all stood to leave. Arin stalked out first, not looking at her, and her sympathy was tempered by annoyance. Even if they'd needed the extra hands—which they didn't—after the way Bear had chewed her out over the last time she had brought the kid along on a drop, she couldn't imagine why Arin would think she'd champion his participation. The others drifted away until only Naina was left, her eyes on the door Arin had just passed through.

"He'll get over it," Naina said, half to herself.

"I hope," Elena said, "what he has to get over is a boring op he was lucky to miss."

Naina met Elena's eyes. She was a good deal older than Elena, perhaps close to Elena's mother's age, round and soft in a way so many civilians were. She was also relaxed and good-natured with a tendency to smile, and Elena had felt less uncomfortable with her than most of the people she'd had to deal with since she left the Corps. After six weeks, Elena was beginning to think of Naina as a real friend, although they had never shared anything deeply personal. Still, it was nice to have someone who would sit with her and chat about ordinary things, instead of frowning at her and reminding her, all the time, how little she knew about the universe outside the Corps.

Naina's dark eyes were gentle, and held a bit of that maternal kindness that Elena would often see in people trying to explain things they thought she should already understand. "You know, Elena," Naina said conversationally, "you need to stop treating us like we're helpless just because we're not Corps."

Well, that was entirely unfair. "I don't think you're helpless," Elena protested. "I just . . . I don't understand the choices you make."

"Because you think, for us, it's about money. *Only* about money."

"No. Not *only*. I just—" *I think your materialism is going to get us all killed.* "I think you've never dealt with a colony going to hell before. And yeah, I think risking your lives over money is fucking stupid. That's my *opinion*, Nai. It's not a put-down."

But it was, and she knew it.

"I don't think you mean it that way." Nai's voice had gone gentle, as if she were speaking to a child. "But you act like you're the only one who's ever been out here."

"Respectfully, Nai, you're an *accountant*."

"I am. I'm an accountant who's far from home, and who wants to get paid so I don't have to do that so much anymore." She smiled. "My sister's having a baby next month, did I tell you? A girl. My mother is thrilled. And my sister could use an extra pair of hands."

"Nai, I understand *why* people want the money. I just don't get the urgency."

"Don't you?" Nai cocked her head to one side. "You know what happened on Mundargi all those years ago."

Elena nodded. She had read about it; it had been a case study at Central Military Academy. "That was before I was born."

"It was not before I was born," Nai told her. "And it was not something I can forget, or leave behind. You have a good heart, I know. But it's not for you to defend us all against the darkness. Even if you could—it's not something we would choose for you to do. We choose, for ourselves, with our eyes open, with as much knowledge as you do."

"It's *one shipment*, Nai." Elena felt like the woman wasn't listening. "And none of that is worth dying for."

"And yet *you're* going down to the surface."

"Well of course I am. It's my job."

"And you're the only one allowed that conceit?"

"No!" She closed her eyes. "Nai, this was my whole career, this kind of bullshit. Not historical horrors that none of us can go back and fix, but this: people wanting to kill each other, and perfectly willing to take bystanders with them. I'm going down because I'm the best qualified to make sure the fewest people get killed."

"And Chi is the best qualified to transfer the shipment, and Bear's the best qualified to make sure we get our money. We're not ignorant, and we're not helpless. You're not the only one who's been in danger, and you're not the only one who's willing to take risks." She reached out and laid a hand on Elena's arm. "We're not in need of rescue. And none of us are going to turn our backs on our families because things are tense on Yakutsk."

"It's not *tense*, Nai. If they're really talking about nuking each other—"

"Do you think those rumors are true?" The question was a serious one.

Elena opened her mouth to equivocate, then sighed and nodded. "I know what Bear said, and I know it doesn't add up. But if it's not nukes, it's something. Jamyung—he's an odd one, but he doesn't panic for no reason. Something has genuinely spooked him. We need to be careful. We *need* to be afraid, or we'll die."

And as Elena looked into her friend's dark eyes, she realized Nai *was* afraid. Nai believed her, even if Bear didn't. Nai understood the risks, and she knew they might all die in the pursuit of this delivery.

And none of that deterred her at all.

"I'm glad you're doing the flying then," Nai told her. She

squeezed Elena's arm briefly before she let go. "And I'm glad Bear is leaving Arin up here."

"I don't know that he'll be any safer," Elena told her, and Nai's comforting smile turned sad.

"Nowhere is safe, Elena. Or didn't you know?"

CHAPTER 2

GALILEO

'm sorry to bother you, sir," Lieutenant Samaras said. "I have *Meridia* for you. Captain Taras."

Captain Greg Foster of the CCSS *Galileo* dropped to a brisk walk, following the curve of the ship's gymnasium track around the corner. "She say why she was comming?"

"No, sir. But . . . she was very cheerful, sir."

Shit. Taras was an acutely intelligent, observant woman, with an oversized personality she knew exactly how to wield. If she had been expansive with Samaras, that meant she was discouraging him from asking questions. Which almost certainly meant something was up. "Thanks for the warning, Lieutenant," he said. "Put her through."

Greg stopped by the door to the locker room, where he had left a towel and a flask of water. Two of his officers passed him running the other way, nodding a greeting; Greg, in self-defense, had long since suspended rules around saluting in both the gym and the ship's pub. He nodded in return, and rubbed the towel over his face. He was sweatier than he had thought.

Taras's voice was in his ear. "Captain Foster. Have I commed at an inopportune time?"

Not cheerful with him—but more interestingly, not, as Taras usually was, painfully loud. Something *was* wrong. "Not at all, Captain Taras. Is there something we can help with?"

Another pause. "I don't know, to be honest, Captain. I am . . . uneasy, and I am hoping that you can provide an alternate perspective."

All the tension he had just run off returned. "Is this about Yakutsk?"

"Nothing so immediate, Captain. I have heard nothing from Yakutsk since our earlier meeting concluded."

From the first news of Yakutsk's terraformer failure, Central Gov had coordinated support and diplomatic efforts with PSI, the informal confederation of generation ships to which *Meridia* belonged. Both Greg and Gov's assigned diplomat had been in touch with Captain Taras daily, discussing issues and strategies, remaining in contact with the Yakutsk dome governments to reassure them that help was coming. Not that the reassurance had made a difference; Yakutsk, stuck with limited food stores and an abruptly space-limited population, was falling prey to old political squabbles and civic unrest. The previous week, the entire Baikul government—six administrators and the governor—had "mysteriously" ended up outside the dome without environmental suits, and a new government had been installed in their place. Worse, rumors had been surfacing for days about a developing black market for pocket nuclear devices—the endgame of more colonies than Greg liked to remember.

Before he had embarked on his run, Greg had spent some time persuading the governments of both Baikul and Smolensk to refrain from any violent coups for a while. He was not confident he had succeeded.

Meridia was a day behind *Galileo,* and Greg had found himself wishing frequently that the PSI ship, with her separate armaments and different rules about interference, was closer. But it seemed, for now, Yakutsk was not Taras's issue.

"Captain Foster. You are aware of *Chryse,* are you not?"

Chryse was the last thing Greg would have expected Taras to bring up with a Central Corps starship captain. And that, somehow, was more unsettling to him than nukes on Yakutsk.

Chryse was *Meridia*'s sister ship, and was known throughout the Six Sectors as the most insular, least communicative PSI ship currently in service. Greg himself, patrolling the same sector as *Chryse,* had only spoken with them twice in his entire career. They had been polite enough, and scrupulously efficient, but it seemed clear that *Chryse* preferred their relationship with Central to be distant. "Of course, Captain," he told Taras, struggling to remember *Chryse*'s current location. "She's out by the Third Sector border right now, isn't she?"

"Actually, Captain, she is headed for Yakutsk."

"As support?"

"One might presume that." Greg detected sarcasm. "But we did not ask for support. More curiously, she's sent us her first officer, Commander Ilyana, whom we also did not ask for, ahead in her own shuttle. Ilyana is in the field, half a day ahead of *Chryse,* and answers every attempt at contact with nothing but an automated telemetry ping verifying that her mission status is green."

It hadn't occurred to him that *Chryse* might be as secretive with her sister ship as she was with Central. "Have you contacted Captain Bayandi directly?"

"Oh, certainly."

"And he hasn't explained any of this?"

"Bayandi," she said archly, "does not explain, Captain Foster. Bayandi is extremely pleasant at all times. He remembers my birthday, and the birthdays of all of my officers, and never fails to ask after my health. But he is evasive like no one I have ever met, and I include all of your Corps officers on that list."

Bayandi, Greg recalled, had been *Chryse*'s captain longer than Greg had been alive. "Respectfully, Captain Taras—do you think he may just be getting old?"

"I cannot know." She sounded frustrated. "I have been focusing on Yakutsk, and to have *Chryse* cheerfully deciding to participate without coordinating with us first—I am perhaps more tense than I ought to be. And . . ." She paused. "You understand, Captain, that it is not my instinct to trust the Corps with this information. You, however, are an individual, and I have always found you to be honorable."

He had tensed as soon as she said *and*. "What's happened, Captain?"

He heard a puff of air, as if she were preparing herself

for an ordeal. "Four months ago, *Chryse* went dark for four days. We thought, at first, that they were hit by that same loopback virus that's been flitting around. The one that hit you a few years back. But when they came back on line, they said nothing. We had to comm them to ask what had happened, and all we got was Commander Ilyana telling us politely that everything was fine."

Four months. "You think this may be related to the equipment failures."

Four months ago, the colony of Odisha had lost one of their polar terraformers. There had been a freighter in the area with replacement parts, and a number of PSI ships able to provide food and staples until the pole was stabilized, but as soon as Greg saw the hardware report on the equipment he knew what had happened. Ellis Systems, the manufacturer of the faulty part, had apologized and offered to provide a full replacement system at a substantial discount, and all was made well. But most people were unaware that Ellis, known galaxy-wide for commercial environmental equipment, was also developing weapons.

That had been the moment Greg had realized how far his own stature within the Corps had fallen. Despite applying all of his considerable powers of persuasion—despite knowing there were people within the Admiralty who knew as well as he did that Ellis was capable of using micro terraformer failures as a type of weaponry—he could not convince his chain of command to suggest to Odisha that they avoid anything manufactured by Ellis. It had been on Odisha that he and Captain Taras had forged something of a personal alliance:

she knew, via her PSI channels, what Ellis had been up to, and she told him that the Fourth Sector PSI ships would keep an eye on Odisha's new terraformer.

That was almost enough for Greg to forget how helpless he had become.

Since Odisha, there had been thirty-seven suspicious equipment failures that Greg knew of, some of which were catastrophic. *Galileo* had been deployed to respond to four-teen of them. But only twelve cases had provided enough data to prove—or suggest strongly—that Ellis-specific equipment was involved.

Privately, Greg had no doubt it was all of them.

"Impossible not to be suspicious," Captain Taras agreed. "*Chryse* was at Odisha a few weeks before the polar issue. It's possible she picked something up there, either that ugly loopback virus or some other malicious system worm. All I know is that they're being entirely themselves and telling me nothing, and I'm rather tired of it. Would you be willing to talk to them, Captain? It would certainly send a different message."

Greg was not entirely sure how to interpret that. "You want me to threaten them?"

Taras laughed. "Oh, goodness, Captain Foster. *Chryse* wouldn't see you as a threat. But if you can get them to talk to you—it might clarify for them that they're a bit farther off-grid than usual, and might want to take a little time to catch the rest of us up."

He set aside, for a moment, the potentially troublesome thought that *Chryse* wouldn't see *Galileo* as a threat. "So you'd like me to ask them if they need help, and let them know you're concerned, and maybe see if I can get them to contact you with more details?"

"It sounds like I'm asking you to mediate a family squabble, doesn't it, Captain?"

He did not believe Taras would involve him in something she thought was that petty. "I'm happy to be helpful, if I can, Captain Taras. I'll let you know what *Chryse* says."

"Thank you, Captain Foster." And she sounded as relieved as he had ever heard her.

Later, Greg stood under the shower, organizing his thoughts, letting the water pummel the muscles in his neck. He couldn't avoid putting the conversation into his official report; her comm would be on record already, and his command chain would want to know what she had said. But because it was neither dangerous nor related to *Galileo's* current mission, he was not obligated to contact the Admiralty immediately. Regardless of his diminished influence, one thing about the Admiralty remained consistent: it paid to stay free of the sticky tendrils of Corps bureaucracy as long as possible. If the entire issue came down to nothing but a single conversation with a PSI ship, they wouldn't be interested anyway.

Even though it's Chryse?

Chryse, he had to admit, was different. *Chryse* was enigmatic on an unprecedented level. Many Corps ships had interacted with *Chryse's* officers, but information exchanges were almost nonexistent. Greg had believed on some level it was because *Meridia* was so uncharacteristically open, and *Chryse* was going for balance. But the Corps abhorred opacity in anyone but themselves, and in PSI specifically. Even the most benign information on *Chryse* would be treated as important intel.

He rinsed off rapidly. "*Galileo,* how far are we from Yakutsk?"

"Three hours."

He frowned. "How long was I running?"

"Two hours, four minutes."

No wonder I ache. He shut off the water and reached for his clothes.

His friends often accused him of running to escape, to avoid the difficult things in his life; but in reality he couldn't remember a time in his life when he didn't run. His earliest memories were of sunrises by the beach, running along the ocean with his mother, his feet getting bogged down in the wet sand. She, with her longer legs, would run ahead, and then loop around to catch him from behind, sometimes sweeping him off his feet, sometimes diving into the ocean and holding out her arms, daring him to jump in after her.

But he didn't, not often. Greg didn't like to swim. Greg liked to run. And as often as he ran to stop thinking, he ran to ruminate, to have a space where he could turn everything over in his head when nobody would interrupt him or ask him to make a decision. Running allowed him to be alone, and these days, the moments in which he was alone were the only ones when he did not feel loneliness.

He wondered, now and then, if he should not be so used to loneliness.

He had just discarded his towel after one final pass over his short-cropped black hair when footsteps intruded on his thoughts. He looked up to find Gov's assigned diplomat:

Admiral Josiah Herrod, retired, who nodded when Greg caught his eye. "Good evening, Captain."

"Good evening, Admiral." Herrod, despite his nearly eighty years, was barrel-chested, sturdy, and imposing— and, Greg reflected, possibly the only person on board *Galileo* lonelier than Greg was himself. That was not because nobody knew Herrod, of course. It was because they knew him quite well—and thoroughly disliked him.

But nobody disliked him as thoroughly as Greg.

"Did it help?" Herrod asked him. "The running?"

Greg had, at first, assumed that Herrod's assignment to the mission on Yakutsk was a thinly veiled threat. Before his retirement, Herrod had not only been highly placed within the Admiralty, but had been part of the Admiralty's unofficial intelligence unit, Shadow Ops. Greg had learned years ago that Shadow Ops sometimes utilized methods that Greg—and, he hoped, most people with any soul at all— found reprehensible. He had never been clear as to whether or not Herrod condoned all of their methods, and the admiral had indeed helped *Galileo* from time to time; but he had also been part of the committee that had taken Greg's chief of engineering from him, and Greg was disinclined to forgive.

But he had learned over the weeks that the man had some diplomatic skill, and Greg had grudgingly concluded that there was a good possibility he had been assigned because he was the best person for the job. In fact, he had more than once wondered why Herrod had not been sent to the Fifth Sector, where Central's relationship with the wealthy Olam Colony was becoming increasingly strained.

But Herrod's combination of tact and bluntness had been keeping Yakutsk's governors at the table longer than Greg would have thought possible. And for the sake of the mission, Greg could be satisfied with the knowledge that Herrod knew exactly why—and how much—Greg blamed him for everything that had happened over the last eighteen months.

"It did, thank you," Greg lied.

Herrod pulled off his jacket and hung it on the wall. It was black, like an Admiralty uniform, but unadorned with piping of any kind. On Herrod, any jacket would look like a uniform. "Used to run," the old man offered. "Found it inefficient. Too much time in my own head." He cocked an eye at Greg. "Suppose that's why you like it."

"Suppose so." Greg shifted; he was no good at small talk, even with people he liked. "If you'll excuse me, sir."

Herrod's dark eyes grew amused. "I'm not an officer anymore," he pointed out. "Your time is your own." But he relented with a nod. "I'll see you in a few hours, Captain Foster."

Greg headed for his office, annoyed, feeling he had been bested in a way he did not understand.

CHAPTER 3

YAKUTSK

In the years when *Galileo* patrolled the Fourth Sector, Elena
had been on Yakutsk more than two dozen times. Baikul,
the dome facing the luminous green gas giant Lena, attracted
some light tourism—she suspected the doomed terraformer
project had been their idea—but she had spent all her time in
Smolensk, the dome facing the stars. Smolensk was service-
able and unadorned, without hotels or restaurants oriented
to off-worlders, but Elena had always enjoyed it. There was
an efficiency to the place and its people, a cheerful *fuck you*
aimed at anyone who expected any non-transactional deference. Elena had received no respect for her Corps contacts,
but her knowledge of machinery and her straightforward
negotiation for the parts she needed had made her solid professional allies, if not friends.

She had seen some vid of the moon's temporarily terra-
formed surface. It had been beautiful: heavy on low-growing
flowers and rudimentary crops, with habitats built by the
wary colonists slowly beginning to spread. The atmosphere,

produced by the terraformers and secured by an artificial gravity field designed to keep the solar winds from sweeping it out to space, had turned the sky a lilac-tinged blue, touched here and there with carefully regulated rain clouds. It had the look of a beginning, a seedling, the start of something that might someday become more substantial. Early days on many planets were beautiful and full of promise, but Elena had seen enough terraformed worlds to have a sense of Yakutsk's fragility.

When the terraformers had failed, she had spoken with Jessica. They both agreed it was most likely Ellis Systems behind the catastrophe. But in truth, she would not have been surprised to find it a simple equipment overload. That the colonists had been prepared enough to maintain the domes, never mind make it back before the entire surface became uninhabitable again, suggested they had never quite believed it would all work. Smolensk, at least, was probably glad enough to see the terraformers go. In addition to ordinary building and repair services, Smolensk had thrived on selling parts found among the debris that was constantly falling on the moon's surface. The atmospheric controls in the terraformers would have deflected much of that supply source, and Smolensk's profits would have taken a hit.

It was no wonder the domes were at each other's throats again.

Between the diplomatic reports and what Jamyung had told her, Elena expected a level of chaos in Smolensk. *Budapest* stocked no hand weapons, so none of the crew were armed. The best Elena had been able to do was make sure she, Bear, and Chiedza were all dressed in vacuum-ready env suits, hoods easily accessible in their pockets, as prepared as they could be for physical attack or attempted ejection from the dome. Even as they brought much-needed food supplies, she expected suspicion and threats, or worse.

But when they reached the colony, Elena found her fears had been misplaced. Smolensk was not chaos. It was a ghost town.

She stood next to Bear as he talked to the import official, with Chiedza behind her double-checking the supplies they'd brought against Yakutsk's intake list. Through the windows of the small depot, she could see the city's normally crowded streets were nearly empty. Not that they weren't lived in—all the walkways were covered in Yakutsk's ubiquitous red dust and littered with footprints—but she saw only three people walk by in the ten minutes she stood next to Bear.

She had seen Smolensk during political coups, a strange hybrid of anarchy and brisk commerce. She had seen drinking and fighting next to mundane business transactions. She had never seen it empty.

"I'll need to verify this with the company," the official said. He didn't seem afraid, Elena noticed, but he was irritable. Ordinarily, Smolensk-level irritable. Nothing to fear?

So where is everybody?

She looked over at Bear. "When are we leaving?"

He shot her a look. It had taken her some time to convince him to let her go look for Jamyung. *This might not be the Corps,* she thought, *but he still wants me to know he's pissed off at me.* "Three-quarters of an hour," he told her. "Do not be late, Shaw. If you are, we're leaving you behind."

She headed out into the city, keeping her hand over the folded suit hood in her pocket. Realistically, she knew it was a useless precaution. If someone wanted to throw her out of the dome, they would certainly think to divest her of her hood first.

She thought of Jamyung's vacated scout and deeply missed the little snub-nosed handgun she used to carry on missions in the Corps. She clutched the hood more tightly.

She had not seen Jamyung in more than two years, but she recognized the shop from a distance: prime real estate, not five minutes from the port, a nondescript and window-less gray building, surrounded by a massive vacant lot filled with piles of junk. Neat piles, of course: battery parts in one corner, nanopolymers in another, carefully insulated crates containing logic core pieces, and one massive bin of conduit and connectors. When she had first seen it, it had seemed like a candy store, but nothing kept outside was particularly valuable. All of Jamyung's specialty parts were inside, in a locked basement vault that was as large as the lot itself.

She rapped on the door. "Jamyung?" she called, and tried the wall panel. The door slid open—unsurprising; these were business hours—but the lights were off. She frowned, leaving the door open behind her, and pulled a pin light out of her tool kit, illuminating the space with cool gray. The room was typically Spartan, containing only Jamyung's desk and a chair; but the desk was askew, revealing the trap-door to the basement vault. He had opened it—or someone had broken in. She stepped over, uneasy, and blinked into the darkness. If he was down there, he was too far afield for her to see his light. "Jamyung?" she called. Her voice slapped flatly in the low-ceilinged space.

"He's not here."

She started and turned, her hand going to her hip for her nonexistent weapon, then relaxed. Clearly this was one of Jamyung's scavengers: short, slim, dark-haired, beige-skinned, and dressed in brown—deliberately nondescript. Dark eyes blinked at her, neither pleased nor bothered.

"Do you know where he is?" she asked.

"Dead."

The bottom dropped out of Elena's stomach. "*Dead*. Are you sure?"

The scavenger nodded.

"What happened?"

"He got vacated."

Shit. "What's your name?" she asked; and then, as an afterthought, "I'm Shaw."

"Dallas."

She took the offered long-fingered hand; Dallas gripped her hand briefly and firmly, then let go. *Polite*, she thought, *and professional, just like Jamyung.* "Dallas, was his vacating part of the political nonsense that's been going on here lately?"

A snort of near laughter. "Nah. Politicians didn't care about Jamyung. He got tossed by strangers." The scavenger waved long fingers at her.

"Like me?"

"Different from you," Dallas elaborated, "but still strangers. Dressed like Baikul agents, but they hadn't grown up in a dome."

41

Damn, damn, damn. It seemed Jamyung had been right about the object after all. "Do you know where he is?"

A nod.

She checked the time: more than half an hour left. *The least I can do is bring him in from the cold.* "Can you show me?"

A shrug this time. "Easy enough to find him. He's not going to get up and walk away."

To Elena's surprise, Dallas met her at the side airlock in a full env suit, tugging a low anti-grav pallet. Despite the lack of visible grieving, the scavenger had apparently already been planning to retrieve Jamyung's body. She was not the only one, it seemed, who had developed some loyalty to the dead trader.

She secured her own hood and let Dallas walk ahead of her to open the door. It was a passive pass-through, like they used for the shuttle docks, with a short corridor used as a buffer rather than an atmospheric generator. She waited while the outer door opened, and together they stepped out into the bleak frigid darkness that was the surface of Yakutsk.

The sky above them was black and dusted with stars, but there was a tiny glowing lip of orange-yellow peeking over the moon's horizon, diluting the severe night sky. The gravity was far lower than it had been inside the dome, and she gave herself a moment to adjust, gripping the edge of the doorway. Dallas was clearly used to it, however, stepping forward confidently, and Elena followed with slow and careful steps, growing accustomed to the bounce. The dome's lower windows were unshielded, and cast artificial light partway onto the flat, dusty landscape; Dallas had turned on a headlight, and Elena pulled the pin light out of her tool kit.

"He's close," Dallas told her.

In fact, she saw them in the shadows, less than twenty meters ahead: bodies, perhaps two dozen, in a haphazard pile. Most of them, she noted, were still wearing env suits, although they were hoodless. Torture, then: keep them alive out here to think about it for a while, and then yank off the hood.

What has this place become?

But Jamyung had not been wearing a suit. She spotted his familiar flimsy overalls, the flat soles of the shoes that had always seemed too small for him. Approaching the body, she shone the light on his face: familiar, frozen, startled, dead.

Shit.

Behind her Dallas brought the pallet. "I'll get his feet," the scavenger said, and positioned the skiff next to the body. Elena walked around to Jamyung's head and slid her arms under his shoulders. Light, here on the surface; probably light inside, too. Wiry and muscly, but never large. Barely as tall as Jessica.

"You're my last hope here."

Damn, damn, damn.

"On three," she said, and counted. They lifted, and laid the body gently on the pallet. Dallas made an attempt to brush some of the red-brown surface dust off Jamyung's overalls. Whether or not it was grief, it was at the very least respect, and Elena was glad of it.

Dallas pulled, and Elena flanked the skiff as they made their way back through the airlock. Caught by an unusual bout of claustrophobia, she tugged her hood off as soon as the corridor pressurized. She looked down at Jamyung; the ice that had frozen around his mouth and nose was already melting. "He won't last long in this warmth," she said.

"Got a place for him," Dallas told her, and she nodded.

And then she noticed something.

Reaching out with a gloved hand, she slipped her finger behind Jamyung's exposed right ear. He'd worn it on his right, she was sure; she had memory after memory of him querying his comm, telling her he was taking alternate bids on what she was buying, trying to drive up the price. She'd never fallen for his trick.

But there was no comm now behind his right ear.

She checked the other side. "Did he take his comm off often?" she asked Dallas.

"A comm means money's coming in," Dallas said. "He wouldn't ever disconnect."

She looked up then, wondering why she hadn't asked before. "Do you know—when he was killed, was there anybody in port? Like we are now?"

Dallas shrugged. "I don't keep track of visitors. Too many."

"You saw them take him." A nod. "Did they scrape off his comm?"

"Nope. Grabbed him. Hauled him off. Threw him out."

"Did he fight?"

"Wouldn't you?" When she glared, Dallas added, "Screamed bloody murder, hung on to the doorway. Took three of them to get him out."

The doorway. It made no difference; she doubted he would have had that kind of presence of mind. Still, he had been right about people being after him, had made the effort to locate her to ask for help . . . She walked up to the door and ran her fingers around the frame.

And when she pulled her hand away, a tiny, blood-covered comm strip was stuck under her fingernail.

Comms weren't guaranteed durable storage, although many people used them that way. Anything important, anything you really wanted to keep, was better passed on to a longer-term system. Most people kept their information on the open network, encrypted with bio codes: vids, games, books, messages from family and friends. Elena, when she had been with the Corps, had saved almost nothing locally; but even so, when she resigned, she destroyed her comm strip rather than turning it in. The one she was wearing now she'd had only for a year, and it held nothing beyond ordinary comms traffic and a few vids from her mother. An older comm, like Jamyung's, would be packed with intertwined data, but recent messages would be easy to retrieve.

And the best place to find a decent scanner that could examine the comm was in Jamyung's vault.

Without looking at Dallas, she dropped into the hole in the floor next to Jamyung's desk. Increasing the output of her light, she straightened, and scanned the big room. It had been, not unexpectedly, entirely tossed; but Jamyung's diagnostic equipment was more or less where he had left it. His comm scanner was on the floor, still in one piece, and Elena wasted no time adhering the comm chip to the tabletop and flicking on the scanner.

And there it was, right on the top, recorded less than two minutes before the comm was deactivated: a message.

She tried to replay it, using her own comm to amplify, but it was encrypted. *Damn.* He had to have left the message for her. What would he have used to encrypt it, with little to no warning that the end was coming? A number? How could she guess? An ident code? A bio key? His own bio key would be invalid now that he was dead, and she was fairly certain he wouldn't ever have had access to hers. Remembering his cleverness, she tried it anyway, but the message didn't budge.

A code word, then. Something he thought she would try.

"Jamyung," she said. And then: "Dallas." Maybe he'd sent the scavenger to meet her for a reason.

Nothing.

Budapest. *Earth. Yakutsk. Smolensk. Rat-fucking murdering bastards.* None of them worked. She was running out of time.

And then it came to her, certain and obvious.

"*Galileo,*" she said, and the message began to play.

"They're here," Jamyung whispered. Wherever he was, he was in hiding; she heard bangs and crashes around him. "They won't find it. Don't let them get it. It's in the back, in the compost. Well, it *was* compost. The cats get at it now. Take it out of here, and don't let them know. I don't know what the fuck it is, Shaw, but you need to keep it away from these bastards. It won't help them, not on purpose. But maybe it won't have a choice. Don't give them the chance, Shaw. Don't—"

Jamyung took a gasping breath, and the message ended.

Elena sat back on her heels, thinking, pushing aside a wave of sorrow at the trader's death. She still found his description unconvincing, and his anthropomorphizing of this unknown object didn't change her mind. But he'd died for *something,* and whether or not the thing was really talking to him, someone had thought it was important.

She wanted to know why.

She checked her comm; she had twelve minutes before Bear would expect her back. She stood, and turned to Dallas. "Where's the compost heap?"

CHAPTER 4

GALILEO

Greg rarely used the off-grid anymore. Earlier in his career, it had been a last-ditch method of communication with parties he was not officially supposed to be contacting: PSI ships, off-schedule freighters, even—occasionally—Syndicate raiders, although in those instances he was almost always delivering some sort of threat disguised as compromise. As a general rule, if he could provide the Admiralty with a positive result, they didn't much care if all his negotiations were on the record with *Galileo*'s comms system or not. The off-grid allowed him to use tactics of which the Corps would not have officially approved.

The Admiralty would know, if they cared to check *Galileo*'s logs, when he had spoken with Captain Taras, and what she had asked him to do. They would not know when—or if—he had managed to contact *Chryse* unless he chose to tell them.

Greg went through the door connecting his office with

his quarters and let it sweep closed behind him. Some of his pent-up tension evaporated in the silence. He was aware it was an odd room, given how long he had lived in it: unadorned with vid, picture, or artwork of any kind, nothing personal except a few physical books his mother had left him when she died. For years, the Corps-issue dresser had held a still picture of his wife, and he had kept it long after he had realized he had no love for her anymore, long after he had resigned himself to hanging on to a marriage that meant nothing to him. Getting rid of it after their divorce had felt freeing, but also disorienting. Some days he walked in still expecting to see her looking back at him, pale and beautiful and not at all what he wanted.

The books, which were a more fond reminder of the tendrils of the life he still had outside the Corps, held half the off-grid, with the other half tucked under his mattress. He kept it in two pieces, just in case. As far as he knew, the only other people who knew its location were Jessica Lockwood, his second-in-command, and Ted Shimada, *Galileo*'s chief of engineering. He trusted both of them to keep it to themselves.

He retrieved the two clear polymer sheets and slid them together, laying the unit on the top of his dresser. It pulsed once, an almost subvisual wave of deep purple, and he keyed in *Chryse*'s ident. Greg's off-grid would show up as *Galileo* on the other end, unless *Chryse* had more detailed data from the last PSI ship that had received communications from this unit. That ship—*Orunmila*—was in the Third Sector, and it occurred to him that, among all of the questions he might have asked Taras, he should have asked how much of PSI's intelligence about the Corps they shared with each other. It might have saved him a considerable amount of time.

Long ago, when he was young and innocent, he had been irritable that PSI seemed so suspicious of Central. At this point in his career, he knew better.

An off-grid comm often languished for a long time, sometimes hours, before it was acknowledged, but Greg's signal was picked up almost immediately. "*Galileo*, this is Captain Bayandi of the starship *Chryse*. To whom am I speaking?"

And didn't that set Greg back on his heels.

Captain Bayandi.

Captain Bayandi.

Nobody spoke with Captain Bayandi. It occurred to Greg there was probably no way even to verify the man's identity. Every meager interaction Central had ever had with *Chryse* had been through subordinates. The voice was baritone, cautious, but with overtones of genuine warmth. *Welcoming,* Greg thought, which fit nothing he knew of *Chryse* at all.

Regrouping, he introduced himself. "This is Captain Greg Foster of the CCSS *Galileo*. I hope I'm not disturbing you, Captain."

"Not at all, Captain Foster." No hesitation. "What can I do for you?"

Tell me who you are, Greg thought. *Tell me what your ship is. Tell me about your crew. Tell me why you never talk to us. Tell me why you never talk to your own people.* "I'm contacting you at the request of Captain Taras," he said.

"Is she all right? Is *Meridia* in danger?"

Instant concern, and convincing worry. In so many ways, this was not the conversation Greg had thought he would be having. "*Meridia* is in fine shape, Captain," Greg assured him. "And I spoke with Captain Taras a little while ago. She is in good health and spirits. But she's concerned about your ship, and asked if I could speak with you."

"I don't understand. We spoke with Captain Taras yesterday. Commander Ilyana should be arriving at *Meridia* in just a few hours."

Greg would have expected annoyance; Bayandi only sounded confused.

"I don't want to speak for her," Greg said carefully. "But I have the impression that she's still worried about your comms outage a few months ago, and the reason for Commander Ilyana's trip."

Bayandi was silent for a moment. "I see," he said at last, and he sounded resigned. "I should have given Captain Taras more detail. I apologize for the need for your involvement, Captain Foster."

Taras was right; it felt very much like a family squabble. "Don't be concerned about that, Captain," he said. "May I ask—is there something *we* can help you with? Yakutsk notwithstanding, I have some maintenance people I can spare if they would be useful."

"That is very kind of you, Captain," Bayandi said, impeccably sincere. "There is nothing for you to help us with. Ilyana should be able to answer Taras's questions when she arrives, and we'll join you at Yakutsk twelve hours afterward. Do you know, yet, if there is anything specific you will need?"

"No, Captain, but thank you." Greg frowned. *Pleasantries,* Taras had said, and it had annoyed her. He was understanding how she felt, but he had no standing to demand answers or details. A PSI ship the Corps had rarely contacted was unlikely to willingly disclose damage information. And if Bayandi had personal reasons for shutting out Captain Taras—that was not a relationship Greg could mediate.

On the other hand . . . Bayandi had offered advice, and that alone might be telling.

"Captain Bayandi, if you have a moment, I'd be interested in hearing your thoughts on the tactical situation on Yakutsk."

If the PSI captain was surprised by the question, he betrayed nothing. "They've been fighting among themselves for a long time," he said. "The terraformer project—its inception as much as its failure—has widened long-standing schisms. There is a great deal of anger there, and unkindness. It seems fixed in their culture. But it is not all of them. There are individuals . . ." Bayandi trailed off. "I think we must be very careful, Captain Foster," he said at last. "I think we cannot underestimate the need of a subset of the population to feel a sense of control and organization. Yakutsk's strategic importance is a double-edged sword. It brings them pride, but there are many people there who have killed for power, and will kill again. They are not the people who will help us, and I think attempting a dialogue with them is, at best . . . procrastination, shall we say?"

"You think we need to start building civilian allies, rather than dealing with the government."

"The government on Yakutsk may have changed again before you arrive there. Negotiating with the government will accomplish nothing."

It was a different direction than Greg had been considering. It was also far less well defined, but he felt, for the first time, a glimmer of hope. "Thank you, Captain," he said honestly. "I'll discuss your thoughts with my colleagues."

"And I will contact Captain Taras immediately," Bayandi promised. "I am sorry that we have worried her. You may rest assured, I will resolve the issue. Thank you, Captain Foster." He ended with something curious: "I hope we will talk again."

Greg folded up the off-grid thoughtfully. Even if he had anticipated speaking with Bayandi . . . the man was not at all what Greg would have expected. Despite his age—reported by some as being north of ninety—he had been lucid and attentive, no waver or uncertainty in his voice. Had Greg not known Bayandi's history, he would have seemed a typical PSI commander.

Greg was missing something. But PSI being PSI, he was unlikely to ever learn what it was, even from Taras.

The door chime went off, and *Galileo* flashed his visitor's name before his eyes: *Commander Lockwood.* He shook off his thoughts on PSI. Those worries could wait until they had stabilized the situation on Yakutsk.

"Good evening, Commander," he said, when she walked in. "What can I do for you?"

Jessica Lockwood stood, not precisely at attention, but with the same compact ease she did nearly everything. She was a small woman—very nearly too short for the Corps, and he had taken care never to confirm her recorded height—impeccably beautiful, and always assembled with flawless military precision. She had a head full of curly red hair that she managed to tame back into a symmetrical bun, and shrewd green eyes. Most people noticed only her round-cheeked beauty when they met her, and missed the deep intelligence in those eyes—and the set of stubbornness in her lips. She had been his second-in-command for two years now. He had argued with and raged at her as he had to no one else ever in his life, and he loved her unreservedly, as much as he loved his own sister. He did not think he could have found himself a better first officer anywhere in the Corps.

"I've got some news on Yakutsk, sir," she said. She did not look him in the eye.

Greg knew what that meant.

Before he had promoted her to commander—indeed, long before she had enlisted in the Corps—Jessica had been a dangerously skilled recreational hacker. Having taken an oath to obey Corps regulations, she was generally loath to use her skills in a way that might have been interpreted as illegal. But ever since they had begun secretly investigating Ellis Systems, he had told her to get her intelligence any way she could. He had not been explicit, and she had not been forthcoming; but he knew a great deal of what they had discovered was unlikely to have been obtained by official means. Including, apparently, whatever she needed to tell him now.

"Off the record," he assured her. "What's up, Jess?"

Immediately she relaxed, all of the military draining out of her. She began pacing the floor of his room. "It's Baikul again, Greg," she said, sounding exasperated. "Oarig, the perpetual amateur."

Oarig, governor of Baikul, had only had the job for two weeks, having obtained it by summarily ejecting his predecessor and her cabinet from the office—a move widely anticipated after the terraformer failure. While this was not an atypical method for Yakutsk to change governing bodies, Oarig's qualifications were difficult to understand. He was short-tempered, entitled, and inclined to violence. Greg was not entirely sure how he had amassed enough dedicated followers to kill for him.

"They've got wind of a food drop at Smolensk," Jessica told him, "and they're threatening to steal it."

He rubbed his eyes. "Oarig, of course, having no trust in the fact that the supplies are going to be shared." Which was not entirely unreasonable of him, despite his hair trigger—Villipova, the governor of Smolensk, was not above denying Baikul resources she had previously agreed to distribute evenly.

Jessica shrugged. "Hard to say. He's paranoid, sure; but really, Greg, I think he's just been planning a coup for so long he doesn't know what else to do with himself."

Which, Greg thought, made a succinct summation of Oarig's personality. "*Budapest* dropped the cargo yesterday, didn't they? So we need to figure out how to alert Villipova without—"

"Actually, sir," Jessica interrupted, "*Budapest* is still there."

Well, hell.

He turned away from her. Most of his crew considered him stoic, even cold; but Jessica could read him too well.

She would know what he was thinking. He didn't need her to see it in his eyes as well. "They should have been out of there ten hours ago."

"They got delayed," she told him. "They did airlift assist at Govi. There were . . . complications."

"Anybody get hurt?"

"Not those kinds of complications."

He knew instantly what had happened. *Airlift assist* meant hands-off recon. Civilian freighters often served that purpose during an evac, using pilots of various experience levels to scan a colony's surface for people in distress. The protocol was to notify the lead airlift ship when a group was found, and move on.

But Elena would never have left anyone in trouble.

"We've got to tell Savosky." He headed through the inner door to his office, Jessica at his heels. "He needs to abort that cargo drop."

He heard her step behind him. "I talked to Yuri a few minutes ago. They're already down on the surface. Import is arguing with them about where they want the cargo delivered."

"The correct answer," Greg said, "is they leave it where it is and let Smolensk sort it out." Civilians. *Dammit.* He hit his internal comm. "Samaras, get me *Budapest*."

But Jessica wasn't finished. "You're not going to talk them out of it," she said. "I tried. If the import office doesn't certify receipt, they don't get paid."

"And they're willing to risk their lives for that?"

"Apparently so."

Shit. "Belay that last order, Samaras," he said, and instead commed Emily Broadmoor, his security chief. "Emily,

I need a shuttle and a security detail." He met Jessica's eyes. "How far are we out?"

"Twenty minutes," she told him.

"Twenty minutes," he said to Emily. When she acknowledged, he turned back to Jessica. "I'm going to get Herrod. Might as well at least maintain the fiction of having diplomacy on the table. You—" He stopped. "Contact Savosky. Tell him we're sending backup."

"Yes, sir. Greg—"

He met her eyes. "No time for that now, Jess," he said, and after a moment she nodded.

"I'll alert Savosky, sir." She turned and left.

Greg left the office and headed back to the gym, putting all the pieces together in his head. Savosky had dropped cargo in some pretty ugly places in the past, and he was well aware of the political situation on Yakutsk. If he was moving forward despite Jessica's warning, then the payoff must be genuinely impressive. Savosky was not naive, and he was not helpless.

And he had at least one pilot who wasn't a civilian at all.

Past is past, Greg told himself.

But it wasn't, and he knew it.

CHAPTER 5

YAKUTSK

Bear's nose wrinkled. "Elena, what the hell am I smelling?"

Elena looked down at herself. Her once pristine env suit was covered in the red-gray dust of Yakutsk's exposed surface, and her arms were caked up to her elbows with muck from the heap of organic material through which she had been digging for the last ten minutes. Her own nose had stopped working shortly after she started, and she was grateful; she didn't think she could otherwise have done the job without getting sick.

"Compost," she said. "Also, cat excrement. I think."

"There some big reason we're all going to have to sit with that on the way back to *Budapest*?"

She reached into her pocket and pulled out the container she had found buried in the garbage. "Jamyung's dead," she told him. "And this is what he left me."

"He left it to you buried in cat shit?"

She tucked it back into her pocket. "It's a long story," she said. "What's going on here?"

She had heard him shouting as she came up the road, his bellowing punctuated by barely audible, utterly unconcerned responses from the import official. When she arrived, the official was walking out the back door, the office itself dark.

Bear grew serious. "We've got two problems," he told her. "First, they want the cargo dropped at the cultivation dome. Second, the Corps has intel suggesting Baikul wants to steal the cargo. I'll leave the exercise of which is more important to the pilot."

She raised her eyebrows. Since the population had moved back into the domes, everything on the surface was disputed territory. The cultivation dome itself was jointly held, but they would have to fly over a substantial amount of open landscape to get there, which would expose them to any ground-to-air fire Baikul chose to throw at them. Worse, the cultivation dome had no established infrastructure or procedures for docking a large-scale cargo ship. They would have to unload cargo without any environmental controls, doing all the work in env suits. They would be almost completely defenseless.

She felt a tingle in her spine. She had been trained for this.

"Let me fly it alone, Bear," she said. When he looked away, she pressed her argument. "Out in the natural gravity, the size of those cargo crates isn't going to bother me at all. I've got the training to fly this kind of mission."

"Chiedza's flown combat," he said.

"Not like this." Elena didn't think the combat Chiedza had flown would have involved much defense. "There's no reason to put everyone through this. Pull the extraneous crap from one shuttle, pack all the cargo on it, and I'll take it out and be back within the hour."

He was still frowning, but she could see it on his face: he knew this was his best choice. Curtly, he nodded. "No risks, though," he added, unable to resist one last admonishment. "And no detours. You drop that fucking cargo and you get the fuck out. Understood?"

"Understood." And for the first time in a year, she felt like she had a real purpose.

She hauled the extra seating out of one of *Budapest*'s two shuttles as Bear and Chiedza shifted their half of the cargo into her ship. It was snug, but they were able to fit it all in. She squeezed between the massive bins of grain and parked herself in the pilot's seat, pulling on her env hood. When she landed, the fastest way to offload the cargo would be to vent the cabin and repressurize later, and she wanted to spend the briefest possible time on the surface.

She flew the great circle route over what passed for a pole, and was treated to an aborted sunrise as she maneuvered toward the side of the moon sheltered by the gas giant. The shuttle's sensors swept as widely as they could, looking for movement and potential attackers. The mechanism had less scope than she was used to, but she comforted herself by realizing that the darkness on the dead surface would make it nearly impossible for a large group of people to conceal any guidance lighting.

Assuming, of course, that they needed lighting after a lifetime exploring the moon's surface.

As she understood it, there were generally no more than five people living in the cultivation dome at one time: a botanical expert and a chemist, a single medic, and one or two horticulturalists, all ensuring the safety and nutritional value of what was being grown in the limited space. They would, she had been told, be expecting her, although she was anticipating they'd be nervous. Purges had been nearly nonexistent during the terraformer experiment; for the ordinary citizens, who had been just beginning to relax into a new life, this would be a jarring return to an uneasy past they had hoped to leave behind. Those were the people she thought of at times like this—not the dome officials, pointing fingers at each other, so caught up in paranoia that they would kill their own without a thought. Most of the people wanted nothing more than their old, comfortable lives back.

She thought of Jamyung, and tugged the container out of her pocket. It was vacuum-sealed, designed to freeze whatever was inside into inertness. Such an environment could wreak havoc on machine parts, but whatever this thing was, it had survived the moon's surface, and the cold shielding would have made it more difficult to find using conventional scanners. Almost absently, she touched the opening mechanism and the lid lifted, revealing exactly what he had described: a cuboid, gray and smooth with rounded corners, its proportions squat and pleasing.

He died for this. Or believed he had.

Curious, she tugged off her glove and held her palm over it. She could not tell how warm it was, but after a vacuum seal, it should have radiated at least a little bit of cold. She frowned at it, and then, on impulse, she brushed one finger along the surface. It *was* warm, like skin, smooth and unyielding, and she wondered what kind of polymer it was. Something sophisticated, certainly, that could withstand such extreme temperatures. Or perhaps the polymer was encasing something, although Jamyung hadn't mentioned that. He would have had it under a scanner, she was sure. Odd that he hadn't—

Without warning, a signal came over her comm, a deafening jumble of sounds. Words, music, shouting, white noise, machines; she could not sort any of it out. There was a rhythm beneath it all, and it built, taking on melody, creeping into her mind, singing one word, over and over again: *Galileo . . . Galileo . . . Galileo . . .* louder and louder and—

There was a lurch, and an alarm, and she reached back to the controls, cursing. She should at least have put the damn ship on autopilot. She wrenched the shuttle back to level and heard her cargo slide, the crates knocking into each other.

And then someone said, "Ow!"

She turned, reaching instinctively for her nonexistent weapon. "Who the fuck is there?" she snapped.

"It's only me," Arin said. He crawled out from between two crates, rubbing his head. "Do you have to fly so rough?"

Shit. "Arin, what are you doing here? Did you have some fugue where you missed the bit where Bear told you to stay on *Budapest*?" At least, she observed, he'd had the brains to pull on an env suit.

"I'm here to help," he insisted. "And don't tell me you couldn't use the extra hands."

No, no, no. This was wrong. "No, Arin, I could not use the extra hands. *Fuck.*" She turned her back to him. The box had fallen to the floor. Hastily tugging her glove back on, she picked up the box and closed it, slipping it back into her pocket. "I need to do this alone so I don't have to divide my concentration making sure you stay in one fucking piece!"

She caught sight of another energy signature and turned again. Behind her, she heard him stumble. "Well I'm here now," he said. "What can I do to help?"

She should never have befriended him. She should never have befriended any of them. *Fuck.* "Get in a fucking seat," she told him between gritted teeth, "and strap yourself down. You'll do me no good if you fly into my head while I'm trying to land."

Arin pulled himself into the copilot's seat, fastening his harness, and her anxiety eased a little. At least he wouldn't break his neck on the way down. She was fairly certain, though, she would break it for him once they got back to *Budapest.*

Right before Bear broke hers.

"What's the plan?" he asked her.

"The plan is we get fifty meters from the cultivation dome," she told him, "we drop the cargo, and we get the fuck out."

"No verifying pickup?"

If she had been alone, she might have scanned for ships, set a beacon, commed them to make sure they knew where to look. "The import official agreed. We drop the cargo and we leave." She shot him a glare; he was still grinning. Dammit, he wasn't bothered at all. A Corps ensign would have had the brains to stop smiling and restrict all his responses to "Yes, ma'am" for the next six or seven years of his career.

Beneath them, she caught the distant lights of the cultivation dome—along with a much stronger energy indicator. Before she could dodge into the moon's shadow again, the shuttle sounded a quiet alarm and said, "We are being targeted."

Big fucking surprise. "Evasive!" she shouted, and keyed in a command to the ship's autopilot. The energy pulse swept past them silently.

Beside her, Arin began unstrapping himself. "What are you doing?" she asked.

"I'll get the cargo ready for the drop."

"Arin—"

"I'm here, Elena. Let me help."

Stupid. Damn kid. "You hook yourself onto the wall," she told him, "and you keep your head away from the open door, do you understand? They will be firing on us. This isn't make-believe. This is fucking war."

She kept her eyes on their attackers as she heard him pull one of the attached lines out of the wall and hook it securely around his waist. She heard scraping as he began shoving the cargo to one side, exposing the ship's side door. If she got low enough, she could open the door, and he could shove the containers out, one by one. Twenty seconds, tops. Maybe less.

"Two minutes," she told him. "Stay behind those containers, dammit. Keep covered."

But before she could steer them lower, the alarm came again. "We are being targeted," the shuttle repeated calmly.

On the tactical display, she could see the small lights moving toward them from three directions this time. Too many, and far too fast.

"Hang on, Arin!" she shouted, and took the controls back to manual. One of the shots would miss, she could see; the other two seemed to be homing in on them. Different firing systems, then; their attackers were neither experienced nor properly prepared. *Which doesn't mean their strategy won't work.* She watched the faster shot get closer and closer to them, and as it closed in, she rolled them abruptly to one side. She heard the containers shift, and the missile swept past them.

But the second detonated not thirty meters from their undercarriage, and they were suddenly pitched forward, nose toward the ground, the ship's engines groaning as they attempted to compensate. "Arin!" she shouted.

"I'm okay!" he shouted back. "Elena, just get—"

They hit the ground nose-first, the front window slamming into the dirt, obscuring her visibility entirely. The harness kept her from dropping onto the ceiling as they skidded upside down through the frozen dust, far faster than they should have; the engines were whining, trying to soften the landing, and she thought they had been damaged. In an instant, though, the engines no longer mattered: they slammed against something she couldn't see, she jerked roughly against her harness, and the engines shut down.

"Arin?" she said, unbuckling herself, her feet dropping onto the ship's ceiling. "You still hooked in?"

There was silence, and everything in her went cold.

"Arin!" She rushed toward the containers. Where they

had been carefully lined up on the floor they were now tossed about the ceiling like huge squares of confetti, on top of each other and in corners, a few broken open, seeds scattered. She saw the safety cable behind one of them and grabbed it, pulling; it resisted. She shoved at the container covering it; the heaviest of them was ninety kilos in this gravity. If she braced herself against the wall she should be able to shift it. Squeezing between the container and the wall, she positioned her feet and set her shoulders, then took a deep breath and shoved. The container slid reluctantly away from her, and fell off to the left.

Arin was crumpled against the wall, unmoving.

She rushed to him, careful not to shift him. She could see his chest rising and falling rapidly, and she felt a glimmer of relief. Where was the damn med scanner on this ship? Under a pile of containers, she realized; she would have to rely on her rusty field training. Pressing her gloved fingers against the thin fabric of his suit hood, she took the pulse in his throat; a little fast, but steady enough. She cleared the debris away from him, trying not to move him, unsure of where he had been hit and how hard. His nose was bleeding; it was clearly broken. As she was running her hands carefully along his arm, he stirred and groaned.

"Sit still," she told him sharply.

"What," he said.

"We've crashed," she told him. "You got hit with a container. Be still; I don't know how badly you're hurt."

He opened his eyes; both pupils, she noted, were even. His concussion couldn't be too bad. "Why'd they shoot at us?" he asked, coherently enough.

"Because they don't want us here."

He looked confused. "We're bringing them food."

"We're interfering in local politics."

"Don't they need us?"

Now was not the time for a lesson. "Lie still, Arin. I'm going to see who I can contact."

She made her way back to the front of the ship and managed to pull up a rudimentary console. No comms at all, but the environmental controls were still on: air, temperature. They could breathe, at least.

Unfortunately, they couldn't shoot, and she cursed. If she'd been running this mission off of *Galileo*, she would have been carrying a sidearm. There would have been half a dozen pulse rifles in the cargo hold, just in case. *Fucking freighters.*

They were lying here, upside down in the dirt, and they were helpless.

CHAPTER 6

You don't have to come, sir," Greg had told Herrod. "I'm guessing there's going to be more shouting and denials than discussion this time."

Herrod had given him a familiar look of mild amusement. "Shouting and denials require diplomacy, too, Captain," he had pointed out. "And while I may not be able to throw my weight around anymore"—here he gestured at Greg's assembled security detail, eight armed soldiers of considerable size—"I can still sling a pulse rifle if the situation calls for it."

Greg had the distinct impression Herrod was having fun.

In the end he had settled for a single platoon with two senior soldiers: Bristol and Darrow, both of whom he knew well, both of whom knew how to be unobtrusive when they needed to be. "With any luck," he told the platoon, "this is a false alarm, and you'll all be nothing more than pomp and circumstance. But keep your eyes open, and stay on your toes."

He could have taken a pilot, or at least a cabin crew, but Greg was fond of flying, and as the ship's captain he rarely got a chance to do it. Herrod had the good sense to settle himself in *Sparrow*'s passenger cabin instead of sitting co-pilot, so Greg had the space to himself. *Sparrow* was an easy shuttle to fly, smooth and responsive, and Greg almost never engaged the autopilot, even when it would have freed him up to do something else. He could watch the stars, see the moon advance through the front window, while keeping an eye on surface scans and nudging their direction now and then.

Almost as relaxing as running. He smiled.

Oarig had denied any plans to intercept the food drop. "Why would we interfere with a commercial shipment?" he asked, and Greg had no rational answer. He hadn't pointed out that few of Oarig's actions since his precipitous instal-lation had made commercial sense. If Oarig was preparing some sort of ambush, it spoke of inexperience. The Admi-ralty had no intelligence on Oarig, but Greg was guessing, based on his appearance, that if he was more than twenty it was not by much. Not enough time to learn real politics, no matter how young he had started.

In contrast, Villipova, the governor of Smolensk, was a grim-faced woman of fifty-four, used to occasional vio-lence, but reasonably skilled at dealing with corporations and trade. Greg had dealt with her under less stressful cir-cumstances, and had found her unfailingly practical, if not prone to overtures of friendliness. During their negotiations she had seemed tired and irritable, and had struggled with letting Oarig speak his mind. She clearly thought the Baikul governor was foolishly inflexible, and much of Greg's challenge had been getting her to listen long enough to understand the areas where Oarig was open to compromise.

When he had briefed Commander Broadmoor on the tactical situation, he had told her to expect both domes to be coordinating attacks on each other. "This attack may just be the start," he'd said. "Keep the troop shuttles on deck, and your people ready to go. And if you detect anything more radioactive than a thorium mine—you alert me instantly, understood?"

Greg had no doubt Oarig would revel in Central sending infantry to Smolensk, but he doubted the governor would sit silent when Baikul received the same treatment. Greg's orders to Emily Broadmoor had been clear: she was to deploy the others if—and only if—she thought a show of firepower was the only way to prevent the colony from blowing itself up.

They were still ten minutes out from the dome when Commander Broadmoor commed him. "Sir," she told him, "we're showing some activity on the surface. Pulse rifles, and what looks like a wreck."

Here we go, he thought. "Any distress calls?"

"Hang on . . ." She was silent for a moment, then: "There's a beacon, sir. It's a cargo ship off of *Budapest*."

Greg hit *Sparrow*'s comm. "Savosky?"

"This is Yuri Gorelik. Captain Foster, is that you?"

Savosky had not yet returned, then. "We're getting a beacon from one of your shuttles down here. Looks like they got caught in some surface fighting. Are you in touch with them?"

"No, Captain, we're not." Gorelik sounded concerned. "Captain Savosky is on his way back right now. Shaw was supposed to be making the cargo drop."

"On her own?" The question came out before Greg realized what he was asking. *Of course* Elena would have managed a way to do it on her own.

But that wasn't what was worrying Gorelik. "She was supposed to be alone," he said. "But it seems we're missing our other mechanic. Arin Goldjani. Captain Foster—" There was a pause. "He's nineteen. Not experienced. He was meant to stay here for this mission. We think he stowed away."

He was also, Greg knew, Yuri and Bear's adopted son. "Are you getting anything from them at all?"

"Just the beacon, as you are."

Shit. "The colonists must have a local jammer," he said. The alternative—that the crew could not respond—was unthinkable. "Your cargo ships don't carry weapons, do they?"

"No, Captain." Gorelik's voice was grim. "They do not."

Greg was changing course even as he commed Jessica. "Commander, get in touch with Oarig and tell him if he's got anything to do with shooting at fucking civilian freight ships trying to bring his own people fucking food, this is no longer going to be a neutral negotiation."

Jessica got the point quickly. "Is it Elena?"

"Of *course* it's Elena. And apparently some green kid who followed her down."

Jessica swore concisely. "On it, sir."

Admiral Herrod appeared at his elbow. "Problem, Captain?"

"We need to divert, sir," Greg said. "Someone shot down

71

a cargo carrier. They've put up a distress beacon, but *Budapest* can't contact them."

He waited for Herrod to lodge a protest, or at the very least grant permission; but it seemed Herrod had grown accustomed to his retirement. "What's our strategy?"

"Our strategy," Greg said, loudly enough for the others to hear, "is to clear the comm signal, get to the civilian vessel, and avoid deadly force as much as we can. Which means we threaten the hell out of them and get them to stand down long enough for us to get our people out. Darrow, Bristol?"

"Sir," they said simultaneously.

"You perceive a credible threat that you can't disarm, you defend, understood?"

"Yes, sir."

He kept *Sparrow* on a clean vector and watched for the shuttle's telemetry: it seemed to have some power, and he held out hope Elena was all right. After several minutes, the wreck appeared on the horizon, and as they grew closer, he saw enough to feel relief. The shuttle, intact but flat on its back, was surrounded by massive cargo bins: the food the colony so sorely needed. Without weapons—*why the fuck do freighters drop in war zones without weapons?*—she had defended her ship with the only leverage she had: the cargo they were trying to steal.

"*Sparrow,* what's in the area?"

"Four hundred and sixty-two people," *Sparrow* said calmly.

"Moving?"

"Yes."

"In the same direction?"

"No."

"Put them up on tactical."

They were clumped in two groups, relatively even in number, and they were moving toward each other. Typical Yakutsk: domes so interested in choking each other off that they missed all of their common ground. He would have left them to their futile devices, but Elena's downed shuttle was right in between them.

He swore again, and tried comms. "This is *Sparrow* calling the shuttle off of *Budapest*." *Pick the fuck up.*

"The other shuttle is not receiving comms," *Sparrow* told him.

"Can they send?"

"No."

"Are we close enough to break a comms jam?"

"No."

"How long until we reach her?"

"One minute seventeen seconds."

Eternity. *Shit.* "Are any of those people targeting the shuttle?"

"Insufficient information to determine target."

"Is the shuttle in the line of fire?"

"Yes."

"How likely are they to light up?"

"Direct impact at a range of less than two hundred meters will result in ninety-four percent likelihood of an incendiary event."

Damn, damn, damn. What he wouldn't give to just open up on both groups of colonists. He recognized it as frustration, but he found himself long over the impulse to rescue people who would shoot at those sent to help.

"What are they firing?" he asked the shuttle. It was remotely possible they were using something old, something that might be vulnerable to a generated EMP or even a radio jam.

"Plasma P7 rifles," *Sparrow* said.

"How many?"

"Five hundred and forty units. Two hundred and twelve with the group south of the shuttle, the rest with the group north of the shuttle."

More guns than people. Never a good equation. "*Sparrow*, keep an eye on *Budapest*'s shuttle. If any of those rifles locks on her, fire on the shooter. Understood?"

"Understood."

If *Sparrow* shot a colonist, it would be an act of war. It might also come far too late to save Elena and Arin Goldjani.

But Greg would sleep better.

Behind him, all nine of his passengers were pulling on env suits. Herrod returned again, and said, "I can pilot, Captain."

Greg met Herrod's eyes through the clear fabric hood of his suit. Serious, military, entirely straightforward. He nodded, and stood. Herrod slipped into his seat.

"The comms jam is broken," *Sparrow* said as they approached.

Greg tied into the colonists' comms. "Drop your weapons!" he shouted. "This is Captain Greg Foster of the CCSS *Galileo*. That shuttle you're targeting contains people in need of medical help. According to the Armed Conflict Act of 2976—"

One of the colonists pointed his P7 upward and took a shot at *Sparrow*.

They were high enough that the shot did nothing but scar the shuttle's hull, but the message was clear. Before Greg could shout an order, Herrod was keying in a command, and *Sparrow* laid down a line of shots ten meters before each group of colonists. Greg saw them stop, saw some of them throw up their arms before their faces, saw a few turn and run. *You guys are the brains of the outfit,* he thought at the fleeing people. Herrod dropped *Sparrow* to the ground in front of the others.

"Stand the fuck down, all of you," Greg shouted over the comm, "or we'll shoot straight next time!"

They did not, he observed, drop their guns, but they stopped advancing and avoided pointing anything at his ship. He stood, grabbing one of the large shoulder cannons from the back of the ship, and slung it next to his ear. "*Sparrow*, keep us covered," he told the shuttle, and opened the door.

The colonists watched him, wary, as his platoon filed out of the door, Greg among them. "Anybody fires," he told them, "the ship will take you out."

"That's illegal," someone called resentfully.

"Your next of kin is welcome to sue." The platoon, weapons raised, gave him cover as he backed around *Sparrow*'s nose until he was completely sheltered by the shuttle's hull.

He turned to the others. "Keep them back," he said, then slung the cannon over his shoulder and ran toward the wreck of *Budapest*'s shuttle. "Elena?"

"I'm here," she commed back. "We need to get Arin out of here."

We need to get both of you out of here, you damn fool.

He covered the last ten meters to the shuttle's open doorway, and squeezed in between the upended shipping containers.

And there was Elena, hanging on to a handle on the wall, hovering over a battered-looking civilian who had to be Arin Goldjani. Goldjani was young indeed: rangy, all knees and elbows, a patch of hair shadowing the brown skin of his jaw. The kid was conscious, and his color wasn't bad, but his nose was clearly broken; through the hood of his suit Greg could see most of his face was covered in blood.

Elena herself . . . well, he had seen her look better. Her env suit was covered in dust and grime, and through the clear hood, he could see long strands of hair hanging in her eyes. He squinted and looked closer; he thought some of her hair was blue instead of her natural dark brown. If she was pleased or surprised to see him, she did not let on. Her expression, beyond concerned, was singularly irate.

"Can you get us out?" she asked him.

"Are you abandoning this bird?" he asked.

She looked as if she hadn't considered the question, and he realized she must be very worried about the kid. "I think we have to for now," she said. "Maybe we can come back for it later."

"I don't think so," he told her. "I think as soon as we get out of here, they're going to throw themselves at each other."

"But we brought food." This came from Goldjani, and he

seemed genuinely confused. "More than enough. What do they need to fight for?"

"I don't think *need* comes into it at this point," Greg told him, but he kept his voice gentle. There were some truths about humanity that were never easy to learn, even when they were laid out before your eyes. "Let's get you out of here, and take you somewhere that has a doctor."

"It'll have to be *Galileo*," Elena told him.

She looked at him, saying nothing else, and he realized what she was telling him: the kid's injuries were beyond the limits of simple first aid. *Worse than he looks.* Whatever she had seen on the shuttle's small med scanner had spooked her. *Budapest* may have had a full-service med kit, but she thought Goldjani needed a surgeon. "You ever been on a Corps starship, Goldjani?" Greg asked him.

The kid smiled. "No, sir."

"As long as you're a civilian," Greg corrected him, "I'm not 'sir.' You can call me Captain, or just Greg, if you like."

"I'd like to see *Galileo*, Captain," Goldjani said.

"Excellent. Then let's get you out of here." He turned to Elena. "We need some kind of a stretcher."

"Come on, Elena," Goldjani put in. "I can walk."

She ignored him. "We'll need to pull one of these containers apart," she said. "We dumped all the usual supplies off this bird to make room for the seed."

They poured the contents of one container into the sand outside the door. Greg took a quick look; the colonists were still milling around in front of *Sparrow*, murmuring to themselves, their hands still on their weapons, eyeing Greg's infantry with increasing boldness. *We are running out of time,* he thought. Behind him, Elena had brought out a power saw and was running it rapidly through the corrugated material of the container. "I'll need to reinforce it," she told him, eyes on her work. "It's too flexible."

"Isn't there anything I can do?" Goldjani asked plaintively.

Elena's jaw set. "You can stay home next time," she snapped, and the boy fell silent. Greg glanced at him; his expression had closed. Goldjani didn't know her well enough to recognize fear.

Just then, Greg heard a hail of footsteps on the ship's hull, and the whole structure shook. He turned to look out the door and saw people jumping to the ground, shooting toward the other set of colonists. His platoon was shouting, but the colonists were leaving them alone. Damn, now they really were in the middle of a firefight. "Move it, Elena," he said.

She finished fastening three horizontal panels on the bottom of the sheeting. "Watch your fingers," she warned Greg, lowering the makeshift stretcher to the ground next to Goldjani. "The edges are a little rough."

Goldjani, subdued, didn't resist when Greg and Elena slid him gently onto the stretcher. If they hurt him further, he didn't let on. Stubborn kid. Greg remembered himself at nineteen, powered by nothing but hormones and self-righteous anger. He would have been equally stupid in Goldjani's situation. "I have to warn you," he said, hoping to cheer the kid up, "my doctor's kind of a dick."

"Then why do you keep him?" At least Goldjani was making an effort.

"Because he mixes really good drinks and lets me win at cards," Greg told him. Goldjani smiled, and Greg thought it was partly genuine.

"Anything here you need to bring?" he asked Elena.

"No. Wait!" She dashed to the front of the shuttle and retrieved something off the floor: a box, about fifteen centimeters across. From the way she lifted it, it was either empty or contained something quite light. She tucked it into her pocket. "Bear's going to have my damn head," she said, giving a resigned glance around the shuttle. Then she looked back at him, businesslike, determined, familiar. "Let's get out of here before somebody drops a nuke on those guys."

She took Goldjani's head, and Greg lifted the corrugated sheet at his feet. He commed Bristol and Darrow. "We're coming out with wounded," he said. "Cover us."

They lifted, and he backed out of the shuttle, steadying himself in the dirt before Elena came out after him. The colonists were all in front of *Sparrow* now, ignoring Herrod's repeated exhortations for a cease-fire, shooting determinedly at each other. Along with the shooting, there were a couple of fistfights. In the training vids, enemies were always expert and organized, with a strategy discernible after a few minutes of observation. In reality, colony squabbles were almost always made up of a bunch of homeowners engaged in a deadly slap-fight with their neighbors.

Before they could make it to the door, a plasma flare sped past Greg's head, and he swore. "One more shot like that," he shouted, "and we'll blow it up, do you hear me? We've got wounded here! Stand the fuck down!"

Another shot went wide, and they started scrambling for

the door. "When we get inside," Greg told Darrow, "fire one shot directly back at *Budapest*'s shuttle, and withdraw."

Goldjani protested. "You really want them to blow up the cargo?"

"Plasma cannon won't breach the cargo containers," Elena told him. "But it'll destroy the shuttle and make a hell of a statement. They'll leave us alone long enough for us to get out of here."

Another shot caught the side of *Sparrow*, and Greg cursed. "Now, Darrow!" he shouted, hauling his end of the stretcher into the ship.

Darrow aimed the cannon and fired, and Greg realized they should have been farther away.

The shuttle blew instantly, the chemical flame lighting up the landscape. The shipping containers, as advertised, were jostled by the blast but undamaged. But the seed they had dumped into the dirt was vaporized, a cloud of dust sinking slowly in the low gravity. Greg knew the colonists could see it, too.

The platoon hustled inside, the door closing behind them. Greg and Elena set Goldjani's stretcher down, and he left her to seal the door while he went to the pilot's seat to get them out of there. Herrod was already standing, giving up his place.

The grain distraction had worked, at least in part. Some of the colonists had rushed over to the cargo containers, tugging at them, desperately trying to pull them aside. *Desperately.* There was a lot of seed, but their actions suggested they needed every bit of it, including what had been destroyed. "Is there more?" Greg asked Elena.

"On Nova Ganymede," she said. "Six weeks away."

Of course. "Get him secure," Greg told his soldiers grimly. "We're getting out of here."

More colonists had surrounded the containers, ignoring *Sparrow*'s weapons. They were squabbling again, shoving at each other. Someone behind the row of colonists began to fire, and the people began to drop, one by one in a row, from both sides. "But—" Arin broke off. "Can't you stop them?"

"We've got nothing to stop them with," Greg said, as gently as he could. And he lifted them off, abandoning the chaos, pointing *Sparrow*'s nose at the pristine stars.

CHAPTER 7

Greg lifted them off slowly, most likely in deference to the people on the ground, but Elena didn't think his consideration would be necessary much longer. She had seen far too many squabbles go this way. In a few minutes, Yakutsk would be down five-hundred-odd colonists, and the dome governments would be back to accusations and raids. Or worse.

And she wouldn't be able to do a damn thing to help.

She sat on the floor next to Arin, gripping the bench as the shuttle rose through Yakutsk's light gravity and began generating its own field, stabilizing them. *Shit.* She was going to have to comm Bear.

"Greg," she said, "can I have comms control?"

Across from her, Admiral Herrod sat in silence. She wanted to tell him to say something; his silence was unnerving. But he had helped, she realized. He had kept the shooters off them long enough for them to get Arin to safety. He had done something good.

Even a stopped clock is right once a day.

"Go ahead," Greg said from the pilot's cabin.

Bear picked up almost immediately. "Shaw? What the fuck? Have you got Arin?"

"He's here," she said. "He's safe. We're headed back to *Galileo*."

"Fuck *Galileo*," Bear snapped. "You need to get your ass back here. Did you drop those supplies?"

"He's injured, Bear."

Bear went silent for a moment. "How bad?"

Even with her isolated existence, Elena knew the tone: the stomach-knotting fear of a parent too far from a sick child. "He's talking," Greg interceded. "He was steady as a rock out there."

"I'm fine," Arin said, trying to sound reassuring.

But Bear didn't want their reassurances. "Elena?"

"He's got a concussion," she said, "and I think a ruptured spleen. But the internal bleeding is under control. We'll be back on *Galileo* in—" She turned to meet Greg's eyes.

"Fifteen minutes," he said. "I'll have a med crew waiting. We'll look after him, Savosky."

"I'll meet you there," Bear said, and terminated the comm.

Elena cursed, and Arin spoke up. "Listen, Lanie, I'm sorry. I'll talk to him. It'll be fine."

"Sit still," she said shortly, and Arin fell silent again, his expression closing. Dammit, she'd hurt his feelings again. He did not understand.

How could he? He's just a kid.

Who you nearly got killed.

She looked up. Herrod was watching her, his black eyes

unreadable. She hadn't seen his face in a year and a half, and he looked older than she remembered. *Much* older. She did the math in her head: he'd be seventy-nine now. She supposed some years were harsher than others.

Not that he didn't deserve it.

She glanced behind her to where Bristol and Darrow were sitting with the others. Bristol blanched, his pale skin communicating his feelings without words, and she nearly smiled. She'd always intimidated him. She wasn't entirely sure why. He was older than she was, and much bigger; but she had to admit he'd annoyed her fairly often, and she'd let him know it. Some people seemed to find her annoyance frightening. When she had been in the Corps, that had been useful.

Rebecca Darrow gave her a friendly nod. "Good to see you, Chief," she said.

I'm not Chief anymore, Elena thought; but she didn't correct her. "You too, Becky," she said. Darrow hadn't changed: tall, sturdily built, straight jet-black hair, smooth, gold-tan skin without anything resembling a line or blemish. She would look the same at sixty as she did now. After eighteen months away, Elena found the effect unnerving: it would be so easy to tell herself it had all been an illusion, from the transfer to her resignation to this awful day.

Just like Becky Darrow, Greg had not changed. He had stormed in—unasked, as usual—and she had fallen into step with him as if they had never been apart. That had been, she had realized since she left the Corps, one of the foundations of their friendship: they strategized the same way. In the field, in a crisis, their communication was fluid

and efficient: no arguments, no power struggles, just solutions. She had always liked working with him, because he
made sense. She had been startled as hell the first time she'd
learned not everyone felt the same.

She tugged off her hood and smoothed the damp strands
of hair out of her eyes. "Can you guys watch him?" she
asked Bristol and Darrow. When they nodded, she climbed
to her feet and headed for the front of the cabin. This was
not the place for their long-overdue conversation, but that
wasn't the only conversation they needed to have.

She slid into the copilot's seat and looked over at Greg.
She wasn't sure why she had expected him to look different;
a year was not so much time. He was still tall, still slim,
still square-jawed and flawlessly handsome, still striking
with his bright gray and black eyes against his dark skin.
Even his hair was the same, cropped so close he was nearly
bald. She had asked him, once, why he kept it so short, and
he'd said, "Because I like how it feels when I have to slap
my head in frustration." Then he had laughed, and she had
never been sure his answer was serious.

She could tell he knew she was looking at him. Years ago,
before things had become strange between them, he would
have asked her what was wrong. *Maybe he doesn't care
anymore,* she thought, and was hit by a wave of unexpected
loneliness. She had to take a moment to swallow it away.

"Thank you," she said, "for coming after us."

"Dumbass place for a cargo shuttle," he remarked.

"We don't make the drop, we don't get paid."

"In a case like this, maybe it's a fair trade." He paused.
"Are you guys going to get stiffed on this one?"

"Bear said the import officer told him as long as the cargo was close enough to the cultivation dome for them to retrieve it, he'd sign off." She sighed. "I don't know if we're going to get stiffed. Our accountant will fight that fight. If we don't get the money, she'll have to figure out another way to make up the shortfall."

"So your accountant is a magician."

Elena thought of Naina, scrupulously honest, dissecting every financial loophole available for the company that employed her. "Yeah, she kind of is. Listen, Greg." That got his attention. "I want to ask a favor."

She half expected him to summarily eject her from the shuttle for her nerve, but he just said, "Okay."

"Do you remember Jamyung, the trader we used to buy parts from?"

He did, and she told him the story, from the comm she had received earlier that day, to arriving in Smolensk to find Jamyung murdered, to Dallas's story of the strangers who killed him. "But that's not the weird part," she said. "The weird part is this . . . thing he left for me. This artifact. I thought he was bullshitting when he said it talked to him, but it talked to me, too."

At that he frowned, that familiar formidable scowl, and she knew then he was focused on the problem. "Show me."

She took the box out of her pocket, and he raised his eyebrows at her. "I should probably have tossed it," she admitted. "But . . . there's something about it. I can't really explain."

He took it from her and opened the box. As he stared at the artifact, his expression eased into curiosity. She wondered if, as she did, he found it beautiful. "His scout found this on the surface? What was it a part of?"

"No idea." He reached out a finger, and she held up her hand to stop him. "Don't do that. That's when it talked to me, when I touched it."

His eyes locked with hers. "What did it say?"

"That's . . ." She struggled to explain the message. "It was nonsense, really. Overlapping voices, noises, rhythm. And then, emerging from the static, one word. *Galileo*. Over and over again."

She hadn't wanted to tell him, but somehow he had seen it in her face. "It affected you," he realized, and she nodded.

"It left me feeling . . . lonely, I guess. And really disoriented. I almost crashed us without the help of those attackers. Greg, if it's some kind of a weapon . . ."

"Not much of a weapon if you have to touch it first."

"Maybe it's a prototype."

"That will evolve into a non-contact weapon?" He kept frowning at the artifact, but when he reached out to close the box, she thought he was reluctant. "What's the favor?"

"I don't have anything on *Budapest* sophisticated enough to scan something like that," she told him. "I was wondering if Ted could look at it. *Galileo*'s deep scanners would give us soup to nuts on what it's really doing."

He nodded. "Of course. I'll pass it on." He looked back at her. "You said this came in over your comm? Can you give me a copy of the message?"

That should have been an easy question to answer. She should have sent him over a copy without hesitation. If it had been Greg alone . . . but she thought of Ted, and the open engineering floor, and all those soldiers, some of whom she didn't even know, listening to her message. *Galileo . . . Galileo . . . Galileo . . .*

"Can you promise me," she asked, "that nobody but you and Ted, and maybe Jessie, will listen to it?"

Anyone else would have demanded an explanation. Anyone else would have told her she was being unreasonable, it was not important, it was just a random impersonal comm. Anyone else would have made her feel foolish for her reticence; after all, this thing was potentially a weapon, and they needed to understand it, no matter how private the message.

But all Greg said was, "You have my word."

CHAPTER 8

GALILEO

Jessica hissed through her teeth when she saw *Sparrow* enter the landing bay. The little shuttle had taken hits—a few bad ones, too—which meant Greg had been hot-rodding again. He had no business doing that. He should have brought more infantry with him, and a larger arsenal. He should have taken something with armor. He shouldn't have risked himself in the first place for fifteen thousand tonnes of grain and a freighter shuttle.

Which wasn't really what he'd done—she knew exactly why he had risked himself—but she was still angry with him.

Greg stuck his head out of the shuttle door and waved Bob's people in. The medics stepped inside, and Greg climbed out, followed by Bristol, Darrow, and the others, and finally Admiral Herrod. Jessica stood at strict attention and saluted; Greg returned the gesture, but Herrod just gave her an amused look.

"What have we got, Commander?" Greg asked her. Formal.

Whether that was for Herrod's benefit or the infantry's, she wasn't sure.

"I've had both Oarig and Villipova pissing in my ear since you deployed troops at the wreck, sir," she told him. It had mostly been Oarig, but she felt obligated to give the two recalcitrant politicians equal responsibility. "They're accusing each other of destroying the cargo, and they're both threatening to send troops to the cultivation dome."

Her captain rubbed his eyes. "The cargo's not destroyed," he told her. "How many troops are we talking about, Jess?"

He knew the intelligence as well as she did. "Between standing militias and official security people? About twenty-three hundred in Smolensk, and another fifteen hundred in Baikul."

"Drop each of those numbers by two hundred fifty," he told her. "*Damn*. We don't have enough people to shut them down by force, unless we're willing to strike from up here, which would pretty much kill any shot at diplomacy. How far off is *Meridia*?"

"Eighteen hours."

"Captain Foster," Herrod interrupted, "let me jump on this. If they're mostly still in the threat stage, we may be able to string together some kind of a cease-fire if we agree to help them retrieve the cargo."

It was not, Jessica thought, an awful idea. Before he'd come aboard *Galileo,* she'd never have considered Herrod a diplomat, although she recognized that was mostly because he'd never had to be tactful with her. Recently, though, she had decided the role suited him: he read people extremely well, and he seemed to know instinctively when to behave with sympathy, whatever he might really be thinking.

Greg, it seemed, thought the same; he nodded. "Very well. I'll be in the infirmary with Goldjani. Let me know what you hear from them. And, Admiral—thank you for your help down there."

That had cost Greg something, but Herrod just arched an eyebrow at him. "I could hardly sit back and do nothing, now could I?" He nodded at Jessica. "Commander Lockwood." And he left the landing bay.

Jessica gave Greg an inquiring look, and he shrugged. "He held off the attackers," he told her. "From inside *Sparrow,* but still. Freed us up to do what needed doing. He was a genuine help."

Despite her approval of Herrod's diplomatic abilities, she still knew too much about him to trust his motives. She couldn't keep the acid out of her voice when she responded. "Could you maybe go on a flight once in your life without getting shot at?"

"They weren't shooting at us, really," he told her. "It's pretty much devolved down there. *Budapest* was set up from the start."

Not my point, she thought, but she knew him well enough to let it go. "How's the kid?"

"Bad."

Minutes later the med team emerged with a boy on an anti-grav stretcher. His brown skin had alarming undertones of gray, but his eyes, as they swept over the storage bay, were alert and shiny. He met Jessica's eyes and blinked, then turned away self-consciously. *Lucid, then,* she thought. It wasn't a guarantee of anything, but it was not a terrible sign.

After him, dressed in a civilian env suit and covered in dust and something that smelled far worse, came Elena.

Her expression was drawn and anxious, and her appearance was uncharacteristically unkempt. Strands of hair had escaped from a loose braid and were hanging over her face, covered in the same red dust; but through the grime Jessica could see streaks of bright blue interwoven with her natural dark locks. A genetic graft, too; the color went down to the roots, and would grow like that until she changed it. It was a pretty color, Jessica thought, but the fact of it bothered her. Artificial hair color was a nod to civilian conformity. For Elena, it seemed like defeat.

"Is it that bad?"

Jessica realized she had been staring. She met her friend's eyes, and suddenly none of it mattered, and she flung her arms around Elena, standing on her toes so she could give her tall friend a proper hug. Elena hugged her back. "You look just the same, Jessie," she said.

Jessica pulled away, aware she was now covered in the same muck Elena was. "You stink," she said. "And no, the color's not bad at all. Why blue?"

"It cheers me up," Elena said. Her smile was wan, and Jessica realized she was worried.

"You want to follow your friend to the infirmary?"

"And get away from the landing bay. Bear will be here any minute, and I can't take him yelling at me just yet."

"It's not your fault the kid decided to follow you."

She felt Greg move to stand next to her, and Elena's eyes shifted to meet the captain's. "I think that's a matter of opinion," she said, and she sounded tired.

"He's awake and alert," Greg told her quietly. "That's a good sign."

Which meant, Jessica realized, that Greg was worried about the boy as well.

The three of them headed for the infirmary. Jessica walked between them, half an eye on Elena. This was the first time her friend had been on board *Galileo* in eighteen months. Jessica had imagined the reunion a dozen times, and it had never been like this: Elena filthy and dispirited, barely noticing the clean, bright halls of her former home. She wouldn't be staying, either, Jessica realized; this would only be a visit.

Maybe being home doesn't mean that much to her after all. Given how long Elena had been away, the idea stung more than Jessica thought it would.

Bob Hastings, *Galileo*'s chief of medicine, was waiting for them and had the med scanner out as the medics shifted the boy to one of the infirmary beds. The doctor frowned at the readout, then waved them away. "Ten minutes," he told them. His blue eyes swept over Elena. "You. Stay close by. You don't look so good, either."

Elena looked as if she wanted to protest, but she hung back, her miserable eyes on Arin. The boy wouldn't look at her.

"Come on," Greg said, his voice gentle. "Bob will take care of him."

Jessica tried to catch Bob's eye as they left, but his expression was grim and focused. Jessica looked down at Arin and made herself smile reassuringly. "Lousy bedside manner," she told him, "but he'll look after you."

Damned if the kid didn't smile back.

Once they were outside, Jessica couldn't wait any longer. "What happened?"

"He stowed away and hid," Elena said simply. "And when we crashed, nothing in the shuttle was secured. All the cargo landed on him."

"After they shot at you," Jessica pointed out. "Elena—"

"Don't tell me it wasn't my fault."

"Of course it's not!" Jessica's temper flared. "How the hell could it be? Nineteen years old is grown-up on every damn colony we've got. And he knew how to secure himself on that ship, stowaway or not. Bob will fix him," she said, "and then you can yell at him for being a stupid ass."

"Where's my boy?"

Jessica started; they should have been warned when Bear Savosky arrived, but she supposed he was too well-known to the crew for anyone to think of him as a guest. Normally Bear was relaxed and smiling, his massive bulk comfortable rather than a threat. But now he radiated rage and fear, and all of his ire was directed at Elena.

Who inexplicably didn't defend herself. "Bob's looking after him," Elena said. "He should be out soon."

Bear took two steps toward the main infirmary, then turned and paced back toward the door. He stopped to tower over Elena. "How did he get down there without anyone knowing it?"

She shook her head. "I don't know. He must have slipped between the cargo containers."

"You didn't pick up the weight discrepancy?"

"I didn't weigh them before I left. I was thinking about how to get them off the shuttle without getting shot down."

"And you fucked that up, too, didn't you?"

At that, Greg spoke up. "Savosky—" he began, but Bear turned on him instead.

"She is not yours to defend anymore, Foster, so stay the fuck out of this." Greg didn't react, and Jessica realized with some surprise that he was deferring to Elena's current commanding officer. *Not the time, Greg,* she tried to tell him with a glare, but he wouldn't look at her.

Savosky turned back to Elena. "I warned you about that boy. I told you he idolized you, and that he'd follow you anywhere. And now he's in there with some old quack, and you're looking at me like he's already dead and you're trying to figure out how to weasel out of all of this."

At last Elena got angry. "That's not fair!" she shouted. "I never wanted him to do this! I told him he needed to be sensible, to learn good judgment, to—"

"To do whatever was necessary to get into the Corps?" Bear shouted. "How the fuck could he understand what that really means? Arin sees you, and Captain Perfect, and the pretty little redhead, and he thinks it's like the vids he's watched since he was a kid. He's *nineteen,* and he thinks he's going to live fucking forever, and you stand there telling me about *judgment?* You remember why the Corps doesn't take anyone under twenty-two, don't you?"

For Jessica, that was enough. "Bear." She said his name quietly.

He turned to her, glowering, radiating fury. "What?"

"Stop yelling in the infirmary," she said simply.

He glared, and loomed, and waited for her to say something else, and she just looked at him.

And then, silent, he turned and stomped out of the room.

Jessica looked back at Greg, and this time he met her eyes. *Play nice,* she thought at him, and by the exasperated look he gave her, she thought he understood. Then she turned and went after Bear.

He had moved partway down the hallway, as if he were removing the temptation to barge back into the infirmary, and was pacing back and forth. *Galileo*'s hallways were wide and tall, but Savosky made every ordinary space seem smaller. He looked up as she approached, and frowned. "Don't start on me, Lockwood," he said. "You know I'm right. She shouldn't have been encouraging him."

"You think that's what's behind this?"

"Of course it is!" He looked away and began pacing again. "Ever since we left Earth she's been talking up the goddamned Corps, telling that kid how good he'd be, all the travel he could do, all the fucking *adventures*. Is this a fucking adventure, Lockwood? Getting shot down and watching a bunch of colonists kill each other? That boy's nineteen, and she could have ended his life today! She—"

"That's enough!" Jessica had never been patient with denial. "You're blaming *Elena* for all of this? You brought her along *because* she was Corps! You threw her at this conflict—when you knew they might be attacking—*because* of her background, *because* she is what she is! You stand there shouting because she's exactly what you knew her to be, what you're *using* her for, and you're blaming her for your own fuckups!"

"I did not make that kid think he could be a hero!"

"What difference does that make?" She knew he knew it, but he was too frightened to admit it yet. "He's *your responsibility*, Bear. Your crew. It was on you to make sure he was where you assigned him. You knew he wanted to follow her down—you should have made sure he didn't!" He turned away, but she wasn't finished. "And by the way, maybe *you* should have been making that kid think he could be a hero. You think he follows her around because she's got a nice ass? He follows her around because she's telling him he can be more than what he is, than what everybody's told him he could be his whole life! You're his *family*, Bear. You should be telling him all that, and if you're not? It's your own damn fault if he doesn't do what you tell him to do!"

"*He is a child!*"

"Not anymore, he's not," she said, more calmly. "He's not grown yet, but he's not a child. And you can't treat him like one just because you're afraid for him."

"And what the hell do you know about being afraid? You've got no children, have you, Lockwood?"

And at that, she truly lost her temper. "Are we playing *who's seen the most death*, Savosky? Because I'm the oldest of *eighteen* children. And do you know how many of us are still around? *Four.* No, I'm not a parent. But don't you dare tell me I don't know how it feels to be helpless when someone you love is hurt, because I will put you off this ship myself!"

He looked enraged, and opened his mouth; and then he turned to the corridor wall and swore for a long time. When he finally stopped, his fists had fallen open, and he seemed less enormous.

"He was thirteen when we adopted him," he told her. "So hesitant. It took Yuri three weeks to get him to tell us what he liked to eat. We found out after he'd been with us a year that he'd been hoarding the allowance we gave him because he wasn't sure when we'd ask for it back, or when we'd want something from him that he couldn't give us. He didn't trust us. He didn't trust that we loved him. He didn't think anyone ever had. I promised—" He broke off, and took a breath. "I promised I would never let anything hurt him. And this, Lockwood. *This*. All I would have had to do was verify where he was before we left *Budapest*. It would have taken three seconds. It's not like I didn't have any warning that he'd do something like this."

"You can't stop him from having a life, Bear," she told him. "And you can't stop him from getting older, or doing dumbass things while he's figuring out what kind of a person he wants to be."

"It's impossible," he told her, "living like this. How do you love someone, and watch them take risks like that? How do you just stand aside while they throw themselves into the void?"

Oh, Bear. "You do it," she said, "because the alternative is never loving anyone. And most of us, thank every god you can think of, cannot survive like that."

He turned toward her. "You've lost a lot of family."

"I have."

"I'm an ass."

"You bet."

At that he broke into a surprised grin, then sobered. "I apologize, Lockwood. I'm not at my best right now."

Instinctively she reached out, placing her hand over his massive forearm. "Don't apologize, Bear," she told him. "You're terrified. You get dispensation for pretty much anything. And all I can tell you is Hastings is the best fucking doctor in the Corps, and Arin is conscious and lucid. Both of these are good things."

"There are days I think having a kid was the worst idea I've ever had," he admitted.

"My aunts always said the same thing," she told him.

Another flash of a grin, and then his eyes fell closed, and she did her best to embrace his bulk, the dust and filth of Elena's env suit between them.

t's not your fault, Elena."

She had dropped into a chair after Bear left, exhausted and helpless, vaguely aware of the state of her appearance. She should find somewhere to wash up, clean off some of the stench, find something else to wear. There would be clothes in the gym she could borrow, maybe even something without a Corps logo on it. She should go after Bear and let him keep yelling at her; she knew him well enough to know he would need to yell until he wound down. Then she thought of Jessica with him, and decided he might wind down on his own. Bear was no match for her friend.

"You can't know that," she told Greg. He hadn't been there. He hadn't seen her with Arin for six weeks, so grateful to have found someone who saw her life in the Corps as something other than some violent, incomprehensible part of her history. She'd been flattered. She'd felt a little less lonely. And she'd come close to getting him killed.

But Greg just looked surprised. "Of course I can. Savosky's the captain of that ship, civilian or no. It was his responsibility to make sure his people were at their posts going into this thing." He was staring at her, his gray eyes clear, as if he believed it.

"Arin's been following me around the whole time, Greg," she confessed. "Wanting to hear about the Corps. Looking for stories of glory. I fed him all kinds of crap. I even started training with him, telling him he could get in if he wanted."

"From what I saw today," Greg told her, "he probably could. He kept a level head, which is saying something in that fucking mess."

"But—" He was doing what she had been doing: thinking about it from the wrong direction. "He's a civilian, Greg. There was no way I could make him understand the reality of it all. I should have kept my mouth shut. I should have shoved him away. The last thing I should have done is encourage him to see the Corps as an option."

"Is that what Savosky told you?"

"I—don't you think he's right?"

Something flashed across his face: annoyance, she thought, or maybe anger. But when he spoke, his voice was soft. "I don't think you really believe that, Elena," he told her. "Savosky's a civilian, too. He doesn't understand."

"He understands Arin better than I do."

"Do you think so?" He was watching her, those incisive eyes studying her face. "Do you remember nineteen?"

She thought back. She had been in college, serious and single-minded, eyes on one thing and one thing only: doing well enough so she would be accepted at Central Military Academy, to fulfill the only dream she had ever had. She had been humorless, fatalistic, and invincible. "I was an idiot," she confessed.

A smile rippled over his lips. "Me too. And if anybody had tried to tell me anything—never mind my dad—I'd have dug in my heels and done exactly the opposite. What happened on Govi, Elena?"

She rubbed her eyes. "That one was *definitely* my fault. We'd found this lifeboat, with seven people, and they were fucking freezing and scared as hell, and there were waves coming in. So I had Arin fly low, and I took a net cable, and I dove into the ocean to hook them so we could pick them up."

He stared. "You dove into the ocean."

"Yes."

"The freezing, toxic one."

"That's the only one that was there, Greg," she said irritably.

And then, to her surprise, he laughed, and sat back, and she thought she caught something resembling affection in his eyes. "No wonder Savosky's been short with you. He must have thought you'd lost your mind."

"I couldn't *leave* them, Greg. I—"

"I know, Elena. And if he'd asked me before you guys hit Govi, I would have told him exactly what would happen." He grew more serious and leaned forward, elbows on his knees. "Here's what I think happened today: I think Savosky fucked up. I think this kid is better at subterfuge than anybody thought. And I think you would have had to lock him in a cargo hold to keep him away from that moon. He's lucky he was with you. I'm guessing it took some flying to keep that bird from shattering on the way down."

She hadn't thought about it. She had flown the way she always did. "He shouldn't have had to see what he saw today," she said, clinging to her guilt.

And Greg's gray eyes grew somber, and she saw grief, deep and familiar. She always forgot how much grief he carried with him, all the time. "Nobody should have to see what he saw today."

"You know," she said, careful and uncertain, "it wasn't your fault, either. Yakutsk is Yakutsk. You got here as quickly as you could."

"It's never enough, though. Five hundred people. Do you think any of them walked away?"

"You cannot fix the universe, Greg," she insisted. She had said it to him before, a thousand times. "You don't have that power. Nobody does."

He met her eyes, and for one instant everything was erased, and he was her old friend, the one who always knew what to say, who always knew her moods without asking, who made her feel stronger and more focused just by being there. His gaze lightened, and she thought, just maybe, for that one moment, he felt the same way in return.

And then a sound came over her comm: a digital hiccup, an audio artifact, like a message that had been overly compressed and resent too many times. She caught a few words, then a phrase, and then the message cleared up: "This is an automated distress call from *Cytheria*, off of the PSI starship *Chryse*. We are in need of retrieval. Repeating." The message played over, this time in a common PSI dialect.

"Greg," she said, "did you just—"

"I received it, too," he told her. His hand was behind his ear. "Lieutenant Samaras, did you just pick up a distress call?"

"No, sir." Samaras sounded curious. "We're clear on comms."

Greg met Elena's eyes, then said, "Lieutenant, I need you to raise *Chryse* for me."

"Yes, sir."

Elena took a moment to digest that. "Since when," she asked him, "are you on chatting terms with *Chryse*?"

"I think that's overstating it." When she kept staring, he relented. "Since this morning. But I don't know that they'll answer me on an official comm line."

But a moment later, Greg's concerns were put to rest. "Captain Foster," said a warm baritone voice. "What can I do for you?"

"Captain Bayandi," Greg said, "I'm sorry to trouble you, but we've just received a distress call from Commander Ilyana's shuttle."

Bayandi. The most elusive PSI captain ever known to Central Gov. And friendly, no less. This was feeling more surreal by the moment.

"Let me check." Bayandi's voice had gone serious, but lost none of its warmth, and Elena tried and failed to reconcile his affect with everything she had been taught about the strange, standoffish PSI ship. After a moment, the PSI captain continued. "I am receiving only telemetry, Captain," he said, palpably worried. "*Cytheria* has dropped out of the stream. Her environmental systems are intact, but I cannot raise Commander Ilyana. If her shuttle is damaged and she cannot reenter the field—she is not close to anything."

"Can you get to her?" Greg asked.

There was a brief pause. "Our travel time would be nine hours and four minutes. I do not suppose, Captain Foster, that you have anyone closer?"

"I could go," Elena put in.

Bayandi said, "May I ask who you are?"

Polite. Not hostile, not reactive; just polite, and faintly curious. "I'm—" How was she supposed to introduce herself? "I'm Elena Shaw," she said. "I'm off the freighter *Budapest.*"

But Bayandi knew her name. "Ah, yes—you were chief of engineering on *Galileo,* weren't you? It's a pleasure to meet you. Can your freighter spare you?"

"Yes," she said firmly, and ignored Greg's raised eyebrows.

"Then I thank you, Elena Shaw," Bayandi said, sounding relieved. "We are most grateful for your help. And if you could let me know what you find—if Commander Ilyana is all right—"

"I'll let you know as soon as I find her," Elena assured him.

"Please tell her—" He paused again, longer this time. "Please tell her that I hope she is well."

The comm terminated, and she stood, ready to move. "If I head back to *Budapest* now," she reasoned, "I can take the other shuttle before Bear has a chance to stop me."

"Wait." He got to his feet, and she stopped. "Elena, I can't send you on a military rescue."

"It's not a military rescue," she reasoned, "it's a PSI rescue. And you're not sending me anywhere. I don't work for you anymore."

At that his jaw set, and she was abruptly aware she might have phrased that more tactfully. But when he spoke, he kept his temper. "Okay, then, how about this? It's irresponsible of you to head off into the unknown in a civilian shuttle. Ilyana's got weapons. You don't."

There was something here she was missing. "Why are you worried about this, Greg?" she asked. "I mean, *Chryse* is *Chryse*, sure; but they're PSI. They've never threatened us."

He stared at her, and she recognized the look in his eyes: *Too public. Not here.* "We're stuck here to deal with Yakutsk," he said, instead of answering her question, "but I can spare you a shuttle. At least you won't be defenseless."

He led her out of the infirmary, and she waited him out.

"Captain Taras is worried about *Chryse*," he told her as they walked toward the shuttle bay. "Apparently they've been acting odd since a comms outage that occurred four months ago."

"Four months." The significance of the time frame didn't escape her. "Taras thinks they've been compromised."

"She didn't come right out and say that."

"*You* think they've been compromised."

"I think it's not a possibility we can ignore."

She shook her head. "Bayandi sounds . . . friendly."

"He does." Greg's tone went dry. "Funny, isn't it, that the

first time we talk to the captain of such an isolated starship, he turns out to be so personable?"

"And the distress call, aimed just at you and me." She was feeling increasingly uneasy. "I don't suppose you could spare me a weapon."

"According to regulations? No." His lips set in a grim smile. "But under the circumstances, regulations can go fuck themselves."

CHAPTER 10

T he Corps is not here as your personal army, Governor,"
Greg told Villipova, "or to teach your people self-defense.
We're here to keep you from blowing each other up."

Greg was seated at his desk next to Herrod, the two governors on vid before them, and Greg found himself grudgingly
grateful for the older man's presence. Herrod's habitual emotional detachment worked well in diplomatic situations like
this one, when Greg was tempted to abort the entire process
and tell everyone involved to grow the hell up. Herrod's reticence reminded Greg that practical diplomacy was less about
making people shake hands than it was about holding people
off of each other until frayed tempers managed to settle.

His own frayed temper included.

Villipova frowned. "It's not possible for you to do that
without taking sides," she insisted. "Oarig's people shot
down that civilian transport. It's his fault the food both of
our cities need lies frozen on the surface."

"We weren't shooting down anything!" Oarig interrupted.

"They were out there confronting *your* people, who were going to hoard it all for themselves! They—"

"That's enough," Greg snapped. *God, this finger-pointing is tedious.* "Gov sent us here to keep the two of you from doing this kind of shit to each other," he told them. "And that means it stops now. You want to hash out who did what to whom—do it afterward, when your people have supplies and safe places to live again. On the other hand"—he felt Herrod's eyes on him—"if you're genuinely inclined to shoot down the people trying to help you, we *are* going to take sides, and it's not going to be with either one of you. Have I made myself perfectly clear?"

Oarig's lips narrowed. Villipova just looked tired.

"So here's what's going to happen," Greg told them. "You are going to clear all of your people off the surface. Once the crash site is clear, I'll send down some infantry to help retrieve the remains of the cargo. They—not your people, on either side—will move the cargo into the cultivation dome. They will dispense supplies in precisely the same amounts to each dome."

"Captain," Oarig objected, "Baikul has far more people. We need—"

"You need," Greg told him, "to make sure your people stand down. Because the second we get wind of either side doing so much as target practice, all humanitarian help will be suspended. We'll drop the seed where it belongs, and we'll be out of there. Understood?"

Oarig looked as if he might object again, but this time a look from Herrod took care of him. He nodded, and Villipova said, "Understood."

When the comm ended, Herrod raised his eyebrows at Greg. "You think that's going to work?" he asked.

"Why not? Being reasonable hasn't brought them anything. They call us, looking for help, we get here and they ignore everything we say. I sincerely doubt Gov wants us to spend weeks here letting them jerk us around."

"Not what I meant, Captain," Herrod said easily. Everything was always easy with him these days, a marked contrast to the short-tempered officer Greg had served under for years. It set Greg's teeth on edge. "I have no quarrel with your strategy. Only your optimism."

He rubbed his eyes. He had not anticipated this day would go well, but it had gone so much worse than he had feared. "Commander Lockwood is pulling the infantry together," he said. "We should be able to protect the cargo, if nothing else."

"What about the civilians?"

"As soon as they start shooting," Greg told him, "they're not civilians anymore."

Herrod's eyebrows went up again, but he didn't argue.

Greg waited until Herrod had left before comming Jessica. "What's the state of the infantry, Commander?" he asked.

"Ready as always, sir," she said.

He could hear it in her voice: she was still annoyed with him for sending Elena after the PSI shuttle. When he'd told her he couldn't spare the infantry, she'd pointed out that fully half of *Galileo*'s 226-member crew were not infantry. "You could have sent a mechanic, or a pilot. You could have sent *me*."

"You're not combat-trained."

She had sworn at him, and he had known better than to laugh. "I am combat-trained to the same degree that Elena is. Just like everyone else on this ship. And most of us know our way around piloting a shuttle, especially one of our own. How the hell is what you're doing any different than Savosky using her for risky missions his own people can't hack?"

It wasn't the same thing at all. But he couldn't figure out how to explain it to her, so he'd just ordered her to drop it. A temporary respite at best, and in the meantime, he could expect her to be short with him.

If he'd had the luxury, he'd have sent Elena after *Cytheria* in one of the big armored troop carriers. Instead, he'd given her *Nightingale*, a ship she knew, and small enough for him to give up without jeopardizing their Yakutsk mission. Herrod's sleek new travel shuttle might have done well enough, but apart from its lacking *Nightingale*'s armaments, Greg would have had to explain why he wanted to borrow it. And Greg wanted, as long as possible, to hide their strange relationship with *Chryse* from a retired admiral who was probably still part of Shadow Ops.

Elena had balked, briefly, at the heavy plasma rifle he wanted to give her. "I'll be on my own, after all," she pointed out. "A hand weapon would be more than enough."

"I wouldn't send anyone into this mess with nothing but a hand weapon," he replied. She'd given him a deeply skeptical look that was achingly familiar, and then lifted the gun effortlessly from his hands and slung it over her shoulder. She was still in her *Budapest* env suit, gray and utilitarian, still coated in dust and grime; but as she strode away from him toward *Sparrow* she looked as military as any other member of his crew.

She looked like she belonged.

Walking back to his office after seeing her off, he found himself unsettled and irritable, and it had taken him all those minutes to figure out what the problem was: from the moment he had seen her down on that moon, covered in compost, determined and furious and terrified for her crewmate, some knot he hadn't realized was inside of him had relaxed, and he had felt more clearheaded than he had in a year. Which was unfair: she had chosen to leave *Galileo,* and she had chosen to resign her commission, guaranteeing he had no way of getting her back on board. He had understood her reasons and had even found them logical; but she had lied to him, back when they had first found out she was being transferred. *They cannot separate us unless we let them,* she had told him.

And then she had let them.

He did not have the luxury of getting mired in all of that right now. She would rescue Ilyana, she would leave with *Budapest,* and Yakutsk would find some kind of irritable peace. And he would figure out, once and for all, how to leave her behind.

"I want the infantry twelve-on, twelve-off," he told Jessica. "No long shifts for anyone. We may need to call them all up together if the situation heats up before *Meridia* gets here."

At that, her tone thawed a little, and she betrayed some of her worry. "Do you think it's that bad?"

"I think when it goes it'll go quickly." He paused. "Jess— did you ever meet Commander Ilyana?"

"I don't think so." Jessica sounded thoughtful. "I'm sure I talked to someone on *Chryse* once or twice, but it would've just been a few words. Whether it was her or not I couldn't say. Why?" He could almost hear her mind working. "Do you think they'd send us a ringer?"

That hadn't been what was worrying him, but it was a good question. "I want everything we have on Ilyana," he said. "As many images and reports as we can get. News, rumor, all of it."

"You should ask Herrod." The tone was back, but at least it wasn't aimed at Greg anymore.

"You think he'd tell me?" He heard her scoff, and he thought he might be forgiven. "And when she gets here, Jess . . . I want her comms monitored, and I want a guard on her. Not a goon, but someone with sharp eyes. Taras can take her when *Meridia* gets here, but I don't want *Galileo* at risk."

"You're thinking maybe rescuing her isn't the best idea?"

"I'm thinking," he told her, "that being kind doesn't mean we have to be stupid."

CHAPTER 11

H ow's the kid?" Ted asked Jessica.

Jessica was seated in Ted's office, her feet on his desk, going over the history of Commander Tatiana Ilyana. The easiest thing, as it turned out, had been to find her original name: Leslie Barrett Millar, born on Achinsk, reported as a runaway at seventeen after a history of run-ins with the police at government protests. What was more interesting than her early history, though, was the reason it was easy to find: the Admiralty had commissioned a similar search on Ilyana nearly twenty years ago. Greg, as it turned out, had been right to be concerned: the Admiralty, although lacking concrete proof, believed she was a fairly accomplished spy.

Of course, with PSI having been allied with Central almost without interruption for hundreds of years, she wasn't sure why the Admiralty would be worried about a spy. She had been thinking, lately—as rumors swirled about colonies in the Fifth Sector wanting to shift the seat of Central Gov to their territory, leaving Earth in political limbo—that

Central had wasted a lot of time over the decades worrying about PSI. PSI was often secretive, and certainly standoffish to a degree that Gov seemed to find puzzling. But in every instance that had mattered, Jessica had seen PSI step up and fight on the same side as Gov, the Corps, and the colonies.

Besides, she thought, thinking of Admiral Herrod, *Central has plenty of accomplished spies of their own.*

She looked up at Ted, who was leaning against one of the office's windowed walls, his back to the open engine room outside. Ted never sat at his desk. Ever since he had been appointed chief of engineering, he had used the office, but never sat in the chair. He hadn't said so, but she knew in his mind it was Elena's. Of course, it might also have been Ted's endless kinetic energy—he was not big on sitting at the best of times—but given how his teeth set every time someone called him *Chief,* she didn't think that was the main reason.

"Stabilized, Bob says," she replied. "If he were one of us, Bob would already have cut him loose. As it is, he wants to sit on him until *Budapest* has to leave."

"So he's worried."

"I think *cautious* is probably more accurate." Or, she thought, possibly *territorial.* For a cynical old man, Bob became deeply possessive of his patients, especially those who had been badly hurt. "If he was worried, he'd tell Bear to delay their next drop and stick around. I'm not so sure Bear won't do it anyway."

Ted was watching her curiously. "This kind of worrying familiar to you, Jessie?"

She met his eyes as neutrally as she could. "More than I'd

like it to be," she admitted. Ted knew her too well. "Ted, you've been around a bit."

"You've been listening to gossip again, haven't you?"

She ignored him. "Did you ever run into this Commander Ilyana?"

He shook his head. "Never dealt with *Chryse* directly," he said. "But one of the guys I originally deployed with—he's out on *Borissova* now—did an airlift with *Chryse*'s help. Said they were unbelievably well organized, but otherwise kind of rude."

"Not surprising, PSI being PSI."

"That's why I remember him remarking on it. They must have been *really* unpleasant."

Which was not unusual in isolation. But Jessica thought of Greg, and his reaction to Captain Bayandi. Greg was both curious and mistrustful of the man, and she did not think he would be so concerned if Bayandi had behaved with PSI's typical coolness.

She shoved aside her research, giving *Galileo* a chance to digest more records. "Did you get anything on that artifact yet?" she asked.

For a moment, she thought he wasn't going to let her change the subject. But then he pushed himself off the wall and began to pace in front of her. "So what we've got there," Ted told Jessica, "is an enigma."

"Haven't you scanned it?"

"Oh yes. I scanned it from every possible angle with everything we've got." He shook his head. "It's shielded. No matter what I point at it, I get a happy little NO DATA back from the system. So whatever it is, it's got better tech than we have, which does not please me."

It did not please Jessica, either. *Better tech* almost certainly meant Ellis.

"But the other side of it," he added, "is that it didn't actually do anything."

Jessica raised her eyebrows. "What about Lanie's message?"

"It's not a message." He leaned across her and hit a panel on the desk. A waveform appeared in the air, and he reached his fingers into the image and pulled it apart. "It's an audio amalgam of comms she's received and sent. There's nothing original in there at all."

Jessica got to her feet, walking around the waveform to stand at Ted's side. "So it tapped into her comm and *composed* something from what it found." She looked up at him. "Is it just me, or is that the opposite of not doing anything?"

"Well, okay, it's not *nothing*," he allowed. "But it's not sophisticated, Jess. It's basically an audio compositor that uses emphasis based on frequency. It's a parlor trick. It's the shielding that's more interesting, and it's possible even that's just a variant of the loopback virus we hit a while back."

She frowned. "I'd feel a lot better if I knew who was after it. Or how to use it."

"I've got one more test I want to try," he told her, "but I've been waiting for you, just in case I pass out or something."

"You're going to touch it."

"Only way, Jess."

"If it goes after you like it did Lanie—"

"I swapped my comm out right before you got here," he said. "If it's doing what I think it's doing, it's going to give me nothing but our conversation. And of course some lovely words from you about how wonderful I am." He grew more serious. "You with me on this?"

She sighed and dropped her feet off the desk to stand. "I suppose I might as well watch the thing melt your brain."

At that, he shot her a grin. "I live to serve."

He led her to a small workroom. When he closed them into the space, she raised her eyebrows at him. He shrugged, looking sheepish. "It's a paranoia thing," he told her. "It commed Lanie when she touched it, but if it's got an interface that gets activated on contact, I don't want to give it access to *Galileo*. This room is comms-locked."

She looked around the small space. "What, always?"

"Sometimes we need a space where things can go wrong without broadcasting to the whole ship."

The box containing the artifact was sitting on a table, next to a haphazard stack of spanners. "Is it safe to open?" she asked.

"The one thing I know," he told her, "is that if there's anything radioactive in there, it's contained by whatever shielding it's got." He gave her a look. "You want to wait outside?"

She shook her head, and he opened the box.

The artifact was, she thought, about as anticlimactic as it could be. It was a flattened cube with rounded edges and corners, done in a gray polymer. If it had been sitting in a corner of the ship, she wouldn't even have noticed it. *Easy to camouflage,* she thought. *Easy to make someone pick it up without thinking.*

Ted took a breath, extended a finger, and touched the cube.

After a moment he lifted his hand and touched it again, then laid his palm on the surface. He took it out of the box and held it with both hands, threaded it between his fingers, tossed it into the air and caught it again. He looked across at Jessica. "Nothing."

"What do you mean, 'nothing'?"

"I mean," he said patiently, "I'm not getting anything, comms or otherwise, and monitoring is showing no signal." He placed it back into the box. "If I hadn't looked at Lanie's comm myself, I'd have guessed she just hit some kind of random interference."

Jessica frowned down at the artifact, suddenly ominous in its nondescriptness. "Is it possible that's what happened?"

"Sure. But if it's not this thing that scrambled her comm, there's something roaming out in the wild doing it. Besides, she said Jamyung heard it, too, remember?"

She looked over at him. Something had occurred to her, but she didn't want to share it yet. "Maybe it's the comm," she said. "Something Lanie's and Jamyung's had in common."

"Maybe it doesn't like the new ones," Ted mused. "I could put my old one on and try it again."

She shook her head. Regardless of the persistent inertness of the thing, risking Ted felt like an extreme response. "We're getting ahead of ourselves," she said. "There's more we can find out without getting reckless. How thick is that inert polymer?"

"About half a centimeter." He caught on to her thoughts. "You want to shave it, see if we get something stronger?"

She nodded. "Slowly. We see anything, any kind of a spike, and we stop right away."

Ted pulled on safety gloves and removed the artifact again, clamping it securely against the tabletop. He could have used a hand spanner, but instead he mounted a mechanical one, setting it over one of the artifact's narrow sides. "This will dig a micron at a time," he told her. "As soon as it hits a variation in any reading at all, it'll stop."

And it was this exercise that gained them a result. The mechanical spanner stopped at 350 microns. "Anomaly detected," it said, and projected what it had found. Jessica recognized it instantly.

Dim, incomplete, and fading: it was the magnetic shadow of a comm signal.

This was Jessica's field. "I need an amplifier," she told Ted, "and something that'll extrapolate for me."

"Extrapolation is awfully inexact."

"Less inexact than just hacking it in half," she pointed out, and he left to find the tools.

She spent the better part of an hour on the shadow, focusing on the smallest fragments she could find, telling *Galileo* what she did and did not want the ship to consider important. *Galileo* might have made entirely different choices, if Jessica had left it to the automated systems. None of this was precise, and it irked her cryptographic mind to be analyzing a potential weapon with what were basically guesses.

In the end, what she had was a muddled mess, but if she

listened to it in just the right way, she could believe it was fragments of someone speaking. "Or dogs barking," she said aloud, disgusted with herself. "Or maybe bats. Shit, Ted, this is *meaningless*."

"Probably," he agreed. "But see what you get from the extrapolator."

They had to give the tool parameters. Yes, they thought it was human speech. Yes, they thought it was a known language. Yes, they thought it was recent. Yes, they thought it was a comm signal. She sat back and listened to the iterations. The extrapolator was focusing on the rhythm of it, the rise and fall of the tone; they had said *speech,* and the extrapolator was finding words.

"This is a chicken-egg thing, Ted," she protested. "Nothing we hear will—"

Cytheria, the extrapolator said.

So much for doubts. She turned to Ted. "Did you hear that?"

He nodded. "Let it iterate a few more times."

But having heard it, she couldn't unhear it. *Cytheria.* And then, a few iterations later, a second word emerged, further down the stream: *Chryse.*

"What the hell?" Ted said, frowning.

But Jessica hit her comm to look for Greg. "Captain?"

He answered immediately. "What's the matter, Commander?"

"Nothing. Everything's—well. We've maybe got something on this . . . *thing* of Elena's, sir. Do you still have the comm of the distress call you received on Yakutsk?"

"Of course. Hang on." There was a pause, and the message played over her comm: *This is an automated distress call. This is* Cytheria, *off of the PSI starship* Chryse. *We are in need of retrieval. Repeating. We are in need of retrieval.*

"*Galileo,*" Jessica asked, "what are the odds that's the message we're trying to reconstitute?"

"Rhythmic and tonal match eighty-five percent certainty," the ship said.

"Greg," she said into her comm, "you should probably come down here."

CHAPTER 12

CYTHERIA

Elena left *Galileo* wrapped in the familiarity of a shuttle she had flown a hundred times. The hum of the engine, the responsiveness of the controls, the curve of the front window with the tactical display overlaying her view of the stars—it was at once soothing and heartbreaking. *Nightingale* didn't sound like *Galileo*, but Elena knew the shuttle's music nearly as well, and she wanted nothing more than to stay where she was, eyes closed, and listening to the engines, possibly for the rest of her life.

Galileo's melodies had not changed. Elena hadn't even noticed until she realized what she was missing: that low-level awareness of an unfamiliar rhythm. During the six-week run from Earth, she had not had time to internalize *Budapest*'s sounds. Yuri was always patient with her questions—as an experienced mechanic himself, he knew how important it was to be tuned in to the ship—but she had always felt vaguely out of sync. She had stepped onto *Galileo*, and something inside of her had stilled, as if she had stopped worrying a wound.

And for that, if nothing else, she was grateful to Arin. Worrying about him had allowed her to avoid the fact that she was just going to have to leave again.

She would have to speak with Jessica, too. During their conversations over the last year, Jessica had volunteered information on Greg, knowing Elena would never ask; but Elena had realized almost as soon as she had seen him that Jessica had left out some important things.

Elena knew Greg had been seeing Andriya Vassily, captain of the Third Sector starship CCSS *Cassia,* and that Jessica didn't entirely approve, worried that Greg had fallen back into the patterns of his failed long-distance marriage. Of course, he also had other lovers, including a journalist for the streamers whom Jessica openly disliked. Elena had seen the woman's reporting, and she could understand why Greg might like her: she came across as quick and good-humored, and she was stunningly, vid-ready beautiful. Jessica had ranted, but Elena had found herself oddly pleased. After the marriage he had escaped, he deserved beautiful women. He deserved legions of them fighting over him. Sometimes, when she thought of him, she imagined just that.

But she had seen it in his eyes as he sat in the infirmary offering her absolution: he was lonely. He had always been lonely, as long as she had known him, but that was supposed to have changed. Over the last eighteen months, Elena had been jealous of his blossoming friendship with Jessica, the professional and personal relationship she was closed out of. She had been happy for them both, and bitterly sorry for herself. But apparently, despite their easy camaraderie, their relationship had changed nothing for Greg at all: he was still by himself in all the ways that mattered.

As long as she had known him, he had lived behind a wall. He would tell her, if she asked, that it was necessary, that he was the captain, that distance was critical. But she had seen it in him from the start, from the first time she met him, when she was an ensign looking for a transfer and he was the captain she wanted to impress. All these years she thought he had done it on purpose, kept himself away from everyone. She wondered, sitting in *Galileo*'s shuttle, if the truth was he had no idea how to let anybody in.

She had a moment of self-awareness at the thought, and nearly smiled. *Always easier to psychoanalyze other people than to understand yourself, right?*

"*Nightingale,* what's our travel time?" she asked.

"Two hours, forty-seven minutes," the shuttle responded.

"Wake me up in two hours and seventeen minutes," she said. Unfastening her harness, she stood up from the pilot's seat and wandered into the back of the little ship. She stripped off her filthy env suit and tucked it into a corner, then turned on the shuttle's utilitarian sink and sponged off, dipping her head under the faucet to wash the dome dust out of her hair. When she finished she pulled on one of the regulation Corps env suits folded neatly in a storage drawer. She had no comb, but she ran her fingers through her long hair, working out the tangles, and weaved it into her usual loose braid.

Nightingale wasn't a troop ship, but she could hold a dozen soldiers in addition to a pilot and copilot. The benches on either side of the cabin were padded and long enough to hold six seated upright. If she lay down, Elena's feet wouldn't even hang over the edge.

She pulled the jacket of another env suit out of the drawer and rolled it up. Almost as an afterthought, she pulled the plasma rifle Greg had provided off the wall rack and laid it on the floor next to the bench. Whatever she was facing, she didn't think it would be a mistake to have her weapon close. Stretching out on the bench, she tucked the extra jacket under her ear and closed her eyes. *Nightingale*'s familiar rhythms seeped into her mind, and she fell asleep.

Nightingale woke her at the appointed hour, and she sat up, feeling more refreshed than she had in some time, despite the unusually eventful day. She took a moment to splash some water on her face, then retrieved the plasma rifle and returned to the pilot's seat, checking the shuttle's status. They were exactly where they were supposed to be, closing in on the location of *Chryse*'s shuttle.

"Has it changed course?" she asked.

"No," *Nightingale* told her. "Speed and trajectory are unchanged."

"Are you detecting any targeting systems?"

"No."

"Ident?"

"Ident verifies that the shuttle is *Cytheria,* off of the PSI ship *Chryse*."

It could all be falsified, of course. For all she knew, she would be coming out of the field on top of a dozen Syndicate raiders, or one black box Shadow Ops fighter ship. Nothing they had found so far had that level of sophistication, but she had long since learned never to underestimate what either Ellis Systems or her government's own special research branch could do.

Giving in to caution, she dropped out early, adding an extra ten minutes to her trip. As she grew closer, both her eyes and *Sparrow*'s sensors told her the same thing: a single ship, running normally at sublight speed, no alarms beyond the automated distress call sent on a narrow, targeted beam.

To me. And to Greg.

But as she grew closer and began to make out details, she found herself surprised. She had expected damage, possibly weapons fire, but the shuttle appeared unscathed. The unexpected thing was not its condition, but its design.

It was *old*.

PSI had a reputation for recycling whatever parts they could find, often to elegant effect, but her image of *Chryse* had been augmented by the fact that everything that ship did seemed to be somehow flashy and modern: automated drops, to-the-second schedules, quick response times, small landing crews with precisely the right set of talents. Flawlessly organized. But this shuttle was older than some of the ones Elena had worked on with her uncle as a child—forty or fifty years by the look of her, in need of a complete hull refit at the very least. Elena could see immediately what had happened: the engine casing had begun to separate from the flimsy hull. Assuming it was designed the same as her familiar Central ships, it would have dropped out of the field and adjusted to automatic mode. It would have been a rough ride, but with environmentals intact, it should not have been dangerous.

Elena sent a general comm. "*Cytheria*, this is the shuttle

Nightingale, off of CCSS *Galileo.*" Automatic, identifying herself as part of *Galileo.* "Are you in need of assistance?"

Silence.

She circled around the ship, looking for other damage, and found nothing. After a moment, she signaled *Chryse,* half expecting the PSI ship to ignore her comm.

But Bayandi picked up almost immediately. "Chief Shaw," he said, his voice anxious. "Have you found her?"

She was not sure why she felt so skeptical that his concern was genuine. "I've found the shuttle," she said, and told him about the damage.

"But the cabin is intact," he pressed.

"As far as I can tell by visual inspection, yes. And all her env systems are functioning." Bayandi would know that; he could read the same telemetry she could. "But if it was a rough drop-out, it's possible Commander Ilyana was injured." She didn't state the worst possibility. "Captain—" She found she could not resist asking. "*Cytheria* appears to be fairly old. Are all your shuttles of this vintage?"

"You have an educated eye, Chief Shaw," Bayandi said. "And no, many of our shuttles are new. But *Cytheria* has longer-range batteries than the others, and she is outfitted more robustly for difficult environmental situations. Given that Ilyana was going alone," and here his voice became concerned again, "I felt *Cytheria* made the most sense."

Elena had an abrupt mental picture of Bayandi: frowning, worried, wondering if his attempt at protecting his officer had led to her harm—or even her death. *There's been a lot of that today,* she thought. "As long as her docking mechanism is standard," Elena said, trying to sound brisk and self-assured, "I shouldn't have any trouble getting in." She thought of telling him not to be concerned, but if he was as old as people suspected, he would know that for a platitude. "I'll let you know as soon as I find her."

"Thank you, Chief," said the subdued PSI captain, and she realized it was far too late to correct him about her title.

Cytheria was outfitted with a locking door on the top. Elena maneuvered *Nightingale* onto her side, linking up the two doors, waiting for the lights to go green. Securing the hood of her env suit, she shrugged on the plasma rifle and settled it comfortably between her shoulder blades. She took a deep breath, opened *Nightingale*'s hatch, and slid open *Cytheria*'s door.

She was greeted with a dim glow: the ship's emergency lights. With some care she slipped through the opening, reorienting to the other ship's gravity, and dropped as quietly as she could to the floor of the cabin. She was standing in a narrow corridor, with storage doors on either side of her. Behind her, the space was unlit, but before her the corridor brightened, turning warmer. She could hear a muffled voice, too quiet for her to make out words or language. It was high, possibly feminine, and the tone seemed leisurely and unconcerned. As she stood still, listening, she heard no other voice replying or interrupting, and after a few moments she thought she heard the rhythm of the speech repeat. A recording? A recitation? Slinging her rifle off of her shoulder, she kept one hand firmly on the grip and pressed herself against the corridor wall, creeping forward.

The hallway opened into a large room, fully as wide as the shuttle itself, and furnished like crew's quarters. There was a bank of drawers along the opposite wall, and a bunk under a long, narrow window, reminding her of her quarters on *Budapest*. Next to her was a large sofa, luxurious and overstuffed, and before the sofa was the source of the voice: a recorded comm, playing in the center of the room. There was a young woman talking, relaxed, dressed all in black as PSI generally were, speaking in a modified version of the familiar Fourth Sector dialect.

". . . know how she is, Mama. Loves school, hates me." The woman laughed, and the expression lit her sober, dark eyes. "I'm happy, really. I don't want her upset when I leave her. They keep telling me I should be jealous that a little girl likes her teachers more than her mama, but I love it. She's learning." The woman sighed. "Well, I know you've got a long trip. I'll see you when you get back, yes? Love you, Mama."

There was a slight digital fillip, and as the message restarted Elena turned to find, lying on the couch, facing the vid with her eyes closed, a woman.

She was short and broad-shouldered, compactly built, with a thick waist and narrow hips. Her skin was dark, and her black hair, cropped short, curled loosely against her skull. She had thin lips and a broad nose, and her eyelids were large and deep-set under thick, oddly graceful eyebrows. Her skin boasted few lines, but something in the softness of her jaw and the faint folds at the edges of her eyes suggested to Elena she was well past fifty.

"Hello?"

The woman didn't move.

Slinging the rifle back over her shoulder, Elena pulled off one of her gloves and moved to the woman's side. She felt for the pulse in her neck: strong and steady. But she couldn't be sleeping, not with Elena poking at her. Elena stood and scanned the small room for a med kit, spying it tucked underneath the bunk. Unlike the kit on *Budapest*'s shuttle, this was a Level Five kit, and she raised her eyebrows. With a little training, one could do bone grafts and neurological treatments with a Level Five. This was luxury, or the expectation that *Cytheria* would be traveling alone for long distances indeed.

One quick pass with the kit's scanner told her what she had suspected: the woman was drugged. The tranquilizer was a common one, and not generally so soporific; but her system was flooded with it. Elena frowned. Ordinarily, injectors would detect dangerous levels of drugs and fail to deploy. Either something had been faulty in the dosing mechanism, or the woman had overridden the safeties on purpose.

The scanner also told her the woman was malnourished, and probably had not been taking in sufficient calories for at least two weeks. Which might explain the drugs, Elena supposed; if she could sleep more, she wouldn't need as much food to survive. She would have to check the shuttle's records and food supply. Perhaps the early drop-out meant *Cytheria*'s journey was going to take longer than the supplies the woman had brought.

The vid looped again, and absently Elena turned to swipe it off.

And in that instant, a hand clamped around her wrist.

CHAPTER 13

GALILEO

"Can you tell if the comm was routed through this thing?" Greg asked Jessica.

They stood in one of the machine room's small utility areas, where Shimada had sensibly chosen to test the object. "I'd have to look at *Cytheria*'s records," she replied.

Greg checked the time. Elena would be arriving at *Cytheria*'s last reported location soon, but he had no idea if she'd be able to bring the injured PSI ship back with her. "For now, I think we need to assume the artifact had something to do with the message going to only Elena and me. Was there any increase in radiation when you started scraping it?"

Ted Shimada shook his head. "All other readings stayed constant. But opening it up, knowing nothing about what's inside of it . . . Its behavior so far has been largely benign, sir, but I think we'd want a very controlled environment before we did that. Like an off-site drone."

He looked up to meet Ted's eyes. "Automated?"

"There could be anything in there, sir," he pointed out.

Greg had a brief, unfair thought—*Elena would not have been so overcautious*—and looked back down at the artifact. Ordinary gray polymer, now with a smooth etched curve on one side where Ted had gently bored into it. Greg had to admit there was something about it, some aesthetic appeal that made the idea of it being dangerous somehow absurd. "Let me ask you two something," he said. "When you look at it, what do you see?"

He met Jessica's eyes. She had that look that suggested he had just asked her something so far outside her realm of experience that she was wondering if he was serious. "Do you mean—what, its physical characteristics?"

He shrugged, not wanting to lead her.

Jessica looked down at it gamely. "It's square on one side, oblong on the other two. Rounded corners and edges. Kind of . . . gray and nondescript." She looked back up at him. "That's not what you were going for, is it?"

"Does it hold any artistic appeal for you?" He glanced at Ted. "Either of you?"

Jessica and Ted exchanged a careful glance. "You mean," Jessica said, "would anyone pay for it?" Jessica had an extensive art collection, some of which Greg liked very much. "I wouldn't," she said decisively. "To me, it reads industrial and uninteresting."

Ted nodded in agreement. "Can't say I'd see it as anything other than ordinary camouflage, sir."

Which opened up a whole host of possibilities. *Coincidence,* he thought. *Surely it wouldn't just be me and Elena.* "You got nothing when you touched it," he confirmed.

Ted shook his head. "It may have scraped Lanie's comm, but it didn't want anything to do with mine."

But Jessica had figured him out. "No," she said adamantly. "Absolutely not. I'll do it, Greg, if you're dead set on somebody else trying it. But not you."

"You can't do it," he told her. "You've got to be ready to deploy the infantry."

"Fuck you, Greg, *you've* got to be ready to deploy the infantry!" Next to her Ted shifted uncomfortably. "You can't take the risk of touching this thing!"

"Jess." He looked down at her, willing her to understand. "If that thing is Ellis tech—if it's a weapon—we need to understand it, and fast. We've had the control test, and Elena's not here. It has to be me. I'm the only other person it's contacted, and we don't have time to wait for the best of all possible worlds."

She closed her mouth and scowled, and he knew he had her. "Just once," she said, unable to keep quiet, "I'd like a world where the best choice isn't one where you need to do something completely fucking insane."

"*Leviathan*," Greg ordered, "decouple yourself from *Galileo*." A moment later there was a brief flash of acknowledgment, and the shuttle was as isolated as if it were in an unexplored sector of the galaxy.

He had taken *Leviathan*, a cramped two-person shuttle, a hundred kilometers outside of his ship. It was not quite as dramatic a solution as Ted's unmonitored drone, but it had seemed a safer alternative to the isolated utility room. Caution still felt unnatural, but he felt mildly relieved his objectivity seemed to be intact. Liking something, he had learned long, long ago, didn't mean it wasn't going to hurt you.

He took a moment to turn the ship so the nose was facing away from *Galileo*, away from Yakutsk, toward the vast empty space past this star system. Nothing but blackness and small, flaring lights, systems too distant to be anything but dust. Silent and beautiful. *I should do this more often,* he thought. It soothed his nerves, cleared his head, gave him a sense of stillness and contentment. He thought he could have watched for quite some time, absorbing the peace and quiet.

But Jessica was already jumpy. If he didn't get moving, she would assume something was wrong and start comming him, destroying the isolated field they had so carefully set up. He got up from the pilot's seat and went to the back of the cabin, where Jessica and Ted had set up the scanning equipment, and stared down at the box on the table.

"Okay," he said, "let's do this."

He opened the box and once again looked at the object inside. Jessica was right, in one sense. It was nothing but a cuboid: gray, flat, and pointless. But it still drew his eye, gave him a feeling of balance, made him want to run his finger over it. He wondered if his artistic sensibilities were so different from Jessica's. Certainly some of the cluttered nonsense she collected was beyond him, but a lot of it he enjoyed in the same way he enjoyed this artifact. The pieces she had that he liked were shaped not like real objects, but like feelings, abstract representations of beauty and humor and happiness and sadness. This artifact was all about longing, this squat six-sided object, rounded and symmetrical, but only on two axes. Almost but not quite perfectly balanced. Almost what it wanted to be.

He took a breath, and reached out his finger and touched it. One second. Two. Three . . .

It began as a low rumble of conversation, like a cafeteria crowd, cacophonous but not distressed. That made sense; most of his comms traffic was chatter, either brief comms to one of his crew, or a debriefing of some sort with an admiral. Aggregated, it sounded mundane, almost soothing; hypnotic in its utter sameness.

Voices began to distinguish themselves in the tumult. His own, of course; perhaps he spent more time talking than listening. He thought he heard Jessica's lilt in there, and now and then Elena's, but he could make out no words. He closed his eyes, letting the sound wash over him, everyone he knew, his whole history.

The first words he made out were his father's. It was the conversation they'd had, all those years ago, when he commed Greg to tell him he was getting married again.

. . . acting disrespectful, to be honest, Greg.

Not as disrespectful as you replacing a dead woman.

Anger. Acrimony. He felt a wave of shame wash over him. He heard his father again, the same sign-off he gave every time they spoke: *I love you, Greg.* Until recently, always followed by Greg's silence.

I'm sorry, he thought; but it was the past, and it was just a sound, playing over his comm, and surely it would end soon.

There was a rhythm beginning underneath it all, at first so low he wasn't sure what it was, but it repeated and repeated and grew louder and he recognized his heartbeat, accelerated as it was when he was running, steady and true, over and over again. Louder and louder.

And then it stopped. Everything stopped. And in the silence, his comm played the last words he'd ever heard his mother speak, from a recording off of a long-dead starship:

. . . dying here while you assholes run off?

He was a child again, running along the shore while his mother went swimming, while she laughed and called out to him and tried to lure him in. He waited on the shore for her, giggling and shaking his head, watching her dive and come up again, dive and come up, dive and . . . she didn't come up this time. *Mom?* he shouted at the sea. *Mama?*

This isn't how it happened, a part of him recognized. *This isn't how she died.* But all he could feel was panic.

He ran into the ocean, but it beat him back, washing over him, shoving him aside. He fought it, scrambling, diving into the surf, eyes open under the water, scanning for her. Surely he would find her. Surely she would be fine. She was his mother. Nothing ever happened to her. She was always there.

He had to breathe, and his head came up out of the water, and he shouted for her again: *Mama! Mama! Mama! Where are you?*

And then he was a grown man, and he was standing on the shore, and he was watching the child struggle in the surf, calling for his mother, over and over, and he couldn't move and he couldn't help, and he watched the boy go under, over and over again, and his feet were rooted and all he could do was cry out:

Where are you?

Where are you?

Where are you?

And then there was only darkness.

CHAPTER 14

CYTHERIA

eave it."

Elena started, and turned away from the vid. The woman was wide awake, eyes open, black and hostile depths fixed on Elena's face. Her expression was haunted, and Elena couldn't tell if she was agitated with fear or anger. *Possibly both,* she supposed. The woman's grip on Elena's wrist was certainly solid.

The woman had spoken in dialect. As gently as she could, Elena responded in kind. "I'm sorry," she said, not pulling against the woman's hand. "I didn't mean to wake you."

Her dialect was rustier than she wanted to admit, but the woman clearly understood. She blinked once, then twice; and suddenly her hostility dissolved, and her expression settled into mildly pleasant blandness. She removed her hand from Elena's wrist and tucked it back next to her side. "That is all right," she said. She spoke Standard this time, undoubtedly clued in by Elena's atrocious accent. "I didn't expect anyone to find me." With what looked like reluctance, she reached out and paused the vid. "Do you know what day it is?"

Elena gave her the date. "How long have you been out here?"

Another blink, then a frown. "Thirty-seven days. I was headed for *Meridia*. Is that why we have dropped out? Are we there?"

"You're close," Elena said. "In the field, they're about sixteen hours off. What is your name?"

The woman's eyes were straying slowly over the room, always returning first to the vid, and then to Elena's face. "I am Commander Tatiana Ilyana of the PSI ship *Chryse*," she said. "I am supposed to deliver a message to the Central Corps starship *Galileo*."

A message? She wondered why Bayandi hadn't mentioned that to Greg. "You're in luck," she said, hiding her reaction, "because that's where I need to take you. *Cytheria* is reparable, but I don't think we should take the time now. You need medical treatment."

Elena wasn't sure Ilyana had heard the last part of what she had said. The woman's eyes had narrowed, focusing on Elena's face, suddenly not seeming at all like someone who had been drugged for days. "I know you," she said.

Elena was certain she had never met anyone from *Chryse* in her life, but it wouldn't have been the first time she had been recognized by PSI. "I'm sure we haven't met," she tried, but the woman was shaking her head.

"No, I have *seen* you. On vid. You are Elena Shaw."

"Yes." She had learned not to say anything more than that.

But the woman was giving her a tired smile. "This is serendipitous. My message is to be delivered to both you and Captain Foster."

Any thought that the distress call had been a coincidence vanished. "Commander Ilyana, did you instruct *Cytheria* to contact us? Captain Foster and myself?"

Ilyana blinked again. "I didn't instruct *Cytheria* to contact anyone."

The woman lay still as Elena dosed her with vitamins and found a nutritional drink in *Cytheria*'s tiny galley. While she was there, she opened the storage bins: food. Horrible, prefab stuff, likely tasteless; but there was plenty of it. For one person, it would last months, possibly years. When she returned to the living room with the drink, she found Ilyana sitting up, regarding the stilled vid with that oddly puzzled look. Elena began to wonder if that was just how she looked when she was thinking.

"Here," she said, and sat down next to the woman. "Commander, among other things, you're malnourished. Is there a reason you haven't been eating?"

For a moment, Ilyana's expression did not change; then she seemed to realize Elena had spoken, and turned away from the vid. "I don't think so," she said, and sounded apologetic. "I expect I forgot. I don't tend to look at the chronometer, and things in here . . . I lose track of time."

Her eyes went back to the vid, and this time Elena asked. "Is that your daughter?"

Blink. "Yes."

"She looks like you."

"Yes. She's back on *Chryse*. She doesn't like it when I travel."

Elena waited until Ilyana had finished all of the drink, then stood. "Do you think you can walk?" she asked.

Ilyana braced her hands against the sofa and pushed. Remembering the woman's original skittishness, Elena offered a careful hand, and Ilyana grasped her wrist, pulling. She got to her feet, looking dizzy, hanging on tight. She was indeed short, barely reaching Elena's shoulder, and after a moment she lifted her other hand to grasp Elena's upper arm. "Just one moment," she said faintly. Her eyes dropped closed again, and Elena saw her take a deep breath and let it out. She straightened and dropped one hand, the other still gripping Elena's wrist. When she opened her eyes, she looked steadier.

"If we move slowly," she said, "I believe I will be all right."

"Is there anything you want to bring?" Elena asked her.

"No." But when Elena turned to lead her out, the woman squeezed her wrist again. "Wait."

She detached herself from Elena and, with more grace than Elena would have expected, stepped over to the frozen vid. She touched the comm behind her ear and whispered, and Elena saw the vid disappear. *Taking it with her*, Elena realized. *Just in case*.

Elena climbed back onto *Nightingale* first, then reached down to take Ilyana's arms. Even malnourished, the woman was sturdily built, and Elena had to brace her feet on the door to lift her with any dexterity at all. Once inside, the woman rolled into a sitting position, her eyes taking in the small space. Her eyebrows twitched together briefly, then she took Elena's offered hand and climbed to her feet.

"If you want to rest," Elena told her, "the benches aren't that uncomfortable."

"I believe I should like to stay awake now," Ilyana said.

Elena guided her to the copilot's seat, then retrieved some prefab meals from *Nightingale*'s meager stores. She saw Ilyana's nose wrinkle, but the woman thanked her graciously enough and ate. Elena wondered if her avoidance of the meals on board the other ship had merely been distaste.

"The food on *Galileo* is better," she offered.

There was a pause, and Ilyana smiled. "I do not think it could be worse."

The trip back to *Galileo* was both uneventful and strange. Ilyana should have been weakened as her system metabolized the last of the drug; instead she seemed oddly manic, pacing up and down, hands running over the bulkheads. She asked questions about the age of the ship, the design, the build; she asked about aesthetic choices, and whether everybody in the Corps liked the blue-gray walls or if anyone ever asked for color. When she had exhausted the subject of shuttle architecture, she asked about the prefab meals: Who designed them? Why wasn't taste prioritized? At that, Elena had laughed and told her some people actually liked them. Ilyana had looked at her as if she had posited the existence of time travel.

There was an inconsistency to Ilyana's communication. When she was opining about the unfamiliar military accoutrements of the shuttle, she spoke quickly, without pause, a surprising number of engineering facts at her fingertips, like every voraciously curious soldier Elena had ever known. When Ilyana responded to Elena's questions, however, there was almost always a pause, the sort that Elena always attributed to silent translation. But the woman's facility with Standard was so fluid, if Elena had met her in another situation, it would never have crossed her mind that she spent most of her days speaking another language. Elena herself was much more likely to comprehend a language than to be able to speak it well; she supposed there should be no surprise in finding someone who was precisely the opposite.

Ilyana did not fit what Elena had heard of her. Officially, she was *Chryse*'s conduit to Central, and the Corps in particular, and was known to be stiff and humorless. Unofficially, there were suspicions that she was a spy. Elena thought of that as she answered questions about the materials used in *Nightingale*'s construction. None of it was proprietary; *Nightingale* had been cutting-edge some years ago, but any technology the Corps might have hoarded had long since been released to the public. Elena had braced herself against questions about weapons, or other missions; but Ilyana had asked nothing. She had seemed, more than anything, delighted at everything new before her.

By far the strangest part of the trip was Ilyana's brief conversation with Captain Bayandi. Elena had contacted *Chryse* as soon as they had decoupled from *Cytheria,* and it was only when she saw the startled look on Ilyana's face that it crossed her mind she should have asked first.

But Bayandi did not shout, or chastise Ilyana in any way at all. He sounded, to Elena, entirely relieved. "I am pleased to hear your voice, Ana," he said warmly. "You are well?"

Ilyana thought about that for a few moments. "I am tired," she said at last. "And rather weak. And hungry."

"The food I'm carrying is not terribly good, I'm afraid," Elena volunteered, and Bayandi gave a brief chuckle. "Sir," she said, "we've had to abandon *Cytheria,* at least for the moment. I want to make sure Commander Ilyana gets proper medical attention. And with the situation on Yakutsk, I'm not sure when we'll be able to go back for her ship."

There was a pause on the other end. "I will try to pick up *Cytheria* on our way to Yakutsk," he said.

Elena wanted to ask Bayandi about Ilyana's message, about why he had sent her to begin with. Greg had said only that *Chryse* was coming to help; but he had spoken with Bayandi about Yakutsk, and no message had been mentioned. She looked at Ilyana, sitting at a strange sort of attention, on the edge of the chair, as if waiting for a command from her captain. *Maybe now is not the best time to ask.*

But she filed it away to discuss with Greg.

They came out of the field close to *Galileo,* Lena behind them, the sterile moon below. Elena engaged the comm. "*Galileo,* this is *Nightingale,* come back."

There was a pause, and she tensed. Then she heard Samaras's familiar voice. "*Nightingale, Galileo.* Landing Bay Two."

She frowned. Bay One was larger; she had flown out of One. Aware of her company, she only said, "Acknowledged." And then, on impulse: "Evan, can you put me through to the captain?"

Another pause. She was not liking this at all. "One moment, ma'am."

She waited, aware of Ilyana's eyes on her. After a moment, Jessica's voice came over the comm. "The captain's indisposed," Jessica said smoothly. Ilyana, who did not know her, would not have heard the tone of anxiety in her musical voice. "Have you got Commander Ilyana?"

Indisposed? What the fuck is going on? "She's all right. She's here with me. But I'd like a medic in the landing bay." At that, Ilyana raised a hand to protest, and Elena gave her a reassuring smile. "Just to make sure."

"Of course. I'll see who Doctor Hastings can spare." And Jessica cut her off.

"Just a few minutes now," Elena said to Ilyana, and maneuvered her ship around to *Galileo*'s port side. Privately, her anxiety level was rising. Ilyana's presence was important, so why wasn't Bob greeting them himself? Was it Arin? Had something happened? Was Greg going to be taking her aside, breaking the news to her, trying to make sense of the nonsensical, as he'd had to do so often in his career?

Why does everything go wrong the instant I look away?

CHAPTER 15

GALILEO

For the second time that day, Jessica met a shuttle in Landing Bay One with a medical team at her side.

He'd better be alive, she thought, *or I am going to kill him.*

Leviathan swept in on autopilot, and Jessica was heading for the ship before its engines had shut down. The door opened automatically and she climbed in. There he was, on the floor, eyes closed; but she could see him breathing, slow and steady, and there was no blood. *Small favors,* she thought, and pressed herself against the back wall to give the medical team room to work.

Bob had come himself to greet the shuttle, his aging features stiff with absolute fury. She had told him what Greg had done, half expecting him to shout at her. But he had simply accompanied her to meet the shuttle, completely silent, and she suspected he was saving his rage for Greg. Bob had great affection for all of them, Jessica knew; but he had known Greg for the captain's entire life. Bob felt a responsibility for Greg that he didn't for the rest of them, which was a good thing. If he reacted with such fury every time any of them did something stupid, he'd do himself damage.

Bob scanned Greg, expression closed, then nodded at the team. He looked at Jessica as the others picked Greg up and carried him out. "No physical injuries," he told her.

"Nothing? Not even a head injury?"

Bob shook his head. "I'll let you know when he wakes up," he said tersely, and left the ship.

Jessica looked around. *Leviathan* was undisturbed: equipment stowed, spare env suits and hand weapons tucked in their places behind her. Even the artifact sat squarely in the center of the shelf where Greg had placed it, its container open, innocuous in its gray mundanity. After this, though, she couldn't help but see its squat corners as somehow menacing.

Stupid, she thought, and closed the box. "*Galileo,*" she asked her ship, "is *Leviathan* still comms-locked?"

"Yes," *Galileo* told her.

"Leave it that way," she said. "On my order. Nobody hooks this sucker up to our systems, understood?"

"Acknowledged."

Samaras's name came up before her eyes. "Yes, Lieutenant?"

"Ma'am, I've got Governor Villipova on the line for the captain."

Shit. Of course. "Put her through to me, Lieutenant," she told him tiredly.

"Yes, ma'am."

The pause before the connection was longer than usual, and Jessica imagined Villipova arguing with Samaras about Greg's lack of availability. Indeed, when Villipova came on the line, she sounded distinctly irritable.

"Commander Lockwood," the governor said, and Jessica knew in advance what her complaint would be. "We have a very serious situation here. Surely your captain can be . . . *disturbed* under the circumstances."

Pompous ass. "I'm fully briefed on the situation," Jessica reassured her smoothly. "What can I do for you, Governor?"

Jessica heard Villipova make a sound, something between a sigh and a grumble. "Baikul is violating the cease-fire even as we speak," she said.

"We've recorded no movement from Baikul." She'd heard nothing from the systems she had asked to monitor the surface. "You're certain?"

"I have received death threats, Commander."

Which is not proof. "Do you have troop activity, Governor?"

"If you've been *briefed*," Villipova said impatiently, "you know that Baikul has infiltrated our dome numerous times in the past. Of course there is troop activity. They are already within the dome."

All of Central's intelligence suggested that threats from within the dome tended to come from Villipova's own people, and with Smolensk's recent economic instability, it seemed the more likely scenario. Under the circumstances, though, that was probably worse than invaders from Baikul: familiar faces, blending in. No way to tell who was who. *What a way to live.* Jessica closed her eyes. "I understand, Governor. Hold for a moment, please." She muted Villipova and commed Emily Broadmoor, outlining the situation. "It's not out of the question," Jessica said, "that Baikul is involved, but we're not here to wrestle with local politics. Do you have suggestions?"

Emily thought for a moment. "Two platoons," she said at last. "Minimal infantry, but a clear showing of defense. Set them in the governor's offices—both of them—and have it be a protective detail, not a combat detail."

"Very well, Commander," Jessica told her. "Get your people together and meet me in Landing Bay One." She brought Villipova back on the line. "Governor, we'll be there in half an hour."

"That seems a long time, Commander Lockwood."

"That's how far away we are, Governor, and that's how long it's going to take." She was beginning to have trouble hanging on to her temper. "We'll see you shortly." And she cut the woman off, then spent the three minutes it took Emily Broadmoor to gather her infantry to hurl every curse she could dredge up out of her memory at Greg Foster's foolishness.

Jessica spoke with Oarig as she led her platoon down the main street in Smolensk toward Villipova's office. Alex Carter had commed her shortly after his platoon's arrival in Baikul to tell her Oarig was trying to send them home, and Jessica had offered to clear up the issue. "I don't need a protective detail," Oarig insisted as soon as Carter had connected them.

The comm was audio only, and Jessica indulged in an eye-roll. "Given the way you were installed as governor— less than two weeks ago, if I remember correctly—I would have to dispute your assessment."

She did not have to wait long for him to digest that.

In truth, Jessica was more worried about Oarig's inexperience—and the destabilizing influence of his recent murderous coup—than Villipova's temper. Frightening him, she hoped, might make him actually consider his behavior. "A threat like that wouldn't come from Smolensk," he stammered, and she thought she might be getting through to him.

At least he's got the brains to understand that much. "No, Governor. But this detail is tasked with protecting you, regardless of who comes after you. Of course, if you'd rather we left . . ."

"No." His response was comically hasty. "Will they do what I tell them?"

"They'll protect your life, full stop. They are explicitly prohibited from taking sides or engaging in politics beyond that."

She had told her people, in fact, that if the situation appeared dire, they were free to tie him up and carry him away against his will, if that was the only way to guarantee his safety. If Baikul wanted another coup, they wouldn't have to kill anyone to get it.

During their descent to Smolensk, she'd had Bristol fly them over the wreck of Lanie's shuttle. Most of it was burned out now—Greg had said they'd blown it to give themselves cover—but past it she could see the storage crates.

Or rather the remains of them.

They had been torn open, every one, their contents spilled into the thin, freezing atmosphere. Months' worth of food and viable seeds wasted on the moon's surface. She closed her eyes and told Bristol to hurry.

Starvation, on top of everything else, she thought. Yakutsk was Yakutsk, and civil unrest had long been part of its cultural DNA; but this was different. This was all of the old territorial bullshit, plus a real, unavoidable crisis.

She commed back to *Galileo*. "What have we got in our food stores?" she asked.

"Twelve tonnes of fresh produce. Six hundred and fifty tonnes of MREs."

Not enough. But it might hold them for a few days, maybe a week. She made a note to herself to contact *Meridia* when she got back to find out what they might be able to contribute.

Smolensk, as it turned out, had a much more organized civil defense force than Baikul. It made sense, she supposed; Baikul relied mostly on tourism, its domed sky exposed to the jewel-green gas giant, and tourists tended to be put off by armed forces. But Smolensk was a trade center, and those in the market for much-needed parts were often less than friendly. Security guards were not only unobjectionable, but necessary. They were also, for the most part, controlled by Villipova's office.

That was going to make her job here a bit more delicate.

The governor's office was no more large or grand than any other building in the city. Villipova had set up shop between two parts dealers, both specialty shops, both low traffic. There was no good place to leave the infantry out here without alerting the public, who were already peering curiously out of windows. Traffic on the streets was minimal—Elena had warned her about this—but apparently the citizens had no qualms about old-fashioned methods for keeping track of their neighbors.

Well, if they were already outed, she might as well take advantage.

"Stay here," she told Bristol. He was not a strategist, but in the eighteen months since he'd saved her life during a particularly ugly firefight, she had come to rely on his steadiness. "Don't stand in formation, don't stand at attention. They think they know why we're here, but let's not slap them in the face with it."

"You want us at ease, ma'am?" he asked.

"Hell, no. I don't want anybody in that building without my explicit approval. And if they come after you? Disarm them if you can, and take them out hand-to-hand. Self-defense only. And nobody kills anyone unless there is absolutely no other choice, is that clear?" She turned to look at each of them in turn, meeting their eyes, seeing them nod. "On your toes," she told them. "These people have lived in what's essentially a war zone for most of their lives. They may not be soldiers, but they're not civilians, either. And if I have to explain to the captain why I lost any of you for a bunch of cranky mechanics, I'm going to be very unhappy. Understood?"

"Yes, ma'am," they all said together.

Jessica thought, in that moment, that this command business was maybe not so bad.

CHAPTER 16

Greg awoke, exhausted and fuzzy-headed, the hangover far worse than the ones he used to suffer when he was drinking. He moaned and shifted, and only then realized he wasn't in his own bed; his eyes opened, and he blinked at the harsh ceiling lights of the infirmary. *Why do we do that?* he wondered, squinting and waiting for his eyes to adjust. *In this place, where people need peace and quiet and time to recover, why do we blast them from the ceiling?*

He grew accustomed to the brightness, and he opened his eyes more widely, trying to remember how he got here. His last memory was the mental image of a child drowning . . . no, that wasn't quite it. His last memory was of agonizing, crippling grief and loneliness. He felt the back of his throat close up as his mind brought the experience back, and irritably he pushed himself up on his elbows. He had no time for this kind of indulgence. He had left that loss behind a long time ago.

"Lie back down," Bob Hastings snapped at him. The

doctor walked into the room, scanner in hand, looking as angry as Greg had ever seen him.

"I'd rather sit up," Greg said. "It keeps—"

"I told you to *lie the fuck down*."

That's new, Greg thought. Warily, he did as he was told, never taking his eyes from the doctor.

Bob waved the scanner over him, teeth clenched, methodically studying the readout. "What in the hell did you think you were doing, Greg?"

"It was an experiment," Greg said. "We had to find out what it could do, and I was the only person around who'd had any reaction to that thing. It had to be me."

"Maybe I'll come to believe that," Bob told him. "And maybe I'll decide not to relieve you of duty over this."

Now Greg found himself getting angry. "*Relieve me of duty?* What for?"

Bob looked up from the scanner, blue eyes blazing. "You have no idea what that thing is. You have no idea how dangerous it is. You've already seen it affect one person—who, by the way, *explicitly warned you not to touch it.*"

I guess Elena's back. "She told you that, huh?"

"She did. She's in the other room with Ilyana, who's being looked after by my head nurse. I believe she's waiting for my permission to come in here and read you the riot act."

Elena was an expert at shouting. Greg thought the experience would be exponentially nicer than the dream he'd had. "We needed to know what it is, Bob. If it's a weapon—" Elena was back from *Cytheria. Oh, God.* "How long have I been out?"

"Two hours."

He pushed himself up again, ignoring Bob's protests, and this time jumped to his feet, hand on his comm. "Jessica."

There was a pause, and then: "This is Commander Broadmoor, sir."

He frowned. *What the hell is going on?* "Commander, where's Commander Lockwood?"

"On the surface, sir, with two platoons. I can put you through to her if you like."

Two hours, and everything had unraveled. And they'd all been talking over comms, as they did with everything. "Not now, Commander. You can brief me in a minute. But right now—everybody on the ship gets a new comm. Immediately. Same for Commander Lockwood and her team. Understood?"

"Okay. Yes, sir." She sounded confused. "Captain?"

"There's a good possibility our comms system has been compromised," he told her. "We need to start with nothing. No data. Let *Galileo* sync us up from scratch. Where's the artifact I was testing?"

Emily, as always, regrouped effortlessly. "It's still on *Leviathan,* sir. Commander Shimada placed it behind extra shielding."

"Still comms-locked?"

"Yes, sir."

He closed his eyes. Everything in him wanted to put it off the ship . . . but if Jamyung had been murdered for it, the last thing he wanted to do was make it easier for Ellis to take it. "I want it secured," he told her. "That comms lock comes off on command code only, understood? Lock the landing bay, and put a senior infantry soldier on duty there. Someone who can stand for eight hours without dropping their guard."

"Yes, sir."

He terminated the transmission, and scraped the comm filament onto his fingernail. He glared down at Bob, who was still looking furious. "You too, Doctor."

Bob may have been angry, but he was a soldier, and he knew when his captain was serious. The doctor didn't hesitate, just swept his hand behind his ear. "I have some blanks in the med closet," he said. "Hang on, and I'll bring you one."

Once Bob was gone, Greg closed his eyes again, reaching out one hand to lean against the wall. His knees still felt weak, and he thought he could conjure up that dream again and weep for days. How had the artifact knocked him out? Had it drugged him? Had it generated vid? How had it projected such a non-memory into his mind?

He wanted to comm his father so badly his stomach hurt.

Bob returned and held out to him the tiny, dark square, made up of hundreds of thin sheets of circuitry. Greg pressed it behind his ear over his temporal bone and let it sync up with *Galileo*'s comms system. He was still leaning against the wall; at Bob's look, he pushed himself upright.

But Bob, it seemed, was done shouting. "Why don't you sit, at least," he said, "and I'll examine you."

Greg sat and let the man run the scanner over him. "Was I unconscious when they brought me in?" he asked.

Bob did not look up from his task. "*Leviathan* did as you'd programmed it, and brought you back once you were overdue. Jessica didn't touch anything, just had the med techs pull you out. She sealed up the shuttle.

"And you weren't unconscious," he added, almost dismissively. "You were asleep."

Asleep? "How did that happen?"

"You don't get enough rest."

But Greg shook his head. "No. I was tired, sure, but no more than usual. There's no reason. Was I drugged? Did it induce a dream somehow?"

"No drugs in your system," Bob told him. "And they got you here fast enough that even the ones that metabolize quickly would have still been detectable. As for it inducing a dream, I can't say. The brain scanner revealed an ordinary REM cycle. You woke up right on schedule."

And right on schedule, Elena stormed into the room, towering over him in vibrating fury. "What the *hell* did you think you were doing?" she shouted.

"Why does everyone yell in my infirmary?" Bob asked, but Greg didn't think he really minded this time.

Elena ignored the doctor. "You know what that thing did to me! You knew I wasn't here, you knew I was hours away from being back, and you risk your life—"

"It didn't kill you, Elena. I had no reason to suspect—"

"*Do not start with me.*" Her expression darkened further. "I am *one person*, Greg. This entire ship depends on you. I touched it because I was *careless,* and because I was a *fucking stupid jackass*. What is your fucking excuse?"

Every goddamned time. "My fucking excuse," he shouted in return, "is that this is *my ship,* and I needed to know what that thing was. You *asked* me to examine it!"

"I asked *Ted* to examine it!"

"So it would have been all right with you if Ted had had his brain scrambled?"

"It *knocked you out,* Greg!"

"It did nothing of the sort. It made me fall asleep."

"How is that in any way *better?*"

That, of all things, made Bob intercede. "Okay, okay," he said. He stepped between them, back to Greg, a hand on Elena's arm, and Greg was annoyed all over again. "I think he gets it, Elena," Bob said gently. "He's all right. I did a full brain scan while he was out."

Over Bob's shoulder, Greg saw Elena close her eyes. She had cleaned up, he realized: changed her clothes and rinsed the grime out of her hair. With her eyes closed she looked worn-out, the way she used to look when she'd worked too many shifts in a row, and he wondered when she'd last slept. He reminded himself that it wasn't his responsibility to look after her anymore, and took a moment to wonder why she seemed to feel it was hers to look after him.

Feeling his anger drain, he switched to a safer subject. "How's Ilyana?"

Elena opened her eyes and looked at Bob. Greg couldn't see Bob's expression, but he could see hers: a flash of worry, and something hollow and sad that passed too quickly for him to identify. Bob patted her arm and retreated to his med console in the corner, and when she met Greg's eyes, she was again the calm professional he'd worked with for so many years. "Redlaw is looking at her," Elena told him. "She'd overdosed on something on the shuttle, but she came with me under her own steam, and she was awake the whole trip home. She says," she concluded, "that she has a message for us. You and me."

Greg frowned. *You and me.* That might explain why the distress call had come to the two of them. Perhaps the magnetic echo was a coincidence, and the comm had nothing to do with the artifact at all. "Bayandi didn't mention a message," he said.

"He didn't when they talked, either, but he knew I was listening."

The implication being that they had something to hide. "Did you tell her about the artifact?" he asked Elena. When she shook her head, he added, "Don't."

"You think she knows something about it?"

"I don't know. Probably not. It's probably just—" He shut his eyes, saw the beach, opened them up again. He looked up at her, and he saw understanding on her face.

"Better to assume until we know otherwise," she said, and nodded. Then her lips set, and she looked away. "Nobody can ever tell you shit, can they?"

A year. They had been apart for a year, and here they were, back to the familiar. "Why do you think I like being in charge?"

"Idiot." But she was smiling.

"You're right," he admitted. "It was a poorly considered move. But . . ." He waited until she looked at him again. "That thing. What it does. I've never experienced anything like that before."

And in that moment, looking into her dark eyes, he thought she knew exactly what he meant.

After one final perfunctory scan Bob released Greg, and he followed Elena into the next room to greet Commander Ilyana.

She was on her feet, standing next to Admiral Herrod, who had apparently filled Greg's traditional role and given her a proper welcome. She was a short woman, dwarfed next to Herrod's sturdy bulk, but she was thick-limbed and solid, radiating a sort of relaxed competence. She looked up when they entered and gave a hesitant smile that steadied when she spotted Elena. For her part, Elena smiled back, reassuring and welcoming, and Greg didn't think anyone but him noticed the very brief look of dislike she threw Herrod.

"You look better," Elena said.

"I am told that my electrolytes have been stabilized," Ilyana responded. And then, still smiling: "If you are all present, I have a message I am tasked with delivering."

Elena met Greg's eyes, and he knew what she was thinking: *Ilyana's not treating it like a secret, so why didn't Bayandi tell us?* "We'll set up in my office," he said. "Admiral Herrod, if you could escort the commander, we'll join you in a few minutes."

Herrod, who apparently had training as a host as well as a diplomat, turned to Commander Ilyana with a smile that was positively friendly, and gestured for her to precede him out of the room.

When they were out of earshot, Elena turned to Redlaw. "How is she really?"

Redlaw, an easygoing man of about fifty, leaned back against the now-empty examining table. "Tell me again what she said about the drugs," he said.

Greg watched Elena frown, concentrating. "Nothing, I think," she told him. "Just . . . when I woke her up, she said she hadn't expected anyone to find her. Do you think she was suicidal?"

"If she was, she didn't know her dosage very well." He looked thoughtful. "At the rate she was taking it, it would have killed her awfully slowly. She probably would have died of starvation first."

"Is she an addict?" Greg asked.

Redlaw hedged. "I did a toxicology backtrack. Her usage goes back four or five months, but until recently it was low-level—not the sort of use that should have triggered addiction. About five weeks ago she started slowly increasing her dose, and she's been OD'ing for the last week or so. But other than that, she's in remarkably good shape. Good nutrition, good muscle tone. She probably wouldn't have passed out if she hadn't stopped eating regularly."

Five weeks. That would have been when *Cytheria* left *Chryse.* "She was very relaxed during the trip here," Elena said. "Cheerful, even. Did you get any psych readout at all?"

"Her brain shows the same signs of trauma as any soldier's," he said. "But without a baseline reading, I can't say how bad it is. Something happened recently, though. I can't say what, or how severe it was, but her cortisol responses are pretty damn suspect."

Greg frowned. "Are you saying she's unreliable?"

"I'm saying, sir," Redlaw told him, "that there's a lot

going on with that woman, and if she were part of our crew, I'd send her to Petra for a proper psych eval before I let her work a shift."

Elena met Greg's eyes again. "We need to ask Bayandi," she said, and he nodded.

"I'll comm him after we talk with Ilyana," he said. "Redlaw, see if you can get Petra to talk to her. Just to get her current condition on the record. There may be no reason to mistrust her, but I want to understand where she's coming from."

He turned, and Elena fell easily into step with him. Before they could leave, though, Redlaw spoke up.

"You know," the nurse said, "it wouldn't hurt either one of you to chat with Petra for a bit, either."

Greg did not look at Elena, but neither one of them slowed down as they left the infirmary.

CHAPTER 17

YAKUTSK

Zinaida Villipova was a grim, square-faced woman with prematurely white hair, thin hands, and bushy, expressive eyebrows. Jessica had never before dealt with her personally, but she'd heard Elena, who knew many of the traders in Smolensk, repeat various unflattering—and often obscene—stories about her. The general consensus was that she was corrupt and corrupting, coldly mercenary, and efficient. Graft and bribery were the norm in Smolensk, but for the most part she made sure enough people kept enough money. Unlike Oarig's predecessor, and the predecessors in Baikul before him, she had held on to power, despite some close calls. She was not without political enemies, but they only turned up dead when threats of a takeover became too severe for her to ignore.

In short: she was a murderer and a dictator, but scrupulously pragmatic about it.

Villipova was seated behind a nondescript desk, hands folded. She did not look up when Jessica entered, but the man seated in a soft chair in the corner of the room stood and crossed the office to stand between Jessica and the governor. He wore a crisp civilian suit that appeared to have never been touched by Smolensk's red dust, and wore his hair combed back severely to hang in a long plait down his back. He smiled an entirely artificial smile and held his hand out to Jessica. "Commander Lockwood. It's a pleasure to meet you."

He was taller than she was as well, although not nearly as tall as Greg, and clearly expected her to shrink from him. Instead she crossed her arms, ignoring his hand. "We can't meet," she said smoothly, "until you tell me who you are."

That smile widened, and his eyes twinkled. Dark eyes, dark hair. Pale skin, almost pale enough to be off of Tengri; but no one on Tengri looked so feral, so aggressive. Jessica thought she might have been romanticizing her home colony a little, but whoever this man was, he was intensely off-putting. "Of course. I can't expect you to have heard of me, the way I've heard of you."

"Given that I spoke with Governor Villipova not half an hour ago," she said, "I'm not in the least surprised you've heard of me." He opened his mouth to speak again, but she took a step past him to talk to Villipova. "Governor. Are you all right?"

Villipova's eyebrows arched, ever so slightly; she knew better than to think Jessica was genuinely concerned for her. "Perfectly, Commander. Where are your people?"

"Outside," Jessica told her.

"How many?"

"How about you tell me who your goon is first?"

The governor's lips thinned, and it took Jessica a moment to recognize she was smiling. "Did you hear that, Gladkii?" she said to the man standing behind Jessica. "You've been upgraded to goon. They'll surely promote you now." She stood and came around the desk. "Commander Lockwood, this is Anatole Gladkoff. A business associate."

Jessica turned, and this time she accepted the handshake. He shook firmly but briefly, and she noted that he was a fast learner. "And what business are you in, Gladkoff?"

"I'm in sales," he told her.

She tilted her head to one side. "That I could tell," she said. "Who are you selling for?"

And at that his eyes shifted, just for an instant, so quickly she almost missed it. "At the moment," he said, "I'm not selling at all. I'm here on a . . . diplomatic mission." His expression recovered. "Our terraformers proved to be insufficient for Yakutsk's needs, and I'm here to shore up their dome environments in any way necessary while they decide whether to proceed with replacing the surface units."

And that explained the studied smarminess. "You work for Ellis Systems," Jessica said. She suddenly wanted to scrub her hands.

"Our dome environmental systems have been allowed to age," Villipova put in. "This was mainly due to our plans to move out onto the surface. Gladkii is trying to convince me he can improve our lives within the dome while we evaluate what to do next."

That was the second time Villipova had used the diminutive of Gladkoff's name, and Jessica began to wonder if the woman was trying to annoy him. For his part, Gladkoff seemed unfazed, and Jessica had to admit she might be inclined to try to needle him herself. "Does Oarig know about this?" Jessica asked.

"Baikul will be upgraded as well." Villipova sounded less pleased by that.

"And you didn't think to tell us?"

"This is not any of your business."

Jessica's eyes narrowed, and she took a step toward the governor. "I have no doubt, Governor Villipova," she said, allowing her voice to grow icy, "that you know all of the history Central Gov shares with Ellis Systems. Your assertion that Gladkoff's presence here is none of our business is . . . disingenuous, wouldn't you say?"

"I think what Governor Villipova is saying," Gladkoff put in smoothly, "is that the Corps doesn't have the authority or the ability to interfere with what we're doing here. And why would you need to? We're here to help."

Jessica did not take her eyes off Villipova. The older woman had let her lashes drop, making her expression more difficult to read. Jessica, on the other hand, wanted hers to be entirely transparent. "Do you really believe they're here to help, Governor?" she asked.

Villipova took a moment to study Jessica's face. "I trust their motives just as I do yours, Commander Lockwood."

Well, Jessica thought, *that's something, at least.*

The rumble was low, building slowly, and Jessica almost mistook it for a ship taking off before she realized how far they were from the spaceport. "Get down!" she shouted, and dove for the floor. Villipova was already there, having recognized what she was hearing. Gladkoff was last, panicking almost comically, throwing himself over Villipova's desk to curl up between the chair and the wall.

Jessica hit her comm. "Bristol, report!"

"Grenade strikes, ma'am," he said unnecessarily. "Three surrounding the building. About a block off. Long-range launchers by the sound of them."

Shit. "Move to disarm them," she ordered. "Send me two officers to—" She glanced at Villipova.

"There is an exit in the rear," the governor told her.

"The back of the building," Jessica finished. "We're coming out. Top priority is to protect the governor."

She had no doubt Gladkoff noted her omission.

"And Bristol—do not engage. Defend if you must, but do not engage beyond getting those launchers off-line. We are not at war with these people. We protect Villipova, and that's it. If they want to occupy this building, let them do it, but *no civilians die.* Am I very clear, Lieutenant?"

"Yes, ma'am." She heard him begin relaying her orders to the others as the comm ended.

Another trio of explosions, these staggered, and the building vibrated again. "They're getting closer," Gladkoff said.

Jessica couldn't be sure if his fear was feigned or real, but either way, she had no time for it. "Then don't slow us down," she told him. "Governor, which way is the exit?"

Jessica stuck by Villipova—keeping one hand on her pulse rifle—as they moved down a side hallway toward a narrow, windowed door. She heard Gladkoff's footsteps behind her, and kept enough of an eye on him to make sure he wasn't trying to ambush her. Neither of these people was her friend, but somehow an Ellis Systems salesman felt far more threatening than a murderous dictator.

Clarke and Brancova were out in the alley behind the building, along with two bulky, nondescript colonists Jessica took for Villipova's people. They swept toward the governor, who nodded to them, and Jessica turned to her infantry as Gladkoff leaned against the back wall of the building, breathing hard.

"Status," she said.

"We make fifteen attackers," Clarke said. "Bristol has sent the platoon to divide and disarm them."

Jessica nodded. Her people didn't know the city like the locals, but neither were the locals used to dealing with soldiers trained in multiple methods of ground warfare. She was putting her money on Bristol. "Keep your eyes on the governor," Jessica told them. "We're here to—"

Brancova abruptly leveled her pulse rifle at one end of the alley. "That's far enough!" she shouted. Jessica turned, her own rifle up, to confront three people, two tall and thin and one much smaller, standing fifty meters off. The tall pair were wearing bright colors, clean and dust-free as if they worked in an office. The third wore the drab brown of a surface scavenger, covered in dust. They were all armed, but their weapons were small and short-range. Effective enough if you got hit, but at this distance, they would have to be either very good or very lucky to get a kill shot.

Where were the long-range launchers?

"Drop your weapons," she told them. "We're leaving."

Two of them looked at each other, hesitant, and began to

bend over, as if to put their weapons on the ground; but the scavenger—short, stocky, stubborn-looking—kept a snub-nosed weapon on the crowd. "You've got nowhere to go," the scavenger said. "The port is closed. We've—"

A shot came from behind Jessica, and the colonist dropped in a bright, incendiary flash. The other two started, lifting their weapons again; Jessica flung herself against the wall as they fired. She had been right; they were terrible shots.

"Who the fuck did that?" she shouted; but she had a guess. Sure enough, there stood Gladkoff, a lightweight but long-range hand weapon in his hand. He was glaring at her, defensive.

"Are you a *complete fucking idiot*?" she shouted. They moved down the alley around the corner and kept running, Jessica keeping her eyes on Villipova and her guards, who appeared to know where they were going. "You really think you're going to blast your way out of a coup attempt? You really are just a salesman, aren't you?"

"They were going to kill us!" he yelled back, managing to sound genuinely outraged. "I came here to help these people, not die in a fucking alley!"

Now, she decided, was not the time to point out how much he'd just jeopardized his own goal. "Listen," she said to him, "your job is to sell these people some fucking shaggy dog story about making their lives better. Mine is to keep them from fucking killing each other. You do your job, and I'll do mine, deal?"

Ahead of them, Villipova's guards pulled her through another door. "Go after them!" Jessica ordered her infantry.

Gladkoff, apparently craving safety in numbers, ran ahead of her to join them. Jessica commed Bristol again. "What's the status of those launchers?" she asked.

"We've got two of them, ma'am," he told her. "No casualties. Still looking for the—"

She heard it before it hit, in that split second before the impact when everything around her slowed to a near stop and she felt certain that she'd reach the doorway in time, get through, close the door behind her, and have the entire back wall of the building between her and the blast. But it was less than a second, and the grenade fell, and the wall next to her flew to pieces, and she didn't even have the time to throw her hand in front of her to keep the red Yakutsk dust out of her eyes.

CHAPTER 18

GALILEO

Greg caught up with Herrod and Ilyana, leaving Elena a step behind him, and tried to reconcile this woman with the person Jessica had described in her report.

This was not the rude, disinterested observer recalled by Shimada's *Borissova* friends. Neither was she a studied, subtle PSI spy. This woman was staring at everything, wide-eyed and palpably delighted, endlessly fascinated by her surroundings. Her fingers skimmed the smooth, clean wall, her palm sometimes flattening against it, and she kept looking up at the daylit ceiling. "It's very consistent, your lighting," she said approvingly.

"It's easy," Greg told her, "over a fairly small space."

When they skirted the edge of the atrium, Ilyana stopped, staring at the greenery. The view was not spectacular—there was very little on this end beyond coniferous hedges and some low-growing herbs—but she gawked as if it reminded her of something. This time it was Herrod who filled her in.

"It's lovely, isn't it?" he said. Herrod's voice was very

nearly friendly, and Greg wondered what that meant. "For someone like me, who's lived most of his life on a planet, it's a real refuge out here."

She smiled and looked at the old man. "Do you miss it, then? Living on a planet?"

Something crossed Herrod's face. Greg did not know him well enough to identify it. "I think we all miss home, wherever that is," he said, with surprising gentleness.

Ilyana stared at him as if he had revealed a profound truth, and then moved on.

Emily had asked about sending Ilyana's guard to the infirmary. "Not yet," Greg had said. "Send them to my office, and I'll find some diplomatic words to explain it to her." He had been thinking of ways to keep from offending the flinty Ilyana of Jessica's report. Watching this woman gape at the corridors of his ship like an enthusiastic tourist, he thought he could assign an armored battalion to follow her around, and she would find it delightful.

Drug addiction, he knew, could cause personality changes; but he wasn't sure he'd ever heard of anyone becoming *friendlier* before.

Elena said nothing during the walk to his office, but he knew how closely she was watching Ilyana. Elena was a mechanic by trade, but he didn't think her year away from the Corps had lessened her instinctive watchfulness. She, like Greg, tended to be far more suspicious of people she liked than those she disliked. He thought she liked Ilyana quite a bit.

Once in his office, Ilyana's body language shifted. She was no longer the rubbernecking visitor, but a PSI official, sober and focused. Perhaps this was what they had seen on *Borissova*. Perhaps, during that earlier mission, Ilyana had simply not had the opportunity to relax.

"May I project over the desk?" she asked, and Greg nodded. Elena leaned against the wall; Greg and Herrod took the chairs.

Ilyana touched her comm, and a schematic of the Fourth Sector appeared in the air. There were seventeen highlighted points, scattered in random positions. Without checking the map's legend, Greg knew what they were.

"These are the Fourth Sector colonial catastrophes that you have confirmed are due to deliberate hardware sabotage by Ellis Systems," she began.

And wasn't it interesting that she had that little bit of intel?

"Here are similar catastrophes documented over the last year."

Another set of highlighted points appeared, most of them clustered. Greg did a quick count: sixty-five. They had missed some. They had missed most.

"These," Ilyana continued, "are situations where we believe the colony either repaired the issue before it could cause damage, or caught the problem early enough to mitigate the harm."

Another scattering of lights. Too many. *How had they missed so many?* But that was not Ilyana's point. Greg leaned forward, reaching toward the image. Slowly he rotated it, looking at it from multiple angles, but his suspicion didn't change.

"Do you see the pattern?" Ilyana asked.

Greg studied the lights. There was a significance there that had nothing to do with location. "*Galileo*," he said, "highlight the colonies that have provided the bulk of the exports for the Fourth Sector."

The image changed again, and all of the most recent victims flared to brightness: Govi. San Sandover. Yakutsk.

"That's not all of them, though," Elena pointed out. "They haven't touched Tonoku, and they ship more hardwood than any colony in the galaxy."

Greg had a theory about that. "Nobody in the Fifth Sector ships hardwood," he said, looking back to Ilyana.

There was a pause before she responded, as something flickered in her expression; and then she gave him a blank smile. "Exactly, Captain. The economic contributions of these particular colonies are direct competitors of colonies in the Fifth Sector."

He had seen it. He had known it, but the scope of the attack was far greater than anything he had imagined. Elena swore, and looked down at Herrod. "They're helping them," she accused. "Ellis is helping Olam and the others with their great hegemony project."

Which was only a rumor, of course, one that Greg had been hearing his entire career. The Fifth Sector was the wealthiest, most stable sector in the occupied galaxy, and that included the First Sector, home to Earth. Many Fifth Sector colonies openly advocated the idea that it was past time for humanity to release their sentimental attachment to Earth and place the seat of their centralized government in a location that befitted its importance. That such a change would cement the Fifth Sector's economic dominance was, of course, only coincidental.

It seemed that not only were the rumors true, but the Fifth Sector was well on its way to implementing a plan.

But Herrod played the skeptic. "That's a big assumption, Chief," he said.

"*Bullshit*," she said, pushing herself off the wall. "We all know it's Ellis taking these colonies down. If they're selecting the ones that benefit the Fifth Sector, they're doing it for a reason. And you know what it is."

"I'm sorry," Ilyana interrupted politely. "Do you have further intelligence on this issue, Admiral Herrod?"

"That's Admiral, retired," he told her dryly. "I'm not looped in to intelligence anymore."

Elena threw up her hands and glared at Greg. "Are you going to let him get away with this?"

Dammit. She wasn't wrong, but she'd never had any sense of subtlety. "Admiral," he asked, "where did we stand with Ellis when you retired?"

Greg had his doubts about Herrod's retirement. That it was true on paper he had verified. And he was aware that even within Shadow Ops, Herrod had never been the most powerful operator, and he was not sure Herrod had always been an enemy. He thought there was a good chance the admiral had been ousted because he was pushing an agenda too many of the others did not want to follow. Either that, or they thought he could learn more this way.

But Greg had no doubt he was still connected.

"Our last direct interaction with Ellis," Herrod told him,

"was over Canberra, a year and a half ago. Accusation and denial, most of which you saw. Afterward? PSI showed them evidence; they said the situation was down to people who had left the company years earlier. They claim errors, spin the public relations machine, and everybody moves on."

"So you're saying their propaganda machine is better than ours," Greg concluded.

Elena scoffed; Herrod ignored her; Greg counted his blessings. "I'm saying people have more motivation to believe them than us," the admiral said. "Especially here. The Fourth Sector has been historically stable, if not as wealthy as the Fifth. Ellis has been a big part of that stability."

"So has Yakutsk," Elena pointed out. "If they're out of play—that opens up a big opportunity for Ellis, doesn't it?"

"Without their exports, though, nobody here has the money," Greg reminded her. "They could do some buying, but it wouldn't be sustainable. They'd only buy enough to build their own infrastructure back up, and they'd still be decades paying off loans." He looked at Ilyana. "Is this all you've got?"

"I have documentation," she said, "of some of the failures you could not prove."

"So what do we do with all of this data?"

Blink. "I'm sorry, Captain. I do not understand the question."

He took a breath, remembering Elena's look outside the door. "Captain Bayandi sent you with this information. What was his reason?"

Another pause, and she smiled again. He was beginning to find her smile disturbing. "I cannot speak to Bayandi's reasons, Captain. He is generally quite logical, but I do not always understand. In this case, though, he did have a message to go along with this information, which is that it is too late."

It was Greg who broke the silence. "Too late for what?"

Ilyana's blank look lasted longer this time. "To stop them, of course."

Out of the corner of his eye, he saw Herrod tense. "Stop them from doing what?"

She shrugged. "Whatever it is they are planning." His face must have changed, because she added, "Even Captain Bayandi is not psychic, Captain Foster. It is clear that Ellis has been working toward something for a long time. What that is, we cannot say. But I am here to tell you that your efforts on Yakutsk are irrelevant. What will happen will happen, and what we must do is prepare a response."

Elena had sobered. "Are you saying they want us to go to war?" she asked.

"We are already at war," Ilyana said comfortably.

Just then there was a familiar sound: a two-tone alert and a shift in the ship's lighting. Greg got to his feet, Elena grew still, and Herrod pushed himself out of the chair from what must have been sheer habit. Before Greg could ask *Galileo* what was happening, his comm chimed, and the words *Lieutenant Samaras* hung in the air before him.

"Did you trigger this alert, Lieutenant?" he asked.

"Yes, sir." Samaras was a nervous stammerer, especially under pressure. This time his words were clear, but the waver in his voice was unmistakable. The man was afraid. "Sir, there's been an incident."

Greg glanced at Ilyana. She should have been disoriented,

on this ship she didn't know, with these people she had only met a few minutes earlier. Instead she was watching her display, that same gentle smile on her face. *She expected this,* he realized. "What's happened?"

"Sir, it's—we've lost contact with the First Sector, sir."

Lost contact. *What the hell does that mean?* "What," he asked, feeling foolish, "*all* of it?"

"Yes, sir," Samaras said. "We're getting nothing from there at all. No comms, no stream, nothing. And everything we send in—it goes nowhere, sir. Bounces right off like they're not even there."

"Is it just us?"

"No, sir. The stream chatter—you can listen for yourself, sir. It's everyone. Sectors Two through Six. Athena Relay isn't responding to anyone, not even with basic telemetry. Nobody can get through to the First Sector, sir. It's like they've just disappeared."

PART II

CHAPTER 19

YAKUTSK

There's a fucking fortune in that wreck."

"Yeah, and there's also a few hundred assholes still shooting at each other out there. How badly do you want the money?"

Dallas sat at a table in the corner, alone, listening to the others talk about the wrecked freighter shuttle. In many ways, it was the same conversation every time: *This is the wreck that'll do it. This is the one that'll make us rich.* Dallas had been scavenging more than twenty years—long enough to be certain that none of the scavengers in this pub were likely ever to save anything beyond weekend retsina money.

"I saw that shuttle when it came into port. Forty tonner, easy, and armored. The nice armor, not the cheap stuff."

"It's the cheap stuff now they've shot it down."

The last remark was followed by a ripple of laughter, and Dallas frowned, annoyed. People weren't respectful any-more. Martine hadn't been gone two days. Jamyung hadn't been gone twelve hours. Dallas was aware of taking their deaths more personally than the usual random accident or political purge that took people Dallas knew; but today, there was not enough liquor to make it worth sitting and listening to this gang. The drink on the table had been Jamyung's favorite; Dallas thought of the dead trader, drained the glass, and stood to leave.

"Oh, come on, Dallas." Friederich had known Dallas for years, and almost always used that knowledge without kindness. "Lighten up. Jamyung was an asshole. You said so yourself more than once."

"Yep." Dallas tossed hard currency on the table; might as well leave a good tip before leaving early. "But Martine wasn't."

Friederich had the grace to look vaguely ashamed before he turned back to the others and began joking again. Dallas turned and left the pub.

It was late afternoon, the businesses along the main road beginning to pack up their merchandise in preparation for closing. When Dallas thought about it, there was no good reason for Smolensk to adhere to a twenty-four-hour cycle, or any specific cycle at all: night and day had no real meaning here. Dallas had been taught that humanity had evolved to function best under Earth's solar rhythms, and that the domes had been constructed to mimic the night and day of the colonists' ancestral home. But Dallas had never been much for sleep, and shops closing for the artificially enforced night was an irritant. And after the last two days, Dallas was feeling particularly resentful of meaningless irritants.

Dallas missed Martine. She had been stupid as hell, and far too sanguine about the idea of spending her life sorting through debris on the surface of a moon. But she had understood the draw of the moon's surface, the headiness of walking in light gravity, the red dust, fine and soft and familiar, that got into everything no matter how hard you tried to keep it out. She had been a good scavenging partner, and good company, and a cheerful loser, even when playing the games she loved the most. And she had been too damn young to die over some piece of scrap that didn't mean anything.

At least the object was gone now. That freighter woman, Shaw, had taken it away, and Martine's killers had no reason to come after any more of Dallas's friends. They might go after Shaw, but she was clearly ex-Corps, and Dallas thought the strangers might be taking on more than they anticipated if they tried to get the object back from her. They'd certainly get more fight than they'd had from Martine.

Stupid kid. Despite the tepid afternoon air, Dallas shivered and walked faster.

The police had come about Jamyung—or rather, the goons that followed Villipova around had showed up—and explained to Dallas that the governor was not responsible for the trader's death. Dallas had done the usual: shrug, nod, be unconcerned and unmoved. But their efforts had been pointless. Dallas already knew Jamyung had been killed by strangers. Anyone who had lived in Smolensk for more than three weeks could tell strangers from up a goddamned city block just by the way they moved. Which did make Dallas wonder why Villipova had been so intent on convincing Jamyung's friends that she hadn't been a part of this one.

Obviously she's hiding something, Dallas thought.

Then: *It doesn't matter.*

That wasn't despair, it was just fact: there was nothing Dallas could do. Finding out who had killed Jamyung would not resurrect him. There were other traders who would buy Dallas's salvage, and maybe even pay a higher price for it. Jamyung's death was wrong, but no more wrong than the usual wrongness that plagued Smolensk. Yakutsk was Yakutsk. Dallas could have left at any time. Surely staying so long was some kind of tacit acceptance of the order of things.

None of your business, Dallas. Villipova's been hiding things your whole life.

Martine was twenty-three years old.

Dallas ignored the first explosion, far off, away from the pub and Dallas's flat and Jamyung's parts yard. Occasional explosions were not unknown in Smolensk, and generally by the time Dallas made it home, all the details were out on the stream and the perpetrators long gone. But the second blast was far closer—near Villipova's offices. Dallas began to walk faster, looking around. There were people running, and shouts in the distance, and far off the sound of plasma rifles.

Fuck. Another coup attempt.

Dallas stopped someone running across the road. "Who is it?"

"Gillanders, I think," she said. "The whole family this time, not just the sisters. But Villipova brought Corps infantry into it. They killed someone."

And at that, Dallas's stomach dropped. *More outsiders? What kind of bullshit is this?* "Where?"

The woman scowled. "The fuck do I care?" she snapped, and ran off.

Dallas picked up the pace and ran toward the governor's office. This turned out to be upstream; most people were running the other way. "They're shooting at us!" a vaguely familiar voice shouted in Dallas's direction. Dallas kept moving, and turned a corner to find the remains of a building façade piled haphazardly in the alley behind the governor's office. Instinctively, Dallas pressed against the alley wall, waiting, listening for the whistle of an incoming grenade or the whirr of a pulse rifle powering up. There was silence, and Dallas counted: ten seconds, twenty . . . after forty, Dallas moved into the alley to assess the damage.

And found a body.

A Corps soldier, although shorter than the other ones Dallas had met. A woman, slim but curvy, skin pale under the gray dust of the rubble, and hair a shade of red Dallas had only seen in vids. The strap of her pulse rifle was looped over her shoulder, but the gun was lying behind her back, and her hands were open. She had not been holding it when the building hit her.

Gingerly, Dallas knelt next to her and held two fingers to her neck. A pulse. At the touch, she moved, and made a quiet sound. Dallas stood. The hospital was close, and she looked small enough. She wouldn't be too heavy for the short distance.

Dallas thought of what the woman in the street had said: *They killed someone.* What would a Smolensk doctor do for a Corps soldier?

Dallas pulled the strap of the pulse rifle off the woman's shoulder and picked up the weapon. A heavy gun for such a small person, but if she was Corps, she would be trained to handle it. Dallas lengthened the strap and shouldered the rifle, then leaned over, grasping the woman's arms. Despite the not-infrequent political purges in Smolensk, Dallas had not hauled many bodies—and none in the full Earth-level gravity inside the domes—but the principle was simple enough. The woman, small as she was, fit easily over Dallas's shoulder; uncomfortably, with her diaphragm compressed against Dallas's sharp bones. But her legs were short enough to stay out of the way of Dallas's brisk stride, and with a furtive glance down the main street, the scavenger carried her back home.

CHAPTER 20

BUDAPEST

Elena borrowed *Nightingale* again to head back to *Budapest*.

At some point, she knew, the full import of what had happened would hit her, and she would have to deal with fear and worry. In the meantime, she fell back on duty, and right now, her duty was on *Budapest*. Nai's lecture notwithstanding, they would not have been through anything like this. They would likely be unsettled and worried, even Chiedza, despite her background. Naina would be thinking of her family, and impatiently checking the comms systems for news. Or, Elena supposed, she might have done what Elena had: set up a private comms alert for any message from home.

Her worry, at this point, was less about her family back on Earth than the reason for the failure. She had no doubt it was deliberate and, despite a dearth of evidence, no doubt that Ellis was somehow behind it all. A few years back, *Galileo* had been hit with a comms loopback virus, effectively isolating the ship; the pattern of this new outage, with Athena's telemetry dropping with no warning, felt familiar. The effects on *Galileo* had been temporary, but the more complex the system, the longer it took for the virus to unravel.

There were ways around the virus, and there were ships in the Second Sector who were already headed to Athena to help, including three science ships from Jessica's home planet of Tengri. This outage was an irritant, and a distraction, and Elena was not happy waiting for the other shoe to drop. Waiting made her worry about things she could not change, and people she could not help.

I haven't spoken to my mother since I left Earth six weeks ago.

She settled the shuttle in the landing bay and made her way through *Budapest*'s corridors. *Budapest* wasn't a bad ship, overall; for a freighter she was positively cheerful, well-lit and adapted with extra temperature zones, allowing for the crew to customize their own comfort. Bear had been flying the same ship for decades, and he'd taken care of her. Working as her mechanic, Elena had enjoyed the solid, comfortable, old-fashioned machinery running alongside the newer tech. There was a familiarity about her, and even though she wasn't *Galileo*, Elena had found some pleasure in the work.

But duty notwithstanding, *Budapest* would never be home.

She climbed the stairs into the ship's main area, and immediately heard shouting. As she grew closer she realized it was only a single voice, and not speaking Standard. Chiedza, then, which made sense: Naina never shouted like that, even when she was angry.

She walked into the kitchen and was completely ignored. Chiedza was pacing and yelling. Naina stood in a corner, jaw set and teeth clenched, arms tensed as if she wanted to hit her crewmate. Elena had noticed nobody on the crew, not even Chi, ever crossed Nai.

Elena focused on the accountant, who shrugged and rolled her eyes. If she was frightened about the First Sector, she was hiding it well.

"Enough," Elena said. When Chi kept cursing, she said it again: "ENOUGH!"

Chi stopped and glared at her. "Who do you think you are? This is none of your *fucking* business."

"Fuck you, Chi," she snapped. "How exactly do you think this helps anyone?"

"Who the fuck is there to help? The whole First Sector is dead!"

At that Naina straightened up. "Stop it, Chi. If you know something we don't, tell us. Otherwise you're as much in the dark as any of us, and you can shut up and panic on your own time."

To Elena's surprise, Chiedza fell silent. She dropped into a chair, staring resentfully at her hands.

Naina looked at Elena. "How is Arin?"

"He's all right," she said. "The doctor says he ought to stay a bit longer. If the two of you want to go over, there's room. They've already set Bear and Yuri up with quarters. Yuri was talking about coming back here in a couple of hours to check on the ship."

"None of that matters," Chiedza said, more quietly. "This is all we have left."

"You don't know that," Elena told her. "You—"

"Don't stand there," she interrupted, "telling me what I know. We all know what you are. We all know you're still in contact with those people. This is some Central military bullshit, and *you know what it is*."

The absurdity of that brought her up short. "Why would Central isolate the First Sector?"

"Who the fuck knows?" Chi leaned back, letting her hands drop into her lap. "Gov thinks they know what's best for all of us. Tariffs and rules and *bullshit,* and if you don't obey, send in the starships and *shoot at people* until they listen to you."

Elena opened her mouth to argue, then closed it again. She knew people who thought that way—her cousin Matthew's daughter had railed at her the last time she was on Earth—and there was little she could say to shift someone's belief in conspiracy theories. It didn't help that there *were* conspiracies within Central Gov; they just weren't nearly as organized as people seemed to think they were. She wondered if somehow people wanted to believe their government had to be more unified than it was, that the inevitable failures were somehow deliberate rather than gaps in a system that had never been better than absurdly fragile.

"I'll tell you what I know," she said, as calmly as she could. She felt Nai's eyes on her. "Whatever hit the First Sector looks a lot like a comms virus *Galileo* ran into a few years ago. And that wasn't Central tech," she added, at Chi's stare. "The original virus came out of Ellis Systems."

"*Ellis?*" Chiedza scoffed. "Pencil pushers. Environmental technologists. They don't make viruses."

190

But Nai did not look surprised. "The company took them off our approved vendor list a year ago. I wondered why."

Interesting, Elena thought, *that we actually managed to hit their commercial reputation.* "Regardless of their public image, most of what Ellis does is stealth weapons research. And their methods tend to be unethical, at the very least." Chi looked skeptical, but at least she was listening. "There's some evidence that the kinds of catastrophes we've been seeing are not coincidence, but coordinated attacks."

"Do you have proof of this?" Chi asked.

"More than you've got against Central," Elena retorted. "But Ellis has been able to hand-wave it away so far. PSI just brought us some intel that may give us more traction. The point is," she went on, before the inevitable protest, "evidence isn't what's important at the moment. Right now we've got to figure out what's going on in the First Sector and what we can do to help."

"We can go back," Nai suggested.

"We're six weeks out. It doesn't make sense for us to move yet."

"But—"

This time it was Chiedza who interrupted Naina. "If we all rush back," she said, her voice finally calm, "we leave everyone out here vulnerable. Which may be the whole point."

Elena felt a wave of relief. Chi believed her, or at least believed enough of what she said to consider it. "Exactly. Unless and until Ellis makes a statement of intent," she said, "we need to focus on what we're out here to do. We came to Yakutsk for a reason. They're still vulnerable. And with this happening, we don't know who else out here is vulnerable, either."

Chiedza's eyes were still full of resentment, but most of her anger seemed to have dissipated. "Fine. But don't tell me we're helpless. What can we do?"

"Funny you should ask." Elena dropped into a chair across from Chi. "Tengri's closest, and they sent a couple of ships with some repair crews to see if they can help at Athena. It occurred to me you might have some contacts in that vicinity as well."

"And who the hell would I know?"

Naina pushed herself off the wall and approached the table. "Chi—" she began, but Elena held up her hand to stop her.

"I don't know what you think I'm thinking, Chi," Elena said seriously, "but I've known some Syndicate raiders in my time. I know their actions aren't always black and white. And I have a small idea what it must have taken for you to leave them." Chi was silent, and Elena knew her guess about the woman's background had been correct. "I don't care who you keep in touch with, and I don't care why. I've worked with you here, and I have no reason whatsoever not to trust you. You accuse me of being Corps on some level? Yeah, I am. I always will be. It's just occurred to me that regardless of your choices, you may feel the same sorts of ties I do."

And then she waited.

"I have some friends," Chi said at last. "They've got a fair amount of comms knowledge."

"Will they help?" Elena asked her.

"Athena Relay is as neutral as territory gets," Chi pointed out. "They use it as much as anyone else. They're not going to exploit this as a business opportunity."

Business. The business of Syndicate raiders was theft, but now was not, Elena knew, the time to get into a philosophical argument. "Would they be willing to give information directly to *Galileo,* or will they prefer going through you?"

"They're not going to talk to the Corps."

Inconvenient, but not a deal-breaker. She stood. "I'll put you in touch with Samaras. He's *Galileo*'s comms officer. He's the one who worked out how to get around the virus last time, and you can pass that on to them. It's not a cure, but it'll be faster than trying to build a temporary relay."

"Assuming," Nai put in, "your loopback virus is at fault."

Elena didn't want to think about what else it could be. "I think the two of you should consider staying on *Galileo* until this blows over."

"Safety in numbers?" Naina sounded amused, but Chi looked outraged.

"You're telling us Central is going to *protect* us?" she said, incredulous.

Elena leveled a look at her. "I'm not talking about official sanctuary," she replied. "I'm talking about *Galileo.* And before you say no, think about how much firepower *Galileo* is carrying, and where you might feel safest."

"We've all got to be communicating," Naina added. "It'll be easier if we're all in the same place. Come on, Chi. I'll stay here for now and wait for Yuri. We can take shifts to look after the ship until Bear comes back."

Chi still looked deeply unhappy. She stood, heading out of the galley, and Elena called after her. "Is that a no?"

Chi stopped and turned. "I'll come with you," she said wearily. "But if Arin's going to be stuck on *Galileo*, we need to bring him his fucking cat."

CHAPTER 21

YAKUTSK

Strange bed, was Jessica's first thought.

Then: *Another concussion. Bob is going to kill me.*

She let her senses explore her surroundings. The bed itself was softer than she was used to, but not unpleasantly so, and a good deal wider than her bunk on *Galileo*. She was under some kind of cloth blanket, lightweight but warm, the nap of the fabric soothing to her skin. Her cheek pressed against a pillow soft enough to mold itself to her face; but she was lying on her ear at a bad angle, and it was starting to irritate her. She was going to have to move soon.

As her perceptions widened, she noticed the way the room smelled: food. Heat and oil, although not heavy; the peaty scent of root vegetables; the bite of toasted nuts and herbs. Pleasant. That must be the sound she was hearing as well: the white-noise sizzle of something cooking. Suddenly she was starving, and she opened her eyes.

She was on a bed set against the wall in a single-room flat. Before her was a table, and across from it a single hard chair, well worn, but curved and attractive, nearly a work of art on its own. Beyond the chair was a counter and cooktop, with a window exposing nothing but the wall of the next building. And before the cooktop stood a figure, slim and slight, pushing at something in a high-sided saucepan and apparently not at all panicked by the recent explosions in the city.

She wondered how long she had been out.

She pushed herself up on one elbow, and her head gave an alarming throb. She cursed, squeezing her eyes shut against the pain, and when she opened them again the figure had turned. Brown hair, brown eyes, light brown skin; fine cheekbones over a straight, square jaw, even and perfect, more nondescript than beautiful. But those eyes looked bright, as if their owner spent a lot of time smiling. *Nonthreatening,* she thought, then noticed her pulse rifle lying on the countertop next to the stove, entirely out of her reach.

"How do you feel?" her host asked. The voice was midrange, slightly musical, oddly calming. *Nature or nurture?* she wondered.

"Like I got blown up," she said honestly. She wanted to lie down again; instead, she swung her legs off the bed and sat up. "Did you find me?"

"Yep." Her host turned back to the stove. "Almost took you to the hospital, but then I saw your uniform."

"Your hospital doesn't take soldiers?"

The shrug told her many things. "Crossed my mind you might not want the publicity, given the circumstances."

"What circumstances would those be?"

Those eyes turned on her again. Still bright, but with a

hint of sharpness that made her think she wouldn't have much luck if she tried lying. "One of our people got shot in that fight."

Fucking Gladkoff. "I know. I saw."

"By a Corps weapon."

"Bullshit." The word came out more forcefully than she'd intended, and her head started throbbing again. "It was . . . *damn.* I didn't get a close enough look at the thing. But I didn't know he had it until after he shot, and he wasn't one of my people."

After a moment, her host nodded. "Maybe not. But that's not what people are saying."

"So I'm safer here than at the hospital."

That shrug again.

"Thank you," she said, and meant it. "Do you have a name?"

"Dallas."

And what are the odds of that? "Would you be the scavenger who worked for Jamyung?"

Dallas opened a cabinet and removed two bowls. "I work for myself. But yeah, I sold to Jamyung now and then. You knew him?"

Jessica watched as Dallas scooped the contents of the saucepan into the bowls. "No. But you and I may have another mutual acquaintance. Elena Shaw."

She saw the look of recognition cross her host's face. Carrying the food, Dallas moved to the table, setting one dish in front of Jessica. She leaned over it, inhaling the spices, and picked up the spoon. "She helped me bring him home," Dallas said, and Jessica thought Elena was right: the scavenger was genuinely grieving. "Is she all right?"

Jessica nodded. "No thanks to some friendly colonists who shot her supply ship down."

Dallas's jaw set; apparently it was a sensitive point. "Not my friends."

"Maybe not," she said, "but nobody's wearing name tags around here. And if your friends think the Corps has been shooting at them . . ." *Shit.* She wasn't thinking. "Do you have a comm system?"

"You want something outside an official link?"

"Just in case," she said. *Dallas catches on quickly.*

A moment later Dallas handed her a small, short-range handheld comm. It took her a moment to contact Bristol, who sounded genuinely relieved.

"Ma'am, where are you? We went back afterward, and none of the hospitals—"

"I'm safe." There would be time for details later, when she was more comfortable with who might or might not be listening in. "What happened to the others?"

"Villipova's people retook the governor's office. She's back there. Nobody's been lobbing grenades at us, ma'am, but people are unhappy. Turns out Gladkoff's weapon was standard Corps manufacture."

A good bet that's deliberate, she thought, frustrated. "Tell them we didn't do the shooting," she said. "Say it once. Say we couldn't prevent it, and we're sorry about that. But don't yell, and don't get into a debate. And for fuck's sake, make sure nobody else gets shot."

"Yes, ma'am."

There was something else in his voice. "What is it, Bristol?"

"Well, ma'am," he said, uncharacteristically hesitant,

"I'm just wondering, since I don't know where you've been . . . have you heard about the First Sector?"

Her stomach contracted. She could feel Dallas's eyes on her. "Could you be more specific, Lieutenant?"

"Nobody can get through. We're suspecting a glitch at Athena Relay, but there's nothing in their last telemetry broadcast to suggest a malfunction."

"How long?"

"It's been down about an hour now."

She swore again. Athena was the oldest relay in the galaxy, and glitches weren't unknown, but something at this level was unprecedented. People would be getting nervous. "Focus on the mission, Lieutenant," she said, knowing she was only saying what he already knew. "Keep your people calm. If you can help pick up after those explosions, reconstruct, rescue people, that kind of thing—absolutely do so. We need Villipova alive, but after that, your priority is making nice with the locals, understand? Gladkoff's stunt fucked things up, but if we're consistent and helpful, maybe we can mitigate some of that."

"Yes, ma'am. We'll take care of it." His voice sounded steadier.

When she disconnected, she looked back at Dallas. "I don't suppose you have anything that can reach a starship?"

Wordlessly, Dallas opened a cabinet underneath the cooktop and pulled out a small, round, clear piece of polymer, about the size of a plate. "I'll need to code it in," Dallas said. "It's not going to look like it's from you, though."

She didn't think that would matter.

Her relief when she heard Greg's voice was nearly overwhelming. "I take off for a couple of hours," she snapped, "and you lose the entire First Sector. What the fuck, sir?"

"Nice to hear your voice, too, Jess," he said, and the gentle humor in his tone eased her anxiety a little. "Why don't you give me your report first?"

Ah, yes. There were more important things than climbing the walls over things she could not change. "Ellis Systems is here, sir."

All of his humor vanished. "Explain."

She told him about Gladkoff, and their escape from Villipova's office. "And apparently," she added, when he was done cursing about the dead colonist, "Gladkoff's weapon is the same design as the ones issued to the Corps."

"You reaching out to the citizens?"

"Bristol's on it."

"What about Dallas?"

Dallas, who was leaning against the kitchen counter watching her, gave another noncommittal shrug. "Dallas has helped me already," she said. "Beyond digging me out of the rubble, though? Can't say."

"I'm a pacifist," Dallas said.

"We're all pacifists," Greg replied. When Dallas snorted, he clarified. "Your skepticism is understandable. But *Galileo* was sent here both to help you recover from the terraformer failure, and to keep you from killing each other."

"Seems to me," Dallas said, "standing troops are maybe not the best way to send that message."

"What would you suggest?" Dallas was silent, and Greg

went on. "My standing troops are there because your current government requested physical protection from the government on Baikul. Are you telling me protecting your governor pits us against the general population?"

Dallas looked at Jessica, and she began to realize exactly how sticky the situation was. "I think that pretty much covers it, sir," she said wearily. "Most of the attacks on Villipova over the years haven't been from Baikul. She's grown very skilled at deflecting them."

"So why," Dallas asked, "did she ask you to come down here?"

"That's a very good question," Greg said. "Do you have any insights on that?"

Dallas shrugged again, and Jessica found herself wishing for vid. Greg was much better at reading body language than she was. "Big difference now," Dallas said, "is Gladkoff."

"At face value," Jessica put in, "his explanation makes sense. Ellis's terraformers fucked up, and they're trying to make amends. With any other corporation, I'd buy it without question." She looked back at Dallas. "Why aren't they just replacing the terraformers?" she asked.

"The real reason? I don't know. But nobody in Smolensk is weeping over that."

"Why not?" Greg asked.

"We've been here five hundred years," Dallas said reasonably. "Why did we suddenly need to move out of the domes? Half of our living is out there. We turn it into crops and housing developments, we're nothing but another generic parts depot."

Patriotism, Jessica realized, *and of a sort that might actually be useful.* "So why do it at all?" she asked, and got nothing but that shrug.

"So Gladkoff's making amends for the failure of something nobody—or at least nobody in Smolensk—wanted in the first place," Greg concluded. "Jess, are you all right? Physically? Can you stay down there?"

"My doctor seems to think I'll survive," she said, and she thought she caught Dallas hiding a smile.

"Does your doctor think you could go incognito?"

Dallas's eyes narrowed. "Don't know. That hair."

"I can dye it," Jessica pointed out.

"Also, she walks like Corps."

"Of course I do," Jessica said, unaccountably irritable. "I spent years learning how to do it."

"I suggest you unlearn it, Commander," Greg said decisively. "Dallas—can we count on you to help us here?"

Dallas shifted against the countertop, and she caught the long fingers tightening against the edge. "I'm Yakutsk," Dallas said. "Not Corps."

"Understood," Greg said. "Right now, I believe our interests are aligned. As soon as you feel they're not, you do what you need to do."

Jessica studied her host. Dallas's face, she was learning, was subtly expressive, conveying thoughtfulness and concentration around the corners of those dark eyes, displeasure with a gentle clenching of the jaw. Right now, she did not think the scavenger was weighing whether or not Greg was worth trusting. Everybody trusted Greg; it was a power he had, a weird force of will that annoyed Jessica as often as she was grateful for it. No, she thought Dallas's dilemma had more to do with how much a career scavenger wanted to get involved in what was likely to become a far more volatile political situation than the colony was used to weathering.

After a moment, Dallas pushed off the counter. "Villipova's opportunistic, but paranoid," the scavenger said. "She'll take systems from Gladkoff, but she'll want local mechs to validate them. I've worked for her before. She'd probably let me in again." Those dark eyes met Jessica's. "Could probably bring an assistant without much fuss."

Jessica grinned. "I think we're good here, sir," she told her captain.

CHAPTER 22

GALILEO

L *ate to the game again. You never learn, do you, Jos?*
Admiral Josiah Herrod, retired, did what he always
did when a crisis hit: he watched. Right now he was watching Greg Foster, calm and professional, talking with his
crew in the pub, reminding them of exactly what they could
and could not control, keeping their duties as unchanged as
he could. Jos felt the palpable nervousness in the room ease a
little, watched soldiers straighten and look more composed.
They would not panic until they saw their captain falter,
and Greg Foster was not going to falter. If the Admiralty
had learned nothing else about him, Jos reflected, they'd
learned that no matter how recalcitrant he was willing to
behave behind the scenes, in front of his crew he would remain the consummate officer.

Shaw had surprised him. After her outbursts during the
PSI spy's presentation, he would have expected her to go for
his throat. Instead she had excused herself to *Budapest* to
look after her crewmates there. Her own ideal of service, he

supposed. Whatever her reasons for leaving the Corps—and he had his own theories on that—she would always do the duty she was assigned.

He was counting on it. They all were.

"We're not getting any environmental data yet," Foster told his crew. "The closest station we've got is a little less than three hours out, so we'll hear something soon. In the meantime—at your stations, on alert. And if anyone hears anything, rumor or otherwise, tell myself, Commander Broadmoor, or Lieutenant Samaras. Keep it off comms, and do not spread rumors. We need to set an example."

Three hours. Without Athena, the other relays would suffer time lags of various lengths as they synced up to compensate for the shortfall. Jos felt, suddenly, the tremendous distance between himself and the home he knew, all that was familiar, all that had tangled itself into the fabric of his life.

You're such a landlubber, Jos, said Andy's voice in his head. *It's amazing you can even climb a flight of stairs.* Andy had meant it as a joke, even a fond one; but he had not been wrong.

Commander Ilyana sat on the opposite side of the pub from Jos—as far away from the windows as she could get, he noticed, or perhaps she only wanted her back to the wall. She was not what he had been led to expect at all. For thirty years the Admiralty had called her a spy, never mind that neither Central nor any of its departments had many secrets Jos considered worth stealing. Jos suspected, if he asked her captain, he'd be told she was simply an expert on Central Gov, the equivalent of the dozens of officers the Corps assigned to keep up to date on what PSI was doing. But she was certainly making no secret of her curiosity, of soaking up every bit she could of what was going on around her. Her disingenuousness might have been performance, but if it was, she was an extraordinary actress.

There was a point in my life when I knew who the enemy was. Today, that thought seemed laughable.

As Foster approached, Jos carefully tucked away his own concerns. Reacting now would do him no good. Letting Foster know what he knew would only make things worse. Best to emulate the captain and keep his fears to himself, and not think about the path to which they were now committed.

Foster sat across from Jos, body language casual, still playing to his audience. But Jos knew Greg Foster well, and he could see the tenseness in his jaw, the annoyance in his eyes. Those extraordinary eyes were always what he noticed first about Greg Foster. Jos remembered the first time he had met the man, when Foster had been a first-year Academy student, twenty-two years old and already described as a leader. Jos had been prepared to find him lazy and entitled—how do you walk through life with that face and not relax into having everything handed to you?—but Foster had surprised him. He had been focused, hardworking, and utterly humorless, and Jos thought he would have easily made Admiral someday.

But he had learned, monitoring Foster's years at the Academy and then his early, exemplary career, that Foster had one thing that disqualified him from the life within the bureaucracy: he believed. Jos had been skeptical at first, but over and over again, no matter how messy the assignment, no matter what horrific loss he had to face, Foster got up and fought again. No matter how much evidence he saw with his own eyes that they were fighting a losing battle, that there was no way to win, he kept going.

Jos told himself that was the only way Foster reminded him of Andy.

"Admiral," Foster said, "do you have any intelligence on what's going on here?"

Polite, Jos reflected, *if only for his crew.* Shaw would have eviscerated Jos publicly, never mind the audience. She might even have done it while she was still Corps, despite his rank.

"I know what you know, Captain," he said. It was only a small lie.

Foster's lips thinned. The expression would give him lines someday, but his skin was still flawless, even at nearly forty. "I'll ignore the patent bullshit of that statement and ask in a different way: Is this the same loopback that hit *Galileo* a few years back?"

Jos wanted to say yes. He wanted it to be true. A part of him, not so old and cynical, the part that had once been young and facing his future with fearlessness, still held on to a thread of hope that it *was* the loopback, that the enemy had considered that enough, that they could get through all of this with nothing worse than some tangled logic cores. "I don't know," he said. Then: "Are the symptoms the same?"

Foster, apparently deciding to believe Jos for the moment, sat back. "Impossible to tell," he said, some of his frustration leaking into his voice. "We've got nobody by the border. The chatter on the stream suggests there may be some Syndicate raiders closer than our people, but God knows if they'll give us any intel. It seems, for the moment, we have to wait and see."

"We could head back," Jos suggested, just to see what Foster would say.

But the captain scoffed. "We're six weeks off from picking up anything at all, never mind anything from Earth." He rubbed his eyes. "How did people survive like this?"

"They didn't leave the solar system," Jos said.

Foster shot him a typically humorless look. "I've sent a message to Admiral Chemeris in the Second Sector," he said, "but she's inundated at the moment. I don't expect to hear back unless she's got specific orders. But there's nobody else out here from the Admiralty."

Jos wondered how long military cohesiveness would last. He let his eyes sweep the room; these people would follow their captain without question. Probably Lockwood as well. She had lost so much of the hesitance he had noticed when he first met her. "So for now," Jos surmised, "we stay on point, yes? We're here for Yakutsk."

Foster nodded. "And things down there are getting a little heated." He told Jos that Villipova's office had been attacked, and that Lockwood was staying down there to keep an eye on the situation. "So we may not have any trouble keeping busy."

Yakutsk, Jos reflected, was unlikely to be fazed by bad news from the First Sector. Like many of the colonies this far out, they saw the First Sector more as a remnant of history than an ally. But he saw something else on Foster's face. "What is it, Captain?"

Foster regarded him for a moment, and Jos realized he

was deciding whether or not to say anything. It was an interesting sensation, seeing this man who'd had to obey his orders for so many years choose whether or not to answer a question. "Ellis is on Yakutsk, sir," Foster said at last.

Even Jos couldn't conceal his surprise at that. "Are you sure?"

Foster had straightened. "We haven't verified the representative's ident yet, but we're as sure as we can be," he said.

Ellis on Yakutsk. Jos had no doubt they'd been responsible for Yakutsk's terraformer failure, but . . . *why are they back?* This was not part of what had been discussed. "That makes no sense," he said aloud.

"Given Ilyana's information, I think it makes a lot of sense."

But Jos shook his head. "Yakutsk is a shipyard. A parts dealership. A big one, yes, and a good one; but it's a commodity business. They're hardly stealing food out of the mouths of Fifth Sector children."

"Maybe the Ellis rep is telling the truth," Foster suggested. "Maybe this is an attempt at good PR. They still need their corporate image."

Not for much longer. "Captain Foster." Jos took a breath. Damn, he didn't think anything could shake him worse than losing Athena Relay. "Listen to me. Ellis is a shrewd player indeed, and PR is part of their arsenal. But there is no way they send anyone—not even some low-level sales drone—to a Fourth Sector shipyard for PR. We need to do more than keep an eye on them. We need to find out why they're here."

Their discussion was interrupted by Foster's comm. "Yes, Lieutenant Samaras?" the captain said.

"Sir." Foster had set his comm to be audible, and Jos

found himself grateful for the courtesy. "Sir, Ellis Systems is making an announcement over the stream. I think—we may want to pipe it ship-wide, sir."

"Go ahead."

A voice, baritone, friendly and comforting, began speaking over the ship's comms, and the room fell quickly silent. ". . . frightening news from the First Sector. Like all of you, we here at Ellis Systems are hoping for a quick resolution to the situation, and the arrival of only good news. In aid of that, we are actively assisting Olam Colony, who has launched their defense fleet to the First Sector. The fleet will arrive there within a few days, and will provide assistance and defense as necessary.

"In addition to assisting Olam, we are offering all colonies in need of parts and environmental repairs free or reduced-price assistance for the duration of this crisis. Please contact your local Ellis Systems representative for more information, or simply reply to this comm." The voice paused with practiced drama. "We are all concerned for our friends and family, but with the help of the Olam Fleet, we will no doubt hear the best possible news very soon. Ellis out."

Jos's eyes swept the crowd. People were talking, and a few looked hopeful; but most of them looked angry. They remembered, he realized. Every officer on this ship, infantry or medical, ensign or commander, remembered Ellis, remembered Canberra, remembered the wormhole.

It wasn't enough. It would never be enough. But that ember of hope clinging to life in Jos's heart flared, just a little, to see it.

"Since when," Foster said, "does Olam have a defense fleet? Our intel has called them VIP starships."

"We've suspected for a while," Jos said. No harm in telling him now.

"And you said nothing."

"You're not a Fifth Sector ship, Captain Foster."

Those bright eyes flashed with anger, and Foster's fist closed on the table before him. "If the Fifth Sector is mobilizing a military," he said, "that's something *everyone* needs to know."

"Possibly." Jos let his gaze harden; retired or not, he still had more experience than Foster. "But that was neither your call nor mine, Captain. And at this point, it's entirely irrelevant, don't you think?"

"Do you really think they're going back there to *defend* the First Sector?"

This time Jos took the opportunity to sit back. His shoulders ached, and his knees; it was difficult sitting in one position for a long time. Pritchard, his aide, had been telling him for some time he should get grafts for his knees, at the very least; he'd only be off his feet for a few days, and it might help. Jos didn't know how to explain to a young, able-bodied man that he felt he had earned his discomfort, the pain and degradation of age, that it was his pride and his shame, and his only reminder of the fact that once, long ago and far away, he had thought he would become a different man. "I think," he said, finding himself wanting to be kind, "it is possible that Olam wants to help, and if that's the case, well, our worries are unfounded. But if it's not—they will not find the First Sector asleep at the switch."

Foster clearly wanted to ask him more questions. Actually, Jos thought, Foster clearly wanted to throw punches, and Jos suspected the captain would, at the first opportunity, adjourn to the ship's gymnasium to run off some of his impotent fury. Jos knew how he felt. He'd had to figure out how to manage impotent fury for the last twenty-seven years of his life.

That temper'll kill you young, Jos. There were days he wished it had.

"We're going to need to talk to Villipova and Oarig again," Foster said at last. His expression had relaxed, but his fist was still clenched. "Whatever Ellis is up to, I don't want them playing Smolensk and Baikul against each other. Maybe this, at least, we can contain." He stood and came to attention, although he did not salute. "Thank you, Admiral."

Jos watched Foster walk away, taking his time going through the crowd, stopping to give reassurances to everyone who approached. Confident, strong, fearless, never mind what he was feeling inside.

And then Jos's eyes fell on Ilyana. She, too, was watching Foster, but her eyebrows had drawn together, and she was frowning, as formidably as any Corps starship captain ever frowned. For a moment, Jos thought he saw rage on her face, in her body, how she sat, how she held her arms and her head: nearly uncontrollable fury, self-righteous and infinitely hot.

And then she blinked, and caught his eye, and smiled at him, and he decided he had been projecting again.

CHAPTER 23

As she disembarked from the shuttle in *Galileo*'s landing bay, Chiedza looked shiftily around as if she were evaluating it for salvage. Of course, Elena realized, that might be her own biases; as a Syndicate raider, Chi would have known what parts she could sell, and what was more trouble than it was worth to steal. Still, it was impossible to find Chi too threatening, even with that look on her face. Her arms were full of an irritable but subdued Mehitabel, who kept glaring at Elena as if the entire situation were her fault.

When Elena had asked if Nai wanted them to wait with her until Yuri arrived, Nai had just raised her eyebrows. "I rather like the peace and quiet," she said. "Especially without that cat."

Elena had argued that the cat could stay behind, that large dishes of food and water would be sufficient to keep the animal for a few days. "It's Arin's cat," was all Chiedza said, and that seemed to settle the question.

Elena sent them off with the duty officer, who had arranged guest quarters on the same deck as Admiral Herrod. It was small and petty, but it pleased Elena to be housing a former thief right around the corner from the duplicitous admiral.

With whom she needed to have a serious talk.

But before she could track down the admiral, Bear commed her. *Lovely,* she thought. *The first call I get on a brand-new comm and I'm going to get yelled at.*

But he didn't sound angry. "Can you come to the infirmary, Elena?"

Her stomach knotted. "Is Arin all right?"

"He's fine. He's recovering. But nobody's telling us anything here."

Of course. Bob got tight-lipped and protective with his patients when things were happening. In most situations, that tactic allowed people to rest. For Bear, never mind Arin, it would be alarming. "I'll be right there, Bear. But the truth is there's not much to tell yet."

When she arrived, Arin was sitting up, Bear pacing restlessly next to the bed. They both looked at her when she walked in, eyes anxious. Even Bear, out here for so many years, in so many ways more experienced than she was, wanted her reassurance.

They think I know something. She wondered if it would be better or worse if they understood how in the dark she really was.

Cautiously, unsure of her welcome, she gave Arin an easy smile. "You're looking well," she said.

"I'd get up if they'd let me." He sounded annoyed, but not with her, and she allowed herself a moment of relief.

"Elena, what's going on?" Bear broke in. "All we're hearing is that nobody can contact the First Sector, and then we get some PR bullshit from Ellis. What the hell does it all mean?"

She took a breath and outlined what she knew. "So it's possible," she concluded, "that what we're dealing with is nothing more than a massive comms failure. I know we can't be sure at the moment," she added, anticipating the question, "but we've hit similar problems in the past, and that's what fits the current evidence we've got."

"Will Athena come back?" Arin asked.

Truth or dare? She chose truth. "I don't know." Bear glared at her, and she glared back. "Nobody knows anything right now," she insisted. "With the relay down, everything has to take another route, and Hemera Relay won't pick anything up for another couple of hours. There are some freighters and science ships heading for the perimeter to see if they can pick up some of the slack, and Chi's going to see if she knows anyone in the area. But we're not hearing anything from anyone yet."

Bear looked away, and she tensed for an angry onslaught. But when he spoke, he was calm and collected, no longer a worried father, but a freighter captain. "So for now, there's nothing for us to do."

"Even if we went full-bore back to Earth, it'd be weeks before we got there. Better to wait and find out what we can from closer ships."

He turned back, regarding her speculatively. "In a situation like this," he asked, "how much is the Corps going to stand on regulations?"

"If you're worried about Chi," Elena said, "don't. I can't believe, under the circumstances, that the Corps won't cheerfully take the intelligence wherever they can get it."

"But you don't know."

She closed her eyes. "No, I don't know. And frankly, Bear, if Chi's friends get burned, they'll get burned because they earned it. But Chi's out, isn't she? Not even the Corps is going to go after her for guilt by association."

It occurred to her then that she and Bear were talking as if the Corps would be in control, responsible for information distribution and relief efforts. They were talking as if this was war.

We are already at war.

As far as she knew, Arin's family consisted of Yuri and Bear; but he was nineteen, and he almost certainly had friends on Earth. Bear, as she recalled, had an older sister. "Syndicates or not," she told them, trying to sound reassuring, "we'll hear something soon. And in the meantime—" She smiled at Arin. "Chi brought that damn cat. I wouldn't count on Bob letting her in here, but you could always try sneaking."

"No more sneaking," Bear declared, and Arin laughed, and for a moment, the universe was normal.

Herrod's door was opened by a man a little younger than Elena: tall, gangly, with a sharp chin and wary eyes. "I'm sorry," he said, stiffly polite. "The admiral isn't seeing anyone right now."

Elena considered him. Jessica had frequently observed that she had a tendency to bash through people, but in her defense, it often worked. "You're Pritchard," she said, and he straightened.

"I'm the admiral's aide. When he becomes available, I will tell him you stopped by."

"Well," she said, "that's very nice of you." She crossed her arms and shifted her weight, leaning ostentatiously against the doorframe. "But as I'll just be standing here until you've done that, perhaps you could do it now and save us both some time."

His eyes narrowed, and she noticed the shadows beneath them. He was focusing on his work, hanging on to what he could control. Not a useless man in a crisis. Perhaps not a bad choice for Herrod's aide, even if he wasn't a trained soldier. Maybe, if he'd had a little more experience, he would have had a shot at waiting her out. After a moment, he gave her a slight nod. "Wait here."

A moment later, the door opened again, and Pritchard stood aside. Herrod was seated at a small table, scanning through a long text document. "Sit down, Chief," he said absently. "And forgive my aide. He's very good at his job."

Pritchard, to his credit, did not respond to this gibe, but removed himself from the room via the interior door. "Does he have people back on Earth?" she asked.

"Everybody has people back on Earth. Even the ones who didn't grow up there." He pushed the document aside but didn't dismiss it. "That's part of the point, of course. The First Sector is humanity's center of gravity. Without it, we're all unsteady, waiting for someone to swoop in and offer us an arm before we fall. And we'll take any arm that shows up."

"You mean Ellis."

"Their concern sounds very convincing, don't you think?" He leaned forward. "What is it you want from me, Chief?"

And wasn't that a good question? "Why are you here, Admiral?"

"I'm sure Captain Foster has already told you."

"He doesn't know any more than I do."

Herrod's eyebrows shot up, and she thought she'd surprised him. "Well," he said, sounding amused, "that will be a disappointment to everyone who worked to get me here."

"So Yakutsk was just a pretext."

"Yakutsk is a serious problem," he said. "And no, we didn't know they were going to lose the terraformers, but with the evidence we've been seeing—that you've been helping *Galileo* to compile, Chief—it didn't surprise us. The timing was serendipitous for me, yes. But I am in fact a trained diplomat, and that part of this mission is quite real."

This time she believed him. She knew as well as he did what would happen in the Fourth Sector if the most popular shipyard there was out of commission long-term. It wouldn't be a paralyzing loss, but they'd be some time replacing the services. Not vital, perhaps, but important enough. "They should have sent more personnel," she said.

"I don't disagree, Chief. But we're not exactly over-whelmed with qualified people just now."

"So you didn't know Yakutsk was coming, but you weren't surprised by it."

"Exactly."

"What about the First Sector?"

He gave her a speculative look. *Not even trying to hide*

that he's deciding what to say to me. "It's a lot more com-plicated than 'we knew' or 'we didn't know.'"

She snorted. "That sounds like bullshit."

"One of the less entertaining things about getting older," he said, "is that you learn that most things that sound like bullshit are actually true. It's easy, in hindsight, to believe people were incompetent, that they should have seen it com-ing, that someone who knew what they were doing could have prevented all of it. But nothing in life is so linear, Chief. And nothing in life is so simple."

That was easy enough to decipher. "You knew the First Sector was a target."

"The First Sector has been a target since before I was born," he said.

Something in the phrase gave her a chill. "That doesn't make any sense. You said it yourself: Earth is the center. Even if we didn't grow up there, we all came from there. Having it host our central government is logical."

He was looking amused again. "You didn't study history, did you?"

She shrugged. "Just what I needed to get through school."

"You're a smart person, Chief. And you surround your-self with smart people. It's one of your defining characteris-tics, or so your psych profile says: slow people irritate you. You don't necessarily like that about yourself, but it's the truth." He folded his hands on the table. "So let me teach you something, Chief: in aggregate, humans are slow. You can pack a colony with the brightest, sharpest, most percep-tive minds ever born into our species, and without any out-side influences they'll become selfish, self-serving, and slow to change. Intelligence does not help. In some situations, it makes things worse."

This is why I didn't study history. "Is there a point in all that pontification?"

"The point, Chief, is that we've seen this coming for decades. Centuries, even. Someone always wants to take power from those who have it. But despite all that history, we didn't see it coming *today*. Nobody does."

For the first time since she had heard the news, she felt a tickle of fear. "Is there nothing in place?" she asked him. "No contingency plans?"

"That we can execute right now?" He settled back in his chair again. "We have one. But nobody likes it much."

"Screw that," she said. "We've got to do something. This is—"

"Offensive?"

She struggled to attach the right word. "It's *wrong*."

"I agree. So what are you willing to do about it?"

"What are you talking about?"

"I need your help, Shaw."

She laughed out loud at that. "Seriously? Why would I help you?"

"I should rephrase. *We* need your help."

"Shadow Ops."

"No, Shaw. All of us. Everyone here."

All of us? What does that mean? "What do you want me to do, set off fireworks? Perform a puppet show so people can take their minds off of the possibility of everything they know and love having been blown to bits?"

"As fascinating as that would be," he said dryly, "that's not what we need from you."

"What is it you need?"

"We need you to stop Ellis Systems."

She blinked at him, his hated face, this man who had lied to her and to her friends, had ripped her away from everything and everyone she loved. "I need," she said, "to get back to work." And she turned and walked out of his office, annoyed and unnerved, to look for Greg.

CHAPTER 24

Greg knew one person who had met Commander Ilyana, and that was Captain Andriya Vassily of the Third Sector science ship CCSS *Cassia*. And ever since he had seen Elena, battered and filthy in a civilian env suit in a wreck on the surface of Yakutsk, he had not wanted to talk to her at all.

He had never spoken of Elena to Andriya. He and Andriya had been lovers, off and on, for nearly a year—sporadically, given how rarely their two ships managed to be in the same vicinity—but Andriya had made it clear early on that she was not particularly interested in emotional attachments, or tales of his past. "I've been married four times, Foster," she had told him, "and I've had enough drama." In the beginning it had suited Greg perfectly well, but as time went on he had found himself increasingly dissatisfied. Their sexual relationship was more than adequate for him, but once the initial novelty of having someone available had worn off, he wondered what it might be like to have someone who satisfied his heart as well as his body.

He had said as much, once, to Jessica.

"Ship is full of people, sir," she had pointed out.

He'd called her on her hypocrisy. Jessica had a string of lovers she had built up over the years, but she hadn't added anyone new in a long time—not since Greg had promoted her to second-in-command. The Corps had no official regulations forbidding people from having personal relationships that crossed rank, but Jessica found the idea too problematic. He had seen enough relationship catastrophes in his career to agree with her.

But he suspected, as observant as Jessica was, that she knew more about his feelings for Elena than he had told her. Jessica would know that Elena, not some set of personal ethics, was the reason Greg would never consider getting involved with a member of his crew. And she would know exactly what it had done to him to see Elena again, and why the last person he wanted to talk to, even in a crisis, was the woman who had been his lover for the past year.

Steeling himself, he sat down at his desk with a massive cup of coffee, and commed *Cassia*.

"You look like hell," Andriya told him. "How's your crew handling the silence?"

Andriya Vassily was short and compact, dark-skinned and muscular, aggressively beautiful, and one of the brightest people Greg had ever known. She had been a few years ahead of him at Central Military Academy, brash and confident and accomplished. He had suffered a debilitating crush on her for months until he met Caroline, who had eclipsed everything else for a long time. During the subsequent years, as his marriage atrophied, he often wondered what might have happened if he had said something to Andriya back then, if he had let her burn through him the way she had so many others. He would never have met Caroline, and he would have met Elena scarred and cynical and free of emotional encumbrances.

Everything would have been the same, you damn fool, he told himself. But he wondered anyway.

"About as you'd expect," he said. "Hyper-focused on their usual duties, and waiting for the other shoe. What about yours?"

"The soldiers are fine," she said. "The scientists, though . . ." *Cassia* was a research carrier, and a de facto mobile hospital; much of her staff wasn't Corps at all. "My psych officer is pulling double shifts so he can deal with all of them."

He took a risk. "What about you?"

Weariness flickered in her fine eyes, and then her expression closed, and she grinned. "Ready for the good fight, as always. Did you comm to talk philosophy, Foster, or do you have a question?"

Andriya's first and last defense against too much intimacy: work. For once, it didn't annoy him. "We've got a PSI officer on board who I think you've met: Ilyana, off of *Chryse*."

At that, Andriya's graceful eyebrows shot up. "Yakutsk must be a hell of a clusterfuck if *Chryse* is there as well. I thought they were out by the Third Sector."

"*Chryse* is en route," he said, keeping his suspicions about *Chryse*'s damage to himself. "Ilyana came ahead. I've read some things about her, but she's . . . not what I expected. I was hoping you could give me your impressions."

Andriya was frowning. "It was a long time ago. Six, seven years, I think. But I do remember her. We were doing an evac of Adsilia, and we didn't have the space. *Chryse* sent some shuttles, with Ilyana to coordinate."

"She was on board *Cassia*?"

"Only in the landing bay."

"But she made an impression."

"Oh, yes." Andriya sounded grim. "Adsilia was a mess. People were dying faster than we could get them off. Whole evac shuttles had to be quarantined. I didn't lose anybody, but Captain Crayne did. And throughout all of it, Ilyana was businesslike and efficient and completely fucking bloodless. I don't think I've ever met anyone colder in my life, Greg."

"Did she help at all?"

"Her ideas were solid, sure," Andriya said. "She suggested methods of transferring refugees, and what we might do with the ones who'd decided they wanted to go back home. Practical thoughts."

"What sort of knowledge did she have?"

"Some medical—enough to understand the contagion issues—but a *lot* of technical. Comms more than mechanics, but still. I'm guessing she's not as good as Commander Lockwood, but I'm betting she could hack her way around a few things."

"Modern knowledge? Up to date?"

"Like she'd trained with my own crew."

Greg thought of Ilyana's reputation as a spy. "You said *bloodless*," Greg pressed. "What does that mean?"

"I know you get compassion fatigue out here. Happens to all of us." Greg thought she was speaking from experience. "But she seemed better at shrugging it all off than anyone I've ever dealt with. She expressed sorrow about the refugees, but it was *polite,* you know? Pro forma. And a lot of people were dying, Greg. A *lot.*"

"Were you speaking Standard? Maybe it was a translation issue."

"Don't think so. Her Standard was flawless. No accent at all. I would have assumed it was all she spoke if I didn't know better."

Greg sat back. What the Corps knew of her was almost nothing. Commander Ilyana of *Chryse* had appeared for the first time, described as a woman in her mid-twenties, seven years after Leslie Millar's disappearance on Achinsk. All of the reports Greg had read more or less matched Andriya's recollections: hyper-competent and emotionless. A cipher.

The perfect spy.

"You're worried about this." For a woman who didn't want any emotional involvement, Andriya knew him very well.

"I'm worried about all of it," he confessed. "And you know how I feel about coincidence. The First Sector may just be having comms problems, but right after we're shipped out here to Yakutsk? And I don't care for Ellis and Olam being so cozy, either, never mind a non-Corps recon fleet. They keep talking about *help* and *stability,* but it's sure looking like a power grab to me."

"And the longer the First Sector is out, the more the Fifth Sector starts looking like an attractive, organized governmental alternative." She shook her head. "Ever think we should just withdraw from the Fifth Sector and move on?"

He chuckled. "I'd say that was a great idea," he said, "if I didn't think that was exactly what they wanted."

"Let them try. They can't survive without us."

But after they had disconnected, Greg thought, *No, that's not it. They* can *survive without us. They just can't survive* alone.

He commed Bayandi from the off-grid, sitting in his quarters again. As he waited for *Chryse* to pick up the signal, his mind wandered toward his father. Even if the disconnect was down to the loopback virus, that meant Earth was not receiving anything outside of the First Sector. Tom Foster never said anything to his son, but Greg knew he worried, even when everything was normal. Something in his face every time he picked up a comm, a brief muscle spasm around the outside of his eyes, told Greg what his father was remembering. One day, twenty-seven years earlier, when Greg was only twelve, his father had received a comm telling him Greg's mother was dead. Greg knew, on some level, his father would always be waiting to hear the same news about him.

Earth has defenses. They will be all right. He resisted the urge to ask *Galileo*—again—if contact with the First Sector had been restored yet.

Bayandi, as he had the first time, replied quickly. "Captain Foster," he said, "I am pleased to hear from you. How is Commander Ilyana?"

"Physically she's doing well," Greg replied, emphasizing

the first word. "My nurse tells me most of the tranquilizer is out of her system."

"I am glad to hear that." Bayandi sounded relieved. "I'll comm her when we're finished to make sure she is all right."

Greg wondered if he had been too subtle. "Captain, I've got a couple of questions about Commander Ilyana, if you can answer them."

"I will answer what I can, Captain. But I must tell you, Commander Ilyana's business is her own. I cannot violate her privacy."

"Of course not." *What does he think I'm going to ask?* "But I've spoken to some people who have worked with Commander Ilyana in the past. I'm finding her behavior doesn't match what I'm being told. I'm wondering if something has happened to her lately, or if she's just changed over time."

"Ah." That one word carried so much: sadness, chagrin, worry. "I believe I can explain without being specific, Captain. Commander Ilyana has been handling a great deal as of late, most of it entirely on her own. One of the reasons I sent her to Captain Taras was that I was hopeful some time away from *Chryse* would help her to relax. I did not think to check *Cytheria* for medications of the type she might misuse."

Greg frowned. *Apparently Bayandi sent Ilyana to Meridia for a holiday.* "Was she exhibiting any self-destructive behavior on *Chryse*?"

There was a silence, and Greg thought Bayandi was struggling with confidentiality. "She was not self-destructive, no." Greg had not expected such a direct response. "What is it you're seeing that alarms you, Captain?"

Alarms was not precisely the right word. "She seems calm," Greg said. "Strangely so. Especially in the face of everything that's happened."

"You mean the First Sector silence."

"You seem calm as well, Captain."

Bayandi made a low sound of consideration. "Please understand, Captain. I am not insensible to how distressing this must be. But my own people . . . we do not see such cartographical divisions. You understand?"

Greg was not entirely sure he did, but he didn't think this was the time for a deep philosophical discussion. "I have one other question, Captain. Commander Ilyana tells us she was sent to deliver a message. Why didn't you mention this when we spoke before?"

And this time the emotion in Bayandi's voice was easy to identify. "I did not send Commander Ilyana with any message, Captain." He was genuinely puzzled. "What message did she give you?"

Greg found himself on his feet, pacing, his stomach in knots. "She told us Ellis was working specifically to undermine the Fourth Sector. She said they're in collusion with the Fifth Sector, and Olam Colony in particular. She showed us some records to support that. She said they've been working at this for a long time." *She said we are at war.*

From his tone, this apparently cleared nothing up for Bayandi. "We do have those records," Bayandi said. "And I would have shared them with you, had I thought they would help on Yakutsk. Much of that information I assumed you already had, especially given your unofficial investigations into Ellis."

"But you didn't send Ilyana to talk to us about that specifically?"

"That would be an inefficient way to transfer such data, wouldn't it? And I had no wish to . . . burden Commander Ilyana with anything." His worry was palpable. "Captain, please—do keep an eye on her. She . . . like so many, Captain, she believes she is strong. She believes she needs no one. She is wrong, of course, but there is no way to tell her that."

Yes, Greg thought. *I know one or two soldiers like that.* "Commander Ilyana has an official escort," Greg told Bayandi. "I'm also monitoring her comms. I apologize if that seems like an intrusion, but under the circumstances, it seems prudent."

"I would do the same in your position," Captain Bayandi assured him.

"Is she dangerous?" Greg asked bluntly.

This time Bayandi's pause was longer, but when he spoke, his voice was decisive. "I have known Tatiana Ilyana for forty years," he said. "In all of that time, I have never seen her deliberately harm anyone, including herself. I imagine I know what your colleagues have told you of her, Captain. I will not tell you they are wrong. But she is loyal and passionate, and she fights tirelessly for her family. Please." His voice softened. "Look after her for me, Captain. When I reach Yakutsk . . . I may be able to help her."

"She'll be safe here," Greg promised.

But as he folded up his off-grid, Greg couldn't help but wonder if Bayandi was asking more than he had said.

He had just tucked the polymer sheet under his mattress when his door chimed, and *Galileo* projected her old, outdated name before his eyes: *Chief Shaw*. Sentiment. Jessica had kept Elena in the system, along with all of her command codes. *Galileo* knew Elena wasn't Corps anymore, but the ship identified her as it had been told to do.

But when he opened the door, Elena wasn't alone. With her was a young woman, in her mid-twenties at the oldest, thin and tall with dark skin and bronzed hair and narrow, cynical eyes. This, Greg deduced, had to be Chiedza, *Budapest*'s supply officer; she was not old enough to be the accountant. Greg had not thought she and Elena were particularly friendly, but Elena was standing close to the younger woman, the look on her face telling Greg she was worried. "What is it?" he asked.

Chiedza straightened, hands at her sides, but Greg saw her fingers trembling. "I didn't have anyone else to tell," she said, mildly resentful. "But—I have some . . . *friends* by the First Sector border, Captain Foster, and I just heard from them. They say—they found out why the First Sector went dark. Athena Relay has been destroyed. They've seen the debris. It's in pieces.

"And all ten thousand people who lived there are dead."

CHAPTER 25

YAKUTSK

"So, what," Commander Lockwood asked, "we just wander into the mech room and start hacking around with stuff?"

Dallas looked down at her, unable to suppress a smile. "Pretty much."

Jessica Lockwood, Dallas had decided, was a difficult person to dislike, despite her profession. On the one hand, she was hyper-competent, talking with her captain and the infantry she had deployed in the city with intelligence and professionalism. She had to be feeling some worry about the First Sector—not her original home, she had mentioned, but intimately tied to the lives of most of the people she worked with—but she had remained calmly focused on her assignment, which seemed to be something between defending Villipova and trying to engineer some kind of alliance between Smolensk and Baikul. Dallas had considered telling her the former might be imprudent, the latter was impossible, and she should quit while she was ahead.

But wouldn't it be interesting, Dallas thought, *to watch her try?*

But when it came to everyday subterfuge, she was deeply uncomfortable, and skeptical of every method Dallas brought up. She had a lot of trouble believing that all she needed to do was put on some civilian clothes and dye her bright hair a nondescript brown in order to blend. Dallas had explained that there were no redheads on Yakutsk, and without that vivid reminder, anyone looking at her would be inclined to fold her into the homogeneous crowd of scavengers that made up the bulk of the city's population.

"I still walk like a soldier, don't I?" she had said before they left.

On that point, Dallas had to agree. She had tried, it was true; but the effect had been stagey and obvious, and Dallas had had trouble keeping a straight face. "You can wait outside the office, then," Dallas had told her after a particularly comical attempt to shake off her military training. "I'll get you an ident."

Convincing Villipova had been almost frighteningly easy. The governor had indeed remembered Dallas, and had issued a set of idents for any assistants required, without asking for anything other than a list of the team's professional qualifications. Dallas had identified Commander Lockwood as "a specialist in logic cores and intra-machine communications."

"That's a pompous title for a hacker," Lockwood had remarked.

"Villipova likes pompous titles," Dallas told her. "And now that you have an ident badge, you look like everyone else. Stop twitching like you cheated the house on game night."

She had done better until they approached the new environmental building. Villipova had not been there, but there had been a half-dozen off-world systems architects, and a ludicrously tall thin person in a bad suit. Dallas frowned at that one. His body language was all wrong—clearly off-world, but artificial somehow. He had been trained—not to fit in, Dallas thought, but to be anonymous.

Dallas didn't like anonymous.

"That's Gladkoff," Commander Lockwood said as they walked closer.

"The killer?"

Commander Lockwood's lips set, but Dallas did not think she was disagreeing. "He howled about self-defense," she said, "but between you and me that's bullshit. Your friends were lousy shots. He had no business doing what he did."

"Will he be prosecuted?"

At that, Commander Lockwood had looked up, and her bright green eyes were curious and speculative on Dallas's face. "Under whose jurisdiction?"

Dallas stayed between Lockwood and Gladkoff. The Ellis salesman didn't even look up at two nondescript locals. By the time they passed through the building entrance, ignored by everyone but a single architect who skimmed their idents, Commander Lockwood was out of breath and moving just as awkwardly as she had been at the flat.

"Don't you Corps people work out?" Dallas asked.

The teasing seemed to snap her out of her mood, and she relaxed, shooting Dallas a look. "I don't do what we just did," she confessed. "The stealth. I'm trained in tech security. Past that, I tell other people what to do, and sometimes yell at the captain."

Dallas had, in fact, noticed a level of informality in her conversations with her deep-voiced superior. "Is that allowed?"

"I wouldn't work for a captain who didn't allow it." Interesting, Dallas thought, that she had the choice. "But I don't lie to people's faces, as a general rule. And I don't sneak."

"Too bad. You're pretty good at it." She was, for an amateur. They had made it through the door, which was more than Dallas had expected when they left the flat. If she kept calm and got better at hiding her nerves, she might do all right.

The mech room was crowded with more systems architects, along with a dozen delivery people. *All off-worlders.* That was curious. Smolensk was full of technical expertise; why would Villipova trust a bunch of strangers without any oversight from her own people? *Maybe,* Dallas thought, *she's counting on me for that.*

And maybe she thinks I'll fail.

The person in charge was obvious: a woman, shorter than Dallas but stockier than the average Smolensk citizen, who kept a manifest hovering by the corner of her eye, occasionally referring to it and talking to the delivery people. Dallas laid a hand on Commander Lockwood's arm. "Wait here," Dallas said, and thought, *Stay calm.*

The woman looked up at Dallas's approach, relaxed and not at all suspicious. Dallas introduced both of them. "I'm Dallas, and that's my comms person. Governor Villipova sent us to double-check the equipment."

"Oh, of course." The woman smiled, unconcerned. "Hang on, let me shoot you a copy of the manifest."

Dallas pulled it up as it arrived over comm, and scrolled through. Nothing at all that looked strange: ordinary environmental equipment, some new parts, some aftermarket. Nothing—on the surface, at least—that seemed like it didn't belong. *No wonder she's not concerned with me.* "Want to stay out of your way," Dallas said. "Where's the best place to start?"

The woman pointed to a tall, slender unit standing in the corner. "If you start there and work to the right, we'll miss each other, more or less."

Dallas returned to Commander Lockwood, and together they headed for the corner. "She seemed normal," Lockwood said.

Normal for what? "Just because there's nothing strange in the manifest," Dallas pointed out, "doesn't mean the deployment is clean."

"She may not know, either."

Dallas looked down at Commander Lockwood for a moment. She was back in Corps mode, eyes shifting over every piece of equipment and person in the room, calculating and suspicious. *What must it be like,* Dallas thought, *to have to doubt every situation you walk into?*

Dallas supposed, back on her ship, she would be able to let her guard down, and feel as comfortable as Dallas did walking through the city streets. But it struck Dallas as a heavy price to pay for a career.

They settled into the work. Lockwood, good to her word, was expert at analyzing equipment, and any qualms she had about subterfuge seemed to vanish. Anyone with rudimentary knowledge would look over her shoulder and see an ordinary mechanic, scanning the function of each part of the system to validate that it was working. Even Dallas, with extensive experience handling equipment that looked like it did one thing but was designed to do something else, had to look closely to recognize when Lockwood was opening the exterior interfaces to check what was going on underneath. She was quick and efficient, and in this task, reflexively relaxed. *Better at lying to machines than to people,* Dallas thought.

Dallas stuck with parts inventory, trusting Lockwood to find anything that was not functioning as designed. The system was, at the very least, radically over-designed for a domed city, which was annoying. *Waste again.* Just like the damn terraformers. So much of what was sold as upgrades was nothing but unnecessary, over-engineered bullshit. Very pretty, though, Dallas had to admit; but simplicity was so much more elegant than this convoluted system of redundancies and over-powered batteries and—

What the hell is this?

Dallas leaned forward, squinting. Had that been on the manifest? Dallas turned and scanned the document. There it was—or at least the pieces. They hadn't logged it whole, which meant they'd shipped it in components and assembled it here.

Subterfuge.

"Lockwood," Dallas asked, "can you have a look at this?"

She abandoned her own unit and moved to stand next to Dallas. The light from her comm illuminated the interior of the cabinet, and Dallas moved aside to give her room. "This is a more sophisticated unit than the others."

Dallas nodded. "It's a controller. What parts do you see?"

She shot Dallas a look, but gamely began a visual inventory. "Logic core," she said, "magnetic memory system, shadow system, volatile storage, comms storage, transmission booster . . ." Dallas could hear in her voice when she began to understand. "A big fucking transmission booster." The frown on her face mirrored Dallas's own. "That looks a hell of a lot bigger than what you'd need to coordinate an environmental system, even if you hooked it up to Baikul."

"Even if you hooked it up to a fucking satellite," Dallas said. "That's outgoing. There's an incoming on the other side."

She voiced Dallas's exact thoughts:

"Why are they building a long-range comms system into a dome environmental system?"

Dallas had agreed with Lockwood that she needed to wait outside the governor's office. Even with her dark hair, she wasn't going to be able to talk to the woman she'd spoken to only a few hours before without being recognized. And Dallas didn't think Villipova would keep trusting Smolensk's scavengers if one of them showed up in her office with a Corps commander in tow.

Dallas affected an even, matter-of-fact tone. "I'm not a designer, Governor." Dallas's eyes took in Gladkoff, leaning in the corner, far too comfortable in the governor's office, and Dallas wondered why Villipova would put up with him. "But a long-range comms system is a big power draw. Waste of battery. Waste of space."

"Well, we can't have that, can we?" The amusement in Villipova's voice was cruel, but Dallas was clear who the target was. "How about it, Gladkii? Why don't you tell me why you're burying a comms system in my free, upgraded env system?"

"I hardly think—" Gladkoff began.

Villipova froze Gladkoff with a glance, and Dallas abruptly remembered that this was the woman whose scores of political enemies had mysteriously ended up outside the dome without env suits. Gladkoff, who had clearly been briefed enough to understand, blanched and swallowed, then straightened, tugging at his jacket, and Dallas reflected the Ellis salesman could be taught. "Governor," Gladkoff continued, far more formally, "I apologize if this aspect of the system was not adequately explained. The comms system is standard in our newest units. It's intended to allow diagnostics to easily be sent back to a manufacturing facility, and for us to perform remote maintenance whenever possible. It is intended purely as a convenience, Governor. I can give you the names of other colonies where we have deployed similar systems. You may speak with them before we continue the installation, if you wish."

Smooth, Dallas thought. *Easier for us if he'd stayed stupid.*

But where Gladkoff could learn, apparently Villipova could not. "I will contact those colonies, Gladkoff," she said. "But don't suspend the installation. We've waited long enough for this system, and the sooner we can get all of our businesses back to full capacity, the better."

And that, Dallas thought, *is the problem with thinking you're invincible.* Villipova had allowed Gladkoff this much access; her ego would not allow her to reverse her position now. Dallas didn't like to think she actually believed Gladkoff was telling the whole truth.

"Excellent, Governor." Gladkoff sounded palpably relieved, and Dallas caught the look of satisfaction on Villipova's face. "I'll send you the list of colonies right away."

Dallas left the office, and Lockwood fell into step as they headed back to the environmental building. "She's not stupid," Dallas said, frustrated. "So why let him continue?"

"Pragmatism," Lockwood speculated. "If he's up to something, she thinks she can outsmart him." She gave the scavenger a look. "*Can* she outsmart him?"

Dallas considered. "Villipova is nobody's fool. She wouldn't have stayed in power this long if she was. But Gladkoff . . ." Dallas looked down at the soldier. "Makes me nervous. Not a lot of people make me nervous."

"Makes me nervous, too." They walked in silence for a moment, and Dallas became aware Commander Lockwood was trying to figure out how to say something. "So at this point," she said at last, "I need to ask you something. How would you feel about a hacker putting an entirely illegal hook into a potentially destructive long-range comms system being covertly built into your dome environmentals?"

How did this person become a Corps soldier? "Better than I would've if you'd asked before we saw all this."

And Commander Lockwood flashed Dallas a bright grin.

CHAPTER 26

GALILEO

Unidentified ship, this is Athena Relay, come back.*"*

Elena heard an exasperated sigh.

"Unidentified ship, this is Athena Relay. Your ident is malfunctioning. This is a monitored corridor. Please identify yourself."

There were muffled murmurings. *"—no idea. Maybe asleep."* Laughter then. *Laughter. "Maybe they're too busy—"* They went on at some length about the sorts of carnal antics a crew might be getting up to that would make them ignore a failed ident alarm. The comms officer had a filthy imagination.

Used to. Used *to have a filthy imagination.*

The final audio was mundane and unremarkable. The joking broke off, and the voice became curious and annoyed. Not afraid. Not even a little bit afraid.

"—the fuck?"

And then a loud, distorted noise, and nothing.

"What's the time stamp?" Greg asked.

"Two hours ago," Chiedza said. "Right around the time the First Sector went dark."

He asked Elena, "Is the loss of Athena Relay enough to explain the outage in the First Sector?"

He was thinking what she was thinking, she knew: *bad design.* "Depending on the orbit of Artemis," she said, referring to the First Sector's secondary relay, "yes. They're out of sync weeks at a time. In theory, once Artemis comes around again, it'll all come back up. But that's . . ." She did the math in her head. "Three weeks. A little more." *Too long.*

Greg turned back to Chiedza. "Your friends. Which tribe are they?"

Chi shifted. She was unused to providing detail to anyone, much less a Corps officer. "They're not my tribe," she said. "They're just old acquaintances." When Greg kept looking at her, silent, Chi relented. "Syncos."

Lucky, Elena thought. Syncos traded in high-tech materials, which meant they would have resources. "What we need," he told Chiedza, "is an interim relay. I don't imagine they'd have all the necessary parts with them, but they'd know where to find them, wouldn't they?"

Because, Elena knew, *they would have stolen similar parts from colonies in the area for decades, if not centuries.*

But Chi answered readily enough. "And how to work with them as well."

Greg gave a decisive nod. "Find Lieutenant Samaras," he told her. "He'll know how to put one together, and he'll be able to get them through it quickly. Can you coordinate that conversation?"

And damned if Chiedza, ex–Syndicate raider, professional irritant, didn't straighten up as if she were coming to attention. "Of course."

Greg gave her directions to comms, and she left, determined and purposeful and no longer in need of Elena's help. When she was gone, Greg slumped back in his chair, rubbing his eyes. "How many people know about this?" he asked, subdued.

"From Chi, or from the Syndicate tribe?" Hesitantly, she sat in the chair across from him. "If it's not out on the stream already, it will be soon."

She waited, knowing what he would have to do next, wishing she could do it for him. After a moment he opened his eyes and hit his comm. "All personnel," he announced, over the ship's comm, "convene in the pub in five minutes." He looked across the desk at her, and she thought she saw, under his usual grim stoicism, a hint of bone-deep grief. "Ten thousand people, Elena."

She knew people on Athena Relay. *Everybody* knew people on Athena Relay. It had been humanity's first FTL comms system, sturdy and iconic and unfailing for centuries. But more than that . . . if Athena had been destroyed deliberately, nobody in the First Sector was safe. "We need to find out what took them out, Greg," she said. "Chi's friends sent a pretty decent chunk of telemetry data. We may be able to ID the type of ship, at least."

"You want to put bets on it being something from the Fifth Sector?"

"To what end?" She had been over it in her head a dozen times since Nai had told her what happened. "I could see taking out Athena in hopes of staging a stealth attack, but that's sort of like setting off a fire alarm to distract people from the flames. Nobody in the First Sector has ever been complacent about defense, never mind Earth. They'll all be on high alert for whatever's coming now."

"I know." He stood, walking around the desk. "Which means either the First Sector isn't the target, or this involves some players we don't know about yet."

"You think the Olam Fleet knew it was coming?"

"I think nobody's going to be upset anymore that they're heading in to 'defend' the First Sector."

She stood with him, and together they headed out the door. There was a weariness about him, even with his straight posture, the crisp salutes he gave everyone they passed in the hall. He was on his own out here, she realized, with no command above him and almost no data, and he was about to tell his crew that what had looked like an annoying equipment outage was actually a tragedy that rivaled anything that had happened in their lifetimes. And there was Greg's father, and his sister, and his nephews, all the people he loved, all the things that tied him to Earth. All the things he had thought he could protect, that might, even as he walked in step with her, already be gone forever.

She wanted to ask him what he was going to do. She wanted him to tell her what to do. She thought of Herrod's words: *We need your help.*

Herrod had known, she realized. He must have known.

Greg stopped outside the pub and turned to her. Her mind was spinning with everything she needed to tell him, but the look in his eyes silenced her. There it was: all his worry, all his insecurity, and she wanted to reach out and take his hands. But she did not expect what he said to her.

"Will you stand with me in there, Elena?"

She was not an officer, not anymore. Most of the crew knew her, but she had spoken to so few of them in the last eighteen months. He wasn't asking for them, she realized, and she felt herself straighten.

"Of course," she told him.

So she stood next to him while he spoke, while he weathered the gasps at the news. Stood with him while he talked, calm and calming, over murmurs and tears. She looked out over their faces, these people she had served with. Most of them looked shocked. Some had covered their faces with their hands; others were clinging to each other; many, like Elena with Greg, were just standing close to their crewmates, not touching, but taking and giving strength in silence. No one said anything until Greg told them about Chiedza's Syndicate friends working on a temporary relay.

"We can't trust them!" Elena couldn't identify the source of the outburst, but there were enough disapproving glares that she didn't think they had to worry about total anarchy just yet.

Greg held up a hand. "In other circumstances," he said, "I'd agree with you. But think it through: the Syndicates rely on Athena Relay as much as any of us."

"How do we know *they* didn't destroy it?" Another unidentified voice, this time followed by murmurs of agreement.

"Because," Greg said, raising his voice just enough to be heard above the crowd, "there's no profit in it." The murmurs died, and Elena saw him square his shoulders. "I need to ask all of you to keep your speculations to yourselves. Right now we don't know anything, and everyone here has been through enough to understand how destructive baseless rumors are. This is going to hit the stream any minute now, and I'd like all of you to use whatever influence you have to focus people away from divisive conspiracy theories. Don't lie, don't embellish. Stick with facts. Which do not include, by the way, any suspicions about the actual mission of the Fifth Sector Olam Fleet."

That, Elena decided, had been a calculated statement. The Olam Fleet was concrete, a defined entity. The crew might not explicitly doubt Olam's motives, but they knew the politics and they knew the capabilities. "Can we intercept, sir?" asked Emily Broadmoor.

"We're too distant," Greg told them. "But *Persephone* and *Tenko* are on the way now, along with *Aganju* and *Novoselov* from PSI. And remember, Tengri's ships started toward the First Sector as soon as the lights went out. If Olam is headed there for antagonistic reasons, they're not going to find the place defenseless."

He paused again, and this time let his eyes sweep the crowd. Elena knew that look from the other side: each of them would feel he was looking just at them, speaking just to them. How he did it with two hundred people, she had never known; but it was undeniably effective. "We were sent here," he reminded them, "to keep the peace on Yakutsk. At this point, our mission has not so much changed as widened. We must keep the peace here, in the Fourth Sector, to the best of our ability. We have knowledge and expertise.

Whatever happened to Athena Relay, we will weather it together. Each and every one of you has my absolute faith."

When he was finished, the crew dispersed back to their duties, and Greg beckoned to Emily Broadmoor. "Commander, I need you to brief Lieutenant Bristol on the surface," he said. "He'll need to tell Commander Lockwood. I can't risk comming her directly, and the off-grid is too unreliable."

Emily nodded. She looked pale, but otherwise her usual determined self. "Do we have any data at all?" she asked.

"There's a little more telemetry with the audio we have," he told her. "Shimada's got it now. We should at least be able to get a better look at what hit them."

"Yes, sir."

She retreated to find Ted, and Elena became aware that Greg was still tense, still unfinished. "I need a favor," he said quietly, so only she could hear.

"Of course."

"In my office," he said. "On the top shelf, behind the left panel. There's something there I need you to get rid of." He would not look at her.

"I'll be right back."

She headed back to his office. The shelf was nearly out of her reach, but on her toes she could touch the panel release, and it slid silently open to reveal a bottle of whiskey. Elena herself couldn't drink, but after observing soldiers drinking for most of her adult life, she knew what he had was very, very expensive. The bottle was still sealed.

She pulled it down, surprised at its heft, and headed through the inner door into his quarters and then to the bathroom. She opened the lid and inhaled the familiar fragrance, then poured the entire contents down the sink. She ran water until the sink was clean, then dropped the bottle and its lid into the recycling chamber.

He had quit drinking entirely two years before. She had never asked him why.

When she passed back through the inner door, he was seated at his desk, eyes out the window. "Thanks," he said, but didn't move.

She perched in the chair across from him. "You couldn't have stopped it," she told him. *Just like this morning.*

He was silent for a long time. "We always know that, don't we? That we can't save everyone? That Canberra, Liriel, Nova Akropola, all of them—that it'd be worse if we weren't trying. That sometimes there's nothing we can do. Sometimes we're helpless."

"Sometimes we are, Greg."

"Bullshit." He pushed himself abruptly to his feet and began pacing behind the desk. "I can't believe that. I can't *live* like that. I stood there, and I told them all to stay strong in the face of disaster. In the face of whatever disaster is coming. Because you know this isn't the end of it. There's no reason to take out Athena, none at all, unless you want to isolate the First Sector. And we're sitting here babysitting two squabbling cities pissed off at each other because they can't see themselves as a single damn colony."

"Yakutsk didn't do this," she reminded him.

"I know. But if we weren't stuck here—"

"Playing that game is pointless, and you know it." She stood and walked around the desk, blocking his path. "Listen." He stood over her, glaring, and she glared back. "Stop, just for one minute, and listen. I can't tell you it's all going to be fine. I can't tell you your father is all right, and your sister. I can't tell you anything because I don't know anything. And *neither do you*, Greg. But what I do know is that the people you love are strong and resourceful, and they know that you love them, and it doesn't matter how long it's been since you've said it. They know it, they feel it, and you are not letting them down."

He glared at her a little longer, then turned away, and she knew she had it right. When he spoke again, he was calmer. "When I was twelve, Elena. The day my father told me my mother was dead . . . I didn't believe him. I thought it was a prank. I couldn't understand why he'd do it. And when I realized he was telling me the truth . . . I wished it was him instead. I said that to him. Do you think he's ever forgotten that? Because I don't think I would."

Oh, Greg. "If I stood here," she said, "and listed every hateful thing I've said to my grandmother over the years, we'd live out our days on this spot." He turned back, and she thought, *The hell with it*. She reached out and took his hands in hers. "You were twelve years old, Greg, and you'd just heard something no child should ever hear. I promise you, your wish was normal. Saying that to your father was normal. And if he's got half your brains, he knew it, too, and didn't hold it against you for an instant." And she suspected Tom Foster would have agreed with his son, and taken his wife's place on that fated starship if he'd had the chance. "Do not do this to yourself. Your father's fate is out of your hands. The fate of the people on this ship, though—

that's in your hands. Focus on what you *can* do, Greg, and not what you can't."

Greg's comm chimed, and for a moment she thought he wouldn't answer it. *Galileo* helpfully projected *Lieutenant Samaras* before his eyes. She saw him focus on the letters, and straighten, and she thought just before he released her fingers he tightened his hands over hers. "Yes, Lieutenant," Greg responded, sounding more like himself.

"I have Captain Bayandi for you, sir," Samaras said.

"Captain Foster," Bayandi said a moment later, "I have just learned of Athena Relay. A horrific tragedy. How are your people faring?"

That same focused compassion. "They're in shock," Greg told him candidly, his eyes never leaving Elena's. "But they're steady. They're well-trained. What about your people, Captain?"

"We have never had ties to the First Sector," Bayandi told him. "But . . . I do think I may be able to help, or at least offer some information."

"Do you know who destroyed the relay?"

"Nothing of that sort, I'm afraid. Rather, my information involves the Olam Fleet."

Greg's eyebrows shot up. "They're not going to be in range of the First Sector for at least another two weeks," Greg said. "And that's assuming they're running their engines at capacity."

"And that is what concerns me, Captain Foster," Bayandi said. He sounded worried, but also curious, as if he were not sure if his news was good or bad. "I have been tracking the fleet, off and on, and I am getting some very odd readings.

Perhaps they are using some new sort of engine, but I'm finding no matter what I try to analyze, I can't interpret the data in a way that makes any sense."

"Captain Bayandi," Elena put in, "this is Elena Shaw. Can you send us the data?"

"Of course. And may I say, Chief Shaw, it is a pleasure to hear your voice again."

This time Elena raised her eyebrows at Greg. Bayandi might be a scattered old man, but he never forgot his manners. "Thank you, Captain."

The data began to stream in, and Greg pulled it up in front of the two of them. She studied it with a practiced eye, teasing out the speed and location information that was relevant, that told them where the fleet was and where it was headed. Except . . . "Captain Bayandi, are you sure of this data?"

"It is precisely as I have received it, Commander. You are seeing what I am seeing, I think."

"Yes." *No.* "I think. It's—" Damn, she'd been away from all of this too long. "Greg, look at their location vectors. And the field limits. And here—that's the FTL fold where they started out, or so it says."

He was frowning, and then his expression cleared, and those gray-black eyes filled with dread. "Oh, hell," he said.

"So I'm not imagining it."

Greg was on the comm to Ted. "Commander Shimada," he said, "drop the Athena telemetry data for now. I want everything you can get on the location of the Olam Fleet."

"Sir?"

"We need to know if there's anything non-standard about

their engines or their field generators. Or both." Greg closed his eyes. "Get me everything you can, Commander. Because if what I've got now is right, nobody's going to be able to intercept the Olam Fleet."

"I think they're in the First Sector already."

CHAPTER 27

YAKUTSK

Jessica decided the thing she hated most about command was having to behave like a professional when all she wanted to do was sit down and weep.

"They're sure about this?" she asked Lieutenant Bristol.

"Audio and telemetry don't appear to be modified, ma'am," Bristol told her, his voice subdued. "And so far there's no evidence the Syndicate tribe had anything to do with it."

"Has it hit the stream yet?"

"A few minutes ago. Aren't they talking about it there?"

Jessica looked over her shoulder at the crowd behind her. She had found a quiet corner in this brightly lit, industrial building that apparently passed for both a public gathering area and a bar. There was a great deal of discussion—most of which, she noticed, Dallas was choosing to stay out of—but none of it was about Athena Relay, or indeed the First Sector at all. "I think they're mostly focused on their civil war," she told him.

Immediately he tensed. "Do you need backup, ma'am?"

"No, thank you, Lieutenant." She smiled, in spite of her mood. "So far the current seems to be away from more violence and toward strategizing. And when that changes"—and she had no doubt it would—"it's not going to be me they're after."

But Bristol, like the good infantry soldier he was, was not satisfied with her answer. "I'm not comfortable with you being there without backup, ma'am."

Me neither. "If I get in trouble," she promised, "I'll send an alert. Will that do?"

"I'd rather send you an escort, ma'am."

"Can't blow my cover, Lieutenant," she said. Behind her, the discussion was becoming more heated. "Listen, I've got to go. But—" She thought for a moment. Bristol's family were Fifth Sector, which had surprised her when she found out, but some of the others were more vulnerable. "How is your team doing?"

Bristol, despite his other limitations, was reasonably perceptive about morale issues. "Varied, ma'am," he told her. "But we're all right. Backing each other up."

"Anybody becomes a danger, send them back to *Galileo*," she ordered. "I'll trust your judgment on that, Bristol. I need you all steady here, which means you take care of each other. Understood?"

"Yes, ma'am."

She disconnected, staring at the wall. She had cousins on Athena Relay. *The bad side of the family,* as her aunts used to say. She had met them only once, when she was about ten years old; even then, her family had been urging her to get away from Tengri, to use her talent for programming in a place where the annual death rate was lower. But she had loathed her cousins, and managed to remain at home for another four years before she had left for school on Earth.

No more loathsome cousins. She almost wailed at the wall.

"Bad news?"

She turned at the familiar voice, and found Dallas standing half a meter away from her, looking down at her with concern in those dark eyes. She was, she realized, susceptible to Dallas's apparent kindness: always polite, never encroaching on Jessica's personal space, but at the same time open, receptive, trustworthy. Impossible to dislike. Impossible to mistrust. Despite counting herself a good judge of character, Jessica knew better than to tell everything to anyone she had only just met.

"Your friends don't do much stream surfing, do they?" she asked, and when Dallas frowned, she relented. "Athena Relay has been destroyed," she said.

"Oh." She saw a flash of surprise, then sorrow, in Dallas's eyes before the politeness took over again. "That explains the First Sector disconnect."

"Yeah."

"You have people on Athena?"

Did it count when she hadn't liked them? "I did."

"I'm sorry," Dallas told her, and she thought again how nice it would be to fall apart for a while.

"Thank you." She straightened. "None of that changes any of this. Did you get me my equipment?"

A long-range comms trace was not particularly technical

or difficult; but her assumption was that signals both in and out of the system would be both encrypted and distorted. She had some hardware on *Galileo* that was, strictly speaking, illegal, but given Ellis's presence, she didn't think it was worth the risk of tipping her hand by having them send it down.

Fortunately, she had realized she was working with a seasoned parts scavenger.

"I've got the pieces," Dallas told her. "But it needs assembly."

"How much assembly?"

Dallas held up a bag. It rattled as Jessica took it, and she shot her host a look. "We do not have time for this."

And at that, Dallas looked away, expression unfamiliar. "I may be able to get you a whole one."

"Excellent." She handed back the bag. "Why didn't you say so before?"

"Involves stealing."

"If you need money to buy it—"

"It's not that." Dallas looked back at her. "The owner is dead."

It took her a moment to figure it out. "You mean it was Jamyung's."

Dallas nodded.

"So what's the problem?"

"Before we retrieved his body, the shipyard was in limbo," Dallas explained. "Now that I've buried him, his equipment is common property."

"Divided among everyone?" When Dallas nodded again, she said, "We can pay for it when we're done."

"Nice idea. But we have to get it first."

Ah. "It's guarded."

Dallas nodded. "Probably Villipova's people."

She swore. "I'm a hacker, not a cat burglar. Any chance you've got a friend who can help us out?"

The smile that came over Dallas's face was positively sly. "What makes you think I need a friend?"

Smolensk was, Jessica discovered, distinctly unlike *Galileo*, which was always lit the same way regardless of the official time. The domed city, in contrast, dimmed and localized the lighting at night, in an attempt to mimic the lighting of a planet orbiting a star. It was the middle of the night, and the streets were largely deserted; but there were bright street-lights and radiant sidewalks all along the path from the pub to Jamyung's parts yard. If they were intent on realism, she thought, they might at least have let the city go dark. She understood the safety issues, but the well-lit areas were an annoying impediment.

A worse impediment was the six guards surrounding Jamyung's shop.

Guards *isn't quite the right word,* Jessica thought. Goons *fit better.* They were dressed in civilian clothes, the same nondescript dark fabrics worn by the rest of the colonists, and they varied in height, age, and gender. But their demeanors declared them a matched set: watchful, superficially casual, jackets designed to drape naturally over the small hand weapon each carried at the hip.

She remembered Dallas's comments about her own body language. "Are they locals?" she asked, keeping her voice low.

They were standing on a corner a few blocks away, facing each other, leaning in as if they were two old friends chatting. Jessica wasn't sure they were fooling anybody, but at least they were doing better than the goons in front of Jamyung's place.

"Two of them are off-worlders," Dallas told her. "The others are local." Dallas sniffed, and Jessica read both derision and disapproval in the sound. "Think they're fucking big shots, carrying pistols for a living. Those pissant guns couldn't light a match."

"Maybe not," Jessica said. "But there's six of them. And unless you're a trained fighter in addition to being a cat burglar, that's a problem we need to address."

Dallas grinned again, and Jessica was beginning to think the scavenger was enjoying all of this. "You good at being quiet?"

"Why would I—" She took a breath. Dallas wasn't going to tell her a damn thing, and she might as well go with it. "When I have to be."

"Good. Be quiet."

Dallas turned and sauntered away down an alley. Jessica followed, trying to mimic Dallas's step: light, she had noticed, here inside the dome, probably because they were used to wearing heavy boots outside to deal with the gravity. But this time subterfuge was irrelevant: there was no one else in the alley, nothing but dirt and trash and—she sniffed, and wondered if this was where Elena had found Jamyung's artifact.

Before her, Dallas had stopped at a doorway. She ran to catch up, and looked down: a fingerprint lock. Archaic. Easily defeated. "I can get through that," she told Dallas, and reached for the lock.

Dallas just looked surprised. "I hacked this lock twelve years ago." One touch, and the door swung inward. Jessica, something of an aficionado of horror vids, was mildly disappointed to find a wide, well-lit, clean corridor, as nondescript as any Corps utility hall. They walked side by side, Dallas relaxed, no stealthiness apparent at all.

The hall opened up on a stairwell, looking more like Jessica's presumptive poorly lit trap. "Where are we going?" she asked.

"Back entrance," Dallas said.

Jessica followed Dallas down the stairs, where they came upon another door. Dallas coughed a few times, then spoke, voice lower than usual. "Fucking scavengers," Dallas said, and the door swung open.

Jessica shot Dallas a look. "That was Jamyung's passcode?"

Dallas nodded. "Took me six months to adapt the lock to take my voice print in addition to his. Couldn't change the phrase."

"It doesn't bother you that he talked about you like that?"

Dallas shrugged. "Always bought my stuff. Paid well. Names don't matter."

"Sometimes they speak to attitude."

Dallas was quiet for a moment. "Jamyung *acted* like an asshole. But he wasn't one. You know?"

Jessica tended to be somewhat unforgiving of that personality type, but she had to admit she'd run across more than one solid Corps soldier who would have fit that description. "You were friends."

"Yeah."

And sometimes, she knew, it really was that simple. "Dallas, do you know who killed him?"

"No." Dallas's jaw set. "But they came from the same place as those two strangers outside. Come on."

The door opened into the back of a storeroom, and here there was no lighting at all. Jessica touched her comm, and a bright beam came over her ear; at Dallas's look, she turned down the intensity.

"It might take some time to find it in this mess," Dallas warned.

"Unless they removed the analyzer entirely," she said, "it's still probably a better bet than that bag of bolts you brought me."

"Wasn't just bolts, you know."

"I'm sure it was full of rare and valuable puzzle pieces." She looked around; the room was huge. "Where did he keep it?"

Dallas threaded through the clutter, and Jessica followed, her eyes falling on objects as she moved. It didn't take her long to realize that this had been Jamyung's treasure chest: unlike the piles of ordinary parts in the yard of his shop, nearly everything here was esoteric and valuable. And, in more than one case, broken. Jessica found herself wishing for Ted, who could have mended a lot of this with only the parts on hand. Or Lanie—Lanie could have constructed a pulse rifle, a comms jamming system, and a waffle maker in under five minutes.

Next to Jessica, a faint light flared, and she stopped. "What's this?" she asked, squinting in the dim light.

Dallas glanced over. "Hardware scanner."

Now she saw it. It was a portable unit, but a powerful one—probably necessary if Jamyung wanted to be specific about what he was selling. He would have wanted to make sure he knew what he was letting go of, that he was getting the proper price for it.

But she couldn't imagine why the machine would have been left on.

She moved closer, brightening her light just a little, and looked at the console readout. Someone had pulled up a previous scan, and the content analysis was still listed at the bottom: 60% INERT POLYMER 40% DELLINIUM ISOTOPE 345.

Holy shit. With panicked fingers she queried her comm for the room's environmentals, and found the radiation normal. She took a breath, calming her pounding heart, and looked back at the readout. It must have been an error, or perhaps Jamyung had been calibrating the machine. Apart from the fact that there were not, as far as Jessica knew, any existing labs maintaining dellinium of any kind, there was no inert polymer that could safely contain a dellinium isotope. The radiation from such a thing would have bled through this room, and the room above, and several surrounding blocks.

The readout had to be wrong, but she was still shaking.

She expanded the readout text to look at the rest of the data in the report. The object it had scanned was apparently small enough to fit in someone's hand, and machined rather than hand-struck. A smooth surface—flawless, as far as the scanner could tell—and slightly warm for a polymer. *Contradicting the inert bit,* she thought. Almost certainly this scanner was malfunctioning, and the flaring light was a part of that.

She started to turn away, and it flared again.

Frowning, she scanned down to the end of the report. And there she froze, looking at a rendered three-dimensional image of the object that had been scanned.

Lanie's artifact. Jamyung's talking cube.

CHAPTER 28

GALILEO

Pritchard was clearing up dinner when Shaw arrived at Jos's door.

Jos had dined with Commander Ilyana. After their earlier meeting, Foster had assigned a polite, tenacious young officer named Hirano to guard her, and she had gone to Jos to ask how to deal with him.

"Is he bothering you?" Jos had asked her.

She had thought about that for some time. "No," she told him at last. "But I am not sure what his purpose is."

That seemed a curious question from the second-in-command of a PSI starship. "If you had a guest on *Chryse*," he asked, "would you allow them to wander around unattended?"

She looked confused. "No, of course not. But that is not the same thing."

In the end he had suggested to her that she treat the young man as a tour guide, and if his behavior became bad, she should let Jos know. "I don't have real authority here," he admitted, "but I can certainly talk to the captain about hospitality. I'm sure he doesn't want you to feel unwelcome."

Her eyes had lingered, briefly, on Hirano's back. "Does he get to rest at all, do you suppose?"

At that, Jos had smiled. "I'm sure Captain Foster knows the limits of his soldier," he said.

The meal had been spent discussing horticulture, about which Ilyana, as it turned out, knew a great deal. Jos had picked up enough on the job to hold an intelligent conversation—the Corps had done a good deal of research on renewable food supplies aboard Central starships—and the time had passed quickly. When they had finished, she had asked if he wanted to accompany her on a walk through the atrium.

"Thank you," he said, "but I have some work I need to catch up on. Perhaps tomorrow?"

She had smiled and left, her infantry in tow.

He had known Shaw would show up when Pritchard briefed him about the Olam Fleet. She was savvy enough to see things unraveling, even if she didn't understand how. When she arrived, he waved her in, then turned to his aide. "You can leave that, Pritchard," he said. "Take the evening. I'll see you tomorrow."

She waited until Pritchard was gone. "Olam is going after Earth, aren't they?"

He turned to the bar. "You don't drink, do you?"

"Does Shadow Ops know they're already in the First Sector?"

"Where did you get that?" He poured himself a finger of whiskey, then doubled it.

"I'll take that as a yes. Why didn't they say anything?"

"It's hardly the first time a Fifth Sector colony has flexed its muscles."

"You didn't think it was relevant."

"We didn't think," he corrected her, "that we had any reason to stop them. The last thing we needed them to believe is that we consider them a threat."

"Are they?"

"Ordinarily, no. But this isn't ordinary, is it, Chief?"

"You said I could help you."

"Are you volunteering?"

She was silent, and he turned around to look at her. Civilian clothes, those absurd blue streaks in her hair; but she stood like a soldier. That was going to be the biggest problem, he realized: camouflage. He wondered if she would understand what he meant if he told her she needed to hide it.

"I don't trust you," she said at last.

"Good." He sat, leaning back. "I'd be worried about you if you did."

"Why me?"

"Because you're Corps," he told her, "and you're not. And that's what I need."

She stood for a long time, and he sipped his drink, waiting.

At long last, she took a step forward and sat down at the table. "If I think it's bullshit," she warned, "I won't do it."

"Fair enough," he agreed. "But before I start, Chief—what I'm going to say to you can't leave this room. Is that clear?"

Her eyebrows crept up again. "Why would I agree to keep your secrets?"

Which meant she hadn't yet told Foster about their first conversation. "You're right." He sipped again. "How about this? I'm telling you that in my judgment it's better if nothing I'm going to say to you gets passed on to any third party. Not your friends, not your family, not your cat. If you hear me out and you disagree—fine. I have no authority over you; I'm sharing this because I trust your judgment. But if we get through this conversation and you think the others should know, I won't try to stop you." *I couldn't stop you.* But he didn't think he would have to. "Deal?"

Another pause. "What do you have?"

With that, he knew he had her. "We have the location of a station Ellis has been using for weapons development," he told her. "Recent intel has told us they're also directing starships through a modified FTL field. A faster one."

"You mean the Olam Fleet." She frowned. "Those raiders we found a few years back, where their telemetry was scrambled so we couldn't tell where they really were. This is built from that, isn't it?"

"That was a precursor," he agreed. "What they have now, though, doesn't just confuse the signals. It's actually a faster field."

She shook her head. "How is that possible? To go that much farther in less time—there are too many variants. Too much instability. People have been working on the problem my whole life, and nobody gets anywhere."

"Ellis," he told her, "has been working on it for longer than that. But it appears, Chief, that one of the ways they got it working was to offload the guidance systems to an external source."

He watched her face as she put it together. "So if we take out that station," she said, "we take out the signal."

"And thus, the fleet."

"They wouldn't just drop out?"

"I'm not a mechanic," he said. "But as I understand it, an uncontrolled drop-out is the best possible outcome. More likely they'd just . . . dissolve."

He saw an involuntary shudder run through her. The thought should have horrified him as well. Those ships were staffed with real people, many of whom probably had no idea exactly how deeply Olam was working with Ellis. But he couldn't believe they were all fools, and even in the Fifth Sector people were aware of how dangerous a military mission could become. On top of that—the attack on the First Sector had been planned for a long time, and whether or not they had sent the drone themselves, they had been complicit in the destruction of Athena Relay and the deaths of ten thousand people who had nothing to do with it at all.

Of course, Jos had been complicit as well. But he, at least, was trying to do something about it.

"You have to tell people about this," she insisted. "Olam is dangerous. People need to be warned."

"If the fleet is already in the First Sector," he told her, "what do we accomplish by telling everyone?"

"We can defend them! We can—"

"Even if we could coordinate, we can't get there in time. We'd panic the entire galaxy, Chief, and for no reason. It's too late to intercept the Olam Fleet. And given what Ellis has been doing, who do you think is going to believe they're behind any of this?" He sat back. "Besides, there's a better answer."

"Your incredible scheme, that depends on spying and secrecy." She sounded derisive. "Why not just take out the station?"

"We tried," he told her. "We sent a recon ship in with a cover story we thought was pretty good. It was vaporized. We got one last telemetry transmission, and then the ship was gone."

She was shaking her head. "So they know you're coming for them."

"Chief." He leaned forward, both hands around his drink. The strength it gave him was purely psychological, he knew; but right now he needed whatever he could get. "We've been working on a counter-weapon based on the small amount of information we got from that attack. We are months away from anything practical, and most of what's been built— both the hardware and the blueprints—is inside the First Sector right now. We don't have time to start over with any of it. Olam is headed for Earth, and there's only one way we can stop them."

"And what's that? We can't attack the station again, and their defenses are on high alert because they know we're looking for them. They may be cocky, given that they just blew the hell out of a—what was the recon ship?"

"An AS-9950 armored cruiser," he told her.

Her eyebrows went up. "Shit," she said under her breath. "So they blew up a 9950, and they know we're scared, but they also figure we'll come back after them. Because we have to, don't we? We know what they're doing. We can't just sit back. Is that why they hit the First Sector now? Because they know that's where we've been building our counterattack?"

We. That was a victory. "It's a reasonable guess."

"So how does that work, when we've completely tipped our hand?"

He sat forward. "Not completely, Chief. We're pretty sure they don't know they've tipped their hand on the accelerated field system."

She threw up her hands. "Even if they did, we couldn't catch them. In a field like that, we've no way to bump them out. We can't stop them in-field, we can't launch an attack on the station, so how—" He saw her work it out. "Infiltration. You've got a way in."

Smart kid, he thought, and shoved aside a wave of overwhelming sadness. "We think so, yes," he told her.

"So you do have a source."

He nodded. "The station imports most of their food, and one of their vendors is based on Io Station. One of the owners goes back a ways with Admiral Waris."

"Waris didn't tell them what was really going on, did she?"

"A coffee vendor? Of course not. She said the station's stealing government secrets and marketing them as their own innovations. Making money off the backs of the people, that sort of thing." He had been impressed by Waris's subterfuge, and glad the company she approached was based in the First Sector. In the wider galaxy—maybe even outside the solar system—it would not have been so easy to find someone whose sympathies lay more with Central Gov than a terraformer company.

"Can't you use them to ship in something that could take out the station?"

His eyebrows went up. "Like what? Explosive hot chocolate? Radioactive beer? They've got safeguards there, and the whole station is built with a system of fail-safes."

"But you know the security systems."

He lifted a shoulder. "Most of them."

"Clearly you have a plan, so why don't you spit it out?"

Here, at last, it was all down to what he had learned about Shaw. If he was right, there was hope, however frail.

If he was wrong, they were all doomed.

"Here's where I go back to my original statement, Chief. I don't think I need to tell you how desperate all of this has become. We knew they'd come after us. But we didn't know they'd do it on the scale they have. And we didn't have Ilyana's data. Ellis is much further along than we thought." Stupid, in hindsight, to have ignored PSI so long, to have allowed them to wander with so much freedom without trying to acquire some of what they had learned. "We have one shot at this. If infiltration goes wrong, they'll lock down completely, and that'll be the end of it. They'll have triggers on God knows how many thousands of pieces of hardware, and they'll have the First Sector wherever they want it. They can play nice and be the benevolent providers, or they can just flat-out tell us to do as we're told or they'll kill us all. We'll have nothing on them at all anymore."

"So why all the secrecy? Nobody in the Corps is going to sabotage a plan like that."

"Maybe not. But what I don't want to do is watch hundreds of thousands of people die because we fuck up this shot."

"Who the hell could I tell who would be that kind of a security risk?"

He glared at her. "Don't be disingenuous. *Everyone* is that kind of a security risk, no matter how circumspect they think they are. You tell someone completely reliable, and they tell their spouse or their doctor, or they mention it to their kid, or just let something slip when they're in the gym. Doesn't even have to be the whole thing; just a germ that someone picks up. *I'm* the one who came up with this plan, Chief. Not even Admiral Waris knows all the details, and she is the only person who knew I was planning to take all of this to you. And it's not because there's no one else I trust. It's because I've seen what a single, well-intentioned remark can do, and there is too much at stake here for me to watch that happen again." He sat back. "So you tell me now, Chief. Can you promise me you'll tell no one?"

But she had latched on to something. "You said *watch that happen again.* What did you see happen before?"

"That's not important."

"Beg to differ, sir. You're asking me for a pretty big commitment here. I think I have a right to know why you think it's so important to isolate me from everyone I love and trust." She paused, and when he did not answer, she said, "Has it happened before? Was there some confidence that you all took advantage of, some leak that caused disaster?"

They'd had a massive fight about it before Andy had left on what turned out to be his last mission. *God, Jos, you don't trust anyone, do you? Not even me. What the hell do*

I have to do to make you believe I'd never betray you? He'd told Andy it had nothing to do with his feelings or his commitment. It was his job, his career, the oaths he had sworn. Andy had left, irritable. Jos had not known he was going to his death. But ever since, he'd had to live with the possibility that he might have prevented it.

"The report you filed on the wormhole two years ago," he said. "Do you remember it?"

"Word for word, Admiral."

When he had first received his copy of her report, he had waited until he was alone to replay the attendant data she had submitted. That short, broken, low-quality snippet of audio, holes bored into it by a deliberately applied EMP, as if Andy was holding out his hand and snatching it away again, even from the grave. "Captain Kelso referred to sending someone a message," he said. "That message was intercepted."

"They can't do that," she said automatically. "Even Shadow Ops can't do that. They can't trap an officer's messages, not unless it's on the record, and it wasn't."

"They didn't trap Captain Kelso's messages," he told her. "They trapped *mine*."

Shadow Ops had suspected what Andy's ship would find, but they'd had no idea of the scale of it, of all the horrific possibilities. And Andy—stunned, exhausted, saddened, and absurdly hopeful—had told Jos all of it, including how he was going to see it all destroyed. Andy's need to reach out had given Jos's colleagues all the proof they needed to know where to focus their efforts. And his betrayal had given them something powerful to hold over Jos's head.

He watched her face as she put it together: puzzlement, incredulity, and then a flash of sympathy that struck something raw in Jos's heart. Andrew Kelso's famous last words to his husband, stolen by cold and heartless fingers, used to manipulate Jos when everything inside of him was ash. When the grief began to wear off, when he began to feel things again, hatred was the first emotion he recognized. These people were fools, and Andy had been right about all of it, and damned if Jos was going to let them traipse along financing weapons manufacturers and starting wars of attrition. Shadow Ops had been fragmented before that, but when Jos began speaking up, the idea of peaceful solutions began to get far more traction. He learned to argue, to persuade. He learned when to lose gracefully, and which concessions would gain him allies. He learned about politics and the roundabout nature of winning.

All because they had stolen his last memory of the man he had loved.

"Did you know," she asked him, "that there was something on the other side of that wormhole?"

"It was a guess," he said. "There had been an EMP flare recorded decades earlier. A flash of a dellinium signature. Everybody put it down to equipment misreading the data due to the pulse, but Shadow Ops spent a lot of time on analysis. They decided there was enough of a chance that it was real that they wanted to send a ship."

"And they didn't tell the *Phoenix* about the dellinium."

"They had some reason to believe that a fairly large percentage of Central captains would balk at the idea of retrieving what would basically be a doomsday weapon."

"You knew."

"Yes."

"Before they left."

"Yes."

"That they'd be trapped in the gravity well. That they might not survive the journey, or even be able to get back."

"Yes." He wondered if that would kill her sympathy for him. He hoped so.

She sat back as well. "I think, Admiral, that you didn't know you were being monitored. That makes your situation a little bit different than mine."

"You think there are no Ellis sympathizers on *Galileo*, Chief? Would you say the same for their family, their friends? And those people on *Budapest*—they're strangers to you, aren't they?"

She held up a hand. "Okay. I take your point. Just—" She sighed. "Okay. I won't tell anyone your plan."

"That is a promise?"

"On my honor, sir."

He knew enough about her to take that as intended. "All right. I'll outline the plan, Chief. But I'll tell you right now: I hope you tell me I'm wrong, that it won't work, or that there's another way in or another way out. Because right now, with the intel we've got?

"Whoever goes in there after Ellis is probably going to die."

CHAPTER 29

Late at night, when her conversation with Admiral Herrod had finally drawn to a close, Elena ducked into one of the small kitchens on *Galileo*'s lower level and pulled up a vid of her mother.

Over the years since Elena had left home, they had fallen into the habit of sending vid instead of chatting over live comms. Elena's mother worked air traffic control, backing up the automated systems over the Alaskan Islands and the Chukchi Sea, and her ever-shifting schedule meant her free time rarely synced up with Elena's. Elena was fond of her mother's vids, full of randomness and acidic observations about people; Maggie Shaw had never much cared what people thought of her, and led her life with cheerful tactlessness. Elena had managed to pick up some of that attitude, although she had never quite managed her mother's complete obliviousness; but the more important lesson her mother had taught was to trust her instincts. And right now, in the face of this fragile, ill-formed mission from which she would not return, Elena needed to remember that lesson.

The vid had arrived a few days after *Budapest* had left Io en route to their first cargo drop, and was little more than a laundry list of meaningless details her mother had forgotten to mention the last time they spoke. Elena watched as her mother, dressed in trousers and boots and kneeling in front of a flower bed, trowel in hand, ran down the mundane school accomplishments of Elena's cousins. Elena tuned out the words, focusing instead on her mother's hands and their methodical digging, her ungloved fingers growing grimier as she made room for seedlings. Her mother had always enjoyed starting gardens more than tending them, and Elena couldn't remember if it was the right time of year to plant.

"Your uncle Mike said to remind you not to cross Bear," Maggie said, cleaning some dirt out from under a thumbnail with brisk efficiency. "I don't know what he means, really. Savosky's a good person. Do you remember, when you were eighteen, and he brought his crew to dinner? There was that nice woman who was not as standoffish as the rest. I showed her my garden. She made polite noises, but she didn't know a damn thing. People think they can fool you, don't they?" She laughed. "Anyway. Mike is full of shit, as usual. He worries what everybody else thinks, and when I yell at him, he says he's too tired to fight. I think some things need doing even when you're tired, don't you?" She dusted off her fingers. "Drop me a line when you can, love. Bye."

Elena played the message three times, studying every moment. She did not resemble her mother. Her mother was short and slight, fine-featured and fair-haired and pretty, like the rest of the family. Elena didn't look like any of them, not her uncle or her cousins or even her irritable, thin-lipped grandmother. It would have been easy to grow up feeling like an outsider, but her mother had always treated her with unvarnished delight, never less than pleased that Elena was exactly who she was.

Elena had met so few people in her life who made her feel at home.

The fleet was still half a day away from Earth, even at their accelerated pace. She and Herrod had discussed a detailed identity, and he had triggered a stealth program to embed a long work history for her pseudonym with the food vendor. She had expected to depart right away, but Herrod had told her altering the vendor's schedule was too risky, and aligning her trip with the delivery drop meant there were hours yet before she could go. The timing left her caught between urgency and inertia. Half a day before she had to worry about what might happen to her mother, and all of her alien relatives.

Half a day to stop the fleet.

The plan was fragile, and relied far too much on goodwill and luck, but given the circumstances, she couldn't disagree with Herrod that it was their best chance. She thought, if she could keep her head, she might be able to stop Olam, never mind that she would never know for sure.

This won't destroy Ellis, she had warned Herrod.

We know, he said. *But it'll damage their power, and most importantly, it'll expose them. They'll lose public support. Sometimes real transparency is the best weapon you've got.*

She didn't point out the irony of Shadow Ops trying to destroy an enemy with transparency.

Restless, she left the kitchen to drift through the atrium. Someone had planted lemon trees, still too small for fruit. She imagined a future atrium, full of row after row of fruit trees, the air heavy with sweetness, the luxury of fresh food. *Galileo*'s food production systems were fully automated, even with fresh ingredients, but she knew there were people in the crew who loved to cook. Bob Hastings, for one, was not bad at pastry, but she thought Redlaw would be the one who did the most experimenting. He had a way with flavors, combining things she never would have thought tasted good together. Fruit and vegetable, savory and sweet, sugar and maple and lemongrass and rosemary. Things she never would have thought of.

She would never taste them.

All of this would be here after she was gone, and that was more comforting than she would have expected. They would all go on as she had gone on, year after year, despite who she had lost. Treharne, gone before her eyes. Jake, the first close friend she had lost. Danny, lover and betrayer. She had carried them and remembered them, and told herself that meant something. It meant nothing to them. They were gone, just as she would be gone, and she supposed someone would carry her as she had carried them.

This is pointless.

She had made a choice, and she wasn't going to change her mind, and what was the point in wandering through the atrium missing people who were still there? Who didn't even know she was leaving? She should be doing something with

278

this time: taking in the view from engineering, the sounds of her ship, the smell of the machine she knew so well, the cadence of the environmental systems, the lights, the gentle vibration of the engines keeping *Galileo* in a precise orbit. She should be opening her heart and soaking up everything that had ever given her strength, all the things that she loved, that gave her this life she so desperately did not want to give up, that gave her so much worth dying for. She should fling open her arms and hold everyone for as long as she could, until she had to leave them to keep them safe. She had so few hours left. Why was she standing in an orchard, determined to be alone?

Who could she talk to, who would let her do nothing but soak up their company without having to explain why she needed it? Who would understand without having to ask?

She went to find Greg.

CHAPTER 30

Y ou can come all the way in, you know," Greg told Elena.
She stood just inside the door, which had slid shut behind her, and was looking around the room, hands on her elbows. Nervous, but Greg didn't know why. She looked tired and anxious, and he couldn't tell if she had been crying, or just desperately needed to. *Maybe it's finally all crashing in on her,* he thought, *and no wonder.* She had been dealing with so much, even before all of this had happened.

Her being home was the only good thing to come of any of it.

He had been reading when she showed up—or rather staring at text, scanning the same paragraph over and over, absorbing nothing. Mindful of the news that Olam was too far ahead of them to pursue, he had kept the crew focused on Yakutsk. He felt certain *Galileo* would be needed in some capacity, but he suspected they would be far more effective out here than tearing back to the First Sector with everyone else. And his crew were tired of sitting and waiting. He had seen them nervous and worried before, but the level of destruction they were being asked to deal with was unprecedented. He thought if he could keep them focused on their duties they might be less inclined to plan revenge.

Not that revenge sounds like such a bad idea.

Elena smiled nervously and took a step into the room. Her eyes went to the window—as always, he realized. Every time she walked into a room, she wanted to see what was outside of it. He wondered, sometimes, what it was like to live like that, constantly restless, constantly looking beyond what was in front of her. For most of his life he had thought himself alone in his restlessness, and then he had met her. Even then, years had passed before he understood why, after a lifetime of uneasiness, he felt so much more peaceful when she was there.

"Do you want something to drink?" he asked her.

She kept staring out the window. "Yes, sure," she said at last. "Tea."

That much hasn't changed. She had always drunk tea with him. In the mornings, at breakfast in one of *Galileo*'s kitchens, it was always coffee, strong and bitter, and she didn't seem in the least bit discerning. But whenever she sat with him, to talk, to strategize, or just to be silent, it was always tea. Just as dark and bitter, though, and he often teased her about it.

Tonight he only handed her the cup. She brought the mug up to her nose and inhaled the fragrance of the dried leaves, flavor slowly leached by the hot water. Her eyes dropped shut, a faint smile crossing her lips. "You always have the good stuff," she said.

He had started buying it because he knew she liked it. After she left, he had never tossed the leftovers. Despite her words, she must have noticed it was old. "Perks of the job," he told her.

He sat down again in the armchair he had been in when she arrived. He still had music playing in the background. Old stuff, from his childhood; probably older than she was familiar with. There were only five years between them, but one of the places the age difference showed was in the sort of music they liked. She danced for exercise, and would play all kinds of things—new, old, ancient. But when she relaxed, she stuck with whatever was current, and stayed entirely away from nostalgia. *Variety,* she had said once; but he put it down to that same rush-ahead restlessness.

She drank the tea, still silent, and he watched her. The ship's running lights shone through the window, and the usual warm gold tones of her skin were cast in blue. The artificial color in her hair looked brighter as well, and the light threw shadows over her face, making her eyes huge and prominent above her wide cheekbones. The expressions that face could take on, from humor to anger to hurt to absolute self-righteous rage. She was not striking the way Jessica was, or even his ex-wife; but he could never take his eyes off of her. He wanted to see every expression she could make, read every line written in her heart.

That hasn't changed, either.

"Do you remember when we met?" she asked him at last.

Reminiscing. Not like her, not really; but he supposed under the circumstances it made some sense. "I do," he replied.

"I was nervous."

She had put in for a transfer to *Galileo* from *Exeter*. He only had one engineering spot left when he saw her application, but he knew before he met her that he would take her. Her reputation preceded her, and Çelik, her previous captain—not one for hyperbole—had praised her unreservedly. But nothing had prepared him for the woman he met, eager and ebullient, not at all like the serious and experienced soldier he had seen in her records and reports. He had quizzed her on everything he could think of, trying to trip her up, trying to shake her out of whatever strange, artificial mood she was in. In the end, he had to piss her off to do it.

"You already had the job, you know," he told her.

"You might have told me." Her tone was mildly reproachful, and he thought her mood might be lightening.

"That would have defeated the purpose of an interview."

"I wanted the job so badly," she said, half to herself. "Jake had coached me over and over, quizzed me on everything I already knew. I needed to get off *Exeter,* but it was more than that. I wanted to come here."

"Why here, specifically?"

Her eyes dropped, and he thought, even in the cool light, that he could see her blushing. "I'd heard about you," she said, and he remembered she had friends who had been serving with him on *Arizona,* classmates of hers from the Academy. "I didn't really believe it. After *Exeter,* I figured wherever I'd go I'd end up reporting to assholes. But they said you weren't like that. That you weren't sarcastic or belittling. That you were different."

He was surprised. "I figured you came for the hardware."

Another ghost of a smile. "*Galileo* was part of it, yes,"

she admitted. "But really, I fell in love with her after I got here. Mostly it was you. I felt like you were my last chance. My whole life, all I'd ever wanted was to join the Corps, and my first year was awful. Just . . . painful. Not just the bad luck and the dreadful missions, but day-to-day unpleasant. I was thinking, *Is this going to be my life? After everything I've fought for, everything I thought I wanted, this is the price of being able to serve?* But when I heard about you, I thought maybe, just maybe, what I wanted was still out there somewhere. I just hadn't found it yet."

He seemed to have something caught in his throat. "You never said," he told her.

She shrugged, embarrassed. "It seemed like a lot to drop on your head," she said. "That all of the dreams of my life were down to that day I met you. But I liked you. Even when you deliberately jerked my chain, I liked you. You made me laugh. You listened to what I was saying. You didn't let me get away with anything, but you weren't obnoxious about it. You were—"

"Familiar," he finished, and she met his eyes, surprised. "By the end of that interview," he told her, "I felt like I must have met you somewhere before. Like we'd known each other as kids, and I'd just lost track." He had not recognized it at the time, but he had fallen into her that afternoon, a cool, soothing lake after a lifetime of hot dry days.

And he had never climbed out again.

"Yes." She smiled. "Like if I suddenly started talking about my cousins, you'd know who I meant. It was odd. It doesn't happen to me much," she confessed, "feeling so comfortable with people."

Why, he wondered, *is this coming up now?* "I have a short list of people like that," he told her. "I'm not even sure about everyone on it. My dad falls off and on."

"Family is a whole different issue," she agreed. "My mother—" She stopped. "It's strange. She is the least like me of anyone in my family. I think that's why we get along so well. She doesn't ever assume she's going to understand what I say or do or want, so she takes my word for it. She trusts that I know myself. And she always—" Her voice broke, and he saw her swallow. "No matter what I was trying to do, she always assumed I'd succeed. And if I failed, she'd pick me up and turn me around to try again. Never scolding, never making me feel bad. Just 'Oh, well. Up you get, Elena!' with the same faith and good cheer." She shook her head. "It's weird. Of all of them . . . I love her the most. And I have the fewest regrets about how I left things with her."

He wanted to tell her she would see her mother again. He wanted to believe he'd see his father again. Somehow, just now, he couldn't see beyond this one night. "I think you're lucky to have each other," he said at last.

The music changed, and she smiled in recognition. "God, this song. I was sixteen when this came out. I played it so often at work that Mike made me listen to it on my comm so I wouldn't drive everyone else mad."

Greg smiled, too, listening to the slow, sentimental rhythm. "I was in my last year of college, and we hadn't heard about enlistment acceptances yet," he remembered. "I was climbing the damn walls." And drinking. Every night, he had been drinking, but he had still been young, and he hadn't lost control as easily back then. "I remember thinking, *If I don't get in, this song will be the soundtrack of my failure.*"

"Did you really think you'd fail?"

"I always think I'll fail."

Her eyebrows knit slightly, as if she were turning something over in her head. "Do you want to dance?" she asked at last.

Say no, something inside of him said. *It's not safe. She's not safe. You are glass and paper with her, and she is fire, and you will turn to shards and ash . . .*

He put his cup down on the table and got to his feet. She leaned over and put her mug next to his, then straightened, facing him.

He took her left hand in his right, and settled his other hand on her waist, careful, not pulling her close, just dancing. Casual. Unimportant. She put her other hand on his shoulder, and he could feel the warmth of her fingers through his sleeve. A scattering of handshakes in their long acquaintance. Two hugs, from which he had harvested vivid memories of her body, her hips brushing against his, her warm softness against his chest, the scent of her hair. One kiss that she had called a mistake, that had burned through him and still woke him in the night.

Stop it, he thought harshly. *Dance.*

They began to sway, just a little, to the rhythm of the old song, and he looked into her eyes, trying to listen to the words, to make his feet move to the beat, to think of anything but how close she was standing to him. She was smiling at him, and singing softly, the nonsense syllables of an old pop song, and she had beautiful lips, why had he ever thought they were not beautiful, full and soft and *hers* and he wanted to kiss her and consume her and swallow her whole, and she had to see it because he could feel nothing else, just the heat of her washing over him, lighting him on fire, and he didn't care anymore if there was nothing left of him at all.

You need to stop this, said that sensible voice again. He cleared his throat carefully. "Elena," he began.

She stood on her toes, dropped her eyes closed . . . and brushed her lips against his.

Oh, God.

She let go of his hand and wrapped her arms around his neck, and she moved forward and he crushed her against him, needing to feel her, needing her close to him, around him, everywhere, it could never be enough. She opened her lips to his and kissed him harder, and she pulled his tongue into her mouth, and his hands went into her hair. *Her hair.* He pulled the elastic from her braid, thinking for an instant of where he could put it where it would be safe; after a moment he slid it over his wrist and combed his fingers through her curls, pulling out the tangles, the blue and brown locks silk and flame against his skin.

She pulled one arm away and slid it around his waist, her fingers pulling at the fabric of his shirt where it was tucked into his trousers. She tugged it free, and he felt her fingertips against his skin, and one last coherent thought went through him—*she doesn't love you*—before he let go.

He broke away from her long enough to let her tug his shirt over his head, and then he reached for her again, holding her body against his, kissing her, hard and insistent and insatiable, torn between pulling her clothes off and keeping her close to him, because any space between them was impossible, unbearable. At some point she unlocked her arms from around his back and—still kissing him—yanked her own shirt off, keeping her legs pressed against his, allowing the cold air between them only for an instant before her skin was against his skin, her breasts against his chest, and God, he was burning, and he needed her like his own breath and he wanted to feel this agony, this craving, forever.

She took a step back toward his bed, and he walked with her, tripping over his own feet, and she kissed him and laughed and he buried his face in her neck, inhaling her hair while she whispered *Greg* in his ear. Trousers. He still had his trousers on, and so did she, and this was a serious problem. "Clothes," he said as he kissed her neck, tasting sweat and flesh and sweetness.

"Yes," she said, and her hands were unfastening his trousers and he was pulling hers down and then they were naked, and her hands were on his waist, and she was tugging at him as she fell backward onto his bunk, and he fell on top of her, hands on either side of her head, and all he wanted was to push inside of her and hear her cries of pleasure in his ears, over and over, for hours, as long as he could make it last.

She slid one hand between them and ran a finger down the length of his erection, and he heard the sound of his own pleasure in his ears. "My God," he said, and she smiled at him, her eyes alight with passion.

"You are so beautiful," she said to him, and one finger became two, and then she wrapped her hand around him and tugged at him, lifting her knees and locking her ankles behind his back, and there was nothing else, nothing else in this universe beyond her body and his need . . . his need . . . his need for . . .

"Tell me you love me," he said to her. "I don't care if it's a lie."

"I love you," she said. Her free hand brushed his forehead, her thumb tracing his lips, and she lifted her head to kiss him again, warm and soft and delicious. She had not hesitated at all. "Greg. I love you."

Shards and ash.

He drove into her, and she did cry out, the loveliest sound he had ever heard in his life, and with all the women he had known he did not think he had ever touched another who drove him to such an impossible ache of pleasure and pain. Over and over he pounded, and her cries took on a rhythm, and he felt, at one point, the tight wet core of her grab on to him, a great powerful pulse, as she arched her breasts against his chest and her cry became constant, a song in his ear telling him to join her, to pulse with her, but it was too soon and so he kept driving, kissing her and tasting her, lips and neck and breasts and nipples, his hands on her body, in her hair, between them to touch her and make her cry out again, and he would have had it go on forever, desire and release, never relenting, never letting her go . . .

. . . and then he felt it, the knife's edge, shoving its way to the surface: impossible pleasure, impossible release, and her legs locked more tightly around him and he drove into her more deeply, harder, faster, listening to her gasp in his ear, until everything he was came apart inside of her, over and over, and he was light and heat and joy and flesh and nothing else mattered at all.

He came to himself in stages, first noticing the cool air on his back. He had broken a sweat, and the air circulating in the room tickled his skin. But he was still warm where her arms were around him, her hands stroking his shoulder blades, her fingers brushing the nape of his neck; and her legs were still locked around him, her hips pressed against his, and they were still connected, warm and one, and he kissed her under her ear.

"Greg," she whispered, not a question, not a statement, just a quiet sigh, his name, warm in her mouth.

He shifted off of her, and they parted, and he felt a pang of loss as they became two people again. He rolled onto his side, facing her, one arm under her neck, and she looked at him, her dark eyes contented, and reached out to touch his cheek. "You are, you know," she said softly. "Beautiful."

Her fingers left trails of fire on his skin. He wondered how long he ought to wait before suggesting they start again. "I think I'm supposed to say that to you," he said, and she laughed again.

"I watch you," she told him, and her fingers traced into the short curls of his hair. "You know when people are look-ing at you. You know when they're reacting to you, when they're making assumptions because of that face." Her fin-gers traced over his skull and down his jaw; once again, her thumb found his lip, and the heat started building inside of him again. "Why does it bother you so much?"

"Because my face isn't me," he told her. If she was touch-ing him, perhaps it was all right for him to touch her. He settled his hand on her waist, smoothed his fingers over her hip. "People look at me and they think they know what drives me, because they see how I look. They're wrong."

"What does drive you, Greg?"

"You do." He reached up, smoothed her hair off of her forehead. "You always have."

He tugged back the covers and they climbed underneath, protecting themselves from the cool room. She lay facing him, one leg over his, her arm over his shoulder, the tips of her breasts brushing his chest. She stared at him, and he caught that odd look in her eyes again, as if she were about to dissolve into tears. He stroked her hair, and leaned forward and kissed her forehead. "Stay," he said to her. "Sleep, if you want."

"I never wanted to leave you, you know," she told him.

So many regrets. "I know that, Elena."

"I don't ever want to leave you again."

There was something in her voice. Sorrow, he thought. Lost opportunity. All that time apart, and all those years before that, friends and not lovers. If his life had been different—if he had been different—could he have known this sooner? Could all their years together have been filled with lust and passion and touch and sex and this bone-deep sense of belonging?

The past doesn't matter, he thought. Now *matters. And maybe tomorrow. But mostly now.*

"Then don't leave me," he told her.

She smiled, and then her expression broke, and she shifted closer to him and burrowed against his chest, and he held her, and she cried for a long time, still wrapped around him like the perfect gift. He said nothing and just held her, kissing her head, rubbing her back, keeping her close to him, offering the only comfort he knew how to give.

After a while he heard her breathing settle, and he thought she was asleep, and the sensible part of himself began thinking again.

You do not know what this is, the voice said. *What she said to you—you asked her for that. You asked and she gave, which is what she does. It doesn't mean anything.*

But did it matter, he thought, whether or not she loved him, if wanting him was real?

That was his loneliness talking, he knew. He was fairly certain he would do anything she asked of him as long as she kept returning to his bed. For Elena, he'd make a fool of himself, anywhere and everywhere, and he'd do it willingly, all for the privilege of being able to touch her again.

You do not know what this is, the voice said again.

I do not care *what this is,* he told the voice, his own eyes dropping closed, *as long as I can keep it forever.*

CHAPTER 31

Her comm woke her, vibrating silently against her skull, gently nudging her out of a deep sleep. She opened her eyes, careful not to move. Sometime after she had fallen asleep Greg had let go of her; he was lying on his side, facing away from her, his breathing deep and steady. His back was rising and falling just a little, and it took an act of supreme will to keep from laying her palm against it. Why had she slept? She should have taken more time. She should have held on and held on and squeezed her eyes shut against all of this.

It would have changed nothing, but she thought, for a while, she could have pretended.

Carefully she pulled the sheet to one side, puddling it between the two of them, alert for any movement. He slept on, and she slipped out of the bed, breathing a sigh of relief when she got to her feet. She found her hastily discarded clothes and shook them out. His undershirt was bunched with hers, and she took a moment to bury her face in it, inhaling his scent. She wanted to take it with her, to carry it like a tactile memory, so it could give her the strength she would need; but he would miss it too quickly.

She put her hands to her face. Her hands smelled of him, too: his soap, his shampoo, his skin, distinctly Greg. One way or another, he would be with her through all of this. She would not be alone.

She pulled on her clothes, then ran her fingers through her hair. She scanned the floor for the elastic she used to tie it back, and frowned. It was missing. It was an older talisman, but not one she wanted to be without. She lifted his clothes again, and scanned the top of his dresser and his bookshelves. It wasn't until she thought back that it occurred to her to look at Greg himself. Sure enough, there it was, stretched around his wrist.

Her throat closed, and she blinked to clear her vision. Somehow, that seemed the right place to leave it.

She left her hair loose and pulled her shoes on, then stopped to look down at the bed. So peaceful, when he was asleep. He must have looked like that as a boy, before everything began to happen to him, before his mother's death and his career and everyone expecting things. She wondered if he had been happy back then, or if he had, like so many children, ached for the amorphous adulthood that he could not yet understand.

Be happy, she thought at him. Somewhere inside of him, he must still remember how.

She slipped out the door. As it slid shut behind her, she felt it cut off the line between them, leaving her standing alone.

I will do this, she thought. *I will do this, and he will survive, and we will win.*

It was mid-shift, and the hallways were mostly deserted again. She passed a few people she knew well enough for a nod and a smile; no one seemed particularly surprised to see her, and no one wanted to stop for a long chat. She was having an ordinary wander through the hallways—the same thing many of them did if they couldn't sleep, or had a few hours of downtime. Wandering was good for thinking, especially after a particularly busy day, and they had all had a particularly busy day.

Bob Hastings was on duty in the infirmary, and looked up when she walked in. "You're up late," he said, unconcerned.

"Couldn't sleep." It was the truth. "I don't suppose Arin's up."

Bob shook his head. "Kid's finally getting some decent sleep. But Yuri's in there. If you're quiet, you can say hello." He frowned. "What's the matter?"

She had been staring. Smiling, she looked away. "Just thinking you haven't changed much," she said. It was a partial truth. In the nine years she had known him, his appearance had changed very little. He did not look like a young man, but he looked twenty years younger than Admiral Herrod, and she knew the two were close in age. There were so many things she had always wondered about Bob—the root of his loyalty to Greg, how well he had known Greg's mother—but she had never asked. It had never been her business, and it still wasn't, but she couldn't shake the conviction that she *should* have asked. She looked back at him.

"Thanks for taking care of Arin," she said. "And thanks for taking care of this lot while I was gone."

"They're the same pains in the ass they were when you were here," he told her, but she knew there was fondness in the gibe.

She slipped quietly into Arin's room. Yuri was seated in an overstuffed chair, skimming a book; he smiled at her as she entered. She looked down at Arin, who was soundly asleep, lying on his side. Curled up behind his knees was Mehitabel, as at home in *Galileo*'s infirmary as she had been on *Budapest*. Somehow Elena was not surprised Bob had given in to Arin. The cat was awake and fixed Elena with her usual expression of feline dislike for anyone not bearing food. Elena reached out and scratched the cat on the head, and was rewarded with a faint rumble.

"Doctor Hastings is annoyed about the cat," Yuri whispered, "but Bear wouldn't take him with him back to *Budapest*. With all the disruptions, it didn't seem fair."

"If Bob wanted the cat out, the cat would be out," she assured him. "How's Arin?"

"Bored. Annoyed. Wants to get up and do something." He smiled. "I expect Doctor Hastings will eject him soon just because he's an irritant."

"And how is Bear?"

Yuri stood and moved next to her. "Bear is coming around," he told her gently. "It's hard for him. Arin's his only child."

"Yours, too."

Yuri shrugged. "I had different role models. My parents were different than Bear's. Better and worse, of course.

I think Bear has always felt more in control of the world around him, and it makes it hard for him when he can't take care of the people he loves." He gave her a look. "A little like you, I think."

"I'm not in control of anything."

"Of course you're not. But that doesn't stop you thinking you should be."

She looked down at Arin, young and brash and brave and appallingly stupid. "I would take it all away from him," she said quietly. "All the pain and disappointment. All the lessons he needs to learn. And if I did . . . he'd have nothing, would he? No joy, no accomplishment, no life."

Yuri said nothing.

"I can't stay," she said at last. She had left it too long already. "But when he wakes up, could you . . . tell him I'm proud to serve with him?"

Yuri smiled, and reached out to pat her arm. "You tell him yourself," he said.

At that, she had to flee.

She resisted the temptation to swing by engineering. When they noticed she was gone Ted would analyze anything she might have said, and she couldn't risk it. She would have to settle for the scent of recycled air in the corridor, the muted sound of the environmental systems. Not that she needed help remembering *Galileo*'s sounds. She had been hearing them in her sleep for more than a year.

Azevedo had been assigned infantry duty alongside the comms officer, and she murmured a quiet prayer of thanks. He had never been the friendliest person, but he knew her well, and it would not occur to him to question what she was doing. He would be focused on infiltrators, or people behaving oddly. He would not find her behavior odd at all.

"Hey, Azevedo," she said, giving him a smile. "Can you clear for me? I'm going flying."

Azevedo frowned. "In what?"

Before she left, when she was a commander, he would have said the same thing in the same tone, adding only her rank. *I am nostalgic for rudeness,* she realized. "Admiral Herrod has given me permission to try his shuttle," she told him. "It's an 860. Brand-new."

Azevedo sniffed. "Rich person's boat," he said. "Can't maneuver for shit."

"Maybe not," she acknowledged. "But it'll blow the socks off of anything *Galileo* has sitting around right now." She thought a silent apology at her ship.

"I'll need to double-check your access," he told her.

"Go ahead."

She let her eyes wander over the shuttle bay. *Leviathan* was still sitting there, severed from *Galileo*'s network, waiting for someone to deal with the artifact that had brought them so much trouble. The small shuttle stood in the wrong corner, away from Herrod's ship, and she hoped she would have no trouble finding the data chip where he had said it was concealed. She would not have much time, and even Azevedo might get suspicious if he caught her there.

Azevedo had finished verifying her access. "I'll depressurize for you, Chief," he said. "Will five minutes do it?"

"Perfect," she said. "Thanks."

He turned away from her, facing the bay controls, and she made a show of walking to Herrod's square-bottomed luxury shuttle. She opened the door, then glanced over her shoulder; Azevedo was still out of sight.

She stepped away from Herrod's ship and hurried toward *Leviathan*.

The little shuttle had been locked to everyone apart from herself, Jessica, Ted, and Greg, but such things had never stopped Herrod. She suspected Jessica could have told her how he'd done it, but he'd have left no tracks unless he wanted to. She slid open the door and let her eyes sweep the cabin; it took her a moment to find what she was looking for. Herrod had left the chip at the bottom of the stack of comm blanks, where it blended almost seamlessly; it was unlikely anyone who hadn't known it was there would have noticed a mismatch. Tugging up her sleeve, she attached the chip to the inside of her wrist, then covered it again.

Step one, she thought, allowing herself a moment of relief, and turned to go.

And then her eyes strayed to the rear of the cabin, where Ted's vacuum crate sat, undisturbed, holding Jamyung's artifact.

The thought came, unbidden: *It would fit in my pocket.*

Absurd to even consider it.

She opened the crate and saw it sitting there, calm and gray and restful. Waiting.

"Don't talk to me," she warned. She took a breath, picked it up, and waited.

Silence. *New comm*, she remembered. *It doesn't like new comms.*

She tucked it into her pocket and closed the lid again, then dashed back out. She made it back to Herrod's ship, and as the door slid closed behind her, she breathed a sigh of relief. She set the artifact on a table in the center of the cabin, then frowned. What was she doing? If Azevedo had caught her, she would have had to make up a story. She had some confidence that she could have convinced him what she was doing was legitimate, but he would certainly have double-checked with Jessica, if not Greg. She had taken a huge risk because—why had she done it? Why the compulsion?

Well, it was done now. And she needed to get moving.

She let her eyes sweep the interior of the shuttle. It was luxurious indeed, but in a way she could respect: everything was efficient, designed perfectly to make optimal use of space and materials. There was a shelf that opened away from the wall to separate the flight cabin from the main area of the ship, effectively providing two private spaces. The shower doubled as a medical closet. Even the flight cabin was comfort and utility: the pilot's chair was dynamically ergonomic, shifting to mold against her back as she leaned against it. When she powered up, the instruments appeared at just the right luminosity before her eyes, responding instantly to her fingers as she manipulated the ship's engines.

"It's locked with *Galileo,*" Herrod had told her. "If you unlock before you hit the field, they'll get a notification. You've got to get far enough away before you sever the connection."

Her last connection to home.

She lifted the ship a few inches off the ground and turned to the opening bulkhead. She nudged the ship forward—slowly, a relaxed pilot going for a relaxed flight, just to pass the time, to clear her head—and crossed the barrier between the bright artificial gravity of *Galileo*'s landing bay and the utter, devouring darkness of space.

The shuttle's interior lights were set low, and the cabin grew dim as she left *Galileo* behind. To her left stood Yakutsk, gray and shadowed, the glow of Smolensk in the distance. Beyond it she could see *Budapest,* squat and stationary, waiting; beyond that, the deep green glow of the gas giant. On her right, there was nothing but empty space, and she turned the shuttle toward the stars.

Of all of them, she thought Bear would be the least surprised. Bear would have expected this of her. If Herrod had approached her anywhere but *Galileo,* he would have found her surrounded by people expecting her to run off and get herself killed. She would have been trapped by suspicion and jaundiced eyes. Ironic, in a way, that the place she felt safest had been the only place she could have done any of this effectively.

"What are you called?" she asked Herrod's shuttle.

"Antigone."

Elena smiled. A good-luck name. Peeling the data comm off of her wrist, she connected it to the ship's core. She waited for the field to spin up, watching out the front window as the stars dimmed and the polarizer kicked in, filtering the bright white field to a soft sea blue.

"Antigone," she said, "separate from *Galileo."*

"Command code required."

Elena repeated the code Herrod had given her.

Five more minutes passed, and then the ship dropped out of the field. She waited, verifying that she was transmitting nothing to *Galileo,* then triggered the second half of Herrod's flight plan. The coordinates were deep in the middle of nowhere, outside every travel and trade corridor, and they were risking that nobody would have found and scavenged what he had arranged to have left for her there.

The first major risk. If she found nothing, her journey would be over. If she found nothing . . . Ellis would have won.

She watched the field coalesce around *Antigone,* then stood, leaving the ship to pilot itself. She wandered to the rear cabin, pulling her pilfered artifact out of her pocket. *What possessed me?* she thought; but as she turned it over in her hands, she felt just a little less bereft. She sat on one of the sofas—absurdly comfortable, and not at all military—and rested her palm on top of the object's smooth, warm surface.

"Just you and me," she said to it.

And then she buried her face in her hands, and she wept.

CHAPTER 32

GALILEO

Greg was not surprised when he woke up alone.

He knew Elena well enough to know that she wouldn't be able to sit long with the intensity of the night before. Whatever had been on her mind, whatever conflagration of emotions had brought her to tears—never mind everything else—she would have tucked it away to be dealt with later. She was most likely in the gym, or back on *Budapest*, tinkering with something that didn't need tinkering.

But oh, how he wished she was here with him.

Andriya Vassily was a beautiful woman, and making love with her was always adventurous, always satisfying. She flattered his sexual ego in ways he had long missed. But he was not in love with her, nor she with him. Andriya compartmentalized too much. It was possible Elena did as well; it would explain a lot.

But Greg did not compartmentalize, at least not for long, and as he lay there, slowly waking up, he found himself wanting to go and find Elena, to pull her aside, to find some secluded corridor or closet and make love to her again. He could still feel her hair in his hands, against his lips; could taste her, warmth and musk and sweat, still feel her heat all around him.

He took a shower, long and cold, and thought about the possibility that she would bolt again. It would certainly be in character, and he would have to figure out how to get her to come back into his bed without making her want to disappear entirely. He thought of what he had asked her to say and cursed; he should have let that go. In the moment it had been everything to him, but it had been too much. She had always been clear about her feelings. At this point, though, even his own feelings were irrelevant. The physical memory of her overwhelmed him, and his body made it very clear that his heart could fuck right off. His heart was used to being alone. His body wanted this woman, and damned if he was going to let stupid vulnerable emotional bullshit stop him. If she was willing to share her body, he would ask for nothing else.

Damn. Why hadn't she stayed?

Crowds, he decided, were the best idea. He took breakfast in *Galileo*'s largest cafeteria, where about a hundred people—some just off shift, some almost on—congregated daily. He sat with some of the infantry. They were still subdued, but they stuck with their tradition of telling combat stories at breakfast; today's were all about victory in the face of adversity, and good outcomes when things looked darkest. It was how they held each other up: *Remember the times we survived?* Voices of hope, against a void of war and uncertainty.

Admiral Herrod entered the cafeteria halfway through the meal. He earned a few resentful glances, but in general the crew left him alone. He took a plate of food and found a table in the corner, eating without a hint of self-consciousness, reading a book. But he looked tired and a little unkempt, and not for the first time Greg wondered about his health. He usually took breakfast in his room, or in one of the smaller kitchens; Greg wondered if, in the midst of all of this, perhaps even Admiral Herrod felt the need for some company.

After breakfast, Greg returned to his room to assemble the off-grid. He stood for a moment, trying to decide where to sit that would not remind him of the night before, and after a moment he carried the unit into his office. Whatever else the day brought him, he was going to have to figure out how to focus.

Jessica picked up in less than ten minutes. "How is everything there, sir?" she asked.

She had not, of course, intended it to be a loaded question. "We're holding steady, Jess," he said. "What have you got for me?"

"Well." She took a breath. "We're off in a little bit to the env equipment area. Dallas is going to keep inventorying the system, and I'm going to see if I can get a signal trap into the thing's telemetry. If it's not activated, of course, it's pointless; but we should at least be able to verify—or not—the idea that it's some kind of maintenance access tool."

"Dallas didn't find anything else strange in there?"

"Not yet," she admitted. "But there's more to look at. Dallas says it's way more complicated than it needs to be."

"New tech," Greg suggested.

"Dallas says maybe, but really? The thing isn't using anything new. Nearly all the standard parts are recycled. Salvage. And the new bits are just connectors and such, so far."

Damn. Ellis had too many tendrils in motion right now. "You find something, Jess," he told her, "comm me direct. Don't screw with the off-grid, or going through Bristol. Even if you verify that yes, the thing is just a super-fine brand-new dome env system, tell me. We don't need this loose end right now."

"Yes, sir. Sir? There's one other thing."

She told him about seeing what appeared to be a recorded scan of Jamyung's artifact. When she said *dellinium,* Greg forgot all about the dome systems. "Did you check ambient?" he demanded.

"Hell, yes, faster than I've checked anything in my life. There's nothing, Greg. All radiation levels are normal for a city this size, and even if my comm was malfunctioning and reporting the readings wrong, I'd have been at least losing my hair by now. Nobody's sick. It was a bogus reading."

"Did you check the equipment?"

"Didn't have time, sir. But the unit had been bounced around a little. It's clearly broken."

"So why are you telling me about it?"

She paused, and Greg rubbed his eyes. "I just—" She broke off. "It's probably nothing, Greg. Except that thing. Jamyung should have seen the same NO DATA scan Ted did. For a malfunctioning unit to yell DELLINIUM in a crowded room? That's a really weird malfunction, don't you think?"

"I think," Greg said gently, "you're getting superstitious

about that artifact. You and Shimada figured out what it was doing. It's a compositor, and that's it. Dellinium isn't used, even theoretically, for any kind of comms system, passive or otherwise."

"Dallas didn't like it. The artifact, I mean."

Oh, Lord. "Why is that relevant, Jess?"

"Because that's another person who reacted to it, unlike me. I look at it, and I see a box. Dallas looked at it and wanted to get as far away from it as humanly possible. Intense aversion. Sort of the opposite of what Lanie's said about it."

He wondered if Elena had discussed the object with Dallas. "Hang on. Let me see if I can get her on the line." He commed *Galileo.* "*Galileo,* where's Elena?"

"Elena Shaw is not on board."

"Is she on *Budapest,* then?"

"No. She left in Admiral Herrod's shuttle at 0423."

He frowned. Elena had a long-standing habit of flying on her own when she felt the need to think; but Herrod's shuttle? That was an odd choice. On the other hand, she would have, under ordinary circumstances, taken something like *Leviathan,* but that ship was tied up. "Can you contact her?"

"No."

He felt vaguely annoyed, and returned to Jessica. "Elena's out flying," he told her.

Jessica, who was no fool, asked, "Why?"

Greg ignored the question. "Listen, Jess. The artifact is contained for now. It's not going to be receiving comm signals from anybody, not even your weird new env system.

Do me a favor, though, and send me everything you have on that upgrade. I want Dallas's inventory list, your notes, anything you can think of." He would have to dig up background on Gladkoff himself; he felt certain, Ellis being Ellis, that any official records on the man would currently be in the First Sector dead zone, but he could dig up any reports that had been distributed. "And be careful, Jess. Anything starts looking cagey, you contact Bristol and get out. Understood?"

"Yes, sir. Greg?"

"Yeah, Jess?"

"How about you? Are you okay?"

She had heard it in his voice; she just didn't know what it was. *That makes two of us.* "I'm fine, Commander," he told her. *And stop being so fucking perceptive.*

He disassembled the off-grid and commed Ted Shimada. "Do we have a portable scanner on *Galileo*?" Greg asked him.

"Yes, sir." Ted Shimada, despite his facile good cheer, was a lot like Emily Broadmoor, answering his commander's questions with easy military efficiency. "What am I scanning?"

"I want you to take another pass over that artifact."

"Yes, sir." As much as he was like Emily, Shimada was still too curious to stay completely neutral. "Any reason why now, sir?"

He told Shimada about Jessica's discovery on Yakutsk, and to his surprise, the engineer laughed. "Sir, I may not be able to find out what's inside that thing, but it's not dellinium. Among other things, that polymer surface? That stuff we scanned with no trouble at all. It's ordinary. It couldn't contain thorium, never mind dellinium."

"She says the scanner was broken."

"That's a sure thing, sir." And then Shimada paused. "Dellinium's a strange thing for a scanner to spit out, isn't it?"

"And unless Jamyung had previously scanned some dellinium," Greg concluded, finishing Shimada's thought, "the artifact wouldn't have had that information to regurgitate back to the scanner."

"So either the scanner has a really odd, specific defect," Shimada said, "or that artifact found a really efficient way to get Jamyung to back the hell off of it."

Which was easily the most unsettling thought Greg had encountered all day. "Scan it again, Commander," Greg told him. "And—put on an env suit this time. It's probably a meaningless precaution, but I don't care for things that change like that."

"I'm all for meaningless precautions, sir," Shimada told him sincerely. "I'll let you know what I find."

Greg sat back. It had to be Jamyung's scanner. There was no way the artifact could have done something like that. Jessica had analyzed the comm Elena had received; Elena had analyzed Greg's. Neither of them contained any new information. Both had been scraped from the comm, cacophony out of order, a heuristically generated message of loneliness. Clever, but not innovative.

Except his dream. Greg's comm signal had not contained the memory of running with his mother on the beach. He had never had a dream of watching himself drown, shouting, helpless. *Only a dream,* he told himself. But suddenly he wasn't sure anymore.

He needed to talk to Elena. She was the only other person who had been through it, who might understand. Contacting the comms center, he said, "Samaras, get me a line to Admiral Herrod's shuttle, will you?"

"Yes, sir." But when Samaras spoke again, his voice was hesitant. "Sir, I— *Antigone* is out of contact, sir."

Greg felt a flash of annoyance. They had all been so focused on emergencies, they had forgotten how to do their jobs. "She's probably just in the field, Lieutenant. Try her again."

Another pause. "I've tried multiple times, sir. She's— I don't know where *Antigone* is, sir. *Galileo* isn't tracking her."

Uneasiness crept over him. "What do you mean, 'isn't tracking'?"

"She's getting no telemetry from *Antigone*. In either direction."

"When did we lose contact?"

Greg waited as Samaras pulled up the records. "0438, sir."

Fifteen minutes after she departed. "Where did this happen?"

Samaras rattled off a set of coordinates, and Greg mapped them in his head. Hundreds of thousands of kilometers off. The middle of nowhere. Could she—was she deliberately getting lost? "*Galileo,*" he said, bypassing Samaras entirely, "why was *Antigone* dropped?"

"*Antigone* was dropped on the request of former chief of engineering Elena Shaw."

He was too stunned to know if he was angry or worried. "Did she file a flight plan? Leave a message? Anything?"

"No."

"So you don't know where she is."

"No."

Every curse he had ever learned floated through his head, but he found himself speechless. "I want a message sent out to every unidentified shuttle in the field that you can scan," he told the ship. What to say? "Just . . . request an ident from them. A destination. Anything. Find that shuttle." *Damn.* She would know how to evade an aboveboard search like that. *Why the hell was she running away?*

You know why, said that voice in his head. But that made no sense. Whatever else Elena was—however she felt about him, or didn't feel, or struggled with feeling—she was Corps. She wouldn't bolt, not in the middle of something like this.

Not unless she had a damn good reason.

"*Galileo,* who was on duty when Elena took *Antigone?*"

"Lieutenant Azevedo."

Perfect. Azevedo was an asshole, but he was an asshole with a nearly eidetic memory. "*Galileo,* get me—" But before he could finish, he was interrupted by an incoming signal. *Commander Tetsuo Shimada,* the ship projected before his eyes. Irritably, Greg answered, "What is it, Commander?"

"Sir. The artifact—"

Greg cut him off. "I'm not interested in that right now. Elena's bolted. I need to talk to Azevedo to find out—"

And Shimada interrupted in return. "I know, sir." Shimada was breathless; Greg realized he was running. "I'm on my way up to see you now. She took *Antigone* out on Admiral Herrod's authorization, but it's more than that. The artifact? The one that knocked you out? That the parts trader got murdered over?

"It's gone."

CHAPTER 33

Everything unraveled too quickly.

Jos had retreated back to his quarters after breakfast. He had enjoyed his brief respite, the bustle of people around him as he ate undisturbed at his little table by the window, watching the surface of Yakutsk below them. He had never liked space travel and had even, early in his career, worked toward assignments that would keep him Earthside; but he always envied the presumptive camaraderie of a starship crew. He had never belonged like that, not anywhere. Not even with Andy. But sometimes, sitting close to the ones who did belong, he imagined he could feel a little of that warmth soothing his old bones.

This time, that fleeting warmth was not enough.

Foster walked in to Jos's quarters without ringing, Security Chief Broadmoor in tow. In addition they had brought a tall security officer, whom Foster ordered to stay by the door. Jos recognized him: Gilbert, he thought his name was. Always came to attention when Jos came in the room, and hid his resentment better than some of the others. Jos wondered if Foster had chosen the man because of that.

Pritchard had jumped to his feet when Foster came in, positioning himself instinctively between the Corps captain and his charge. Jos had not moved at all, but took a moment to brush aside the book he had been reading. "It's all right, son," he said to Pritchard. "Stand down."

He saw the boy's fingers clench, but then Pritchard stepped aside, standing stiffly, eyes on the wall. And Jos had a clear look at Foster.

He had learned, Jos realized, since he had been the fire-eyed cadet Jos had met eighteen years ago. Foster had a sharp intellect, and an analytical mind, but emotionally he was prone to volatility, and when he was hurt, he torched everything within reach. He rarely lost his temper, but when he did, that was when everything went to hell. Now, at nearly forty, Greg Foster seemed to have that dragon contained. Jos could see it in his eyes, the blind rage, the desire to strike out; but he was standing at attention, almost respectfully. Some of that, Jos conceded, might be Commander Broadmoor's presence. Jos didn't know Emily Broadmoor, but he knew her reputation. She was dispassionate, dedicated, and scrupulously by the book. If the Corps survived all this, Emily Broadmoor was the sort of officer who would keep them together.

"Perhaps Pritchard could wait somewhere else," Foster said.

Pritchard didn't move, but Jos saw his jaw clench. "It's all right, Logan," he said gently. "I'll call for you later."

He thought for a moment the boy wouldn't listen to him,

but then, obedient as always, Pritchard pivoted on his heel and stalked out of the room.

Jos looked back at Foster. "He has nothing to do with any of this."

Foster nodded. "Noted, sir." Almost as an afterthought, he sat in the chair opposite Jos, where Shaw had been sitting only the night before. Foster really did have absurdly long legs; he looked almost like a grasshopper, folding himself into the soft upholstery. "Admiral. What have you done with Elena?"

He was out of uniform, Jos realized suddenly. Around his right wrist, he wore a thin band of black elastic. Unobtrusive, but blatantly non-regulation. "She is where she is of her own accord, Captain," he said.

Out of the corner of his eye, Jos saw Commander Broadmoor shift. Foster said, "That's not an answer, sir."

"I don't owe you an answer, Captain."

"That's not true, I'm afraid," Foster said. "Elena's a civilian."

Jos scoffed. "She's no more a civilian than you are, Foster. That woman was born Corps, and that hasn't changed just because she made the impulsive choice to resign."

Jos thought Foster might be fairly close to leaping out of that chair and throwing a punch. "Regardless," Foster said stiffly, "she is not currently a member of the Corps. Involving a civilian in a military operation is a court-martial offense."

Jos suspected if he mentioned his own civilian status, Foster would not consider it relevant. "You don't think that's a little hypocritical, Foster?" The captain shot him a glare, and Jos went on. "You think we don't know what the two of you have been playing at all this time? Exchanging intelligence, trying to piece together a case against Ellis, preferably one that implicates Shadow Ops, and me specifically? You think we stopped watching her when she shucked off that uniform? We may be low on resources, Captain, but we can track one mechanic."

It had been easy. Good mechanics were a rarity, and their comms fingerprints were lit like neon. The only way she could have hidden would have been to stop working, and he had known that would never happen. It was one of the reasons they had started watching her in the first place. Unlike Foster, she was predictable.

"Hypocritical or not," Foster told him, "I'm placing you under arrest."

"Given that I've committed no civil offense, what gives you the authority?"

Foster leaned forward, and just a little bit of his rage escaped into his voice. "The fact that this is my ship," he said. "And my security people, and my allies in this sector. But if it makes you happy, sir, I'll put Commander Lockwood in charge when this is all over, and you can have your friends court-martial me while you're serving time." He sat back. "What have you done with Elena?"

Jos took a moment to look over at Commander Broadmoor. She seemed to find nothing objectionable in her captain's statements. *Not that she would say a word in front of me,* Jos thought. He could not help but approve of her. Slowly, feeling his joints objecting, he pushed himself to his feet. "Can I get either of you a drink? I know it's before lunch, but under the circumstances, I don't think it's inappropriate." They didn't respond, and he turned to the bar. "What about you, Lieutenant Gilbert?" he called to the man at the door. When the security officer was silent, Jos poured himself half a glass of scotch. He wouldn't drink it all this time, but it would give him something to hold.

"Amazing, isn't it," he said, half to himself, "that you still get the good scotch here. I'm sure you feel like you've been screwed over, Captain, and indeed you have been. But they know what they have, the Admiralty. Or at least some of us do." He drank.

"'Us.' So this *is* a Shadow Ops operation," Foster guessed, and Jos shrugged.

"As much as it's anyone's. But to be honest with you, we've been pretty divided on what, if anything, to do. The last time I spoke to the others, they were leaning against my idea. I barely convinced Waris, and I would have thought she'd have been the easy one. But I think they'd feel differently now. I'll make sure to ask them, if we ever get the First Sector back. If they're even still alive."

"Where did you send her?"

"I can't tell you that."

"When will she be back?"

There was no avoiding it. "She won't."

He kept his back to them. If Foster was going to hit him, it wouldn't help to see it coming. If he was going to shoot him . . . let the man shoot him in the back, if his temper was really so hard to control.

"Captain." That was Broadmoor, her voice low, warning.

It took Foster a very long time to speak, but when he

did, his voice was almost composed. "What's the mission, Admiral?"

"The mission," Jos said, "is to take out the strongest piece of Ellis's assault plan. They have a research station that has not only been manufacturing weapons, it has been triggering the equipment failures. Right now, it's controlling the Olam Fleet. We can't be sure it's their only station, but it's the focus of what they're doing."

"You have proof?"

"Yes."

"Where?"

He shook his head. "As much as I'd like to share that, Captain, Ellis has people in the Corps as well."

"Not on my ship."

He shrugged; it didn't matter. "You don't know. You can't. Some of the officers you've got have only been here three months. If Ellis planted them a decade ago, you'd have no way to tell. Hell, neither would we."

"Why didn't you send a warship to take out their station?"

They were consistent, Foster and Shaw. "We did."

When he said nothing else, he heard Foster rise from the chair. "They took out a *warship,* and you sent her there *alone* in your shuttle?"

"Do you think we're stupid, Captain Foster?" He turned then; Foster was standing, much closer to Jos than he had thought. The captain's eyes were furious and sharp and his fists were clenched. Despite having a slighter build than Jos, he was taller and forty years younger, and he was doing an impressive job of looming. Jos moved past him, close enough for Foster to reach out, to grab him, to hit him.

The captain did none of those things, and Jos was mildly impressed. "She has a cover story and a way in. She's going to take the place out from the inside."

"Just like that?"

"Just like that."

"On her own?"

Jos took another drink. "Yes."

Foster shook his head. "Why?"

"Put it together," Jos said irritably. "We haven't the time to do anything else. And you name me one person better qualified than she is."

"Me, for one," Foster said predictably, and Jos scoffed.

"You're good, Foster," he said. "But apart from the fact that we need you to keep being a captain, your face is known all over the galaxy."

"So is hers."

"Not in the same way. And it was easy enough for us to plant false stories on her location, put her in some Third Sector gray market repair shop, manufacture some blocky surveillance vid. She's been nothing but a struggling ex-soldier for the last year, as far as the streamers are concerned. On top of that—this is a research station, and anyone going in to destroy the place is going to need mechanical knowledge of a depth that you just don't have. A mechanic was our best bet."

"And it had to be *her*?"

Foster was shouting now, and Jos closed his eyes. He knew what Foster felt for the woman. They all knew. It had been noted early, listed in his profile, a potential vulnerability, something they could exploit. They always saw attachment that way: *weakness.* It had been Jos's weakness, certainly, and Andy's, and after Andy's death Jos had seen the wisdom of their perspective—or at least the utility. But it didn't make him any happier. "She's the best chance we have," he said simply, and it was the truth.

But Foster, unsurprisingly, was not thinking logically. "Bullshit." Foster walked up to Jos, so much more vital, more angry, than Jos had ever been. "Elena's not fucking *magic.* Shadow Ops could have sent any Corps mechanic on this mission. Shimada could have done it. Hell, if you want to take out a station, send Jess, for fuck's sake. She could probably hack the place from here, if you got her the access. You sent Elena because *you knew she'd go.* That she'd never turn you down, because she couldn't bear the idea of having someone else die in her place. You've been watching her like you watch all of us, and when the time came, you used what you thought you knew. She went willingly, because she loves these people, and you knew it would never occur to her to fucking say *anything* to *anybody* about it." He stepped back. "We're just tools you hold in reserve until you need us."

Foster's assessment was remarkably close to the truth. What he didn't know was how close Jos had indeed come to asking Jessica Lockwood instead, or Foster—or taking the mission himself. Technically, it was possible he could have done it; he had a decent knowledge of mechanics, he was a better hacker than Lockwood, and he had decades of experience on top of it. But there was no way to shuffle an aging, cynical old man into a research lab in any way that was remotely anonymous. And underneath it all . . . he was tired. Not returning from the mission wouldn't have bothered him, but he wasn't sure he would have had the passion to fight hard enough to succeed.

Excuses, Jos? So like you. Home where it's safe, while the rest of us die.

"Your assessment of our motives is fascinating, Captain Foster," he said, "but ultimately irrelevant. She's out there, and she will succeed or fail with or without your outrage. And nothing she does will change what has already happened. If we're lucky, though, it might give us a solid base of support from which to move forward."

"Move forward with what? What is it you want, anyway? Shadow Ops wants unity through war."

"Not all of us."

Foster laughed, a humorless sound. "Great. You send an officer off to her death and you can't even say why you did it."

"You don't think stopping the Olam Fleet is enough?"

"Stopping the fleet is the only thing you and I agree on, Admiral," Foster said. "But you cannot make me believe that sending one woman on her own is the only way to make this work." He straightened, containing his emotions. "I'll ask you again, sir. Where did you send her?"

Jos just looked at him, silent, and Foster's lips tightened.

"Very well." He became an officer again. "Admiral Herrod, you are under arrest for involving a civilian in a military operation. I hereby strip you of your diplomatic authority pending an investigation by a full committee authorized by Central Gov. You're restricted to quarters until further notice."

"And what if there's no committee to investigate me?"

Something dark and vengeful flashed in Foster's eyes, and it crossed Jos's mind that the Admiralty had, despite all their carefully compiled psych profiles, underestimated how dangerous he could really be. "Then I'll handle the investigation myself. Sir."

Jos kept the glass in his hand, never dropping Foster's murderous gaze. He caught Broadmoor shifting again; she was uncomfortable when Foster got like this. *Smart woman,* Jos thought. Slowly, deliberately, he took a sip of scotch, and waited.

Without saying another word, Foster turned and left.

CHAPTER 34

INTERSTITIAL

*A*ntigone's interior lights faded briefly to green. "Field termination in thirty seconds," it said.

Reluctantly, Elena put the artifact down on the bench next to her and stretched. Somewhat to her surprise, she had slept, although she hadn't gone under deeply; weeping had exhausted her, and she had managed some prefabricated food before she lay down and closed her eyes. Her mind had drifted, full of anticipation and regret and every hard, cold engineering fact she thought she might need in the ordeal ahead. She would have expected nightmares, or anxiety dreams, the sort where she couldn't quite see and she couldn't quite move but if she failed everything would be lost. Instead she had dreamt of *Galileo,* clean and bright, the atrium full of flowers, her friends relaxed and laughing. She woke feeling strangely peaceful; it had been years since she'd had an *everything will be all right* dream.

It had, she supposed, been some time since she'd needed one.

She'd grabbed the artifact as she sat up, wondering again

what she'd been thinking, bringing it with her. She put it on her knees and stared at it, feeling its strange warmth through the fabric of her trousers. *Odd thing,* she thought. And then she said it out loud: "Odd thing."

It said nothing, of course. Whatever it was, it was a machine. She found herself vaguely disappointed that she would never know where it had come from. Nor would anyone else, if her mission went as planned.

Unless there were more somewhere. She hoped there were more. *And when did that happen?* she thought. *When did I go from believing it's a weapon, to wanting it to survive?*

She strapped herself into the pilot's seat and watched the field through the window. She knew what she was supposed to see when she came out of the field, but she was still a soldier, and that meant being prepared. *Antigone,* as it happened, had a fairly substantial complement of weapons. She wondered whether Greg had authorized that, or if they'd somehow been hidden when Herrod brought the shuttle on board. She supposed Greg had found them and had *Galileo* neutralize them; she couldn't imagine him allowing Herrod of all people on board without going through every single search the regulations allowed.

Three . . . two . . . one. The field dissolved cleanly, and she came out into an ocean of stars, no systems within reach, the galactic middle of nowhere. She did a quick scan; nobody in the near field, other ships folding space in other directions, unconcerned with this nondescript chunk of space.

She could see it in the distance: a small white dot at first, details resolving as she flew closer. It was a ship, some kind of utilitarian vehicle; not sleek and graceful like *Antigone,* but boxy and drab like any small freighter or bulk transport. But unlike the commercial craft Elena was used to seeing, it was bright white, and absolutely pristine. She circled around it, giving it a cursory external examination: the engine vents were clean to the point that she couldn't tell, from the outside at least, if they'd ever been used.

She had asked Herrod how he'd obtained it. "They have people with Central," he'd said to her, "and we have people with them."

"Trustworthy people?"

"You'd better hope so, Chief."

Unlike most commercial shippers, it was stamped with the vendor's name: Cesium Industries. Commissioned and built for the company, Herrod had said, and it made her wonder why nobody asked why a food distribution network would require—or could afford—proprietary shipping shuttles. Cesium, it seemed, had an exclusive contract with Ellis; it was part of what had led Herrod and the others to speculate on the location of the research station.

"They had to know an external contractor would be a security risk," she had pointed out. None of this seemed secure. "Why didn't they just make space to produce their own food?"

"Full food production isn't so easy," Herrod said. "Even PSI brings in supplies. And this is an elite station—they're treating their people well. Fresh coffee is critical, never mind precision-brewed beer."

"How many people?" She had avoided the question for a long time.

"One hundred and forty-three."

She shoved that knowledge aside. Collateral damage, of course. Most of them probably knew what they were doing, that they were engaged in activities that were killing people. *Most* of them. And they all had to know the risks. The risk that an infiltrator would show up and tear apart their walls and bulkheads and expose them to the vacuum of space. One hundred and forty-three people that she would be murdering.

Worth the cost, to save millions on Earth, but that didn't change the fact of it.

Finished with her flyby, she maneuvered *Antigone* next to the clean white ship and aligned the doors. Once she had a seal she shut down the engines but left the generator running. She would need one more burst of power from the craft before she was finished.

The lights came on as she entered the freight carrier, and with a quiet *whoosh* the room filled with both warmth and air. The cabin was large but crowded with shipping containers: stack after stack of crates labeled coffee, soy, beans, dried fruit. There was indeed beer, in two large vats wrapped in a coolant shielding, prominent seals on the latches. Even Cesium, it seemed, had to guard against pilfering by its employees.

The whole thing reminded her too much of *Budapest*'s shuttle, now burned out on Yakutsk.

She moved deeper into the freight ship and found the pilot's cabin, small and squat. Not designed for comfort, then, and she frowned in disapproval; the pilot would almost always be flying alone, and for days at a time. Whoever was benefiting from this enterprise, it wasn't the pilots of these bright, sterile little boxes.

As Herrod had told her it would be, the uniform was folded on the ship's seat, along with a change of underwear. Down to every detail, she thought grimly, and picked up the clothes. Making her way back to *Antigone,* she stripped off her borrowed clothes and put on the crisp white items from the other shuttle. Everything clean, everything flawless, although the uniform might have been laundered a hundred times. Crispness was obviously branding for this company.

Elena frowned down at her artifact. It was not white, and it was not crisp, and she was not sure how she would explain it if asked. She slid it into one of the suit's pockets and zipped it up. She would be unlikely to be allowed to keep it, she thought, but at least now she had some time before she would have to explain why it was with her. She wondered if they'd believe it as art; certainly some of the most expensive pieces in Jessica's collection looked to Elena like nothing more than oddly painted storage materials. Then there would just be explaining why she felt she had to carry it everywhere she went, which somehow seemed easier than leaving it behind.

She looked around the cabin, her last view of the Corps, making sure she hadn't left anything she needed. She checked the time: easily on schedule. Five minutes ahead, even.

She sat back down in the pilot's seat and recorded a message.

"Send it with delayed delivery," she told *Antigone* when she was done.

"Specify time frame."

Everything would be over in less than fourteen hours. "One day," she said. *Antigone* winked acknowledgment and sent the message off.

Then, climbing to her feet, she gave the ship one final order: "Thirty seconds after the other ship has cleared the blast radius, I want you to detonate all the weapons you have on board." *More destruction.* She had grown numb to the thought.

"Authorization required."

Elena recited the sequence Admiral Herrod had taught her, and let *Antigone* reread her biometric information to confirm her authority. Another brief flash to green; the ship acknowledged the order. She turned and went through the door to the freight shuttle, and when the door slid shut, she did not look back.

Moving to the tiny pilot's cabin, she sat, then said the words Herrod had taught her: "Execute resequencing order B1829."

The designation number for the wormhole where Herrod had lost Andrew Kelso. She did not think the choice of program name was a coincidence.

"Enter biometric data," the ship said smoothly. An androgynous voice, like *Galileo*'s but with a flatter affect; cheaper AI, she thought.

She let the control panel scan her palm, then waited as it tied in to her comm and read her data. After a moment, there was a benign chime. "Resequencing complete," it said.

"What are you called?" Elena asked the ship.

"I am the commercial freighter *Wanderlust*," it said, and she took a moment to wonder about the pilot who had named it. Was the pilot Herrod's mole? Or had they been killed to obtain the cargo? Was wanderlust really what the pilot had felt in this small seat, in this tiny, claustrophobic cabin?

She shook herself; none of it mattered. "What's our travel time?" she asked.

"One hour and fifty-eight minutes," it said.

"Very well, *Wanderlust*," she said. "Let's go."

The field spun up nearly silently, the blue glow closing around her, the stars one by one absorbed by the brightening light. And then, with a minute vibration, the window polarizers engaged, and they were in the field.

Elena sat back to wait out her journey, eyes on the obscured windows, one hand absently covering the small, warm object in her pocket.

CHAPTER 35

GALILEO

When Jos's door chimed nearly an hour later, he knew who it would be. Gilbert, his jailor, answered the door, and met the eyes of Lieutenant Hirano; and then he turned. "Admiral," he said, with flawless politeness, "you have a visitor."

Jos saw Commander Ilyana peer shyly around the doorframe. Relaxing a little, he nodded. "It's all right, Lieutenant," he said, knowing Gilbert did not need his approval. "I'm happy to talk with Commander Ilyana."

Ilyana smiled, that hesitant expression that never quite reached her eyes, and slipped into the room. Hirano placed himself outside the open door, back to the room; Gilbert returned to his post in the corner, eyes never leaving Jos. Herrod knew he would listen to their conversation and report every word that was said. A steady officer. Herrod had always liked steady officers. Even in tight corners, they always did exactly what they'd been instructed to do—nothing more or less.

"Can I offer you anything, Commander?" he asked her. "Something to drink? I think I've got some food in here somewhere, and I suppose they'd bring us something if I asked."

Her eyes always looked a little lost, a little bewildered. When she blinked, he had the sense she was clearing her head. "You are kind, Admiral. But I'm not hungry at the moment." She turned and looked at Gilbert, massive and well-armed, and her eyebrows twitched together. "That seems like overkill," she remarked. "Where would you run?"

"I think the idea is to keep me from wandering through the halls and fomenting insurrection," he said dryly.

"But they don't listen to you. How could you foment insurrection?" She frowned, and he had forgotten how literally she took everything.

"I almost certainly couldn't," he agreed, "unless they disagreed about how they were going to kill me."

Blink. She looked more sympathetic. "I have heard some of this in the hallways," she said. "It's why I'm here. They're upset with you because you have sent their friend away."

"Yes." He was rather upset himself. "They don't see the necessity of it, at least not the same way I do. They think I had options, or could have sent someone else. They always think there's someone else."

"That is a luxury." Something in her voice had hardened; she was looking away from him, out the window where there was nothing but the stars, and he could not see her face. "Sometimes the answers are bad, but that doesn't keep them from being the answers."

"You think like a campaigner," he told her.

She shook her head. "I think like a mother. That's what Renate always says. It's funny, since my own mother—" She broke off. "Where did you send her?"

"That's exactly what I can't tell people," he pointed out.

"But this place she is going. This mission. It will hurt them, Ellis?"

It is our only hope. "Yes," he said, "I believe it will."

"Fatally?"

"That's probably up to the people dealing with the consequences."

"So this is a first step."

He supposed her curiosity was based in wanting to know that he knew what he was doing, but her questions were growing oddly specific. He hoped she wouldn't push the point on the location. "Yes," he said, "but I think it's a good one. We'll be able to fight."

"We must all fight them." When he said nothing, she looked at him, and he noticed, for the first time, that her dark eyes could be something other than misty and unfocused. They could be sharp and clever and angry. "What happens if Chief Shaw fails?"

He spread his hands at her. "I can't say. Earth may have enough defenses to defeat Olam. If they do—we are where we are today."

She frowned and turned away. "That is not acceptable." She shook her head. "He's going to keep asking you, you know."

"Who?"

"Captain Foster. He's going to keep asking you where you've sent her. He loves her, and you don't let go of the people you love. You don't let them get ripped away from you, either. You kill for that."

Was she worried for him? "Captain Foster isn't going to kill me," he assured her. "He's disillusioned, and all of this is going to disillusion him further. But he's a soldier, still, and beyond that he is moral." It was a failing, sometimes, Jos reflected; but in this case it would save his life. "He may disagree with my duty, but he's not going to kill me for doing it."

"No, he won't kill you," Ilyana agreed. "But you do know where she is."

"If I tell him that, the whole mission falls apart. He knows that."

"He doesn't, really. He thinks he can do it instead of her. He'd go after her, and they'd find out he was coming, and she would fail. You would fail."

"And that's exactly why I won't tell him." Herrod was puzzled. "What's troubling you, Commander? Is there something I can help you with?"

She sagged a little then. She was still turned away from him, but he could see part of her profile, and he thought he saw her lower lip tremble a little. "You know where she is," she repeated. "And they can't know. Not ever. It's too important."

And she turned back, and she shot him.

It was an astonishing sensation, being shot. He found himself most curious about where she had hidden the weapon. She would have been searched when she came on board, so she'd stolen it from somewhere. Foster would have heads for that oversight. It hurt, being shot, more than anything else he had ever felt, but somehow his mind moved sideways, and he could feel all of it but he was not actually in his body. He opened his mouth to say something to her, to reassure her again that he wasn't going to tell, but she had shot him and that was over and it was the past and time didn't work like that. Gilbert was moving, and Hirano behind him; one of them clamped his arms around Ilyana, who dropped the weapon and did not resist. Her face. *Her face.* She was weeping, and her eyes were black with bottomless rage and grief, and he wanted to tell her it was all right, it would be all right, he understood now, it made sense, *I'm sorry, Ilyana, Ana, I'm sorry, I'm sorry Andy I'm sorry I'm—*

THE SILENT WAR

Greg strode back to his office, Emily Broadmoor at his heels. He was nearly incoherent with rage, but whether he was angrier with Herrod or Elena, he couldn't say.

"*Galileo*," he barked, as soon as he got through his office door, "status of those unidented ships."

"Seventeen responses," *Galileo* told him.

"Any of them *Antigone*?"

"No."

Of course not. She wasn't going to answer. This was futile. "How many outstanding?"

"Three hundred and twelve."

Too many. How was he going to unravel anything from three hundred and twelve ships? He took a breath. "We took specs on *Antigone* when Herrod came aboard, didn't we? I want you to filter the data on those three hundred and twelve ships to exclude anything that couldn't be Herrod's shuttle."

"Data is inexact. Precision will be impossible."

"Understood." Even if *Galileo* could eliminate one, it would be better than none. "And keep requesting idents. Get threatening if you have to." Elena wouldn't respond to threats, but others might, and anything that cut down the list was a help.

"Sir."

He looked up; to his surprise, Emily Broadmoor was still standing there, at attention. He bit down on annoyance. She wasn't Jessica. She wouldn't understand how very much he needed to be on his own right now, how hard he was working to untangle his duty from the knots of fury and anguish in his head. "I'm sorry, Commander," he said. "I don't need anything right now. You're dismissed."

But Commander Broadmoor, perennially compliant and dutiful, just straightened, at attention, her eyes on the back wall. "No, sir."

Greg was too astonished to be angry, but instinct kicked in. "You want to restate that, Commander?" he asked, keeping his voice cool.

"Sir. With Commander Lockwood on Yakutsk, I am effectively first officer. It's my duty, sir, to assess your state of mind, and to behave in a way commensurate with ensuring you are in the best possible position to perform your duties."

He was pretty sure that was a precise quote from the regulation job description. "You think my state of mind requires company at the moment, Commander?"

"Yes, sir."

He paused, then, and took a good look at her. Emily Broadmoor was close to sixty, her hair iron-gray and straight, cropped so close to her head it stood up straight on top. She had a sturdy build and a sturdy face, as if designed from birth to be a career soldier. He had been worried, when she had been assigned to him, that she would be bothered reporting to someone so much younger; but he had learned that his actions were all she needed. He did not think it would matter to her if she liked him or not, and in fact he had no idea what her personal feelings were. For her to stand there like this . . . he owed it to her to take her seriously.

He sat back in his chair and rubbed his eyes. "I'm all right, Commander," he told her. "I just need to untangle this mess."

"If you'll forgive me, sir, I don't see much of a tangle."

He very nearly laughed at her. "If you can see all of this clearly, please, lay it out for me."

Commander Broadmoor was silent for a moment, and he realized abruptly she was trying to figure out how to be tactful. "Assuming we can take Admiral Herrod at his word, sir," she said, "it seems to me the mission Chief Shaw has taken is a fairly routine one."

"Come on, Emily. She's a *civilian*."

"Permission to speak candidly, sir."

He could count on one hand the number of times Emily Broadmoor had said those words to him. "Of course."

"Admiral Herrod is wrong about a lot of things," she said. "But he's right about that. I know she resigned her commission, but she's *not* a civilian. I don't think she knows how to be one. And you, Captain, are not seeing this clearly. You're not seeing *her* clearly."

"You want to be more specific, Commander?"

"Sir, what's the point of tracking her shuttle?"

"Do I need a reason, beyond stopping this insane suicide mission?"

"Captain, if Herrod is telling the truth about that station, her mission isn't insane. I understand how you feel about the predicted outcome—"

And that pissed him off. "Do not presume you know how I feel, Commander," he warned her.

But Emily, as it turned out, had a temper of her own. "Sir, do you know how old soldiers get to be old?"

And where is this *going?* "Sure. They survive."

"That's only one part of it, sir. We get to be old soldiers because we see all the shit, and the bureaucracy, and the futility and the failure, and we stay anyway. You think I don't know how you feel? What do you know about my life, what I've seen, had, lost? I've known Elena Shaw nearly as long as I've known you, sir. I know what kind of a soldier she is, and I know she wouldn't have taken this mission if she did not believe, with her intellect as well as her heart, that it was the best possible choice she had."

Of course she believed it. Elena always thought she could fix everything. And he believed in her, too . . . didn't he? "She doesn't have all the facts," he tried.

"Possibly not, sir. But neither do we. And if you don't mind my saying so, sir, I think you need to stop thinking like a man worrying about someone he loves, and start thinking like a commander with an operative in the field who may need help."

"I—"

Well . . . fuck. I guess I should have talked to Emily sooner.

"All right, Commander," he said. "Give me your assessment."

Commander Broadmoor squared her shoulders, and Greg thought she looked mildly relieved. *I wonder what she thought I would say to her?* "As I see it, sir, we have three emergent situations at the moment. The first is Ellis Systems on Yakutsk, which Commander Lockwood is handling. The second is Commander Shaw's mission to this station. That's trickier, because we don't know what kind of intel she was given, and our only source is not entirely trustworthy."

Greg found her description of Herrod overly polite.

"Based on what we know, though," she continued, "it would be my suggestion that we maintain her cover, and focus instead on obtaining the location of the station. Which is intelligence that Admiral Herrod has. Extracting it will be a challenge, but I don't believe an impossibility."

"Why not?"

At this, her expression softened just a little. "Admiral Herrod is career Corps as well, sir."

He was not so sure an appeal to duty would do it, but it was a legitimate place to start. "Go on."

"The third, and most urgent situation," she said, "is the Olam Fleet attacking the First Sector."

"We're too far away to stop them," he pointed out. "Everyone is."

"Yes, sir. But people need to know what's going on. They have a right."

He agreed with her, but it wasn't his call. "I commed

Admiral Chemeris," he told her. "Either she's ignoring me, or she's too backed up. I can't move unilaterally."

"Respectfully, sir, I think you have to."

At that, he raised his eyebrows at her. "Advocating insubordination, Commander?"

"I think we're beyond that here, sir," she said. "The Admiralty on Earth is very likely to be under attack soon. We don't know what we'll find when all of this unravels. Olam is flying under the auspices of Ellis Systems and presumptive goodwill. Their deception isn't going to stop if they hit Earth. The word needs to go out, and it needs to go out now. Worlds besides Earth may need to defend themselves, and it's our duty to see that they aren't left blind."

He had thought of that. He had thought of so much more. "The trouble is," he told her, "not enough people are going to believe us. Ellis has been warm and generous and useful through all of this. The Corps has been reactive and slow. We don't have the credibility to—" He stopped. "Except maybe we know someone who does."

He contacted Samaras, and within moments Captain Taras's voice filled the room. "Captain Foster," she said, "has something happened?"

"A great deal has happened, yes," he said. "I have a favor to ask."

He outlined the situation to her, and for once she reined in her outsized personality until he was finished. "PSI has more credibility in this sector than we do," he concluded. "Possibly in the other sectors as well. If you can put this intel out on your network, I believe it'll gain better traction than if we do it on our own." He glanced at Emily Broadmoor; she still stood at attention, but he thought if she objected she would have said something by now.

"And you will back up this information?"

"We can release a statement at the same time if you like, Captain."

Taras took a moment to think. "Let us get the word out first," she told him. "We will mention that we are with the Corps on this mission, but give it perhaps half an hour before you back us up." Her voice grew more subdued. "When I have worried about war, Captain Foster," she said, "I never saw it starting like this. Perhaps I should have."

"Perhaps we all should have, Captain Taras," he told her. "But I am, in this situation, glad to know who my allies are."

When he disconnected, Emily was still standing at attention. "What I just did," he told her, "isn't going to go over well with the Admiralty."

"Understood, sir."

"It probably *is* insubordination, if you parse it out. Especially when you realize a lot of what I just told her could be considered classified."

"Yes, sir."

"You may want to distance yourself from this situation," he said. "For career reasons."

"My career is *Galileo,* sir," she said, and he felt an unexpected wave of affection for her.

"What do you think," he asked, "is the best way to approach Herrod?"

"Well, sir," she said, and he could tell she had been thinking about it, "if what we know of him is accurate, his advocacy with Shadow Ops has leaned more toward peace than war. Given the potential downside of Chief Shaw's mission failing—which is a possibility, with her on her own—I would think he'd—"

This time it was Commander Broadmoor's comm who interrupted them, and she frowned. At Greg's nod, she connected. "Lieutenant Gilbert?" she asked.

"Ma'am." Gilbert was breathless, flustered; Greg straightened in his chair. "Ma'am, there's been an incident."

Greg got to his feet. "Report, Lieutenant," he snapped, and Gilbert regrouped.

"Sir. It's Admiral Herrod, sir. Commander Ilyana—she shot him, sir. She came to visit him, and she had a weapon, and she shot him. There was nothing we could do for him, sir; she was too close. He's dead."

CHAPTER 37

YAKUTSK

"What do you mean, it's cracked?"

"It's cracked." Dallas set the part down on the table in front of Villipova's goon. "See that line? That's four millimeters deep. Thing is useless."

Jessica stood next to Dallas, trying to look disinterested, trying not to stare at the weapon Villipova's guard was carrying. She was not entirely convinced that this strategy would work, but when she had told Dallas she might need as much as an hour to hack into the env comms system without having her tap detected, her host had said only, "Okay," and told her to follow. Jessica had expected Dallas to come up with some shaggy dog story about a system that needed extra vetting, or even to call the guards over to look at something.

Accusing the Ellis representative of trying to pass off crap seemed less low-profile than Jessica had been hoping.

"Can't you fix it?" the guard asked irritably.

"Not a mechanic," Dallas replied, equally irritable. "I'm

not here to fix this stuff. I'm here to validate it for the governor. No way I'm signing off on this part. Your guy needs to replace it."

"Won't they be able to find out you did this?" Jessica had asked, after Dallas casually swept a narrow spanner blade through the molded polymer surface.

"You got scanners on your starship that can date damage like this?"

"I—" That was a question for Ted. "I don't know."

"Possible," Dallas told her, "that they'd be able to see what's clinging to the inner surfaces of the crack I just put there. Possible they could date something on a molecular level. Possible they've got equipment that sensitive in the pockets of those nice suits they're wearing. Really, really unlikely, though, that they'd even check. At least in any time frame we care about."

Jessica wasn't sure what would happen to Dallas if Villipova found out later on that they'd deliberately damaged a piece of the dome environmental system. *When this is finished,* she thought, *I'm going to offer Dallas a place on* Galileo. She was sure she could convince Greg.

Villipova's guard picked up the part and squinted at the crack. Then he sighed, shot Dallas a look of resignation, and said, "Fine. I'll tell Villipova."

Dallas nodded. "I'm double-checking everything we looked at yesterday." Jessica had never heard Dallas sound so decisive. "Carefully. Tell her that, too. I don't want to live in a dome if the fucking air handler is going to reverse and suffocate me in my sleep."

The guard looked vaguely alarmed at that, and Jessica

had to hide a smile. That was the advantage of working with someone who knew a place: Dallas, born and raised in the domes, knew exactly which fears they all shared. What surprised her, a little, was how reflexively easy it seemed to be for Dallas to lie. From her angle, it was easy to tell when Dallas was doing it; but she wasn't so sure she'd be as aware if those shrewd, dark eyes were turned on her instead.

The guard stalked off, part in hand, and Dallas turned back to Jessica. "If he comes back, I'll handle it." They walked together back toward the line of equipment. "Do what you have to do. You've seen his level of knowledge."

"What if he brings someone back with him? Gladkoff? He'd know what I was doing."

Dallas thought for a moment. "Code word. Something I wouldn't say."

"Sunrise?" Jessica suggested, and Dallas grinned.

"Sunrise. I say *sunrise,* you move on to . . ." Dallas's eyes scanned the room. "That one, back there. Big-ass redundant viral detection system. Even Gladkoff would believe you'd be hours checking that out."

She shot Dallas a look. "I said *hour,* not *hours.*" And she got that grin again.

Dallas took the unit closest to the door and began doing, as far as Jessica could tell, exactly what they'd explained to the guard: rechecking each part, slowly and methodically. She wondered if Dallas ever got bored, and if not, what sorts of thoughts wandered through a scavenger's head. Elena had often told Jessica that rote work was relaxing and inspiring; her mind could go anywhere, trusting her hands to take care of what needed doing.

Jessica's task, of course, required a lot more mental focus than a safety check.

The interface to Jamyung's comms tracer was clumsy, despite all the work Dallas had done overnight to try to give it some finesse, and it took Jessica nearly ten minutes to figure out how to gesture clearly enough for it to understand. But once she had established detente with the machine, hooking it into the odd comms system was not as difficult as she feared. The Ellis equipment did appear to be a basic long-range comms setup, without any embellishments, which suggested to Jessica that any subterfuge and encryption would be attached to the source and destination signals. Before she activated the trap, she took some time to write some code to shadow the incoming and outgoing signals. It was a simple trick—take a copy and trap that, and leave the original alone—but it was delicate to implement. She only knew one other hacker who had done it, and for a moment she wished for Admiral Herrod's company and expertise, never mind his divided loyalties. She had been breaking into systems since she was a little girl, but she never got past the butterflies of worrying about getting caught.

It took her nearly the full hour she had claimed, and then she leaned back. "Done," she told Dallas, and wiped the back of her hand against her face. Damn, that had been as tense as a marathon run.

"Close it up and get off it," Dallas said. "They're coming back."

She tried to affect casual swiftness as she closed up the comms system, verifying through her own comm that she was trapping the signals. There was something coming through: encrypted, of course, but she was getting a clear shadow.

Before she could look closely at it, though, Gladkoff came in, guard in tow. He looked more frazzled than before, she thought, turning to a different environmental unit. She turned her back to him, bending over a cooling unit, cracking open the lid and opening it as she had seen Dallas do earlier.

But Gladkoff wasn't interested in her at all. "This wasn't broken when we installed it," he snapped at Dallas.

Dallas, slighter than Gladkoff and far shorter, did not back down. "Not my problem when it broke. It's broken now, and we can't use it. Aftermarket parts."

"Our aftermarket parts are fully vetted!" Gladkoff yelled.

Jessica tuned out the argument, touching the comm behind her ear. "Bristol," she said quietly, "get me a line to *Galileo*."

"Ma'am."

A moment later, a low tone sounded in her ear, and she was connected to the ship. She fed in the shadow signal, and waited. It took the ship less than thirty seconds to perform a preliminary analysis.

"Fully encrypted signal," *Galileo* said. "Unable to decode."

She hadn't expected the ship to be able to untangle it immediately. "Can you get any shape on it?"

"Specify reference point."

Jessica frowned. "Is it exporting diagnostic data from this environmental array?"

"Probability 19.2 percent."

Not impossible. "What's more likely?"

"Define parameters."

Someday, Jessica thought wistfully, *someone will invent an AI that actually understands what the fuck I want it to do.* "Is it a personal message? Natural speech?"

"Probability 1.3 percent."

So not machine data, and not speech. "Some kind of hardware signal?"

"Probability 83.4 percent."

That was more like it. "What kind of hardware signal?"

"Six thousand, four hundred and twelve possibilities."

"Okay, okay." She thought. "Can you narrow that down?"

"Analysis will take four hours, twelve minutes."

She sighed. "Yeah, okay, do that." Then she paused. She always forgot to ask the simple questions. "*Galileo,* you can't tell what it is, right?"

"No."

"Can you tell where it's going?"

There was a pause, and Jessica felt a glimmer of hope. Not that it mattered; it was likely going to Gladkoff's shuttle, or some random Ellis lab somewhere. It would be foolish to send an open comm signal like this to anything nefarious or proprietary. Ellis was arrogant, but rarely foolish.

Galileo returned. "The signal is calibrated and tuned to a ship currently in the field."

Which would muck up the location data. Jessica's hope disappeared. "Any ident on that ship?" she asked.

"Yes. The signal is contacting the PSI starship *Chryse.*"

Jessica stilled, no longer worried that Gladkoff might overhear what she was saying. She touched her comm and brought in Bristol again. "Lieutenant," she said, "I need you to connect me with Captain Foster.

"Right fucking now."

PART III

CHAPTER 38

INDUS STATION

Indus Station," Elena said, "this is *Wanderlust,* requesting docking privileges on Level Five."

She waited.

There were not a lot of possibilities. They could, of course, just ignore her; but she thought that was vanishingly unlikely. Out here, in the middle of nowhere, a field-shielded station wouldn't be approached by a random shuttle. If they didn't identify her as one of their own, she would be deemed a threat, and all her worries would be over in a flash of laser fire and vacuum.

And yet she couldn't quite convince herself they'd open their loving arms and let her in, either.

The reply came at last. "*Wanderlust,* Indus. What have you got for us this time?"

His voice was deep and mildly disinterested. He was undoubtedly in the middle of checking her ident, and despite the lack of indicators on her dashboard, she was sure she was already being scanned. "Vending supplies," she said, trying to sound equally bored. "Coffee, mostly."

"We're not out of coffee," the voice said, beginning to sound suspicious.

There was a freedom, she was discovering, in knowing she was going to die anyway. She let out all of her exhaustion and irritation in her reply. "What the hell do I care if you're out of coffee?" she snapped. "They sent me with the damn shipment, and I've been flying for sixteen straight hours with this shit. You want me to drop it, or you want me to space it? Because I don't care, as long as I can tell them I made the damn delivery."

There was one moment of tense silence, and then the man laughed.

"Relax, *Wanderlust*. Nobody's giving up coffee today." A light flashed on her dashboard. "Docking privileges granted. Proceed to Level Five."

Well. Step Two completed. Somewhat surprised, she nudged the ship forward and connected with the station's autopilot. While she was being pulled into Level Five, she stood and checked her cargo one last time. Seventeen cases of coffee, three of dried nuts, and the beer. She should have mentioned the beer. *Greg would have thought to mention the beer.*

She suspected they'd be happy enough to see it anyway.

She turned back to the window, and watched Indus Station grow larger and larger.

It was an inelegant structure, blocky and asymmetrical, made up of what had to be radiation-graded shipping crates connected by narrow corridors. It seemed to have been constructed for a purely utilitarian purpose, with no sense of home or personality. Not made for humans. There were windows here and there, but not many, and it occurred to her that she might be seeing the stars for the last time in her life.

She switched the viewer to the rear of the ship, and watched the stars get swallowed by the hangar while she landed.

Wanderlust's feet touched the floor, and Elena took one last look in the mirror by the rear door to make sure her uniform and ident badge were tidy. She had the door open before the ship was powered down, and did her best to move easily, casually, with confidence and little care. *Don't be a soldier,* she told herself. *Efficiency, but not precision. You're a delivery person. You do this all the time. You belong here.*

She hit the decking with a bounce in her step, and, without looking at the white-uniformed duo approaching her ship, she walked around to the back and opened the cargo hatch. "Have you got a lift?" she called to the couple, without turning around.

"We need your shipping number."

She looked up, the irritability on her face completely genuine. "Fine. But can one of you get a lift?"

She hit her comm to pull up her documentation, and one of them, a bored-looking man with rather fine eyes, tugged it away from her. The other, a stocky woman with a cheerful smile, said, "I'll start unloading," and headed to the other side of the hangar to pick up a lift.

"You need to wait until I check," the man told her.

"She's got *beer,*" the woman said, not slowing down.

He frowned, but he seemed more exasperated than worried. He scanned through Elena's documents as she cultivated a look of boredom and vague impatience.

"All set," he said at last. "You need help with that?"

Elena did her best not to sigh with relief. "No, I think we've got it," she said. The woman had already pulled the beer off the ship and set it on the lift, heading back inside for more.

Elena went in after her, wrestling with coffee crates. "If I'd had any idea," she said conversationally, "I'd have asked for more beer."

"They never send enough," the woman agreed. "Always coffee, of course, because they want us all to stay awake. Like we're going to work double shifts just to be nice about it." She laughed. She had an easy laugh, loud and unselfconscious.

"Next time," Elena assured her, and felt a pang of guilt.

No next time. And no guilt, dammit. You knew this. These people you're killing—it's a trade, remember? An eye for a thousand eyes.

They unloaded the cargo, and Elena followed the woman out of the hangar, the cargo on the lift before them. "Sixteen hours you were out?"

"Yeah." Elena made the syllable sound exhausted. "Out of Shixin."

"A lot of tourists this time of year, aren't there?" The woman shook her head. "I went to Shixin a couple of years ago. You couldn't even walk through the spaceport. They were all there rubbernecking like they'd never seen a domed city before."

"They probably hadn't," Elena remarked.

"Which is fine," the woman said, "except what were they doing standing and staring at it from inside the spaceport?" She laughed again. "I'm Jats. Mika, to my friends." She held out a hand as they walked, and Elena shook it.

"Taylor," Elena said. "Olivia Taylor. It's nice to meet you."

The woman's smile widened. "After sixteen hours," she said, "I'll bet you're wanting something to eat."

The kindness, Elena thought, might kill her before anything else. "That would be lovely," she said, and meant it.

"Of course, it means a body search." Mika sounded apologetic. "No way around that, unless you want to sit in your ship until turnaround time."

"For food, you can search me twice."

At that, Mika laughed, and gestured to a door in the corner. "Once should do it, but no promises."

As Elena approached the doorway, she felt a brief flare of warmth against her leg. *Damn.* "Oh," she said, and stopped. "I've got—something to declare, is it? I forgot I had this with me."

Mika stopped. Her smile hadn't faded, but her eyes had gone wary, and one hand moved to rest on her sidearm. "What is it?"

How would a civilian handle this? Elena thought. She moved her hands away from her body, palms forward: *I am not a threat.* "It's a sculpture. My brother gave it to me the last time I was home, and I stuck it in my pocket. I meant to take it out before I left." She kept her expression apologetic. "You want me back in the shuttle?"

Mika had spied the lump in her right pocket. "There?"

she said, gesturing, and Elena nodded. She sighed. "I'm going to have to ask for help. Just—don't move, okay?"

Elena nodded and kept still. A moment later, the man who had scanned her documents returned. He was not smiling.

"She has something in her pocket," Mika told him.

He shot Elena an exasperated look, then reached down, unzipping her pocket to remove the artifact. *Behave, behave, behave,* Elena thought at it desperately.

The man frowned, turning it over in his hands, then tossed it to Mika. "Put that in the scanner." He faced Elena again. "Against the wall," he told her, "hands above your head."

She forced herself to remain relaxed, and rested her palms against the wall. He ran a scanner over her, and then his hands, thoroughly investigating every fold of her borrowed uniform. He ran his fingers through her hair, feeling the contours of her skull; he checked her neck, her spine, her ribs, every part of her. She kept her eyes closed. It was necessary, of course. It made perfect sense. It was impersonal, and he was scrupulously professional. But she had to clench her teeth to keep from shuddering, to repress the urge to turn and punch him just for touching her.

It didn't matter. Mika would run the artifact through whatever scanner she had, and see the NO DATA bounce back. Its cover as a sculpture would be blown. She wondered if she could break away, run back to *Wanderlust*, trigger some kind of self-destruct that would destroy the rest of the station . . .

"It's clean," Mika called from the scanner station. She

turned, tossing the artifact into the air as she walked. "Polymer, through and through. Like they use in the interior bulkheads. Pretty, though, isn't it?" She gave Elena another smile, her suspicions gone. "Where'd your brother get it?"

The man searching Elena had reached her feet, and was probing her boots carefully. "Not sure," she said. "He goes to these art fairs. Buys off the tables using hard currency. He thought it had a nice shape."

"Yeah." Mika kept tossing it. "Fits right in the palm. Ian, you want to hold it?"

Ian glared at her, and Elena had a sudden impression of two people with disparate temperaments who had worked together for a long time. "No, I don't," he said clearly. He turned back to Elena. "You're clean. But listen . . . don't bring toys in here again. I don't have time to waste on this shit." He stalked off.

Elena pushed off the wall and ran a hand over her mussed hair. Irritably, she pulled the tie out of the back of it and pulled out the tangles Ian had introduced. "I should have cut it off," she complained, and Mika shot her a sympathetic grin.

"He's not as bad as some of the others," she said.

"That's something, I suppose." Elena did not find it at all comforting. "I'm going to tell my brother to stop giving me presents."

"Ask him where he got this first," Mika suggested. "And bring another one next time. We could use a little aesthetic beauty." Somewhat reluctantly, she held the artifact out to Elena. "Around here, it's easy to forget that form over function isn't necessarily bad."

Elena took the object back. Its surface was cool, just like any other ordinary polymer, just like the solid object it had told Mika's scanner it was.

It . . . lied.

She had no time to consider the implications of that revelation.

Slipping back into her role as exhausted delivery person, she unzipped her pocket and dropped the artifact back in. "We all need a little beauty in our lives," she agreed.

As she followed Mika out of the landing bay, she felt the object in her pocket grow warm against her hip, and the irrational part of her mind wondered if it was laughing.

CHAPTER 39

GALILEO

In the tiny storeroom where Greg's security people were keeping Ilyana, the PSI officer was sitting in a chair, arms folded before her on a small table, that bland smile on her face. Greg, monitoring on vid from the next room, could hear her humming, her voice low; sometimes the sound would get louder, and she would rock, just a little, before growing still again.

"Did she say anything?" he asked Commander Broadmoor.

The security chief shook her head. "Hirano says she didn't resist at all. Shot Herrod and just wilted."

"Where'd she get the weapon?"

"It was Herrod's, apparently. She must have lifted it before we arrested him, because Gilbert found nothing when he tossed the room." She looked over at Greg. "Hirano's beating himself up pretty badly, sir."

He should have found the gun, Greg thought, but he couldn't bring himself to lay too much blame on the security officer. Greg's own instructions had been to treat Ilyana as a guest. And even with all his own habitual paranoia, he would not have seen her as a physical threat. "They were friendly, Ilyana and Herrod. There was no reason to suspect she would have hurt him. I'll have a word with him later, but let him know that he won't be disciplined for this."

Emily Broadmoor raised her eyebrows, but said nothing. She would think he was being too lenient. It was possible he was. But he could not see this as anything other than his own dismal failure.

Jessica's revelation about *Chryse* should have surprised him, but it hadn't. It was the last piece that knit all of this together, but he still didn't understand what any of it meant. And he hadn't realized how hard it would be, telling Jessica that Herrod was dead. Despite the man's evasiveness and divided loyalties, Herrod and Jessica had always worked well together, and Greg believed—despite her frequent denials—that she'd been fond of him. She had gone very quiet when he had told her, and sworn only once.

"I want you in touch with Shimada," he ordered. "I'll get him an off-grid, and have him keep the line open. Find out what that comm is sending."

"Do you think Herrod knew?"

Irrelevant. But he did not say that to her. "I'll find out what I can from Ilyana," he told her, "but I'm guessing that might be an uphill battle."

He had said that before realizing Ilyana was essentially catatonic.

Petra Arapova, *Galileo*'s head counselor, stepped into Ilyana's makeshift cell and sat down across from her. "Commander Ilyana," she began, "I'm not here to interrogate you. Nothing you say to me can be used to prosecute you in any way. I am here to evaluate your mental state, and that is all. Do you understand?"

At Petra's question Ilyana met the counselor's eyes, but said nothing, still humming.

"I'm going to ask you a few things, Commander, and I'd like you to answer if you can." Petra gave Ilyana a reassuring smile, but the woman still did not respond. "Can you tell me where you came from?"

No change.

"Were you born Leslie Barrett Millar on Achinsk?"

No change.

"Have you been living for the last forty years on the PSI ship *Chryse*?"

The humming grew louder, and almost imperceptibly, Ilyana began rocking.

"Why did you leave *Chryse*, Commander Ilyana?" The rocking stilled again. "Would you like us to contact Captain Bayandi for you?"

That, of all things, seemed to get through to her. Ilyana blinked that strange, slow blink, and finally focused on Petra, giving her a friendly smile. "Thank you, Commander Arapova," she said formally. "But that is not necessary."

After a moment her eyes lost focus, and she began to hum again.

Petra tried a number of other questions, but Ilyana responded to none of them, only rocking, just a little, every time Petra mentioned *Chryse*. There was something there, and Greg found himself growing angrier. Bayandi had vouched for her. He had said she was not violent. Something was missing. "Samaras," he said, connecting with the comms officer, "get me Captain Bayandi on *Chryse*."

Greg was not sure what time it was on *Chryse,* but Bayandi, as always, picked up instantly. "Captain Foster," he said, and his voice sounded pleased. "How nice to hear from you again. What can I help you with?"

Tell me why you're coming to Yakutsk. Tell me what you know about Ellis. Tell me why Admiral Herrod is dead. "We've had to arrest Commander Ilyana."

There was a long silence on the other end, and when Bayandi spoke, Greg heard no surprise. "Was anyone hurt?"

"Yes."

"Badly?"

"A man was killed." Greg waited, and heard nothing. "Captain Bayandi, I think I've been extraordinarily patient throughout all of this. You've stonewalled nearly every question I've asked you."

"I would like to speak with Ana, please."

"She's not talking to anyone," Greg said. "But after I'm finished talking with you, I'm going to sit down with her and find out how *Chryse* is involved with Ellis Systems, and exactly why you're receiving data comms from Yakutsk."

The silence was longer this time. "I would like to discuss all of that with you, Captain Foster." He sounded apologetic. "But for now—please. I must speak with Ana. You may listen, of course. But—please understand. She believes she is alone. I need to let her know she is not."

There was something in Bayandi's voice, something that

made Greg think the man was not asking purely as a commanding officer. *And don't I know what that's like?*

Greg commed Petra in the interview room, and told her what he was going to do. The counselor's lips tightened—disapproval, of course—but she nodded, sitting back to watch her charge.

"Commander Ilyana," Bayandi said, when Greg patched him through.

The change in Ilyana was instant. She stopped humming, pushed the chair back, and stood, spine stiff at attention. "Yes, Captain."

"I am told, Commander, that you killed someone."

At that, Ilyana's face crumbled, and Greg caught an expression he was not sure he could identify—anger, perhaps, or sadness. "Yes, sir. It was necessary, sir." Her voice was awkward, stilted.

"Violence is never necessary, Commander." That got Greg's attention; he had not heard Bayandi sound harsh before.

"It was for *Chryse,* sir."

Greg expected Bayandi to challenge her. Instead, the captain was quiet for a moment, before he said, much of his harshness dissipated, "That was not your mission, Commander."

"Yes, Captain."

"You will have to be disciplined."

"I understand, Captain."

"You will do as these people say, Commander Ilyana, without question. Do you understand?"

"Yes, sir."

"And you will hurt no one else, no matter what the reason. Not even if you are attacked." His voice was stern, as if he were scolding a recalcitrant child. "Am I making myself clear, Commander?"

She looked appropriately chastised. "Yes, sir."

"Very well, Commander. At ease." Ilyana sat again, and began to hum, and Bayandi said, "Captain Foster, if you and I could speak."

Greg took the comm private, his eyes on Petra through the window. "What is to become of Commander Ilyana?" Bayandi asked.

There would be tests, Greg knew. It was possible Ilyana was faking her mental state, but Greg didn't believe it. Ilyana being PSI, she would likely be released back to her own people; but if *Chryse* was working with Ellis . . . "We're still unraveling what happened, Captain. Can you tell me why she would do something like this?"

"Commander Ilyana has been under unprecedented pressure, Captain Foster. Having said that—forgive the question, but is there any way this was self-defense?"

Greg thought of Herrod: stiff, old, mentally brutal, physically frail. "No. There were two witnesses."

"And what do they report?"

"Ilyana and Herrod were talking," Greg said. "They'd talked before." *They were friendly. It made me suspicious, just not of the right person.* "Based on the witness reports, she wanted to keep him from revealing a particular piece of information."

"What information?"

Something I don't know, that you might. "Without going into detail, Captain— Herrod was attempting to punch a hole in Ellis Systems."

At that, Bayandi's voice sharpened. "This Herrod person was trying to stop Ellis?"

Greg wondered if Herrod had known about *Chryse,* if he might have left Elena alone if he had. "His methodology was flawed."

"She silenced him because she was concerned he might change his mind?"

That seems like a strange conclusion to draw. "I can't speculate as to her reasons, Captain."

"Captain Foster," Bayandi said decisively, "Commander Ilyana's state of mind is unhealthy at the moment. Your own medical people will verify this. I would like to make a formal request of Central Corps that she be remanded to *Meridia* for punishment by her own people."

Greg frowned. "Why *Meridia?* Why not *Chryse?*"

Bayandi paused again, this time for so long Greg began to wonder if the line had dropped. "It is past time for you to pay me a visit, Captain Foster," he said at last.

Greg should have found it menacing, to be invited to *Chryse,* her ties to Ellis exposed. But there was something in Bayandi's voice, something unutterably sad, something that reminded him of the tune Ilyana had been humming, over and over, as she rocked.

"Very well, Captain," he said. "I'll come to you."

Greg was checking in on *Galileo*'s search for *Antigone* when Pritchard appeared at his door.

The number of ships that *Galileo* thought might be Elena's shuttle had been reduced by nearly half, and Greg thought that perhaps by next year he might narrow it down to a small enough number to actually investigate. His rogue installation query had produced slightly more interesting but equally pointless results: seventeen cities on established colonies that he had already speculated were related to Shadow Ops research, four moons that were officially uninhabited, and no fewer than forty-seven "free-floating structures of unknown origin and purpose." Forty-seven bits of space junk, any one of which might hold Ellis's research station. *Useless.* Greg was finding nothing, and his last link to Elena was dead.

"Come in," Greg said to the man, and watched as Herrod's aide crossed the room. Herrod had called the man *son,* but he was not much younger than Greg: over thirty, at least, by the look of the lines around his eyes. Of course, under the circumstances, he probably looked older than he was; he wore an expression that suggested something between grief and anger.

But when Pritchard spoke, his voice was measured and polite. "Captain Foster. I'm sorry to bother you."

"No bother, Mr. Pritchard." Greg gestured at the chair before his desk, but Pritchard shook his head. Greg rubbed his eyes. "I'm sure you know the admiral didn't have a lot of fans on this ship. But his death is unacceptable, and I don't believe you'll find that any of us will treat this as anything other than a serious crime."

Pritchard was frowning. "I understand that, Captain. That's not what I need to talk to you about." He relented, sitting in the chair, but he stayed stiff, as if he wanted to be sure he could run if he had to. "I . . . have been going through the admiral's things, and I've run across something . . ." He broke off. "I am quite sure I shouldn't be showing this to you, Captain. But it's beyond anything I'm capable of handling, and I think you need to hear it. It relates to Athena Relay."

Herrod had said he knew nothing. *He lied.* Greg supposed, at this point, it was his own fault if he was surprised. "Wait a moment, please." He commed Emily Broadmoor. "Commander, can you join me in my office? She's my security chief," he explained to Pritchard. "I want her to hear this, too."

Pritchard nodded, still uncomfortable, and Greg tried again to parse the expression on his unfamiliar face. Greg was beginning to see more anger there than grief.

Emily arrived quickly, and Greg let her stay at attention in the back of the room. "Go ahead, Mr. Pritchard."

Pritchard turned so he could look between Greg and Emily as he spoke. "He doesn't—didn't have much with him," Pritchard told them. "So it was mostly his documents, and his comms. His documents I know, because I generally wrote them up for his signature. But his comms—I expected his confidential messages to be locked, even bio-keyed. With his encryption skills . . ." He trailed off.

"You didn't think any of us would be able to read them," Greg concluded, and Pritchard nodded.

"But . . . he'd bio-keyed them, Captain. Just not with his bio key. He'd keyed them with mine, and when I accessed the list, they started playing."

You can't do that with bio keys, Greg thought. But Herrod, of course, was not bound by the same rules as anyone else. Jessica, who was the most remarkable hacker Greg had ever seen, stood in awe at Herrod's skills. He'd always thought she was just a bit starstruck, or happy to have someone to talk to who understood the intricacies of her field. *I owe her an apology.* "You said this was about Athena Relay," he prompted. "What did you mean?"

"I mean—" Pritchard swallowed. "They knew, Captain."

Greg became aware of Emily Broadmoor's eyes on him, but he kept looking at Herrod's aide. "Knew what?"

"That it was going to be destroyed. They knew, and they didn't warn anyone."

"Wait," Greg said, his head spinning. "Who knew? How?"

"Just listen." Pritchard touched his comm, and a message started playing.

"Request denied," said the voice on the comm, and Greg knew her immediately: Admiral Ilona Waris, copiously decorated, highly placed in both the Admiralty and Shadow Ops itself. While she was capable of expansive generosity in public, Greg knew her to be cold and ruthless on a level he had rarely encountered in anyone else. "We talked about this before you left, Jos. We can't afford to be clouded by sentiment, especially not now. If you send her before the relay is destroyed, she's going to think she has time, and she's going to figure out that she doesn't need to destroy that station to stop the fleet. Which means all of the data that Ellis has on the Admiralty—which they've been holding over our heads all this time, Jos, and that means yours, too—is at risk of going public. And when that happens, how long do you think it'll take before the colonies decide having their government in the Fifth Sector isn't such a bad idea after all? You want your comfortable retirement here on Earth, Jos, you'd better remember what you're doing out there. Waris out."

The Admiralty. *Not Shadow Ops,* Greg thought, cold radiating in his stomach, *the Admiralty.*

All *of them.*

"There's one other," Pritchard said, almost apologetically, and Greg nodded, unable to speak.

On this one, Waris's voice was less formal. Whatever Herrod's response to her previous message, it had made her lose her temper. "Well, then, break those ties, Jos! We've been following her because she's an independent agent. If she starts ingratiating herself with the *Galileo* crew again, you're going to lose any leverage you've got over her at all. I don't care what you have to do, or how many white lies you need to tell! Once that relay goes, everybody is going to know what Olam is up to. If you lose her, the fleet reaches Earth, and I'll be damned if I'm going to sit here and wait for a pack of Fifth Sector usurpers to stage a firefight in my backyard. You wait for the relay to be destroyed, and you get her out. And if you have to shoot all of her friends to keep her isolated, you fucking do it. I hope it's clear this time, Herrod." No sign-off, just a terminated comm.

Emily broke into Greg's jumbled thoughts. "Sir."

"Yes, Commander?"

"Does that mean they sent the chief under false pretenses, sir?"

She sounded stiff and stilted, as if she were fighting to

control her own temper, and Greg met her eyes. This time, it seemed, she was the one who needed him to be steady. "I think," he said, keeping his voice calm, "only partially. They did send her to stop the fleet."

"And to cover their asses. Sir."

Emily's fists were clenched, and Greg stood, instinctively, to walk over to her. "It looks that way, Commander."

Emily looked up at him, and close up, he could see the rage growing in her eyes. "All those people, sir, because they didn't want to give up power?"

"It sounds like it."

Emily Broadmoor swore, and out of the corner of his eye, Greg saw Pritchard flinch. "They knew it was going to happen. Before they sent us out here. Before they sent *him* out here." And he saw her digest the knowledge that her chain of command may have deliberately allowed ten thousand people to be murdered. "Captain, we've got to get Commander Shaw that information."

"I've got *Galileo* tracking her down," he told Emily, with more confidence than he felt. "But in the meantime, we've got these messages as proof." He turned to Pritchard. "Don't we?"

Pritchard had stood. "I'll give them to you, Captain. But there's one thing."

Isn't there always? "What?"

The man inhaled and exhaled, and Greg realized he was shaking. "I didn't know Admiral Herrod for long, Captain," he said. "I have no illusions about the kind of man he was. And to go along with this . . . scheme was unconscionable. If he was going to share these messages, it would have been better to do it before he died. But he *did* share them."

"You want me to acknowledge his great altruism?" Greg couldn't keep the sarcasm out of his voice.

"I don't expect that. But . . . as I see it, he might not have been able to stop the destruction of the relay anyway. He's left us with concrete evidence of Admiralty involvement. He didn't have to do that."

He didn't have to send Elena to die, either. But Greg thought, for now, he could keep his lack of generosity to himself. "I understand, Mr. Pritchard," he said, and tried to keep his voice calm. "I appreciate your coming forward with all of this."

When Pritchard left, Greg turned back to Emily. "I've got to head out," he said. "I've got to get to *Chryse* and find out what's going on. But I want you on this, Commander. Two audio comms is a start, but we need corroborating data. Times that Herrod was talking to people, off-grid traces, anything. Whether Elena succeeds or fails, we're going to need our own evidence."

"Are we going public with this, sir?"

Ten thousand people. Ten thousand people, and Elena, all for politics. Everything he had known, his career, his command—none of it was what he had thought it was. "I don't know what we should do with it yet," he said. "But we need to focus on why we're here. Our mission is still a good one, no matter what the Admiralty has done. I need you to keep your people focused on protecting this colony, is that clear? We'll deal with the Admiralty bullshit when we've figured out what's going on with *Chryse*."

She nodded, and looked steadier. "If you find the chief, sir," she said, "will you be able to get her the intel? Will you have time to stop her?"

I have never had time to stop her. But all he said was, "I hope so."

CHAPTER 40

YAKUTSK

'm sorry about your friend," Dallas said.

"He wasn't my friend."

They were standing outside the equipment room with the others, Ellis delivery people and colonists together, on a de facto meal break. Dallas had offered her a sandwich, and she had refused. She had no idea why Herrod's death was hitting her so hard. Surely she should be more worried about Elena, running off to save the galaxy with no weapons and no backup, or Greg, still believing on some level that he could save her, regardless of the fact that he never had been able to save her before. Not that Elena ever wanted anyone to save her anyway.

Everything Herrod knew, Jessica thought. *He could have decoded this signal with his eyes closed. I never asked him. I never asked him anything.*

Herrod might not have had to decode the signal, she told herself. If he was in it hip-deep with Ellis—or even just Shadow Ops, whoever's side they were on this week—he might have already known what it was saying. She would never make sense of it. She would never learn anything from him, about S-O or Ellis or hacking. He was dead, full stop, and nobody was ever going to learn anything from him again.

Dallas was just looking at her, expression neutral, leaning against the alley wall. Keeping her company. No hovering, no proffered handkerchief. "Everybody hated him," Jessica said. "But I couldn't, not really. He never patronized me. Never pretended I didn't know what I knew."

"He respected you."

She nodded. "I don't know that he was a good person, you know? But this."

"Death is an extreme punishment for being a jerk," Dallas agreed, and Jessica had to stop herself from laughing. *Stress,* she thought. *Too much, all at once.*

"He might have been worse than a jerk," she confessed. "But . . . that wasn't all there was to him." She shook her head. "I don't have time for this."

"Doesn't always matter," Dallas said.

"It does, though." She pushed herself off the wall. "Ted's going to be getting in touch at some point. I've got to keep him in the loop. I need to find out what that damn signal is."

Dallas pushed off the wall with her. "Thinking we should just shut it down."

"We do that," she pointed out, "they just turn it back on, and Villipova shuts us out completely—or gets some of the usual suspects to toss us out on the surface. We need to find out what's in that signal, and what *Chryse*'s involvement is."

"Your captain is on that, isn't he?"

She looked up at Dallas. *No fool,* she thought. But Dallas

was a native, and had never been off Yakutsk. And of course Dallas would have had no experience with the unrelenting stubbornness and absurd, persistent optimism of Greg Foster. "You sell to PSI, don't you?"

"We sell to everyone."

"How much do you think they'd tell you about their operations if you knocked on their door and asked?"

Dallas's dark eyes gleamed for a moment in comprehension. "This signal is the bird in the hand."

She nodded. "And the best chance we have at finding out what the fuck is going on here is if we can find out what that fucking bird is saying."

She waited as Dallas vanished for nearly ten minutes, returning with what appeared to be an ordinary handheld scanner. Only when she turned it over in her hand did she see what it really was: a camouflaged signal analyzer, and a fairly powerful one. "The interface is pressure-sensitive," Dallas told her, almost apologetically. "That was the only way to keep the parts small enough to fit."

"It's amazing," she said, and was treated to a smile.

Back in the environmental room, Dallas began a back-and-forth discussion with some of Gladkoff's suppliers about what kind of materials they could use to fill in for the damaged part until something new could be acquired. For someone who didn't talk much, she realized, Dallas was pretty good at drawing out an argument, but she wasn't going to take any risks with her time. She leaned over the signal and began pulling it apart, thread by thread, nanobit by nanobit. Separate into component parts, look for patterns.

Reconstruct, hypothesize, reject what doesn't fit. Slow, methodical, repetitive. Pleasantly familiar. This was something she could do, she was certain; she just wasn't sure she could do it in any kind of a useful time frame.

She had been less than ten minutes separating the bits of the shadow signal when she hit a block.

Frowning, she backed up the scanner and picked up the same thread again, following it more carefully. There it traveled, paralleling the live signal, pulsing in the pattern that she was beginning to recognize. The same signal, over and over again, complicated and encrypted, but repeated. And—

There it was again. The live signal continued, streaming out into the ether, into the FTL comms field, to the PSI ship. And her shadow signal was dragged off parallel and terminated.

Shadow tracking had its drawbacks, but she had never seen abrupt termination like this anywhere outside of a lab. There was something else in this comms system, something already linked in parallel, something blocking her from shadowing the signal.

Turning off the scanner, she rubbed her eyes, then looked back down at the hardware. There was the comms system, ordinary and blind, receiving and transmitting just as it should, agnostic about content. There was the conduit connecting the comms system with the power source. It wouldn't draw much power, not for a machine instruction signal like this; vid used far more power. Voice would need a bigger boost, but not by a lot. A machine telemetry system would need nothing but a small stellar battery and the occasional charge.

Her eyes swept the room. The units were all connected, all of them powered by the same central system. Except this comms setup.

She could hear Gladkoff's excuse now: *The comms system should have its own power source. It needs to be available even if everything else goes down.* Redundancy was not a bad idea, of course, and if she took the design at face value, it made an excellent excuse.

With one glance over her shoulder at Dallas and their argumentative friends, she drew her spanner over the comms conduit and opened up the power source.

And there, sequenced into the system, were five squat, unobtrusive, pocket-sized nuclear bombs.

She needed Ted. Jessica had some hardware background, but this kind of subtle wiring called for an engineer, someone who knew how to take this stuff apart as well as put it together. She had no idea what the trigger was, or how to discover it, never mind how to defuse it. For all she knew, she had started some sort of countdown just by discovering the things.

The time for subterfuge was over. "Dallas," she said, and looked over her shoulder.

But Dallas wasn't there, nor were Villipova's guards. The only person there was Gladkoff, that same Corps-manufactured weapon in his hand, this time pointed at her. "I think you've tinkered enough, Commander Lockwood," he said, and gave her a cheerful grin.

CHAPTER 41

INTERSTITIAL

reg took *Leviathan*, divested of its comms-locked cargo, mostly for its speed. He could make it to *Chryse* within sixty minutes, roughly half the time it would take *Chryse* to reach Yakutsk. He had never paid much attention, but *Chryse* seemed to be slow for a PSI ship. He remembered Elena's description of Ilyana's shuttle: old, constructed from disparate bits of hardware. He wondered if *Chryse*'s engines were similarly constructed. They would have been better off, he reflected, having traded up by now.

Traded up. Of course. God, he had forgotten he knew her.

"*Galileo*," he said, maneuvering *Leviathan* away from the ship in preparation for taking the shuttle into the field, "I need you to narrow that search for unidented ships. Prioritize ships that emerged from the field in an isolated location, but with another ship or structure within reasonable sublight distance."

Elena, no matter Herrod's manipulation, would never have been foolish enough to agree to infiltrate an Ellisowned station in Herrod's own shuttle. *Antigone* might be a civilian craft, but she was fully idented and traceable, and not even Herrod's formidable skill would have been enough to completely camouflage her. With the cover Herrod had provided, Elena would be as close to untraceable as a person could get—as long as she indeed remained unrecognized. Even her Corps ident chip was long gone, decommissioned. In any official capacity, she was invisible. Shadow Ops would have built her a new identity that would withstand the scrutiny of a place like Ellis.

And they would have found her a new ship to go with it.

He waited, impatient, as *Galileo* sorted through the data, and then she came back. "One ship matching those criteria."

Got you, he thought, and he was half furious and half elated. "Where is it?"

"Last received telemetry at 349.001.224."

"What's near it?"

"Unidentified. Parameters match multiple civilian cruiser classes."

"How fast?"

"Matching civilian cruisers range from .5 to .82 of *Antigone*'s FTL speeds."

Slower than *Leviathan*. There was still a chance he might catch her.

He checked *Chryse*'s position; the detour was going to delay him, but not by much. He would still reach *Chryse* well before the ship made it to Yakutsk. He keyed the course into *Leviathan,* and sent one last signal to his ship to let Emily Broadmoor know he was taking a detour.

Greg was hanging most of his hope on the theory that Elena would have left him clues.

She did not, after all, trust Herrod any more than he did. She would not have accepted this mission unless she believed it was the right thing, yes; but she would have held on to her skepticism, doubted Herrod's words, taken everything as suspicious. He wondered if that was why she had taken the artifact with her; perhaps she thought it was part of the whole scheme. Perhaps Herrod had said something to her about it. Perhaps Herrod knew enough about Ellis to know what it was.

She might have left him a message. He might be able to follow her after all.

He tried to shake off the conviction that she had come to him, finally, only because she knew she was running away. But it was the only way it made any sense. With everything they had been through, all the ways they had let each other down—she had told him, bluntly, that he did not have that part of her heart, and she had neither said nor done anything since to suggest that it was not still the truth. Not even this. Why else would she have put her arms around him, made love to him, said what he asked her to say, except that she knew he would have no more memories of her?

What would he say to her if he found her?

I should never have met you, he thought, bitterness overwhelming him. *I should never have brought you onto my ship, into my life. You have been poison, all this time, and I've taken it willingly.*

Would he really give her up, if he could do it all over? All the years of laughter he would not have had? Would his marriage have survived if he had not had Elena to talk to, to share his good and bad days—or would it have ended sooner, before he and Caroline had torn each other to pieces? Would it have been worth giving up all of that joy to avoid this pain?

You left me to go to your death, he thought. *You gave me everything, and then you left me forever. Why couldn't you choose to live instead?*

"Field termination in thirty seconds," *Leviathan* said. "Debris detected."

Debris. He sat forward, dread in his stomach. "Get as close as you can," he told the ship, and watched the field fade away to starlight.

And he came out into the classic debris field of a shuttle that had blown its weapons banks.

So much for wanting me to follow.

He scanned, knowing it would be futile. She would have been careful, making sure the logic core went up with everything else. The shuttle was too small for a flight re-corder, but it wouldn't have mattered; she knew exactly how to take care of those.

"Scan for other ships," he ordered. "Anything that might have left here around the time of the blast."

Leviathan scanned. "Seventy-two ships within range," it said. "Sixteen without idents."

Sixteen was not insurmountable. "How long ago was the blast?"

"Two hours, thirty-four minutes."

Too far ahead. "Get me the destinations on those seventy-two ships. Extrapolate for the ident-free ships."

Leviathan paused. "Sixty-four destinations acquired."

"Why the discrepancy?"

"Eight ships are untraceable."

"Why?"

"The field generators are not providing sufficient information to allow the destination to be calculated."

"Are all eight ident-free ships?"

"Yes."

"Keep track of them, then," he said, frustrated. Where sixteen had seemed optimistic, eight seemed impossible. "Let me know when they drop out."

Another pause. "Drop-out data may not be accurate."

"Understood."

He leaned back, closing his eyes. He was grasping at straws, shooting in the dark. Even if he figured out which ship was Elena's, she had too much of a head start. Catching up with her before she did whatever it was she was doing would be nearly impossible. He felt it rising in his chest, a bubble of frantic frustration.

I never want to leave you, she had said.

Liar.

"Incoming message," *Leviathan* told him.

He opened his eyes. "Play it," he said.

"Playback is delayed."

Which told him who it was from. "For how long?"

"Twenty-one hours, twelve minutes."

Whatever she was doing, she thought she would be done in twenty-two hours. At least that gave him a time frame. "Override," he said.

"I cannot."

He rattled off his command code.

"Message is locked with a non-Corps command code," *Leviathan* said.

"How the—" He stopped before he could finish the thought, and stared out the window at the remains of Admiral Herrod's shuttle. She had beaten him, then. Becoming a civilian, of all things, had taken away the last hope he had of being able to follow her. Whatever she had to say to him, he would not hear it until it was too late, until she was irretrievably gone, until his rage and fury would be piled upon a ghost.

There was nothing on *Leviathan* he could punch, and that had been shortsighted of him.

He had nothing. Nothing to move toward, and nothing to go back to. Elena was gone, out of his reach, unable to even explain the mission she thought she was fulfilling. She was caught in Herrod's trap, finally pinned by Shadow Ops, and they would have what they wanted: the First Sector back, the Fifth Sector shamed, and all of their power structures fully intact.

And what would he have left that would mean anything to him at all?

He closed his eyes. None of this was finished. Commander Broadmoor had it right: Elena's was only one piece. He might lose her, might never see her again; but she was acting, might still be able to stop the Olam Fleet. With Herrod's comms and Jessica on Yakutsk, he was not helpless. Or useless.

He commed Captain Bayandi.

"Captain Foster," Bayandi said, and sounded puzzled. "You are not in the field."

"I had to take a brief detour," Greg told him. He could not keep the defeat out of his voice. "I have . . . a missing officer." He thought, under the circumstances, Elena wouldn't mind the conscription. "Captain, do you know what information you are being sent from Yakutsk?"

Bayandi paused, as he often did. Greg wondered why he had never found those pauses ominous before. "I am not sure I can know," he said, and his voice held that reflexive apology.

Greg frowned. "What does that mean?"

"I cannot explain, Captain. This is something you must see."

Greg knew he should not have gone alone. *Leviathan* had sturdy defenses, but nothing that would match him against a PSI starship. And he could not forget Taras's surprised laugh at the idea that *Chryse* would see even *Galileo* as a threat. He was too vulnerable, and he had too little intel. And he was so close to an answer he did not care at all.

"I'll be there in a little under an hour," he said.

"I will drop out of the field when you arrive," Bayandi promised.

Greg found Bayandi no less ominous when he was pleased.

CHAPTER 42

YAKUTSK

It had to be a setup, Dallas realized, running down the block. Someone had recognized Lockwood, or something in what she had found had alerted someone. Which meant they wouldn't have killed her, because if they'd been planning to kill her, they would have killed Dallas as well and not thought twice about it. They would have both been on the surface by now, cold and dead, eyes staring eternally at the stars. Dallas, bland and invisible as always, and Lockwood, who would fight them every step.

I only left her for three minutes.

If I'm alive, she's alive. It was the only acceptable scenario.

When Dallas had taken a flat so close to the governor's office, the other scavengers had found it funny: *Dallas has nothing to hide from the government because Dallas has nothing.* The flat was big enough, and it was cheap. Today, Dallas would have paid twice the rent without thinking.

The portable off-grid comm was right where Lockwood had left it, on the table where Dallas had given her breakfast. *Work,* Dallas thought furiously, keying in the code, waiting for the telltale purple pulse across the small surface. *Please, let there be someone on the other side.*

As it turned out, Dallas only had to wait two minutes. "Jess?" said a suspicious voice.

"Who is this?" Dallas asked.

There was a pause, then: "I'm Commander Tetsuo Shimada. Who is this? Where's Commander Lockwood?"

Dallas took a breath. "I'm Dallas. And they've got her."

The voice instantly sharpened. "Who's got her?"

Dallas explained what had happened. "I left for less than three minutes. It couldn't have been anyone but Gladkoff."

"You need to go to the Corps infantry," Commander Shimada told him. "They—"

"Can't." *Do I have to explain everything to these people?* "They're attending Villipova."

To his credit, Commander Shimada seemed to grasp the situation without explanation. "Hang on, Dallas, I've got to call some people." There was a silence for more seconds than Dallas wanted to count, and then a new voice came on the line: a woman's voice, lower than Lockwood's, but with the same reflexive authority.

"Dallas?" she said. "I'm Commander Broadmoor, chief of security. I'm in charge of the infantry. Do you have Commander Lockwood's location?"

"No." *Where would he have taken her?* "Won't be far, though. Hasn't been time. Office, maybe. Behind the environmental building. Small building, no windows."

"Okay. That's . . . half a kilometer from Villipova's office. Dallas, I'm going to contact Lieutenant Bristol and—"

"Can't. Villipova kills people."

"Bristol is a professional," Broadmoor assured him. "He's not going to tip our hand. In the meantime, do you have anyone who might be able to help you?"

Dallas thought of the other scavengers. *Friends* was pushing it for most of them, even though Dallas had known some for decades. Martine had been a friend. Dallas remembered the look on Friederich's face when Dallas had mentioned Martine. *She wasn't just* my *friend*. "Maybe."

"The more the merrier," Commander Broadmoor said. "If you can get to Commander Lockwood without us—"

"Villipova might not even have to know we found her."

"Dallas." This was Commander Shimada. "Gladkoff might have information."

"Meaning don't kill him?" Dallas considered. "No promises."

Most of the other scavengers were out on the surface at this time of day, some of them already stalking the wreck of the freighter shuttle, where there were still skirmishes taking place. Dallas reflected that perhaps the sorts of people who would run through plasma rifle fire for a one-day payout were not necessarily going to be helpful in this situation anyway. But Dallas was still dismayed when arriving at the pub to find fewer than two dozen people, all looking deeply skeptical.

Dallas outlined the situation. None of the skepticism faded.

"She's not our problem," someone volunteered.

"My problem," Dallas said. "Grabbed right under my nose."

"How is that our fault?"

"She's been trying to help us."

Friederich scoffed. "Come on, Dallas. They shot Blair. One of our own people. Just because she looks at you with big, sincere eyes doesn't mean—"

"She did not shoot Blair. Gladkoff shot Blair."

"So *she* says."

"She has no reason to lie about that."

"They're Corps. They lie all the time."

And at that, all of Dallas's frustrations erupted. "I'm the one who found the embedded comms system! Am *I* lying, too?" Friederich frowned and looked away. "Fuck's sake, all of you. We put up with Villipova's bullshit and graft and purges our whole lives. Our parents, too. Shake our heads and say this is how it is, even when one of our own gets fucking vacated."

"That was off-worlders," Friederich pointed out.

"Yeah, and who is it this time?" *We have been so blind for so long.* "It's not the off-worlders sitting on their asses waiting for someone to sell them a shot so they can drink off the day's bullshit. It's not the Corps waiting passively for the next wave of purges, for the next governor who's going to do the same fucking thing this one is doing. Who's supposed to change all this?"

Friederich took a step over to Dallas. "Why should we be fucking heroes? Paying protection to Villipova beats the hell out of sucking vacuum."

Friederich was big for a Smolensk native, taller than Dallas and not quite as slim, and Dallas wondered if somewhere in the man's bloodline was a foreign ship that had passed in the night. Dallas didn't back down. "That why you live your life like this? Because you're afraid?"

"I'm not afraid of anything." But Friederich looked stung. "Scavenging is good fucking work. You've said so yourself."

"Scavenging, yes. Cowering, no." Dallas looked over the others, who were all watching with wide eyes. *Guess I don't yell much.* "Commander Lockwood is trying to help us. Not to fix it for us, or to install a new government, or to take over. She's trying to help us keep control of our own lives, and this Ellis asshole is doing something else. I know who *I'm* helping. You can all fuck off." And with that, Dallas turned and stalked out of the bar.

But walking angrily back toward the environmental dome, Dallas heard footsteps following. Dallas stopped, and turned. Not all of them, but more than half, including Friederich. Dallas met the tall man's eyes, and wordlessly they came to detente.

"Jamyung stashed pulse weapons," Friederich said.

Dallas had sold him some of them. "Not all working."

"We only need them to see one taking a shot," said someone else. "The rest can be props."

Dallas nodded. "What else?"

Friederich looked strangely uncomfortable. "Well. Seems to me if we're going to fight this guy, we should know more about him."

Dallas's eyebrows went up. "You're talking about a comms hack."

"I have this thing I put together," Friederich said, almost apologetic. "I mean, I'm not the best cryptographer ever, but it does a pretty good job."

And in the midst of all the urgency and worry, Dallas couldn't help but grin.

CHAPTER 43

INDUS STATION

The meal consisted of soup and sandwiches, nondescript but fresh, and coffee that was, indeed, very nice. Elena ate sparingly, but her companion managed to both talk and eat at the same time. Mika talked with her hands, and Elena grew fascinated by how often a chunk of sandwich would fly through the air as Mika was gesturing. The woman talked mostly about her next holiday, which she had planned on Circe, in the Fifth Sector. She wanted to go skiing.

"I used to ski when I was a kid," she said. "There was this one trail they blocked off because too many people got hurt. A couple of times people went right into trees, and that was all she wrote, right there." She spoke of it with grim delight. "I'd go down that hill with the wind in my hair and my eyelashes icing over, and I'd think, *Go ahead, trees, kill me. Because this is how I want to go, with the cold filling my lungs, going faster and faster.*"

"So why Circe," Elena asked, "instead of going back to . . . where are you from?"

"Saroseka," she said, easily enough. She seemed entirely willing to trust. "All the trails on Saroseka are dull. Circe's got a drop that's unparalleled. You have to sign a release even to get on the lift to go up. Sixteen tourists a year get killed. Can you imagine?"

"I don't think I'd like hitting a tree."

"But can you imagine what a run it is if you don't?"

I'm sorry, Elena thought. *I'm sorry you won't get to die with your lungs full of cold air.* "Circe's six weeks there and back," she said. "Do you get that much time off?"

"I'm coming up on three years," Mika said proudly. "At three years, I get six months off, with pay."

"That's impressive," Elena said. "Why do they give you such a good deal?"

Mika seemed to become aware that she had been talking too much. "It's a good job," was all she said. "I'm lucky to have it."

Not today. "Well, it sounds like it beats delivery," Elena said. "You don't have any openings, do you?"

At that, Mika perked up again. "I'm not sure, to be honest. But I can find out for you, if you like. You don't have to take off right away, do you?"

"I've got another two hours I could spare and still make my next pickup on time."

"Great. I'll dig around after lunch."

Just then Elena felt a flash of heat against her leg, and she flinched, and cursed. Mika frowned. "Something wrong?"

Elena unzipped her pocket and felt for the artifact. It was still warm from burning her, but it was cooling rapidly. Irritated, she tugged it out and set it on the table. "It digs into my hip sometimes," she complained. "I should have brought the box it came in." *What did you do that for?*

But Mika was grinning at it. "Can I pick it up again?"

Elena shrugged, and the other woman took it off the table, her fingers tracing the edges. "Undoubtedly done by machine," Mika said with certainty. "Nobody does these things by hand anymore. And if they do, they're not this clean. Oh!" She frowned at the underside. "It's got a scratch down there."

"I dropped it at the warehouse," Elena lied.

And silently, her comm vibrated, and data began streaming in. There was no audio associated with it, but Elena kept still, not reacting, letting the comm store the information.

"I wonder if you could sand it down?" Mika wondered aloud. Then, reluctantly, she replaced it on the table. Immediately, the data stream to Elena's comm ceased. "You about done?"

They left the cafeteria and walked through a narrow corridor. Elena remembered the exterior of the station, and wanted to put her hand on the wall to feel if it was cold. The ambient temperature was perfectly comfortable; if this was one of the narrow conduits, it was spectacularly well insulated. Solid technology. *So much good that could be done.*

They didn't run into many people as they walked, and Elena began to make plans.

Mika brought her to a small room with a narrow door. Elena slouched in the hallway, hand in her pocket. The anesthetic patches had been designed to blend with the fabric of the suit, and had fooled the station's scanners, but Elena was not at all sure how powerful the dose of such a substance could be. Mika brought up an input console, which scanned the woman's face before bringing up the documents Mika asked for. "I think," she began, "that if you're willing to—"

Elena palmed the anesthetic, touching the patch to Mika's neck. The stocky woman slid to the ground in oblivious silence.

Elena pulled Mika's simple spanner kit off of her upper arm, tucking it into her pocket next to the artifact. She rolled the woman over, looking for her comm; but Mika didn't have an ordinary dermal comm filament. The comm behind Mika's ear was embedded, grown into her flesh like a parasite. Even if Elena had the medical knowledge, she would be unable to remove it without killing the woman.

You're killing her anyway, she thought.

But even if she could extract the comm, she had no way to tap into it. She'd knocked someone out, risked revealing herself, and for nothing. "*Shit,*" she said aloud.

And instantly, a map of the station appeared before her eyes.

She blinked once, then waved her hand through it, dismissing it. "Map," she said this time, and it reappeared.

She looked down at the bulge in her pocket. "What else did you get me?"

A chaotic amalgam of video and audio began streaming through her comm, and she shut it off as quickly as she could. "Quite a bit, then," she said. Calling up the map again, she began scanning for the main data access points.

She had not been sure, when she saw the station, that it

would be configured the way a typical station was configured, but there it was: one primary data carrier, and right next to it, the main power source. Indus was run by one large, very hot battery settled at the bottom of the station, using the vacuum outside to help it cool. A simple, reliable system, powerful enough to provide energy for the station as it grew, and only a single point to be secured.

Elena couldn't help but think that any decent mechanic would have balked at a single point of failure.

Elena dragged Mika into the corner where she wouldn't be seen from the doorway, then she let the door close behind her as she left to make her way down to the power station.

She wasn't sure if this area was more crowded than the one she had walked through with Mika, or if she was just more aware of being a stranger. She kept walking like she knew where she was going; most of them ignored her. A few nodded, and some smiled, cheerful and professional. *Strangers are not unknown, then.* They all seemed so ordinary, going through the day, fulfilling all of the small, mundane duties that were necessary to keep a place like this running. How many of them knew about the experiments? How many of them knew what Ellis was really up to? Were there any innocents here? How many of them was she going to kill?

Stop it.

She strode casually past the power station access hallway, her eyes flickering to the end as she passed. Unattended. She frowned. Were they so certain of their security?

Did she have to go in blind?

"Do I have a shift schedule?" she asked.

Silently, a list of names and times appeared before her eyes. "Just for the power station," she said, and most of the names disappeared. She zeroed in on the current time, and noted the overlap. *Shift change.* Someone was slacking off. An opportunity, but undoubtedly a very, very brief one.

She turned back, walking as slowly as she could without being conspicuous, waiting until she could dash undetected down the corridor. The power station room itself was open—no door at all, she noted. Easier to defend, perhaps; or maybe only easier to access. How much did they prepare for infiltrators? How much did they assume their preemptive exterior defenses would be sufficient?

It doesn't matter as long as you can blow it up.

She crept inside, pressing herself against the wall, taking in the setup. The battery was fully exposed, contained by radiation shielding; even so, her comm obligingly warned her about long-term radiation exposure. *Sloppy.* She supposed the station crew got inoculations, but surely it'd be easier to just contain the battery properly. All they would need for something like this was some liquid shielding, or even just a stronger gravity field. It might even be spun as a cost efficiency, if that was what they were worrying about. She could probably even work with the radiation shielding they had, bumping up the strength without tapping the battery too badly. It wouldn't take her half an hour.

Exactly the opposite of what you're here for, Elena.

Detonating a stellar battery wasn't the easiest thing in the world, but once set up, the process was effectively destructive. The batteries were not particularly incendiary in and of themselves. The connections, filters, and amplifiers that tended to surround them were far more volatile, but even those needed a decent trigger. Centuries of hideous accidents had made designers cautious. She was not, given the materials at hand, going to be able to cause an abrupt explosion.

But it would be a simple enough task to remove the shielding, and let the radiation from the battery itself eat through the connectors. It would take nearly three hours for the system to destabilize enough to attract attention, and by then it would be too late to stop the chain reaction. It might even credibly look like an accident.

Not her priority, but the thought of it gave her an unexpected sense of professional satisfaction.

"Live and die a mechanic, Elena," she said aloud, crouching down to access the battery from below. The field controls were live and on the surface, but locked. Elena pulled a spanner out of Mika's kit and tuned it to the narrowest setting, working slowly, alert for any alarms. None came, and in a few minutes, the lock assembly disengaged, and the controls were activated.

The battery output was calibrated to the station's demands, in constant but moderate flux. There were three fail-safes, designed to shut down the battery if the radiation output became too great; those she disabled with little trouble. And then she mocked up the station's inputs, slowly increasing the power demand. The radiation shielding would prevent the overload from triggering external alarms for at least three hours; even if the battery assembly began complaining before that, nobody would perceive it as an emergency.

Three hours. If she could keep her work undetected for three hours, there would be no way to reverse it.

Pocketing the spanner, she crept back to the doorway and out into the hall. She began walking again, and someone rounded the corner, absorbed in what he was reading, oblivious to her. When she passed, he did not react at all, and she began to breathe again. She wondered if she could make it back to *Wanderlust* after all, if she might overcome the landing bay lock, if she might in fact escape before the explosion; but she needed to be careful until her scheme hit the point of no return. There could be no alerts, no security alarms, nothing that might make them check their systems early. She would need to blend, as she had been blending, just a little while longer.

She nearly jumped when her comm chimed. "Incoming message from shuttle *Wanderlust*," it said, in a light baritone, loud and echoing against the walls of the corridor. Was that the voice of the station?

Why is the shuttle comming me? "Can you play it?" she asked.

"Command code required."

What? She had no command code. And . . . there was something odd in the station's tone. "Repeat, please," she said, listening closely.

"Command code required."

It sounded different that time, lower, flatter, less expressive. She thought of the long, convoluted command code Herrod had given her, and wondered if she ought to start reciting it. Was this something he had forgotten to tell her? Was this something he had left out deliberately?

"Excuse me," said a voice behind her, "but I don't think you're supposed to be here."

And she was discovered.

CHAPTER 44

CHRYSE

*C*hryse had dropped out of the field at Greg's approach, and for several tense moments, Greg kept his hands over *Leviathan*'s weapons controls.

But *Chryse*'s weapons were registering cool, and the ship made no threatening moves, just drifted at a leisurely sub-light speed on its course toward Yakutsk.

The ship was, in many ways, a typical PSI configuration: a boxy core of indeterminate age, with graceful extensions of wings and branches built up over time. Overall, *Chryse* had a modern look, sleek and avian, and Greg thought she had been rehulled, at the very least, within the last few years. *Chryse*'s shape still gave him that alien feeling he always got from PSI generation ships, as if she had grown from an entirely separate evolutionary branch from *Galileo;* but there was nothing about her that was alarming, or even remarkable.

"Welcome to *Chryse,* Captain Foster." Captain Bayandi

again. *Always Bayandi,* Greg realized. *Never anyone else.* "I trust your trip was uneventful."

"Yes, thank you." He could manage politeness, at least. Whatever else was going on, he would learn soon enough, and then he would know what to do.

"I think you will find our port-side landing bay to be the most convenient for your ship. Will you be able to land yourself? I am afraid our autopilot is not working."

Greg frowned. Uniqueness of PSI ships aside, an autopilot was generally part of a starship's autonomic function. He wondered how serious *Chryse*'s hardware issues really were. "I shouldn't have a problem," he said. "Is your gravity working?"

"Yes. We keep it slightly lighter than you may be used to, however; about .98 Earth normal."

Enough to notice, but not enough to make a difference. "That should be fine, Captain."

He flew around to *Chryse*'s port side, and found the landing bay wide open, waiting for him. It wasn't until he grew close enough for his eyes to take over from his sensors that he noticed there was anything wrong. For one thing, there were no other ships in the bay. For another, the whole place, floor to ceiling, was covered in fine, crystalized ice. With a shiver, he realized the landing bay wasn't sealed: despite the ordinary lighting and the gravity, it was exposed to the vacuum, and probably had been for some time.

He flew *Leviathan* close to the interior wall, then set it down gently, turning off the shuttle's artificial gravity. His stomach gave a mild lurch as he adjusted.

"I apologize," Bayandi said, contrite. "I am afraid I have no one available to meet you."

"That's all right," Greg said. "I can come to you, if it's easier."

"That would be ideal, Captain. Thank you." Bayandi paused. "But you will need your environmental suit."

Greg tensed again. "Why?"

"The interior areas between you and me are uninhabitable." Bayandi said it easily, casually, as if Greg should have known.

Greg unstrapped himself and stood, retrieving his environmental suit from the rear of the shuttle. It was probably only vacuum and not contamination, but he took no chances, testing and retesting the seals at his ankles and wrists, double-checking the readouts in his hood. "Repressurize after I leave," he told *Leviathan*, and opened the door. With a quiet *whoosh*, the small amount of air he had brought with him osmosed into the shuttle bay, and he stepped onto the floor.

The layer of ice was thin, and his feet left a slight depression, but the crystals were dry and not slick. He checked his suit: the temperature in the bay was 2.7 kelvin. Vacuum temperature. Apparently the ship's systems weren't generating enough ambient heat to warm anything. He took a moment to check the bay for casualties before he realized anyone who had been exposed had probably been vented outside. He shivered again, and walked up to the inner door to open it.

The interior corridor was crystalized as well, but this time, there were people.

Across from the doorway lay a man, his short hair golden and straight, eyes staring upward, his face forever confused. He had slumped to the floor, but his elbows were still braced; he had died semiconscious, Greg suspected, when his blood sublimated and froze. Thirty to ninety seconds, they had all been taught. Greg dealt with the remains of people who had died in vacuum, but he had never seen it happen.

Here, it seemed, it had happened to a great many people.

"If you will turn right, Captain Foster," Bayandi said pleasantly, "you will find me two levels up in the bow of the ship."

Greg turned, taking in all of the people he passed. A couple, clutching each other, collapsed in the middle of the floor. A small child, curled in a corner. One person, sprawled in agony against the wall, a shaggy, long-haired dog draped protectively over their stomach. Belatedly, Greg began to count: twelve, twenty, forty. By the time he reached the stairwell at the end of the corridor, he had counted nearly eighty.

"How much of the ship is like this?" he asked Bayandi.

"There is a small area in *Chryse*'s nose," Bayandi said. "Forty square meters. Enough living space for Commander Ilyana. Still, it is not perfect. Even here . . . it is cold, sometimes. I haven't been able to properly repair our heating systems."

Greg climbed the stairs. *Eighty-two, eighty-three, eighty-four . . .* "What happened?" he asked.

"Sudden depressurization and temperature reversal," Bayandi told him conversationally. "It was over before I knew it was happening."

"Couldn't *Chryse* compensate?"

There was a pause, and then Greg knew. "It was over before I knew it was happening," Bayandi repeated.

Greg climbed two levels and headed once again toward the fore of the ship. At one point he saw a wide opening to his left, and he stopped, looking into the cavernous room. It was a nursery, a line of cribs in one corner, pens throughout the room, a larger table, and a play area for older children. He took a step inside, meaning to count; instead, he found himself drawn to the cribs. They were occupied, all of them, nearly two dozen. Two contained twins in matching fuzzy onesies, feet futilely bundled in green and yellow felt. He turned away, only to be confronted by the pens, toddlers lying next to blocks and stuffed animals, boards and art toys. The older children all lay in one group. Up against the wall, Greg saw a soccer ball.

And then he could not see anything anymore.

He stumbled out of the room, horrifically conscious of where his feet were falling, and leaned against the wall next to the door, unable to look back inside. "How many children do you have?" he asked.

"They are all my children," Bayandi said simply. "But if you are speaking of those that are not fully grown . . . one hundred and eighty-five."

Which meant he had not even seen all of them. "How much farther are you?" he asked.

"Twenty meters," Bayandi said, and Greg heard gentleness in his voice. He had realized, perhaps, that Greg was not indifferent. "I am at the end of the hall."

Greg did not look at any more bodies in the corridor as

he made his way to the closed doorway. "Is it airlocked?" he asked.

"No," Bayandi said. "But I can rapidly repressurize this small space. Be quick and you will cause no trouble."

Greg opened the door and stepped through, and the door slid closed behind him. The room before him was entirely different from the ship he had walked through. The walls were free of ice, and were colored a cool cerulean blue, calming and welcoming. The floor was dark, and made of some soft, springy polymer that was kind to his feet. There was another door opposite where he was standing; Ilyana's quarters, he supposed.

And in the center of the room was Bayandi.

The console resembled what stood in *Galileo*'s engine room, a control center allowing easy access to all of the core capabilities of the ship's systems. But the main display was far simpler: no readouts at all, just a row of six green lights. As Greg watched, one winked out, and then another; they came back a moment later.

"Is this you?" Greg asked, feeling foolish.

"As much as anything is," Bayandi told him, his voice still coming through Greg's comm. "I do not really understand the self in the same way that you do. I have tried, for quite some time, but no one has been able to adequately explain it to me. I suppose we are all limited."

"You're a machine, then?"

"That is the closest correct description, yes."

"How old are you?"

"I don't know." Bayandi sounded regretful. "When I was made, I knew very little. I could not measure time properly. I could not communicate well. My children taught me eventually, but I cannot explain how long I was here before that."

"How long have you been able to measure time?"

"Seven hundred and forty-nine years."

Good Lord. Central had known *Chryse* was old, but this was beyond their understanding. "Who made you?" he asked.

"I don't know that, either," Bayandi said. "I believe I did, at one point. But in order to learn to speak with my children, I had to forget other things. Does that make sense?"

No. "When was *Chryse* attacked, Bayandi?" he asked.

"One hundred and forty days ago," Bayandi replied.

"Right around the time the disasters began to happen."

"This cycle of disasters, yes."

"That can't be a coincidence."

Bayandi was silent for a moment. "It was not," he said. "They knew of me, Ellis Systems. I believed I was prepared for any attack they made, but I was mistaken. They accessed *Chryse* via an environmental component obtained six years ago from an unregistered trader. It would have occurred to none of us to check its provenance."

"It was probably designed to hide," Greg said.

Bayandi paused again. "I am, as I have said, a machine, Captain Foster. But I find that explanation . . . insufficient. It is my purpose to protect my children. I have failed. That I was outsmarted by another piece of machinery makes it no better."

"You protected Ilyana."

"Ana was not here," Bayandi said. "She was returning from a supply drop. I was temporarily incapacitated when we were hit. I could not warn her. She came home to this."

Greg tried to imagine it: walking onto *Galileo* and seeing everyone he knew and loved dead before him, deck after deck, his ship silent and impotent. He would want to rewind every moment of his life. He would want to save them. If he could not save them, he would want to go with them. "How did you look after her?"

Bayandi sighed. *Sighed*. What an odd affectation for a machine to develop. "I am not well-versed in psychology, Captain. Many of my children were, so I never saw the need. I told her . . . I asked her to please not leave me alone."

Greg felt his throat close up again.

"She acquired a routine," Bayandi went on. "She would visit them, her daughter and her granddaughter. One day she returned and started talking with me about them, as if she had had a conversation with them. It seemed like a good thing to me, that her mind had brought them back. She had not left me alone; she should not be alone, either. Will she be alone, Captain Foster?"

Greg no longer had any idea what to do with Commander Ilyana. "I promise you," he told Bayandi, "she won't be alone."

"Was he a particular friend of yours, this man she killed?"
Greg shook his head. "I didn't like him."

"But he did not deserve this."

"Actually, he might have," he admitted. "But that's a personal reaction. Right now, I could use him around, professionally. And he had some information I needed."

"I am sorry," Bayandi said, sounding aggrieved. "Had I

known she had such violence in her, Captain, I would not have sent her to *Meridia*. But it had become more and more obvious that she could not stay here."

So in the end, Bayandi had been left alone anyway. "None of us saw it," Greg said. "We saw aspects of her that seemed odd, but we explained them away. And Admiral Herrod—the man she shot—he liked her. He was fond of her."

"Is it a strange thing to say, Captain, that I am glad she had someone who cared for her?"

He supposed it was. Then again, he supposed most reasons people cared for one another were strange. "What can I do to help you, Captain Bayandi?"

He waited out another pause.

"Captain Foster, I have been damaged. I have been able to repair some systems, but others . . . Dropping out of the field for you required far more finesse than I would have thought, and I cannot change my course."

"The signal from Yakutsk. From the environmental system."

"I believe so. I find . . ." Bayandi sounded curious. "There are things I know that I cannot say. Strange. I have assumed it is part of the damage, but perhaps I am wrong. Perhaps this signal you have found is the cause. How is it you found it?"

Greg thought of how to relate the story concisely. "The people of Yakutsk are more curious than Ellis assumed they would be."

"What I do not understand about humans," Bayandi said, "is how often they underestimate one another. That was a foolish oversight by Ellis." Then: "I don't suppose they can turn off the signal."

"We're fighting that fight," Greg told him, "but I'm not sure we'll win. What are you going to do when you reach Yakutsk, Bayandi?"

"I don't know, Captain Foster. I am . . . concerned at how difficult it has been for me to exercise free will. You must not wait. I am under compulsion, and I cannot believe that is for any good reason. I could not save my own children. Whatever Ellis Systems wishes to do on Yakutsk, I cannot believe it's something I would choose to be part of. Can you destroy *Chryse*, Captain Foster?"

No. It was an instant, visceral response. "Let my people figure out how to shut down the signal," he said.

"You hesitate to destroy me."

"Yes."

"Why?" When Greg did not answer, Bayandi spoke gently. "If it is out of compassion, Captain Foster, please understand. Even if I were not a danger to Yakutsk, it would be my wish to stop."

"But why?"

There was a long pause. "If it were your crew, Captain Foster," he said at last, "what would be your wish?"

CHAPTER 45

YAKUTSK

I t's all stream shit," Friederich said, looking at the comms tap. "We can't trap anything like this."

They were standing in the alley behind the environmental building, just two scavengers idly passing time before dinner. Friederich had tapped Gladkoff's comms easily, but there was nothing moving in and out. Dallas, a dubious-looking plasma rifle hanging over one arm, scowled. "Doesn't matter."

"It does," Friederich chided, "if we can get a picture of what's going on in there."

"Working on that," Dallas told him, and signaled Shimada. "Commander. You there?"

"Just about set up here," Shimada told him. "Where are you?"

"We're behind the building," Dallas said. "Trying to tap Gladkoff's comms. He's streaming everything."

"Give me a few," Shimada said. "I might be able to get something from here." There was a pause. "Can you take anything off his comm?"

Dallas raised an eyebrow at Friederich, who frowned. "What am I, a detective?"

"It's easy," Shimada said. "You just need to reverse the tap."

"With what? A folk song and a whiskey shot?"

Shimada laughed. "What are you using to trap?"

Friederich described the device, and when Shimada whistled, he looked vaguely proud. "Nice setup," the Corps officer said. "Streamlined interface though, I'm guessing."

When Friederich looked confused, Dallas said, "He's trying to tell you it's too simple."

"But that doesn't mean we can't make it work," Shimada put in. "Now listen." He started talking to Friederich.

Dallas stepped away, counting on the other scavenger to call when he had something, and looked cautiously around the alleyway corner. No extra guards around the building Dallas thought Jessica was in. The front windows were still exposed, no curtains, nothing to hide them from the eyes of the people who occasionally wandered past. No suspicious guards, or strange shielding on the roof, or anything to tag the building as anything other than another random business office.

No side entrance, either. No way to get in with any stealth.

"Psst."

Dallas reluctantly turned away from the building to return to the other scavenger. Friederich looked up, and for possibly the first time, Dallas saw the man genuinely angry. "Listen to this fucking shit, Dallas." And Friederich turned up the volume.

Dallas first heard Gladkoff's voice, but his tone was far more deferential than it had been with Villipova. "How should I accomplish that?" he was asking, and Dallas realized they were hearing the middle of a discussion.

"Come on, now, Gladkii," said an unknown voice. This one was full of derision, and Dallas wondered if Villipova's attitude had crawled under Gladkoff's skin more than he had admitted. "This is not a difficult assignment. We want *Chryse*. You are to get us *Chryse*. You have any number of strategies open to you."

"Well," said Gladkoff, "he won't want the colonists hurt, will he?"

Who? thought Dallas.

"That's our assumption, yes," said the other voice.

"This should be easy, then," Gladkoff said, sounding both decisive and relieved. "I'll daisy-chain some pocket bombs in with the system. If he wants the colonists saved, he agrees to come with me." He paused. "Are you sure the signal is secure?"

"You let us worry about the signal," snapped the other voice. "Just get us *Chryse*. And don't blow yourself up, Gladkoff. Nobody wants to do that paperwork."

The comm ended, and Dallas and Friederich stared at each other. The tall scavenger was looking more and more outraged by the second, and Dallas had to resist the urge to laugh at him. "You think this guy was going to be friendly, Friederich?"

"Fuck him," Friederich said decisively. "Fuck all of them. The Corps hates this guy?"

"Yep."

Friederich brandished his own weapon, a battered hand-gun that Dallas was pretty sure wouldn't hit a broad bulk-head. "Then I'm with the fucking Corps on this one." He hit his comm. "Rankine. Where the fuck are you?"

"On the other side of the building from you, asshole," snapped Rankine. "Who the fuck put you in charge?"

"This fucking asshole," Friederich said, and played the snippet of comm for Rankine. The woman began to curse. "You still have people in Baikul?" Friederich asked her.

"Cousins. But we don't talk much."

"Well, they need to know this shit. Tell them what's going on. If they've got some fancy new comms system going in, they're in fucking trouble, too."

"Fucking off-worlders," spat Rankine, and disconnected.

Dallas's feet were getting itchy. "That ship. *Chryse*. If Lockwood was right, it's only ninety minutes out. We need to get in there *now*, Friederich."

Friederich rolled his eyes, and Dallas wondered when they had become a team. "You say the word, Dallas, and we'll go in."

"Word," Dallas said. "Now. We get her out now."

CHAPTER 46

'd like to apologize to you, Commander Lockwood," Gladkoff said smoothly. "I'm usually a better host than this. My usual entertainment budget has been somewhat . . . curtailed."

Jessica looked around the room. They were still in the environmental center, but in the rear of the building, where the space had been divided into a half-dozen generously sized offices. Gladkoff had made himself at home quite nicely. Apart from the lack of windows, the room was well-furnished and comfortable, and were it not for the two armed guards standing by the door, it would have passed for a business office, or even a room at a luxury hotel.

She eyed the guards. They were dressed in grays and browns, typical for Yakutsk natives, but even Jessica knew enough about body language to know they'd never pass for colonists. They were both constantly scanning the room, and she recognized their deceptively relaxed stances from her own infantry: they were on alert, and were undoubtedly very good at quickly dealing with threats.

Gladkoff had seated Jessica in a high-backed chair next to a table containing an urn of pleasant-smelling coffee. He sat behind a desk set near the rear wall, ignoring the guards entirely, his regret at the situation apparently genuine. She had always imagined corporate shills like this, apart from the handgun pointed at her head.

You're less likely to miss if you aim for the body, you idiot, she thought, then remembered the dead colonist.

"Gotta say, Gladkoff," Jessica said, just as smoothly, "your story about the long-range comms was pretty good. I wasn't even sure until I tracked the signal that you were lying about it."

"I wasn't lying about it," Gladkoff said. "The system is multi-use. And Governor Villipova is comfortable that I am doing what is best for her city."

He seemed undisturbed that she had discovered the target of the comms, and she grew more uneasy. *I'm missing something.* "I suppose it's not worth mentioning that if those nukes go off, you'll be as dead as anyone else."

Ted would have tried to comm her by now, which meant he likely knew she was missing. He wouldn't be able to try Dallas's off-grid; he'd need someone local to make the connection. He'd certainly comm Bristol, who would discover that her comm—stripped by Gladkoff before she left the environmental room—was off-line. Bristol wouldn't have much trouble finding her, especially with Ted's help, and they'd be able to stop Gladkoff's plan. Assuming they found her before he executed that plan.

But her own fate wasn't her only concern. *Where is Dallas?*

Gladkoff smiled, as if he were pleased with her deduction. "You needn't be worried about any of this, Commander. All of this will be over in an hour or so. Villipova will get her environmental upgrades, and *Galileo* can go about her business."

An hour. That was a very short time. Jessica wondered if Bristol would connect with Dallas, and if the scavenger would know where she was being held. She let her eyes narrow at Gladkoff. "You're *bluffing* with nukes? That seems shortsighted."

"Only if you don't plan things out."

"So your 'plan,' such as it is," she said, "is to sit here with me until . . . something happens. Something with *Chryse*."

"Unless you make me shoot you. I don't like shooting people."

"Tell that to the colonist you killed."

At that, Gladkoff looked annoyed. "That was self-defense. You were there. I didn't come here to get shot at."

Sensitive, she thought. *And ego-driven.* Whatever he was doing, he must have believed it would benefit him directly. "You didn't come here to install an environmental upgrade, either," she said.

"I did, actually," he told her, relaxed again. "It's a nice one, too. That was my idea. There's no reason not to do something good for these people in the midst of everything else. They'll remember that, when all is said and done, not the rest of it."

"Oh, they'll remember the rest of it, Gladkoff," she said.

"Yakutsk doesn't get that many visits from PSI starships. And nobody gets a visit from *Chryse*."

When she said the name of the PSI ship, Gladkoff sat forward, all eagerness. "I know! Isn't it amazing? I knew, when the others lost that first piece of hardware, that this was an opportunity. One little square component, and they screwed it up. And here I am, looking at a whole starship. This is what I've been working toward for years."

"Well, I hope you get a promotion out of it, Gladkoff," she said. "Because an awful lot of people have died for this all to be for nothing." *What does he think he's going to be doing with* Chryse?

"That's not my operation," Gladkoff insisted. "I have nothing to do with the Fifth Sector. After this, though . . . I hate domed cities, you know? Give me a properly terra-formed planet any day."

And before Jessica could call him a snob, the door behind her burst open and the room was full of people.

Startled, Gladkoff jumped to his feet, holding up the gun; Jessica, hoping the people behind her were from her own side, flung herself out of the chair and over the desk. She connected with Gladkoff's midsection, and both of them fell to the floor, but he managed to keep the weapon in his hand. He fought to point it at her and she scrambled to pin his flailing arms. *He's better at this than I thought he'd be,* she realized; and as he grabbed her wrist and yanked her toward him, she jerked up her elbow and caught him square in the nose. He gave a startled shout, and she took the moment's distraction to twist the gun out of his hand. She saw his eyes widen and his palms open, and she wanted to kick him: *I'm not interested in you, jackass.* "Stay down," she ordered, her hand firm on the gun, and turned to see who had come to her rescue.

And found a crowd of scavengers.

There were at least ten of them, and so far they weren't doing a terrible job with Gladkoff's guards. She could tell immediately that they weren't professional hand-to-hand fighters, but they had moved in quickly and started hitting, keeping both guards off-balance enough to prevent them from getting one of their rifles in position for a shot. She saw Dallas, and caught that dark-eyed glance; and then the scavenger was swinging the hilt of an aging pulse rifle at the head of one of the guards. The man staggered, and almost dropped; and then the other guard turned, rifle in hand, and aimed.

"Dallas!" she shouted.

A pulse charge fired . . . and the guard went down.

Jessica joined Dallas in regarding one of the other scavengers with a surprised look. The other was taller than Dallas, and bigger, and was staring down at the dead man looking as shocked as any of them.

"I didn't think the gun was working," he said.

"I didn't say they were *all* rubbish, Friederich," Dallas said. Friederich's eyes stayed on the body, stunned, but Jessica didn't think Dallas was angry with him.

Moments later Jessica heard the cadence of footsteps, and Bristol and his platoon ran into the room, weapons raised. Evaluating the situation quickly, they disarmed Gladkoff's downed guards, and moved them into a corner. "The boss is under the desk," Jessica told Bristol. "And it's nice to see you, Lieutenant."

"Yes, ma'am." Bristol, who was not prone to insubordination, looked very much like he wanted to tell her he'd told her so. She just grinned at him.

Behind Bristol, Dallas was talking quietly with his friend Friederich, who looked more than a little nauseated. *Surely with all the executions around here,* Jessica thought, *this shouldn't bother him.* Then again, she knew from her own experience that nobody ever really got used to death—at least, nobody she ever wanted to rely on.

She took a step toward them, meeting Friederich's eyes. "You did the right thing," she said firmly, banking on her authority as a soldier.

Friederich blinked. "I didn't think I was doing anything. I just—it was—"

"Instinct?" When he nodded, she said, "Staying alive is instinct. Sometimes, so is saving someone else. He would have killed Dallas."

"Don't go thinking I owe you," Dallas said to him, with what Jessica hoped was mock seriousness.

Friederich grinned a little, and steadied, and turned back to the others. Jessica faced Dallas.

"Nice to see you breathing," Dallas said easily, as if they'd met in a grocery store.

"Yeah, well," Jessica said, "it would have been nicer to have avoided some corporate sales drone getting the drop on me. Did you know there were nukes in the env system, Dallas?"

And to her surprise, Dallas said, "Yes. Also know why. Can you cut that signal, Lockwood?"

"I can try," she said. "But what's going on?" Irritably she

realized she was without a comm, and she waved Bristol over. "Give me a blank, will you, Lieutenant?" He pulled one out of his uniform pocket and gave it to her, and she pressed the small chip behind her ear. "Ted?" she began, hoping he was already connected.

Ted's signal came through loud and clear. "Hey, Commander," he said easily. "I see your scavenger friend pulled you out of the fire. Also," he added, before she could snap at him for his frivolity, "Yakutsk is bait."

At that, Gladkoff, who had been yanked unceremoniously out of his hiding place by Jessica's infantry and handcuffed with the guards, objected. "Don't be silly. Yakutsk isn't bait. It's just a base of operations." He looked at Jessica. "I'm here for *Chryse*. As soon as the ship gets here, we'll take it and leave."

She frowned. "What do you mean, take it?"

"It's his mission," Dallas told her. "Get them *Chryse* at any cost." Dallas's accent changed, and Jessica recognized skilled mimicry. "*Come now, Gladkii. This is not a difficult assignment.*"

Gladkoff had to be in some pain. His nose was broken and was bleeding freely down his face, the blood dripping on his fine suit. But he seemed unfazed by both the mimicry and the handcuffs. "They say things like that all the time. But they're right; this is an easy assignment. All I needed to do was activate the hardware control, and wait."

"But . . ." Jessica was puzzled. "*Chryse*'s a PSI ship. They're not just going to sail off into the sunset with you."

"The crew's expendable," Gladkoff explained.

"Just like Jamyung and Martine," Dallas said, and Jessica

was suddenly conscious that the nose of Dallas's mangy-looking pulse rifle hadn't wavered from Gladkoff's chest.

"Did he kill them, Dallas?"

"Him? I doubt it. But his people"—Dallas swept the rifle's nose in an arc before aiming it again at Gladkoff's chest—"yes. Them. That thing that Martine found. Jamyung was right: it's not a thing these people should have."

But that, of all things, seemed to cheer Gladkoff up. "Do you know where it is?" he asked eagerly. "I'd pay you for it, legit. That'd be a bonus, bringing that artifact in as well."

Jessica revised her estimate of his intelligence downward. "I don't think you're going to get a lot of these folks willing to trade with you today," she said.

"You see, *Gladkii*," Dallas said evenly, "vacating people is not a good business strategy." Dallas turned to Jessica. "Can you get in touch with *Chryse* and tell them what's going on? They may be able to disconnect from their end."

Before Jessica could hit her comm, Gladkoff laughed. "You people have no idea, do you?"

"No idea of what?"

But Gladkoff just straightened, his expression utterly unconcerned, as if he stood in handcuffs every day. "Kill the long-range comms. It's fine. It's too late anyway."

Dallas turned to Jessica. "They've already shut down the new env systems in Baikul. Their people are on the way here to help us."

Unity? Now? "Why?"

Dallas gestured with the gun toward Gladkoff's relaxed figure. "Nobody likes outsiders," the scavenger explained, and Jessica grinned.

"Let me back in the systems room," she said. "I'll get in touch with *Galileo*. We'll see if we can give *Chryse* back her guidance systems."

"Waste of time," Gladkoff said.

And Dallas, that rifle never wavering, took a step closer. "I don't know if this gun works," Dallas said conversationally. "But I didn't know about Friederich's, either."

"Oh, come now," Gladkoff said, and Jessica was impressed at how well he almost hid the tremble of fear in his voice. "You're not going to kill me."

"Eye for an eye."

"You already killed one of my guards!"

"That was for Jamyung," Dallas said. "You killed Martine as well, didn't you?"

"I didn't kill *anybody*." Gladkoff was beginning to sound pleading.

Dallas only shrugged. "Boss is responsible for his people."

At that, Gladkoff turned to Jessica. "I have information," he said. "You can't let some scavenger kill me."

"What does the Corps say?" Dallas asked her, eyes never leaving Gladkoff.

"The Corps has no jurisdiction here," she said, and waited.

"Wait! You've got to help me!"

Jessica shrugged.

And after a long moment, Dallas dropped the nose of the rifle. "I guess," the scavenger said, "I really am a pacifist."

Jessica, more relieved than she wanted to let on, couldn't help but smile. "Aren't we all?" she said, and strode out of the room.

CHAPTER 47

GALILEO

The trip back to *Galileo* took less than an hour, but to Greg it seemed eternal.

He had mentioned to Bayandi, in passing, Elena's message, and *Chryse*'s captain had offered to try to get past the time header. "I can't unlock it," he explained, "but it's possible I can fool it into thinking time is not what it believes it to be." Greg had spent the entire trip home with his eyes shut, trying to imagine what she could possibly want to say. She would not have done anything as useful as given the explicit coordinates of where she was going; she did not, after all, want him to find her. But there might be clues, or at the very least reasons why she would have done this without telling anyone at all.

Bayandi had been prepared to host Greg on *Chryse*. The small oxygenated space held both food and entertainment, and even enough room for Greg to stretch out and sleep if he liked. But he could not shake the need to get away from that frozen cemetery. Before he had left, he had walked all of *Chryse*'s decks, looking into as many faces as he could. Bayandi had names, but there would be no way to trace the origins of all of them, and Greg thought someone should take the time to memorialize them all.

He had Emily Broadmoor meet him by Ilyana's cell. She had assigned Hirano to guard duty, and Greg returned the man's salute, ignoring the haunted guilt in the young officer's eyes. It would not matter, he realized, if he disciplined the man or not. Hirano would carry this as a failure forever, and how he processed that would dictate the direction of the rest of his life.

Greg watched Ilyana on the monitor. She had stopped humming, but was still seated at the table, staring straight ahead, her hands folded in front of her. She had that same serene look on her face, and Greg wondered, taking in her wide, absent eyes, how he could have missed the signs of utter devastation.

He knew devastation. But he had never known it at the level she had.

He stepped into the room and stood at the table, across from Ilyana. She looked up at him and smiled, that same polite, tranquil smile she had worn the day she had arrived. "Captain Foster," she said. "Please, sit down."

As if it were her home.

Greg nodded. "Thank you," he said, and pulled out the opposite chair. Greeting him seemed like progress, and he hoped he wasn't about to derail her again. He sat, and leaned forward, folding his hands to mirror her. "I've just come from *Chryse*," he told her.

"Ah." She smiled more widely. "I'm glad you've had a chance to see her. Did you speak with Captain Bayandi?"

"Briefly," he said. "He told me what happened."

No change in her expression. "It upset him very much at the time," she said, lowering her voice as if in confidence. "It was days before he would speak to me. Even then he didn't want to tell me, but in the end I got the story from him." She shook her head. "It was very hard on him. He works so hard to protect us, you know."

"Did you always know he was a machine?" Greg asked.

Ilyana nodded. "Oh, yes. I met him when I first came on board. It was a privilege. Not everybody knows, even now. Renate does, but she could hardly not; I had to bring her with me a lot, when she was little. When she was older, I could leave her with her friends. But then I missed her. Do you have children, Captain Foster?"

"No," he said.

"We have more children than *Meridia*," Ilyana said with pride, "and she has more people. The littlest was born—oh, what was it? Last January? She'd be five months now. Did you see her?"

"Yes," Greg said. He had seen them all.

"I haven't seen them in so long," Ilyana said wistfully. "I used to visit, now and then, but even in an env suit I would get too cold. I kept asking Captain Bayandi to warm the place up, but he couldn't. Something about resources." She frowned. "He can be very stubborn. Like sending me here. I didn't want to come." She focused on Greg again. "I don't mean that personally, Captain Foster. Your crew has been very kind. But I don't like leaving my family. They need me, you see."

"Captain Bayandi says he didn't send you with a message," Greg told her.

She leaned forward conspiratorially. "He wouldn't, would he? He's far more clever than you lot ever gave him credit for. He's more clever than I am, by far. I had to figure it out for myself. He wouldn't make me leave my family unless it was terribly important. And you were here, with *Meridia,* and when you didn't understand, the message I needed to give you became clear. Do you understand the message, Captain?"

I understand nothing. "I thought I did," Greg said. "You said we were too late. I thought you meant the Ellis experiments. The sabotage."

Her smile brightened. "Oh, no. I mean, I can't blame you for thinking that. That's what I thought at first, too. But Ellis—if it was not them, it would be another. I meant all of us. We're all going to die."

"How?" Greg asked her.

"Don't you see it? I can see it. I didn't, at first. But if you look, you see the pattern. Things fall apart. Over and over again. We turn on each other. We kill. We die. And nothing we do changes that. It's too late, Captain Foster. It's always been too late. We've just been too foolish to see it."

She sat back, satisfied, and it took Greg some time to work out why those words made him so angry. He agreed with them, didn't he? Hadn't he and Elena discussed just that? He had been a privileged kid, with every possible advantage, and he'd had his heart destroyed for the first time when he was twelve years old—ripped out by the sudden loss of his mother, and he had never had it back, not really. Instead he had watched it as if it were separate from him as it had been run over, time and again, by orders and missions and loss and everything he cared about that he couldn't save. Elena. His father. *Galileo,* his ship, his home; and her crew, who trusted him. Even Herrod, so convinced that he could fix it all with just one more proffered sacrifice. All of them, standing up, again and again, no matter how certain the failure, and Greg along with them, because he didn't know what else to do.

This woman was saying none of it mattered. That love didn't matter, that friendship didn't fix anything, that the bright, brief experience of life was unimportant. She was saying they should all give up.

"If it's too late," Greg asked her, "why did you kill Admiral Herrod?"

Ilyana frowned then, and for the first time her serene expression flickered. She glanced away, her eyes suddenly skipping around the room, dancing over the window and the ceiling and the small bed, resting on everything but Greg's face. "She needs to succeed," Ilyana said at last, the odd hesitance back in her speech.

"Who needs to succeed?"

"Chief Shaw." Ilyana's fingers clenched, and she shifted in her chair. Greg felt apprehension begin to tickle the back of his neck.

"Why?" When Ilyana said nothing, he pressed the issue. "If it's too late, Commander, if we're all going to die—why does she need to succeed? What does it accomplish if she succeeds?"

"She stops them."

"You mean Ellis."

Ilyana began to rock, just a little, back and forth. "Yes. She stops them, and they pay."

"Pay for what, Commander?"

The rocking intensified. Ilyana took her hands off the table and hugged herself, her eyes out the window again.

"Commander. What happened? Why did you kill Admiral Herrod?"

"He would have told you," she said softly, almost apologetically. "He said he wouldn't, but he's soft, and you matter to him, all of you on this ship. He would have told you, and you would have gone after her and stopped her, because you think you can fix it. You think you can fix *everything*. You think because you win small battles that you can win the war just by strength of will." Her eyes snapped into Greg's then, and her face was suddenly ugly, enraged. "You're a *fool*, and I won't have it, do you understand? Because they need to die."

"We're all going to die, remember?"

"They need to die first."

He needed to push her. He needed to hear it. "Why?"

Ilyana's teeth were clenched, and Greg couldn't hear it at first; but slowly, it became audible: a keening, a high wail, first soft, in the back of her throat, and then louder, stronger, more shrill. And then she was screaming, over and over, rocking in the chair, rage and grief and something worse, all of her fractured humanity howling in that room.

And Greg, who had not four hours ago been ready to kill her, stood up, and walked around the table, and wrapped his arms around the wailing woman, and clung to her as she rocked and screamed over and over and over again, howling into a void nothing was ever going to fill.

"So *Chryse* has no crew," Jessica concluded.

After everything he had just told her, *that* was her summary. "Not anymore, no," he said.

"Then it's Bayandi they want."

Greg was sitting outside of Ilyana's detention room, utterly drained of energy. Jessica had commed him while he was still holding Ilyana, and he had made her wait until Bob Hastings could arrive with a sedative. When Jessica had updated him with the situation on Yakutsk, he had suddenly wondered if his unwillingness to hurt *Chryse* was an error after all.

"He says," Greg told Jessica, "that he's being forced to come to Yakutsk. He can't stop. He dropped out so I could get on board, but even that was difficult for him." He closed his eyes, saw recent horrors, opened them again. "What happens after that he doesn't know, but I don't like the sound of those nukes."

"They're daisy-chained with the comms system," Jessica told him. "But I don't think they're on a comms trigger."

"Can you disarm them?"

"Working on it." She sounded grim. "Gladkoff's an asshole, but he's an asshole with some knowledge. He's biokeyed them, which means we have to hack around them instead of disabling them, and that is going to take a while. And I'm not sure that's a while we've got."

"Keep on it, Jess," he said, then frowned, puzzled. He

could see the problem if *Chryse* was armed and aiming at Yakutsk, but this situation seemed exactly the opposite. "Did Gladkoff say *why* they wanted the artifact?"

"No. And that one worries me the most, Greg. It's almost certainly Ellis tech, and Lanie's got it. Have you found her yet?"

"No," he told her. "But Bayandi's looking into something for me. And we may still get a hit on the location of their lab."

"Yes, sir." She sounded as tired as he felt. "What's going to happen to Ilyana, sir?"

"I'm going to talk to Taras," he said. "*Meridia* should have the right facilities, or know someone who does."

Jessica paused for a moment. "Greg. Are you okay?"

No, he was not. He had never been okay. All of his life he had been shattered, and he had never seen it until now. He fell back on the reflexive lie. "I'm fine, Jess. You watch your back. And tell Gladkoff if he goes after you again, I'll come down there and kill him myself."

CHAPTER 48

INDUS STATION

The man who addressed Elena had gray hair and a bland smile, and seemed neither alarmed nor suspicious.

"I—" *Don't panic. You are a vendor. You are benign.* "I think my ship is having some trouble," she told him truthfully. "It's telling me it has a message, but I can't get it to give it to me."

"Yours is the shuttle in Five, right?"

She nodded. *So much for lax security.*

He frowned, but she thought he was only thinking about the problem. "That's an older one. The eighteen series sometimes had comms glitches. When you get back, you should have them upgrade you."

"No shit," she said, "especially if it's randomly talking to me." She needed to get rid of him. "I suppose I should go back and find out what it wants."

He gave her a smile. "It's a long walk back. Let's see if we can figure it out from here."

Why is everyone here so accommodating? "I don't want to trouble you," she said.

"It's no trouble. I'm a comms jockey on this station. I see hiccups like this all the time. I'll bet we'll have that message in two minutes, tops."

He led her into another side room, a small utility station, smaller than the room where she had left Mika. If she knocked him out, she'd have nowhere to hide him. *You're a mechanic,* she chided herself. *Use your head. Try something other than drugging him.* She stood, watching over his shoulder, as he pulled a spanner out of the kit around his wrist and opened a panel on the wall.

"Indus," he said, "tie into . . . what's your name?"

"Taylor," she told him, and managed a smile. "Olivia."

He returned the smile. "Tie into Olivia Taylor's comm."

"But—" She swallowed her objection. *It's all there,* she thought. *Everything I said to* Wanderlust. *Everything I stole from Mika.* All of her original discussion with the shuttle, taking on her new identity, Herrod's command code . . .

She should have blown the shuttle as soon as she arrived.

Her rescuer didn't notice her reaction. "Indus, can you capture the message *Wanderlust* is trying to send?"

There was a pause, and this time the man did frown. "No message from *Wanderlust,*" the station said. It was the voice she had heard the second time, monotonic and bland.

"It's on the comm," she objected, and the man held up a hand.

"Indus, run a comms diag. What's the lag about?"

Another pause. "Origin stimulus overload," it said.

What the fuck does that *mean?* Elena thought; but the man seemed relieved by the information. "Indus, verify that *Wanderlust* was the source of the comm sent to Olivia Taylor."

"Verified."

"But *Wanderlust* has no message?"

"Correct."

He looked over at her, resigned. "It's on your shuttle's end, then," he said. "You probably need an overhaul. When was your last maintenance check?"

"I can't remember," she said, grateful for the opportunity for honesty.

"Don't put it off," he advised her. "It starts in the comm system, but with those old eighteens you can end up with your field generator out of tune, and then the real trouble begins."

She wondered if she ought to tell him how many times she had rebuilt 18-series shuttles from their component parts. "I'll bring it up when I get back," she promised. "If they can fit it in the schedule."

He laughed at that. "The maintenance people are always too busy when it's someone else's life, aren't they?" he said, and she felt that wave of guilt again. "Are you leaving soon?"

She shook her head. "I don't have to go for another couple of hours." She might as well be consistent with her story.

"Come on, then." He turned and led her out of the small room. "There's an access terminal around the corner—we can check on your shuttle from here, and then you can get back to . . . what were you doing?"

She caught up, falling into step with him. It took no effort for her to look guilty. "I was looking for the cafeteria," she said. "I think I got lost."

"Actually, you're pretty close." He rounded the corner and stopped in front of a translucent panel mounted into the wall. With a wave of his hand, the controls lit up: a simple lock interface, waiting for access. "Indus Station, this is Nikolai Botkin. Connect me with the shuttle *Wanderlust* on Level Five."

The screen went briefly blank, and then she saw a full schematic of her little shipping vessel. "What can we do from here?" she asked him.

"Pretty much anything," he told her. "Indus, run a comms diagnostic on that ship." The schematic was bisected by a bright yellow line that divided, scanning slowly fore and aft. After a few seconds it completed, flashing green. Botkin looked over at Elena. "Must be an intermittent error," he told her, and she realized she was lucky he'd overheard the message. "Let's see if we can open it up a little, hm?"

He chose hand controls this time, most likely to avoid using codes in front of her, and she watched his fingers. The schematic disappeared, and Botkin began to swipe through screen after screen of information, some of it simple renderings of ships or systems, some of it line after dense line of numbers. It took her a moment to recognize what she was looking at: this was a full-spectrum multilevel remoting system. And with the structure of the battery she had just sabotaged, she suspected it had more than enough power to run a continuous telemetry line into an FTL field.

This was the system they were using to control the Olam Fleet. And if she could get access to it . . . she could disconnect them. All she would have to do is get through the top-level security, mock Botkin's—or maybe even Mika's—access, and flip one switch.

She didn't have to destroy the station at all. She didn't have to kill anyone. She didn't have to die.

And Herrod must have known. With all the details S-O had on what kinds of experiments were happening on the station . . . he hadn't sent her to destroy it to stop the Olam Fleet and save Earth. He had sent her for another reason. He had sent her to die, and he had lied to her about why.

She looked over at Botkin. *How do I get rid of him?* Her hand went toward her pocket. There were too many people around for another anesthetic patch; she'd have no way to drop him without attracting attention. She was suddenly acutely aware of the time: ten minutes, easily, since she had sabotaged the battery. She'd have time to stop it, if she went back now. She might even beat the lax shift change . . . but how would she get into the system to stop the fleet? She needed the overload as a backup. She needed to stop the fleet first. She needed Botkin's access, and she needed him out of the way.

Another flash of warmth in her pocket. *What?* she thought at it. *What do you want me to do?*

And as she opened her mouth to say something to Botkin—question, threat, flirtation, she had no idea—the lights dimmed, and a deafening klaxon filled the air around them.

CHAPTER 49

GALILEO

A re you certain," Captain Taras asked at last, something hollow in her voice, "that no one is left?"

Greg wanted to tell her he had been wrong, that there was some hope. "I walked the whole ship, Captain," he said. "And I took a look at the environmental readouts myself."

She whispered quietly to herself. He thought, at first, that she was swearing, but then he recognized the words: not Standard, not dialect, but an ancient liturgy for the dead. "Bayandi should have told us," she said.

"I don't think he could," Greg told her. "Beyond whatever this compulsion is from Yakutsk, he's been damaged. He can't even articulate how."

She sniffed something that might have been a laugh. "This explains a great many things," she said. "I find I'm rather pleased to find out he is a malfunctioning machine. I was beginning to worry for my own sanity." She grew quiet. "We will be at Yakutsk within the hour, Captain Foster. How are you planning to handle this?"

He had thought, long and hard, about the best way to proceed. "Strategically, I want to find out why *Chryse* is being brought to Yakutsk, and I can't do that if Bayandi is disabled." *And I don't want to kill him.* "But if he becomes a direct threat . . . it's our mission, you understand, to protect the colony."

"No less ours," Taras said, and sounded tired. "I shall trust your judgment, Captain, and PSI will hold no grudge against Central if you deem *Chryse* too dangerous to survive. Bloody hell." The swearing went on, more familiar to Greg than the prayer, and in far more languages. "Forgive me, Captain, but I need to tell my crew. We will be some time mourning this loss, I think." She heaved a sigh. "I envy Bayandi. On days such as this, I wish very much I was a machine."

Greg did not think Taras understood the sort of machine Bayandi was, but he did not correct her.

In the end, Bayandi was able to drop more than eighteen hours off of Elena's time-delayed message. "I must apologize, Captain Foster," Bayandi said. "Altering the time skew meant I had to directly access the message. I am afraid I have intruded."

"You haven't," Greg told him. "You've helped me. Please don't worry about it."

He had stopped, he realized, asking himself why he was speaking to a machine as if it were human.

He watched the message in his office. It had occurred to him he might want a more private space, somewhere he would feel free to react; but all of his instincts gravitated toward his desk, where he took all of his professional correspondence, where he and Elena had had hundreds of discussions and arguments, military and nonmilitary alike. Privacy was unnecessary. Falling apart was not an option.

Still, he was unprepared for his own reaction to seeing Elena again, so few hours after he had let himself drown in her. *Antigone*'s cabin was behind her, absent any kind of personalization from either her or Herrod before her. She was sitting in the pilot's seat—of course—and had found something to pull back her hair. Her clothes were white and not black—whatever fictional uniform Herrod had found her. But it was still her, those dark eyes, the angles of her cheekbones, her beautiful lips, her skin, colorless in *Antigone*'s cold blue light, making his fingers tingle from the memory of touching her. He clenched his hands into fists, and promised himself to listen all the way through before he lost his temper.

"I imagine you're pretty pissed off right now," she said, without introduction.

Right in one, he thought.

"But there are some things I need to say to you. There are things I should have said to you a long time ago, and there's no time now. I'm sorry about that. I meant it, you know. That I didn't want to leave you."

Her eyes closed and she took a breath, and despite himself he thought she was telling the truth.

"By the time you get this, you'll know why I had to do it. Or maybe you won't. If it goes as planned, maybe nobody will know for certain. But we'll have them. It'll be down to you, and I'm not afraid of that. I know who you are, Greg, and I know what you can do. I wouldn't have done it this way if I thought there was another answer, you know. But it had to be now, and it had to be me, and I hate it, but here we are.

"And here's the thing, Greg. I know who you are, and I need to tell you something, which is this: you matter. Not Captain Greg Foster of *Galileo,* the hero, the man who can do anything. Not the iconic Corps officer who works miracles. Not Kate's child, following in his mother's footsteps, doing everything she never had time to do, fulfilling the destiny she was denied." She smiled a little. "You know, nobody ever talks about your dad? He's done a few things with his life, too. But you're not Tom's child, either. You are yourself. You make a difference. You have made a difference in my life, just by being my friend, listening to me, letting me see who you are. I've been a stronger person because I've had you. I'm strong enough now because I've had you. You matter, Greg. And it's not just to me, and it's not just because you're the boss. It's because you are brave and faithful and you do everything with your whole heart. Fuck the Corps, Greg. You matter. Don't forget that.

"I've always loved you. I don't know if it's what you thought it was, or wanted it to be, or if it was ever the right kind of love for you, or enough of it. But I love you and I'm pissed off that I'm leaving, and if I could change it I would. But never forget that. No matter what you think of me, never forget it."

And she disappeared.

He stared at the space above his desk for a long moment. He had been so ready to be angry with her, to rail at her pale self-justifications, to use her words to find a way to hate her, to let her go.

Fuck the Corps, Greg. You matter.

"I am sorry for intruding, Captain," Bayandi said gently, and Greg thought, for a machine, he was pretty perceptive.

"That's all right," he said. It was. Somehow he felt better knowing someone else had seen the message. "It's—" *Not what I wanted,* he was going to say. And it wasn't. It told him nothing. It told him everything.

"I'm not always good with subtext, Captain," Bayandi said, "but—have you mislaid her?"

What an odd way of putting it. "She's left on a mission she doesn't expect to return from," he explained. "I have no way of finding out where she's gone."

"But that's not true," Bayandi said, and he sounded relieved. "I can tell you exactly where she is, Captain Foster, because Chief Shaw is with me."

Ted Shimada was fascinated. Emily Broadmoor looked vaguely alarmed.

"He called it a lifeboat," Greg told them, pacing behind his desk. "He said it was launched automatically after Ellis attacked *Chryse*. Destroyed them."

"So it's, what, a backup?" Ted asked. "No. Too small. A comms interface? Some kind of remote?"

"He couldn't really explain it to me," Greg said. He was familiar with that from Bayandi now, and he wondered if he would ever know if it was damage Ellis had done, or if Bayandi's programming had been so altered throughout the centuries that facts had been genuinely lost.

"Is it dangerous?" Emily asked.

Leave it to my security chief. "I don't know," Greg said honestly. "He couldn't tell me."

"Or wouldn't."

"If you're asking me if Bayandi is a threat," Greg said, "I will tell you yes, absolutely. And I say that believing he has no intention of harming anyone. But he's under compulsion right now, and he doesn't know what they're going to ask him to do, and I need the two of you here working with Jessica to figure out what's happening before more people are hurt. That means," he told them, shoving aside his visceral reluctance, "if *Chryse* becomes threatening, you take her out, no questions asked."

When he had dismissed them, he sat back down and straightened his jacket, fingering his collar, and connected to his comms center. "Samaras," he said, "get me Admiral Chemeris. And don't take any *she's too busy* bullshit this time. This is a priority call."

"Yes, sir."

Samaras must have been uncharacteristically persistent, because Admiral Chemeris sounded positively irritable when she came on the line. "Captain Foster," she said shortly, "unless this is about the First Sector, you are wasting my time."

"It is, ma'am. It's about the Olam Fleet headed toward Earth."

"That," she said decisively, "is a hysterical rumor being spread by PSI. Although don't think I don't see your fingerprints on this, Captain Foster. None of us have time for your petty vendetta against Ellis Systems right now."

He wondered, then, if she was deflecting because she was

protecting herself, or if some of them genuinely didn't know what was happening. "Admiral Herrod is dead," he told her.

And at that, she grew quiet. "How?" she asked at last.

"You'll get it all in my report," he told her. "But right now, I need you to listen. Before he died, he told us about the Ellis Systems research station that you—that Shadow Ops—had tried unsuccessfully to destroy. He sent a single officer to infiltrate and deal with the situation, which is, in my opinion, a woefully inadequate plan. And as we now have the location of the research station—"

Admiral Chemeris interrupted. "How did you—"

Got you, he thought. "How we obtained the data is not relevant, Admiral." Now that he knew she was Shadow Ops, he had no compunction about protecting Bayandi from her. "I'm comming you to request permission to assist in the mission that Herrod began."

She regrouped quickly. "Captain Foster," she said, "if you're aware of the subtleties of the situation, you're aware that we chose infiltration for very specific reasons. *Galileo* is a fine ship, but the defenses on that station are like nothing we've seen. Unless you can camouflage your starship, there is no realistic way for you to assist."

"We've been working with a commercial freighter here on Yakutsk. Request permission to accompany that ship on an assist mission."

"Absolutely not, Captain Foster. If your freighter friends want to risk their lives, that's their business. But you are an officer of the Corps, and possibly one of the only ones we've got left. You are absolutely not to accompany any ship, civilian or otherwise, to that station. Is that clear, Captain?"

He straightened in his chair. *Be precise,* he thought. "To be specific, Admiral: you are forbidding me from going after this Ellis research station."

"I am forbidding any member of the Corps under my command from doing so, Captain. And if you try to split hairs on that, I promise you, I'm not going to be shy about making a loud, severe example of your ship and everyone on board, never mind what's happening in the First Sector."

He wanted to tell her he knew she was an imposter. He wanted to tell her he knew she was a murderer, that they were all killers, that he had the evidence tying them to Athena Relay. But now was not the time. Now he needed to protect his ship, and his crew. Justice could wait.

For a little while.

"You don't need to be concerned about the crew of *Galileo,*" he told her truthfully. "My people know their duty, and they know who is in command."

"Excellent." The admiral paused. "At what time was the mission initiated, Captain?"

He swallowed a bitter retort. "0423," he told her.

She sighed. "Then it'll be over soon, and we can talk again. There's a great deal to do, Captain Foster." And she disconnected.

Greg took a moment in the silence. His office, the space where he had spent nearly every day for the last nine years: desk, shelves, alcove where that bottle of scotch had whispered to him, his inanimate safety net. Decisions made here.

Messages sent and received. Realizations. He looked out the window: Yakutsk floated below, lovely from this height, gray and smooth, the bright light of Smolensk looking up like one wide eye.

Galileo. His ship. His command.

Fuck the Corps, Greg. You matter.

He stood and took off his uniform jacket, draping it carefully over the back of his chair. And then he commed the landing bay, and told them to ready *Leviathan.*

CHAPTER 50

INDUS STATION

Botkin had gone rigid. "Wait here," he told her tersely, and hurried up the hallway.

She stared at the wall. The panel was still open, Botkin's access still active. Around her, people were running past, paying more attention to the alarm than one woman standing alone. They wouldn't be able to hear her in the chaos. "Indus Station," she whispered, "show me the Olam Fleet."

The display went blank for a moment, and then she saw a familiar FTL field telemetry reading: six ships, in loose formation, traveling far faster than any field she'd ever seen. Her mind immediately leapt to the implementation details: *How are they generating the extra power needed? How are they keeping the field stable? Off loading guidance only saves them ten, maybe fifteen percent—what else are they using here?*

None of that mattered. "Indus Station," she said, "terminate telemetry to the Olam Fleet."

The interface winked blandly at her. "Authorization required."

Of course. It wouldn't be that easy. She thought of all the cryptographic lessons she'd had, all of the unauthorized things Jessica had taught her—or tried to teach her. *If this was all they wanted,* she realized, *they would have sent Jess.*

She wondered, then, if Shadow Ops wanted this plan to succeed at all.

She heard Botkin's steps at the end of the hall, moving back toward her, the opposite direction of everyone around him. She swept her hand through the fleet display, returning the panel to its previous state, and turned, tense, half expecting armed guards. Instead, she found Botkin in different clothes: he was dressed in an orange reflective env suit, which she recognized as both radiation- and fire-resistant. And under his arm, he carried another.

"Put this on," he told her.

"It's a fire alarm?" she asked.

"Probably false," he said. "But we don't take any chances. It's too small here, and too many of the labs are oxygen rich. Here." He shook out the jacket for her, handing her the trousers, then turned back to the panel, quickly logging off.

As he turned away, pulling a clear cloth hood from his pocket and shaking it out, Elena's comm sounded. Her own voice echoed in her ear: *I don't ever want to leave you again.*

She must have looked puzzled, because Botkin stopped what he was doing to look at her. "Are you all right?" he asked.

"I—yes. It's my comm again. It's—" The message repeated: *I don't ever want to leave you again.* This time, though, it was not her voice, not precisely. It was modulated, flattened, like the message she had heard earlier.

And a brief flare of heat hit her hip.

But what do you mean? she wanted to shout. *You're not leaving me. You're in my pocket, safe, and—*

This time, she heard Greg's voice: *Then don't leave me.*

Reflexively her hand opened, and the trousers dropped to the ground. "Oh! I'm sorry." She bent down to reach for them, and her companion bent next to her.

"That's all right," he said, sweeping them up with one hand.

Behind his back, Elena pulled the artifact out of her pocket and set it on the ground, shoving it against the wall. It should have stood out, square and gray and not flush; but as she released it the color changed, precisely matching the background. She blinked; it seemed to be growing flatter, or larger, or something, but it became hard for her to focus on it, and she had to look away. She wanted to keep watching it, see what it would do; but he stood up too quickly, blocking her view. He handed her the trousers.

"Thank you," she said, and pulled them on rapidly. He returned to fastening his hood, and he never looked toward the floor at all.

"Come on," Botkin said, as she started shrugging the jacket on. "We need to get out of here." He ran up the hall and she dashed after him. The corridor was crowded, everyone moving in one direction. Urgency, she noted, but no panic. They trusted this place. They headed back down the hallway she had followed earlier, and she glanced down at the entrance to the data center. There was a guard there now, but only one, armed but as relaxed as the rest of the staff of this place. She would never have a better chance, but how to escape her rescuer?

"This way," he said, leading her back toward the cafeteria. "It's fireproof in here."

The cafeteria was full of people—at least eighty, she thought, giving a quick count. More than half the station complement. Botkin began talking with some of them, demanding explanations, speculating about what was happening. She let herself drift backward, into the crowd; he caught her eye once, and she smiled at him.

And then she was in the back of the room and out the door, and she was amazed to find herself free.

She turned and ran back down the hallway. Someone passed her and shouted, "Where are you going?" She gestured vaguely ahead of her, and as she passed, she said, helpfully, "The others are in the cafeteria." The person turned away from her and kept running.

She reached the access panel, and as she approached, she saw the main interface appear, unlocked. But before she could reach it, a man appeared at the end of the corridor: a single guard, large and armed. *Damn.* She slipped her hand into her pocket to find another anesthetic patch. This guard was big and purposeful; she didn't think he'd fall for apologetic incompetence.

But she had to try something.

"Excuse me," she said, stepping into his path. "Shouldn't you be in the cafeteria?"

"No, ma'am," he said formally. His hand, she noticed, rested on his rifle. "But you should."

He kept moving toward her. "But everyone's there," she said. "They're trying to figure out the source of the alarm. Nobody seems to know what's burning."

"Just get back to the cafeteria, ma'am," he said, and she saw his fingers tightening on the barrel of his weapon.

"I'm only asking—" she began; and then she rushed at him, as quickly as she could, her hand out; and he lifted the barrel of his rifle and said, "Stop!" and then, for no visible reason, his eyes squinted shut and he doubled over, as if he were in pain; and she slapped her palm on the back of his neck. He gestured once with his hand before he dropped, senseless, to the ground.

She leaned over, taking his pulse rifle. "Was that you?" she asked.

I don't ever want to leave you again, said her comm.

"Thanks," she said. Then she added, "Do you think maybe you could pick a different identifying phrase?"

After a moment, her comm said, *Galileo . . . Galileo . . . Galileo.*

"That'll do nicely," she said, and turned back to the panel on the wall. "Indus," she said, "show me the Olam Fleet."

She studied the schematic, and found herself grudgingly impressed. However they had made the ultra-fast field work, it was the guidance system that was true genius. The ships themselves had required very little modification, because all of the spatial calculations were done externally. All of Indus's logic core power could be devoted to this problem.

Origin stimulus overload. All of Indus's logic core power *was* being devoted to this problem.

One of the targets on the schematic was a different color,

and she realized it was decoupled from the system. Emerging, and probably over Earth. The others were still in transit. *Time's up.* She swept her hand through the controls, looking for a guidance switch, attempting to shut it off; and then a map came up, with the winking lights of the fleet indicators within it.

They would be close behind the leader. She had no time for subtlety. No time for regrets. No time for wondering how many people must have been on those five ships, whether they were trained soldiers or civilians, if they had understood the risks. With a simple swipe, she redirected the targets to the far side of the galaxy, past the Sixth Sector, into territory they had only just begun to map.

As far as she knew, there was no technology allowing for changes of direction in-stream.

One by one, each of the lights faltered and disappeared.

"I don't like killing people," she said, half to herself.

The sound was gentle in her ear: *Galileo . . . Galileo . . . Galileo.*

"Thanks," she said quietly.

And then another alarm went off, very different from the klaxon that had proclaimed the fire. This one was higher, and louder, and was accompanied by an announcement. "Intruder on Indus Station. All hands, report. All registered visitors, report."

Damn. She still had to repair her sabotage of the station. She turned and took a moment to scoop up the prone guard's plasma rifle. The power station shift change would have happened by now, and she wouldn't have the luxury of finessing her way past a guard at this point. She desperately did not want to kill anyone else, but one more was better than letting all 143 on the station die for no reason. She broke into a run. She was sure she remembered the corridor, it was just ahead, there was plenty of time—

"Stop where you are!"

She stopped and turned. It was another guard, twin to the first, down to his very large, very activated plasma rifle.

CHAPTER 51

GALILEO

Greg had worried that Savosky would take some convincing, but he had, before Greg had finished explaining the situation, volunteered.

"*Budapest* is a freighter," Savosky said, getting out of the chair next to Arin's infirmary bed. Arin himself was sitting up, legs hanging over the side of the bed, eyes following Savosky around the room. Greg thought he knew what the kid was thinking. "They won't fire on us out of hand—if they nuked every commercial ship that skulked around them, they would have been long exposed by now. We've got a shot at getting in close, taking out their defenses. Maybe even taking them out ourselves."

"Or getting some people off the station," Arin said.

Savosky shot him a look. "Why do you think you're coming?"

But something must have changed between them. Arin just grinned, and pushed himself to his feet. Behind him, the orange tabby cat that had been haunting his bed stalked gingerly toward the pillow, ignoring the human chatter in favor of positioning herself for a nap. She caught Greg's eye and froze for a moment, then twisted her neck and began licking her shoulder. "You need hands, Bear," Arin said. "And you know I'm fit enough."

Greg raised his eyebrows in question, and Savosky shrugged grudgingly. "Hastings said I could take him home. Wasn't counting on taking him home to stage a raid."

Arin took the opening. "If we really have a chance of keeping the fleet away from Earth," he pressed, "I am going to help. Besides." He grew somber. "She'd come after me."

She was right about this kid, Greg thought. "Regardless of what needs to be done to stop the Olam Fleet, we know Shadow Ops is trying to hide information by lighting the place up. Even if we have to do that, we need to take a shot at sucking every bit of data off of that station that we can." He looked at Arin. "You hack as good as you fly?"

"No, sir," Arin said, and Greg didn't correct him this time. "But I'm a fast learner."

For a moment, Savosky looked furious; but then his expression faded into simple annoyance. "Not going to listen to me anyway, are you?" he said.

"No, Captain." Arin was grinning.

"Then I might as well keep an eye on you." His eyes went to the cat, still bathing herself, radiating calculated disinterest. "I think Hastings just inherited himself a pet."

Greg let Arin pilot *Leviathan* back to *Budapest,* and commed Taras during the brief journey. "I don't know that a PSI ship would be any safer than a Central starship," he confessed, after telling her the plan. "But given everything, maybe you could hang behind us, stay in the field, just in case. If we fail, I'd like someone there who can at least witness what happened."

"Of course," Taras said. "And with *Chryse* having a contact on the station, we may be able to approach more closely anyway." She paused. "Captain Foster, are you sure about this?"

He was, strangely enough. His plan was rash, impulsive, based on few facts and substantive speculation. And he could not remember the last time in his life he had been so sure he was on the right side of the fight. "I believe," he said to Taras, "that we have an obligation to help Elena succeed in this mission, especially since she's out there without all the facts."

"You can't come back from this, you know."

"I know." In his heart, it was already done, and he could not bring himself to feel regret.

"Very well, then," she said. "We will make our way to the station coordinates. As to where we will come out of the field—I will leave that decision until we are there. As should you, Captain. You may find you do not have an opening at all."

He would have, if he'd had to, taken *Leviathan* on his own to go after Elena. He might not be able to save her—and hadn't she run away often enough for him to stop trying?— but he could help. He could stand by her in this fight that they both believed in, in this war that they had been fighting long before they even knew they were on the battlefield. She had said it to him, once: *We never get it wrong until we for-*

get that none of this is about us. And that's what gave him certainty: he was not fighting for Elena, or even for himself. He was fighting for what he believed, and for the first time, he was doing it without rules or constraints. The right thing, at last.

Even if it killed him.

"I'll be careful, Captain," he promised.

"You know," she said, before she disconnected, "you have alternatives here. I know one part of your course of action is already decided. But . . . you and I have always worked well together, Captain Foster. Should you so choose, I would be pleased to continue that relationship."

He understood. He knew of only one Corps officer who had left to join PSI, and the political rumbles had never settled down. *Still, not a terrible option,* he thought. *Assuming I survive.*

"Thank you, Captain Taras," he said. "I'll consider it."

They reached *Budapest.* Yuri, Chiedza, and Naina were still on *Galileo,* but Savosky had no trouble handling the ship on his own. "Rest of the crew is just for company," he said with a grin. "Foster, stay on weapons. Arin, get our data systems ready to grab whatever we can get."

The journey to Ellis's research station would take less than an hour. Greg found the timing frustratingly long, but it was not nearly long enough for him to do what he needed to do before they arrived. The official comm would be easy, he thought; he had already composed it in his head. Chemeris would ignore it, deliberately or otherwise, for as long as she could, but that would make it no less regulation.

Telling Jessica was going to be a far different experience. With her presence on Yakutsk exposed, he was able to comm her directly. "What's your status there, Commander?" he asked, reluctant to get to the point.

"Well, nobody's murdered Gladkoff yet, if that's what you're asking," she told him. "All of our readings are the same. *Chryse* is still fifty minutes out."

"No luck breaking Gladkoff's lock?"

"I'm not sure it's his," she confessed. "It's him on the nukes, for sure. But the data signal? I'm not even sure Gladkoff knows what it's doing. Based on his comms, sir, I don't think his own people trust him very much. They don't think he's a traitor, but they seem to think he's kind of . . . unimaginative."

Greg thought of all the times he'd used the term writing evaluations for his own crew. It was almost always a euphemism, and he tried to leave it out unless he felt it was irretrievably true. Gladkoff's superiors, apparently, thought he was not very bright. "I've cleared it with Taras," he told her. "If *Chryse* goes rogue, *Galileo* is going to take her out. You should be all right there. Focus on those damn nukes."

"You're getting sentimental in your old age, sir."

"It's not just that." He took a breath. "It's that your ship is going to need you."

"She needs all of us, sir."

He said nothing. And Jessica being Jessica, she figured it out.

"Greg. You *can't*."

"I have to, Jess." It was not just his heart. It was the only practical solution, the only thing that would keep his crew and his ship safe and strong and able to continue doing the work they so critically needed to do. "I have to do this, and it has to be me. If I don't resign, either the whole ship goes AWOL and every one of them gets court-martialed, or we risk Olam reaching Earth. Elena believes this mission is worth giving up her life, and I trust her judgment. That means I back her up, and that means I cut ties to the Corps so my crew stays safe."

"You don't even know what this mission is!"

"If we live through this, I might." *How can I explain this to you?* "I could go AWOL all on my own and have them throw me in jail, but this seems more honest. And less likely to result in prison. And it leaves you and *Galileo* and the crew indisputably in the clear."

But she hadn't had as long to think about the decision. "There has to be another way," she said desperately. "Chemeris doesn't understand the whole situation. You need to explain to her that—"

"Do you know," he interrupted, "that I always had an idea *Galileo* would be yours someday?"

"I do not want her to be mine!"

"That's exactly why I thought she would be," he told her. "You never wanted the job, because you could see, much better than I ever could, everything that has to go into it. You see every corner of the workings of that ship. And you've already been in command of her, Jess. You've commanded her through boredom and battle. The crew will stand up and die for you, just as they would me. And I need you to take care of them. I need you to take care of *her*." *Damn,* he thought.

I always seem to be giving people field promotions. "By the book, Jessica. Okay?"

She swore.

"Commander Jessica Lockwood," he said, "you are hereby promoted to the rank of captain, said promotion to be effective immediately, pursuant to regulations. Do you accept this promotion?"

She swore again. "Yes, sir."

"Thank you, Captain Lockwood." He steadied himself. "And I hereby resign my commission as a Central Corps officer, and my command of the CCSS *Galileo*. Do you acknowledge this change in command?"

"Yes, sir." He wondered if she was crying.

"I'm not *sir* anymore, Jessie," he said. He was smiling. He was not sure why. He thought his heart might be broken, but he was not sure how he would know. "Now. As far as this mission goes, I'm going to hand any intelligence we get over to you as well as *Meridia*. As a Corps officer, you'll of course do whatever you need with it; but I'm guessing Taras is going to make it all public."

"And what if she gets blown to bits with you?"

Jessica was angry. She always got angry when the people she loved were at risk. "Then you keep fighting, Captain," he told her. He could not give her orders, not anymore; but he could give her advice. "Every day. One mission at a time. You know how to do all of this, Jess, and you have the best soldiers in the fucking fleet. Don't forget it."

"I'm not filing this resignation until you get back, Greg."

The official message would be routed through Commander Broadmoor, now acting second-in-command; Jessica's objections would make no difference. "Do what you need, Jess." He took a shuddering breath. "It's been an honor working with you, Captain."

"Fuck you, Greg. Stay safe, and get back here, because I want to wring your fucking neck in person."

And at that, his shuddering breath turned into laughter.

CHAPTER 52

YAKUTSK

Jessica looked at her hands.

She had been told, all of her life, that her hands were small. Jessica herself was small, but she had never felt that way. She was exactly the size she was; it was only that most other people were bigger, some by quite a bit. She had met some, from time to time—Bear Savosky, for one—who were so impossibly huge she couldn't really believe they were of the same species. She'd had lovers who dwarfed her, who'd been afraid they might hurt her until she had reassured them.

She was not small. She was herself, the size that she was, and it was enough.

It would have to be.

She hit her comm. "*Galileo,* this is—" *What do I even call myself?* She gave up. "Samaras, can you get Commander Broadmoor for me?"

"Yes, ma'am," he said steadily. Good man in a crisis, Samaras. She would have to remember to tell him so. It was her job to look after him now.

Emily was quick. "Yes, Captain?" she said.

And there it was. "Did he tell you," Jessica said wearily, "or did you pick it up in the paperwork?"

"I was notified as soon as he entered his resignation officially," Emily said. "And between us, ma'am, I'm not surprised by any of it." If Jessica hadn't known better, she would have thought Emily Broadmoor was proud of what Greg had done. "Do you want me to wait to notify the crew?"

Jessica suspected it had hit the rumor mill already. "No," she said. "I'll speak to them in a moment. First, though, I need *Galileo* on battle alert. *Chryse*'s due soon, and I don't know what's going to happen when she arrives. We need to be ready to take her out if she becomes a threat."

"Yes, Captain."

"We don't know her capabilities," Jessica warned, "but the captain"—*what else am I supposed to call him?*—"has some intelligence suggesting they may outgun us."

"Unusual for a PSI ship," Emily remarked, but she didn't sound alarmed. "We'll be ready for her, ma'am."

"Thank you. Commander, how widely known is the Admiralty's involvement in Athena Relay?"

"It's still at the rumor mill level, ma'am, but most of them have heard it by now."

Okay. She took a breath. She wasn't sure she'd breathed properly since she got off the line with Greg. "Put me on ship-wide, will you, Emily?" *Commander. You should call her Commander. She's earned it.*

But Commander Broadmoor forgave her the mistake. "Go ahead, Captain."

Jessica looked at her hands again.

Let's go.

"All hands, this is Jessica Lockwood." Enough hedging. There was no changing it now, anyway. "A few minutes ago, Captain Foster officially resigned his military commission in order to distance *Galileo* and her crew from the consequences of pursuing the mission to eliminate the threat of the Olam Fleet, a task he was explicitly forbidden by the Admiralty to pursue. Prior to his resignation, he promoted me, and put me in charge of *Galileo*.

"I know how you're all feeling right now." That was a lie. She didn't even know how *she* was feeling right now. "Your loyalty to the Admiralty is strained, at best. But I would ask that you set aside your resentments and remember why we're here. It's not for the Admiralty, or for glory, or even for ourselves." *Or Greg Foster.* "We're here to keep these colonists safe. Right now, Ellis Systems is luring a PSI ship to this location with the express purpose of capturing it for their own uses. Regardless of the Admiralty's crimes, we all know what Ellis is capable of. We will remember who we are, and how we've been trained, and we'll do what we've always done: work together, and stop them.

"I have high hopes this won't come to battle at all," she said. "But if it does, I have no doubt that each one of you will rise to the occasion, do your best, and fight as a team, as you always do. I can't tell you, right now, if this is a skirmish or a war; but I can tell you, as long as we hang on to each other, we'll win.

"Captain Lockwood out."

The voice came from behind her. "Good speech," Dallas said.

She turned and found the scavenger leaning against the wall, relaxed as always. "Thanks," she said. Then: "I didn't want this."

Dallas shrugged. "Life goes that way sometimes."

She wondered if, with repetition, she would find Dallas's quiet acceptance too passive. At the moment, however, it was reassuring. "So as it happens," she said, straightening, "I've got a little more authority here now." Even Chemeris's tepid order was working in her favor. "We need to evacuate the domes."

Dallas's eyebrows shot up. "Not going to fly."

Not the first time colonists have refused to act in the interest of their own safety. "Gladkoff is sitting in there, smug as hell, certain those nukes aren't going to go off. But Gladkoff is an idiot, and seriously, Dallas, these are *nukes*. In a domed city. Overkill, but the end result is the same: lots of vacuum, very fast. Efficient little bastards, nukes."

"People live here."

"I'm not talking about a permanent evacuation." She strode around Dallas to the end of the alley, looking up and down the road. She was disoriented.

"Jessica."

"I'll bring some ships down. We need to get people to the spaceport."

"*Jessica.*"

She stopped, and looked around.

"They don't trust Central," Dallas explained. "They're

not going to climb on Corps ships. Doesn't matter if you say 'nukes,' it's not happening."

She caught herself before she reached up and rubbed her eyes. "Okay, then," she said. "You must have transports of your own. You salvage from orbit, too, don't you? And some of your manufacturing takes place on ships, doesn't it?" When Dallas nodded, she said, "Then take those. It doesn't matter how: people need to get off this rock."

"Who's going to tell them this? They're not going to listen."

"You need to make them listen."

"This isn't the Corps. I can't just declare myself the boss."

"That's how everybody on this colony ends up in charge, isn't it?" Dallas's eyebrows climbed at her remark. "I've seen you with them, Dallas. They respect you." Dallas looked away, and she wanted to use her small hands to throw a punch. "And you can cut that shit. You think I'm standing here thrilled to pieces because someone put me in charge? I *hate* this. I don't want to be the one standing up and telling people what to do. But you know what? Someone has to do it, and I can, and my people listen to me. And right now, Dallas, you need to stand up and make your people listen to you, because I don't know what's going to happen, I don't know if any of us can stop it, and I'll be damned if I'm going to stand here watching you wring your hands while we all die."

Dallas's impressive glare, she realized, rivaled Greg Foster's. Jessica had never thought much of her own glare, but she had found, over the last couple of years, that she had power of her own. So she stood her ground, and glared back.

And then, without comment, Dallas straightened, looked away, and nodded.

"Good." She turned to head back into the environmental room. "I'm going to keep on Gladkoff. You get as many people off the surface as you can. And contact Bristol anyway. You may need the ships." Before Dallas could speak, she glared again. "I don't want to hear again how we're off-worlders. There's only one enemy here, and it's not the Corps."

Dallas straightened, and saluted, and she found herself rather pleased that after such a brief acquaintance she could recognize sarcasm. But she saluted back anyway, then returned to their prisoner.

CHAPTER 53

INDUS STATION

Elena had spent the first several minutes banging on the door and yelling anything she thought might make them listen to her.

She started with the truth: "I've sabotaged the station!" she yelled. "If someone doesn't stop it, this whole place is going up!" She didn't say she wasn't sure she could stop it at all. That would depend entirely on the power of the shielding, and how well-constructed their connecting conduits were. She could only hope, on an Ellis research station, that they'd gone for super-paranoid over-insulated conduits. If they restored the battery shielding, the conduits might not give, and the station might be salvageable.

None of which mattered if she couldn't get out.

The door was solid, with no window, and she had no idea how thick it was. The room she was in was tiny, barely large enough for the table and single chair shoved against one wall. She supposed she should be grateful there was a light, from a single anemic panel on the ceiling, but she suspected it wasn't a massive improvement over full dark. *Dank.* Why did cells always look dank?

She returned to yelling, resorting to threats and fictions.

"My shuttle is rigged to blow, and I'm the only one who can stop it!"

"I'm here on a special mission from Ellis Headquarters!"

"Please, I'm having an allergic reaction, and I can't breathe in here!"

But there was nothing, no sound, no footsteps, no answers.

They had left her comm, but she had no doubt it was being monitored. Even if she could speak to the artifact—and how was she supposed to do that, without addressing the entire system?—nothing she said would help. She hadn't hacked software; she had taken down an entire shielding system. Unless the artifact grew hands and a spanner, there was nothing it could do, either.

But the artifact had capabilities beyond basic hardware.

"Can you warn them?" she said, not bothering to shout. "Can you do something, say something, give some alarm that will at least get them off the station?"

Silence. Perhaps her comm was blocked after all. She felt abruptly furious, and she turned and pounded on the door again. *I didn't have to kill these people,* she thought. *I didn't have to die. Herrod lied to me, and now this, and it's all useless.* She wanted to bang on the door until her hands were bleeding and numb.

And then, abruptly, the door slid open, and a hand caught her arm mid-swing.

He was her height, more or less, with white hair and wrinkled skin, darkened by age or nature she could not say.

He had full, fleshy lips, curving downward, and a narrow, straight nose. And his eyes. Elena knew better than to judge someone by a single expression . . . but this man's eyes, as they took in her face, were cold, detached, and very slightly bored. She repressed a shiver and stared back, willing her own expression into that same detachment, and waited.

He let go of her arm. "Why don't you sit?" he said. "We'll be talking for quite some time."

"No, we won't." Creepy and cold or not, at least he was listening. "The station's been sabotaged. If you don't get to the power core in"—she did some quick math in her head—"ten minutes, fifteen at the outside, you're not going to be able to stop it at all."

His expression did not change. "I said, why don't you sit?" And so quickly she didn't see it coming, he slapped her across the face.

She stumbled, reaching out instinctively to brace herself against the wall. *A good hit,* she thought, detached; her vision went briefly double, and a spot around her molars had gone numb. He had not, it seemed, entered the room in answer to her pleas. "You can beat me up all you like," she told him. "The story doesn't change. This place is going up, and you need to stop it."

He stared at her for a moment, then hit the comm behind his ear. "Cage," he said, "check the power systems." He lifted his chin at her. "Sit down."

She blinked again. Her vision was clearing, but she thought sitting was probably not the worst idea. She lowered herself into the chair by the table.

"Who are you?" he asked.

This part was easy. This part was unchanged. She might be able to save this man's life, and the lives of the others on the station, but Ellis was still the enemy. "I'm not going to tell you who I am."

"Then why tell me what you've done?"

"Because," she said, as patiently as she could, "I'd rather not see anybody else die. Which I know isn't a concern of yours, but we're not all inhuman bastards."

His eyebrows went up, and a hint of amusement hit those cold eyes. It didn't improve his expression. "As you've just confessed to coming here to kill us all," he pointed out, "I'm not sure you're in much of a place to judge." He hit her again, this time on the other side. "Who are you?"

That slap was not quite as effective, but it still smarted. "I'm nobody."

"We do not let nobodies in here. You came in on a provision ship. How did you get past our background checks?"

"You are wasting time," she said, her frustration building. "You need to stop the overload!"

"My people tell me there is no overload."

"Then they are idiots." They were depending on read-outs, she suspected. And . . . could the artifact be covering for her? *It's not alive,* she reminded herself. *It's not like it would understand the subtleties. Or maybe Herrod designed it to make sure everything happened this way.* "Tell them to look at the thing. Not just the reports, not just the indicators. Go into that room and *look at the fucking battery.*"

This time it was a punch and not a slap. Her vision dimmed briefly, and when it returned, she could not focus at all. "What are you trying to distract me from?" he shouted. "What are you trying to keep me from finding?"

She closed her eyes against intensifying nausea. "*Nothing.*" Then she remembered. "The fleet," she told him. "I've destroyed the fleet."

And that provoked a reaction. Those cold eyes grew wider, and a glimmer of heat, sharp and angry, crept in around the edges. "Cage," he said to his comm. "Find the fleet. *Now.*"

"The battery sabotage was only a backup," she told him. No need for him to know that she'd been lied to, that she'd trusted the wrong people, that she'd fucked this up from the beginning. "With the fleet gone, there's no need for the station to be destroyed. *Please.*" She didn't need to exaggerate the pain in her voice. "Send someone to look at the battery. You need to put a field around it. You need—"

But her interrogator wasn't listening to her. Those lips grew longer, thinner; those eyes grew angrier, cold and hot at the same time, a hint of madness around the corner. *You don't lose often, do you?* she thought, just as he rounded on her.

"*Where did you send the fleet?*" he demanded.

"It's not relevant!" she shouted back. "They're gone, and you need to—"

He hit her again. "You do not decide what you do and do not tell me. Where is the fleet?"

That punch made her bite her tongue, and the pain briefly cleared her head. "If you keep hitting me like that, I won't be telling you anything either way." She reached up to rub her jaw. "You know where the fleet is." *Those people are already dead. The rest of you don't have to be.*

He straightened, his fury barely contained. "The warship made it to Earth, you know," he told her conversationally. "All of this, everything you've done? Pointless. Earth can't stand against a warship."

My mother. He had to be wrong. Earth had defenses. What she had done was give them a fighting chance. "I suppose I'll never know," she said. "But of course, neither will you. Unless you *get someone to check that battery.*"

"You're a liar," he said to her. "This is a trap."

"It's only a trap if I've somehow managed to rig the battery to go up when someone looks at it." *Please,* she thought at him. *Please, even if you kill me, please get these people out of here.*

It took him an eternity to nod his head.

CHAPTER 54

YAKUTSK

G ladkoff, still in handcuffs, made a great show of checking the time. "Nearly there," he said comfortably.

This asshole, Jessica thought, would find a glare from her nothing but a victory at this point. Instead she briefly met Bristol's eyes, and watched as he edged, very subtly, closer to where Gladkoff was standing. The Ellis salesman twitched and glanced over, his eyes taking in Bristol's weapon, pointed politely at the floor. Gladkoff blanched, just a little, and looked away, and Jessica felt very slightly better.

Dallas had had moderate success convincing the colonists to remove themselves from the surface. Forty-seven Smolensk ships, mostly maintenance trawlers and tugboats, were now hovering above the little moon, carrying nearly two thousand people—more than ten percent of the city's population. But she had been truly surprised to see another three dozen ships—all of them smaller, but still—lift off from Baikul. Eight of them had stopped at Smolensk to take on extra passengers. Baikul had found no nukes in their systems, but there was enough new Ellis hardware that even Oarig had become suspicious. He had contacted Villipova, and in three minutes they had hashed out what the two domes hadn't done in twelve decades: a binding cease-fire. Baikul had offered the extra space on their ships, and in return, Villipova had pledged all necessary medical aid, should the situation become violent.

Jessica suspected most of the people who had been fighting on the moon's surface were still squabbling, but this was more of a step toward peace than she had thought they would ever see. *Ellis Systems, everyone's common enemy.*

She hoped she'd live long enough to be smug about it.

"Captain." Emily's voice in her ear, and it still took her a moment to remember she wasn't listening in on one of Greg's calls. "*Chryse* is coming out of the field. She's on the other side of the moon."

"Maneuver to greet her, Commander," Jessica said calmly, knowing Emily was already moving the ship. "And put me through to *Chryse,* if she'll take the call."

"That won't be necessary." Gladkoff, suddenly neither idle nor intimidated by Bristol, reached up with his bound hands and touched his comm. "Captain Bayandi, I presume," he said. "How nice to finally meet you."

There was a pause, and then Bayandi's voice came over Gladkoff's comm. "Who are you?"

He did not, Jessica thought, sound like a congenial old man anymore. Any hint of warmth or pleasantness was gone.

"Who I am is not important," Gladkoff said.

"Don't be so modest," Jessica snapped. "You're the one who's been controlling him."

"Who is speaking?" Bayandi asked.

"It's Commander Lockwood, sir," she said. *Captain Lockwood now.*

"And are you working with this . . . person?"

Absolute frigid disdain. *So he* can *be intimidating.* "I am not, sir. I'm here to protect Yakutsk, and you, if it's possible."

Gladkoff broke in, his voice reassuring. "I'm here to protect Yakutsk as well. And you can help me with that, Captain Bayandi."

There was a pause. "Yakutsk is at peace," Bayandi said. "The fighting on the surface has ceased. Several thousand colonists are currently off the surface, but the others are alive. Breathing. Warm." Jessica thought she caught something in his voice with that last word, and had to remind herself he was a machine. "I think you are a liar."

Gladkoff laughed. "I'm many things, Captain, but a liar is not one of them. My proposal for you is simple: come back with me to one of our research stations, and Yakutsk will be quite safe."

"And if I refuse?"

"If you know the people in the domes are currently alive and well, then you know what I can do."

And just then, there was a quiet voice in Jessica's ear. "Lockwood."

She stepped backward, whispering. "Dallas?"

"That long-range comms, Lockwood. It's broadcasting, and not just to the PSI ship. Whatever you're talking about in that room, it's going out to someone else."

Shit. "Where are you?"

"I'm in the machine room."

"Why the hell didn't you get off the planet?"

Dallas made an exasperated sound. "Can we encrypt the signal without triggering the nukes? Screw up what they're getting?"

She shook her head. "It would take too long. And without knowing how Gladkoff's set up the nukes, it'd be too dangerous. Try to find out where it's going."

"Not a comms hacker, Lockwood."

"Well, do the best you can." She thought she knew who it was going to; the precise location was irrelevant. "If you're going to be stupid enough to stay here, make yourself useful."

"Yes, Captain."

She had the distinct impression Dallas was saluting her again. "But really, screw that. You should get off this fucking rock, Dallas."

"You be careful, too, Lockwood," Dallas said, and disconnected.

She turned; Gladkoff was still explaining the nukes to Bayandi, who surely already knew it all. "It's very simple. Airlifts or not, there are still twenty thousand people on this moon. And if you refuse to come with us, they will all die."

"As will you," Bayandi pointed out.

"But you won't allow so many deaths," Gladkoff went on, as if Bayandi had not spoken. "I know what you are. I know your programming. Twice the population that was lost at Athena Relay. Give us control of your nav systems, Captain, and I will disable the weapons."

There was a long silence, and it took Jessica a moment to

recognize what was strange about it: she could hear Bayandi *breathing*. And then, his voice no longer cold and threatening, he said, "No."

Gladkoff blinked. "What?"

Bayandi sighed. "You say that you know what I am. I am afraid that I know what you are, as well, Gladkoff." And with a shiver, Jessica realized Bayandi knew far more about the situation than Gladkoff had assumed. "You are human. You have approached this with a human calculus, with the perspective of a human life span. I have lived more than seven hundred years. I have seen far more than twenty thousand people die. I have no wish to cause more deaths, but I know what Ellis would do with me, and I know twenty thousand people is not all there are." He paused, and his next words were full of his old familiar gentleness. "I am sorry, Commander Lockwood."

Her throat abruptly thickened. "That's all right, Captain," she told him. "I think my calculus is closer to yours."

Gladkoff looked confused. "I—you *can't*," he said. But Bayandi wouldn't respond anymore.

Gladkoff's comm sounded again, and he touched his ear apprehensively. "Yes?" This time he kept the response silent, but Jessica saw him go white. "I—yes. Of course." He disconnected, and turned to Jessica. "I've been instructed to disable the nukes. I'll need to get to the machine room."

She and Bristol escorted him. Dallas was there, frowning at the comms readout, scrolling through the data and squinting. She glanced at the display; Dallas hadn't been able to encrypt the signal itself, but the destination was highlighted on the map: Ellis's secret station. Where Elena had gone.

Why am I not surprised?

Gladkoff went up to the panel with the exposed nukes. "What's to stop you from killing me when I shut them down?" he asked.

Jessica shrugged. "It's not my call, really."

Dallas was still working with the comms data, and did not turn around. "You'll be tried for the shooting from yesterday. Deportation is most likely."

"But you won't space me."

Dallas's smile was dry. "Not today."

Gladkoff turned, and laid his hand against the panel's controls, and spoke a few words. "They're off."

Jessica hit her comm. "Captain Bayandi. Are you still under compulsion?"

There was a pause. "Yes, Commander."

She glared at Gladkoff, but he was only frowning. "I don't understand," he said, mostly to himself. "I've turned it off. The nukes are off-line. The nav directive should have ended."

"Commander Lockwood," Bayandi said, and his voice sounded strange and distant. "I have been redirected."

Well, this can't be good. "To where?"

"I am . . . directed to fly into the surface of Yakutsk."

"And what will that do?"

But she knew before he spoke. "It will kill everyone," Bayandi said, confirming her fear. "It will pull the moon apart."

CHAPTER 55

INDUS STATION

ell, open the damn battery up," Elena's jailor was saying. "I don't care what it's reading." Another pause. "If it's radioactive enough to kill you, you idiot, we're all dead anyway!"

The lights in the brig flared brightly, then went off. A moment later the emergency lighting in the floor came on, illuminating her captor's odd features from below, and then an alarm began to sound.

Every thread of hope she'd had disappeared.

Her captor shouted over the comm. "Cage. Cage!" Then he turned, leaning over her and grabbing her shoulders, shaking her, making her head hurt. "What have you done?" he demanded again.

"I told you." She had no energy anymore—frustration had drained her of fear. "I've destroyed your station."

"How do I stop it?"

Too late. "You can't."

His wide eyes were furious. He threw her back in the

chair and opened the door, stepping out into the hall, where all the lights had gone red. She could hear running footsteps; as he stopped someone, she heard an explosion in the distance. "What's going on?" her captor shouted.

"The generator blew," the man said hastily. "The fail-safe, too. This whole place is going up in less than ten minutes."

"How do we fix it?"

"There's no fixing it." The man wrenched away and ran.

Her interrogator stood for a moment, and she saw his fists clench. Then he turned, fury on his face, and stormed back into the room. "You will stop this!" he shouted at her.

"I can't."

"You think you'll get back to your ship? You'll die with the rest of us."

"It wouldn't matter if I did get back to my ship," she told him. He knew all of this. "The landing decks are locked. Nobody is getting off this station. No matter how highly placed they are."

He could see it in her face, she knew: the truth of what she had done, the truth of his own death. He raged, hitting her again, over and over, until she thought she would black out; and then he pulled his gun and braced the barrel against her forehead.

"If I'm going to die," he snarled at her, "I'll see your brains on that back wall before I go."

She kept her eyes open, staring at him—

—and something outside the room exploded, taking out the door and most of the section of hallway. Elena was flung through the air and into the rear wall. She slid onto the floor, and something heavy dropped on top of her. When everything around her stopped falling, she opened her eyes, and saw her captor—or rather, part of him. The left side of his face was burned black, and most of the back of his head was gone. One staring eye pointed more or less in her direction. Flesh, bone, and blood were dripping onto her face.

Good timing, she thought.

As she listened to the klaxons her vision began to dim. She could not find it in herself to be too sad. She had succeeded, after all. She had stopped the Olam Fleet—or most of it, anyway. Earth would survive, she was sure. They would be all right. All of them—her mother, Greg's father, their families. That this whole place was going up, and everyone with it—the guilty and the innocent, all at once—was not perfect. Not how she had wanted to die. But at least she was dying in the line of duty, and that was all right.

A pair of legs appeared next to her, feet in short boots standing next to her head. She had not heard the steps. As she frowned at the toes of the boots, wondering why they looked familiar, the person squatted in front of her. Bright hair, blue eyes, petite, lovely in a way Elena had never been: her mother. *Her mother.* What was she doing here?

"Are you going to die here," her mother asked, "underneath a dead lunatic?"

Elena blinked at her, waiting for her to disappear. She didn't.

"I don't think it matters, Mama," she said.

"If you get up," her mother suggested, "you could make it to an airlock. You could see the stars."

"One last time?"

"You could leave the station," her mother said. "You

don't have to die here. You could be out there, with the stars. In the open. At home."

That . . . that sounds lovely. "I'm tired, Mama," she said, and she was.

"Some things need doing," her mother said gently, "even when you're tired. Get up, Elena."

CHAPTER 56

BUDAPEST

Weapons live," Savosky said.

"You've got shit for weapons on this thing," Greg pointed out.

"She's got enough to take a bite out of them before they kill us. Arin?"

"Data capture is ready," Arin confirmed.

Greg hit his comm. "Captain Taras?"

"We're ready here, Captain."

He did not correct her. For her, he supposed it was a part of his name. There would be time later—perhaps—to establish new protocols. "Then let's do this."

They had decided, in the end, to have *Meridia* drop out first. Greg had argued with Taras on that, believing that an errant freighter would be less likely to be seen as suspicious; but she pointed out that a PSI starship was a drastically different political entity than a commercial freighter. "Blowing away one little freighter can be brushed off as a mistake, if anyone notices at all," she said. "If they shoot at us, they'll expose themselves, and make an awful lot of enemies they do not want."

Privately, Greg held out hope that Bayandi would be able to do something via the artifact. He wondered if Elena knew what it was, or if she had only brought it along out of sentiment. Bayandi said it had been active for a while, which meant she had been in contact with it. He wondered if it had spoken to her again, and what it might have said.

He wondered if she would listen.

He wondered if she was still alive.

Meridia dropped out, and he held his breath, waiting for a warning comm from the station, waiting to hear the telltale alarm indicating she had been fired upon, or destroyed. But there was silence, and Savosky, paying more attention to his flying than Greg's anxieties, dropped them out of the field.

The station was hanging there, industrial and utilitarian, not looking at all like the place that would build stealth weapons or direct an invasion fleet to Earth. It might have been any other commercial manufacturing station, except that it was silent.

"Taras?" Greg asked.

"Their sensors are live," Taras said, puzzled. "As far as I can tell they should've detected us. But they're not reacting at all. No weapons locks, no comms, nothing."

"On your toes," Greg said, his stomach knotting. "Herrod said it came suddenly. If we—"

The bottom of the station, as blandly geometric as the rest of it, burst suddenly into a fireball and dissipated into pieces.

Elena. "What was that?" he asked.

Arin replied. "Their battery containment. I'm pulling data now, and it's telling me . . . the station's going to go up, Captain."

Greg abandoned the weapons console and ran down the hall toward *Budapest*'s landing bay. "How long?"

"Ten minutes. At the outside."

Taras took care of sending the message for them. "Indus Station," she said, "we are prepared to offer airlift to your people. Proceed to the airlocks. Leave your weapons behind."

"What's the complement on that station?" Greg asked.

"According to what I'm seeing here," Arin told him, "one hundred and forty-three."

They had nothing like enough space for that many. *Damn*. "Taras?"

"Our enemy is not going to be space, Captain Foster. It will be time. They have five airlocks—with you and Captain Savosky, we will have eight ships."

"Arin," Savosky was saying, "stay here. If we get caught in the blast, get away from here, and get that data out. Stream it raw if you have to, but make it public." He appeared at the doorway of the landing bay, and headed for the shuttle next to Greg's. "You ever flown a freighter shuttle, Foster?" he asked, as Greg climbed aboard a shuttle and powered up the engines.

"Sure," Greg told him. "Twenty years ago, when I was still living with my dad."

"They steer just like a fighter," Savosky told him, "except you feel it all the way down to your heels."

"I have no idea what that means," Greg said, and Savosky laughed.

"It means," he said, "don't crash my ship, Foster. Now let's haul some people out of there."

Greg did not dare hope Elena would be one of them.

CHAPTER 57

INDUS STATION

Elena got up.

She shoved the interrogator off her, and more bits of him came off. The smell of the dead man was appalling, but it was rapidly overwhelmed by the odor of burning metal and chemical from the hallway. She rolled to her knees and almost collapsed. There was something terribly wrong with her right hip, which seemed to be unable to hold her weight or to make much progress controlling her leg. She put a palm on the wall and pushed herself to her feet with her left leg, but the pain nearly made her black out.

"It's not far," her mother said. "You can do this, Elena."

I don't know about that, she thought. But she levered herself forward, lurching against the wall toward the door. She was leaving great smears of blood on the dank gray walls; hers or his, she didn't know. The contrast of colors was almost beautiful.

Out in the hallway, her mother was looking from side to

side, watching the people go by. "It's faster this way," she said, gesturing toward a small auxiliary corridor.

Elena frowned. "Then why are the others going that way?"

"They're looking for escape ships. You only need to get outside."

How do you know that? She grasped the doorframe and gave herself a push, reaching out for the opposite wall. Her weight shifted briefly onto her right foot, and agony shot through her, toes to scalp, so sharp it woke her up even as she nearly blacked out. Suddenly she felt everything: the arrhythmic vibrations shuddering through the walls and the floor beneath her feet, the lights, dim and bright in turns, the smell of electricity and human sweat and, yes, blood, not just on her, but all around. Her eyes swept the hallway. The blast that had taken out her captor had taken out three people on the other side of the wall. Or maybe more; she couldn't identify all the pieces. Carnage and suffering. *My doing.*

"You can't help them now," her mother said gently. "Come along, Elena."

Everyone was yelling, and there were alarms, and for a moment it was too much. Someone ran past her and bumped into her, and she collapsed again, cursing. *Stars,* she thought, and clung to the wall again.

Her stomach lurched briefly; the gravity systems were going. Her eyes skimmed the wall; no grip. Gravity might give her hip a break, but she'd have some trouble guiding herself through the unfamiliar halls. Straightening as best she could, she limped forward, pushing at the wall, doing her best to keep the weight off her bad leg, ignoring the motes flashing before her eyes every time her right foot brushed the ground.

She came around a corner and stopped. There was the familiar utility room, and there were Mika's feet, just where Elena had left them.

"Elena," her mother said, warning in her voice.

"I need to bring her." Mika had screwed up and allowed Elena to succeed, and she was going to miss her vacation and die because she had been kind. She deserved the stars, too. It was all Elena could give her.

Elena thought her mother would argue, but instead she only said, "You need to hurry."

Elena pushed herself into the room and looked around. Mika's uniform was too fitted to hook anything into it; Elena would need to find something she could loop around the woman, something she could use to drag her. Spying a cabinet, she pulled it open and found a long cabled loop of temporary lighting. She pulled out a length and tugged experimentally; she'd have to double it, but it might be strong enough. Her hands were shaking, and she was grateful her plan required no fine work.

She doubled the loop and ran it around Mika's chest and under her armpits, then ran it around her own waist, threading it through a loop in her trousers. She took an experimental step and had to stop, gasping; Mika's weight pulled at her hip, and Elena could feel things giving inside of her that weren't supposed to be moving at all. But she didn't lose consciousness; indeed, the motes grew no worse. Whether that was a good sign or a bad one, she didn't know.

Her lurching was much less efficient, but she managed to keep Mika sliding along behind her, still unconscious. Or possibly dead—it hadn't occurred to Elena to check, and there was no time now to stop. *Why does it matter?* a part of herself asked. *Because it does,* came the answer, and she nearly laughed when she realized that was all the logic she had left.

She could feel it in the wall, every step she took, every time she slid her palm forward: the station was coming apart. The vibrations were becoming stronger, and a rhythm was taking over: pressure was building, trying to escape, and eventually it would find a way, taking them all to pieces.

She turned a corner, and forty meters ahead she saw the airlock door. Her heart actually leapt when she saw it: she would have her stars after all. "I don't know how to open it," she said.

"Hang on," her mother said, and ran ahead of them. She did something Elena couldn't see, and the inner airlock door slid open. The outer door was translucent, but the hallway was too bright for her to make out many stars from here.

She would have to go out. She would see better when she went out.

Twenty steps, then ten; and then she was dragging Mika into the little room. She unhooked the makeshift harness and fell forward, hands on the airlock door. She blinked into the darkness, and they came into focus: all those tiny lights, a million million suns, places she had never been, would never see. Peaceful, eternal, welcoming, giving her warmth and company all of her life, since she was a little girl. *Do you remember,* she wanted to ask her mother, *when*

I told you I wanted to sleep on the roof? You said no, and I was so angry. And you put in a skylight in my room, and I slept under the stars anyway. You never told me I was silly. You never told me I was wrong. My first memory, Mama. My last memory, too.

She was on the floor. She glanced up at the wall; the air-lock controls were above her, out of her reach. This would have to be enough, then. She let herself slump against the door, and put her palm against it. Insulated against the vacuum: she couldn't feel the cold. She knew the cold would be too harsh for her, uncomfortable, but she felt a pang of regret. So close. *So close . . .*

The light crept into the corners of her vision, and brightened until she couldn't see. She blinked against it, hearing voices around her; someone was talking over the comms system. Warnings, instructions, something; the usual cacophony of disaster, of people denying the inevitable. *Stars,* she thought. *Stars.*

And then a shadow appeared in the light, and she blinked at it. Not her mother this time. Someone much larger, much wider, and when she saw the light reflecting off of a bald head, she knew. "Bear," she said, and smiled. "I didn't think it would be you." She supposed it was all right, that it was Bear. Maybe it meant he had forgiven her. Maybe it meant she had forgiven herself.

"Be still, Lanie," he said.

He looked worried. *How strange,* she thought. *He shouldn't worry. Everything's all right now.* "Everything's all right now," she said, trying to reassure him.

"Hush." He was reaching out toward her, but she couldn't feel anything. "I've got you. I've got her," he added, and she wondered who he was talking to.

She kept looking at his head, covered in intricate tattoos. She had thought they were all abstract, but here, in this bright light, she thought she could see faces in there as well. She had always meant to ask him about them, to find out what they meant to him, but it had seemed such a personal question. "Do you know," she said, "you have the most beautiful head I've ever seen."

"Don't talk," he said shortly.

"My uncle thought I'd be scared of you," she told him, thinking back to their first meeting. "But you weren't scary at all. You treated me just like everybody else." She frowned. "Do you know, I don't think anybody had ever done that for me before? Just treated me like a regular mechanic. Not like some stupid kid playing at being an adult. And then your pilot did that awful inversion, on purpose just to get at me, and made me throw up. I was so mad."

"Sweetheart." There was something strange in his voice. "Be still. Don't move, honey."

"Doesn't matter," she told him. "It's nice to see you, Bear. I didn't think it would be you, but I'm glad it is." She wasn't sure her words were coming out of her mouth as clearly as they sounded in her head. "I should have thanked you earlier, you know. For helping me. For giving me a place to go, and a purpose. I should have thanked a lot of people. There's never any time."

Bear was shouting at someone, and she could see other

silhouettes behind him, and she was getting so tired. She couldn't see her mother anymore, but that was all right; she was here with her friends, and there were stars, even if she couldn't see them anymore. She was warm. She was safe. She was home.

"Tell Greg," she said, and that was all.

CHAPTER 58

YAKUTSK

ommander?" Jessica said into her comm.

"We're moving," Emily Broadmoor said. "He's on the other side of the moon." There was a pause. "Captain . . . we're not going to make it in time. Once we get there, if we shoot him down, the debris will shred the whole place."

"You've got to try anyway!" Jessica shouted. "At least there's a chance."

"Commander Broadmoor is right," Bayandi said. He was sounding more detached. "I will be far too close by then. If I . . ." He fell silent.

"Can you self-destruct, Bayandi?" There was nothing, and she rounded on Gladkoff. "Turn it off!" she shouted at him.

"I—" He still looked confused. "This makes no sense. The nukes and the comms were linked. I turn off the nukes, the comms compulsion goes off."

"Did you write the programming," Jessica asked, "or did they?"

"They wouldn't set me up like that." He sounded so certain.

"If *Chryse* crashes into this moon," she said, "there's a good chance her logic core will survive, not to mention her other components. Not as good as having Bayandi whole and operating, but a whole lot better than nothing. You're expendable, Gladkoff. Just like the rest of us." She turned to Dallas. "We need to get this comms system shut down."

"If it's dumped programming into him," Dallas said, "it won't matter."

"We have to do something!" she shouted. Furiously she began rummaging through the system that had become so familiar to her. "Gladkoff, are you sure these nukes are off-line?"

"I—I'm not sure of anything anymore."

They want Chryse. They don't want a heap of radioactive melted metal. "Help me shut this shit down," she snapped at him.

"I don't know how."

"You installed it!"

"They gave me plans. They—"

"Then use the brains you were born with and reverse-engineer what you did!" She began terminating connections, severing each line to the outgoing telemetry. But every time she took one out, another one sprouted. *This thing is a fucking Hydra.* Beside her, Dallas was doing the same with what appeared to be slightly more success; the outgoing stream was growing thinner.

Even with Dallas's skill, they would never make it in time.

"Dallas, is there a dome breach alarm? Some kind of siren we could sound to let everyone know to jump into their suits?"

"In Villipova's office."

"Go," she said. "Trigger it. I'm going to shut down the power to this whole installation." She glared at Gladkoff, daring him to challenge her. "You may want to find a suit somewhere," she said to him.

"So might you," Dallas pointed out.

"Unless you have a better idea, go set off that alarm!" she shouted. Dallas fled, and she kept terminating connections; she was getting ahead of the tide, but not by much. "Bayandi?"

"I cannot stop." He sounded misty, like a sleepwalker. "I cannot stop."

"Hang on," she told him.

A moment later a klaxon sounded, through the air and over the comm system. *How long does it take people to get into env suits? How long will the air last once I pull the power on this thing?* No time for calculations. No time for safety margins.

She looked up; directly above them, growing larger against the dark sky, was the bright shape of *Chryse,* listing drunkenly toward the surface, aimless and deadly.

First day of command, and probably the last.

She shut down the power.

CHAPTER 59

BUDAPEST

The employees of Indus Station may or may not have been loyal to Ellis, but they had no qualms about getting the hell off of a station about to explode. Greg was ready for them, a pulse rifle in his hand as he opened the door to the airlock.

"Back the hell off!" he shouted at the crowd. "One at a time, in the door, until I say stop. There are ships behind me. Anybody tries to bring a weapon, I blow this shuttle right here and take out your airlock with it. Understood?"

There was still shoving and shouting, but they managed to push onto the shuttle no more than two at a time. Greg had no idea what the vehicle's official capacity was. He would take as many as would fit, and count on the autopilot if he found himself unable to get back to the pilot's seat.

They were about half full when he heard from Savosky. "I've got her," the freighter captain said, but something in his voice made Greg's stomach drop.

"Savosky?"

Thirty-nine, forty, forty-one . . . the ship was filling up. He would have to shut the door soon, and that would not go over well.

"Savosky, is she alive?"

"Yes," he said. "But it's bad, Foster. Hurry the fuck up."

Greg looked into his shuttle: packed. He turned to the people still in the airlock. "There's a ship right behind me," he promised, hoping *Meridia*'s shuttle was close. "Hang on." There were protests, and pushing. He had to pry hands off the hull in order to get the door closed, and they cursed him from the other side. His other passengers stood, crushed together, many stunned, some looking sick, some staring in anguish at the door.

"Can't you—" someone began.

"We'll get everyone we can," he promised. "But I have to get us out of here so the next ship can come in, understand?" He had the autopilot decouple and launch, then pushed his way to the front of the shuttle. By the time he reached the pilot's seat—nearly hidden by the crush of people huddled against the walls and on the floor—they had dropped away from the station and were speeding back to *Budapest*. Behind him, some people began to argue; the shouts grew too loud for him to ignore. He hit the internal comms, making sure his voice was amplified. "Shut up, all of you, or I'll open that door right here!"

In the moment, he thought he'd do it.

They reached *Budapest,* and he had the door open before the shuttle hit the deck. "Out, quickly," he said. "Arin, how much longer before it blows?"

"Four minutes, eight seconds," Arin said.

Greg turned the shuttle around, spilling the last few people unceremoniously to the ground, and sped out through the atmospheric barrier. He might have time for one more run. He might have time to save a few more.

It's bad, Foster.

If he couldn't save her, he could save someone.

Meridia's shuttle was pulling away as he got back to the station. "Two minutes, twelve seconds," Arin told him. Greg connected with the airlock and opened the door; there were mercifully few people standing there.

"Get in now!" he shouted, waving at them. He'd worry about disarming them later. "Twenty seconds and these doors shut. Get moving!" He headed back toward the pilot's seat, not watching what they were doing.

He had no idea if they'd be able to get far enough away.

"Full power the moment that door seals," he told the shuttle, and a few seconds later he was thrown to the floor, the artificial gravity unable to keep up with the inertial shock of speeding away from the dying station.

And then Indus blew.

Greg grabbed the arm of the pilot's seat, half blinded by the explosion, and he wondered for a moment if it would engulf them, if brightness would be the end of all of it. He was flung forward as the shuttle pitched, caught from behind by the blast wave; they spun, the engines struggling to compensate, and he could not see *Budapest* or *Meridia* or even the stars.

CHAPTER 60

YAKUTSK

D allas had always been prepared to die on Yakutsk's surface, victim of an env suit leak or an air supply problem, or even one of Villipova's purges, which occasionally encompassed scavengers. But Smolensk—the dome itself—had always seemed invulnerable, impenetrable. Eternal safe haven.

Stupid.

For a few moments, Dallas thought the light was getting brighter, more blinding, that *Chryse* was filling the sky, blocking out the darkness, an instant away from crashing through the invulnerable windows, depriving them of air before destroying Smolensk in a flash of bright fire; and then Dallas heard the voice coming from Jessica's comm, no longer cloudy, no longer distracted. "I believe, Commander Lockwood," Bayandi said, "that I can control my ship again."

Dallas heard the familiar roaring whine of a sublight engine engaging, and the light receded, and all that was visible through the windows of the dome were the dark night and the shrinking outline of *Chryse*'s pale hull. Dallas could hear, distantly, the cheers from outside, and next to Jessica Gladkoff had collapsed against the wall, sinking to the floor.

Alive. A wave of relief and euphoria swept through Dallas, and Jessica was standing right there, and impulsively Dallas hugged her, shouting her name, and she kept saying, "I can't believe that worked," and over her shoulder Dallas could see the dome's backup kick in, activating their old air handlers, leaving Gladkoff's new system inert.

Bayandi had been freed.

When the captain spoke again, his voice came over the general comms, echoing throughout the dome. Dallas supposed he was speaking to Baikul as well, and probably all of the people on the surface, their endless civil war interrupted by the sight of a starship descending to destroy them.

"Gladkoff," Bayandi said, "you may tell your employers that your task has failed." He sounded imperious, dismissive, and very, very angry. "To the people of Yakutsk, I extend my personal apologies. While my guidance systems were, in fact, under the control of Ellis Systems and not myself, I take full responsibility for allowing them to take control of *Chryse*. There has been loss of life." Bayandi fell silent for a moment. "For that I cannot atone."

No, Dallas thought. *You can't.* But Dallas thought Martine would have forgiven him.

"But I would suggest that you remember this day, and remember that all of you together fought this threat. You have seen, for so long, two sides: Smolensk and Baikul. From what I have seen of you, from what I have learned of you, I would say there is only Yakutsk. You have lived here for hundreds of years. You have built homes and businesses. You are known throughout the sector for skill, talent, and ingenuity. And I would say to you, as an old man who has seen more than you have . . . war is lazy. War is an easy answer. Perhaps, after this day, you might consider trying something else."

When Bayandi spoke again, his voice was only in the env room. "Gladkoff. You are there?"

Gladkoff's skin was damp and shiny, and he was still catching his breath. "Yes."

"Your station is destroyed."

Dallas didn't know what Bayandi was talking about, but Gladkoff clearly did. He nodded. "I understand."

"Many of the employees were saved. The events were vidstreamed by *Meridia,* and are currently being rebroadcast throughout the sector. Ellis cannot play the benign savior any longer."

That seemed to bring Gladkoff back. "The nukes were supposed to be a bluff," he said, crestfallen. "I would have died with the rest of them if you'd crashed into this rock. Why would they do that to me? What was the purpose?"

Dallas thought the purpose was obvious.

"I don't know the ways of the amoral, Gladkoff," Bayandi said. "But in your shoes, I would be seeking a different employer. In fact, I might consider not going home again."

Gladkoff blinked. "I did everything they asked." He was beginning to get angry; he looked, Dallas thought, more human than he had since the moment Dallas had met him. "They can't do this to me."

Under whose jurisdiction? Jessica had asked, when Dallas had suggested prosecuting Gladkoff. "I'd be more worried about what *we're* going to do to you."

Jessica still had her arms around Dallas. She smelled rather pleasantly of soap and flowers, and a little bit of Yakutsk's persistent red dust. When Dallas spoke she let go and took a step back, becoming professional again. "As a Corps representative," she said to Dallas, "I would like to officially request that you try this man under your current justice system."

Dallas was not sure Gladkoff had earned a trial. Gladkoff was not one of the individuals who had thrown Martine outside, who had dragged Jamyung out as he screamed, but he worked with the ones who had. *Who are we going to be?* Dallas thought.

Not a city where one person decided the fate of a killer.

"Not entirely my call," Dallas said at last, and something at the corners of Jessica's green eyes relaxed.

"I've made my request," she said. "My obligation is completed." She shot Gladkoff a look. "You could always ask for extradition to the Corps justice system. Or PSI's. But I suspect you'll get a better deal here." She hit her comm. "Lockwood to *Galileo.*"

"Yes, Captain." That was her Lieutenant Samaras. Apparently he had adapted to Jessica's title quickly—more quickly, Dallas thought, than Jessica was going to. But all she did was smile.

"Stand down from alert status," she told her starship. "*Chryse* is no longer a danger."

CHAPTER 61

BUDAPEST

The light faded, and the ship stabilized, and they were cruising sedately toward *Budapest*'s landing bay.

For the moment, Greg was still alive. *With any luck, we both are.*

He climbed to his feet and turned. Most of his passengers were on the floor, and some were bleeding; but they were all moving, and that was the best he could hope for. He counted quickly: seventeen. He wondered how many had been left behind, lost. He wondered how these people were feeling, whether they were defensive, belligerent, guiltless, frightened.

"Anybody armed?" he asked.

Hesitantly, three people raised their hands.

They did not protest as he relieved them of two hand weapons and a folding knife. He pocketed the contraband, and stepped to the back of the ship, opening the first aid kit. "Who's got medical knowledge?" he asked.

It turned out six of them had been trained in rudimentary

first aid, apparently as a requirement for the job. He did not ask about their employer, or what they had been up to; instead, he worked with them, attending to the wounded, disinfecting cuts and applying analgesics to bruises. There was miraculously only one broken bone, and the woman had obtained it not on the station, but when their shuttle had pitched and rolled in the shock wave. He gave her a strong painkiller, and promised her *Galileo*'s doctor would look after her.

Punishments could come later. Right now, they were refugees.

"Are we under arrest?" someone asked.

"I don't know," Greg told them truthfully. "I don't think too many people are going to be happy about what was going on at that station."

"We were doing research," said someone else. Greg shot him a glance, and he fell silent.

"Right now," he told them, "I think we should focus on the injured and the dead. We'll need your help figuring out who's missing. And if anybody's signed any kind of nondisclosure or binding contract that's going to keep them from doing that," he added, anticipating the objection, "call your fucking lawyer after we've cleaned up this mess."

The shuttle landed back on *Budapest,* and he ushered the passengers out into the landing bay, where the others had set up a triage station of sorts. Savosky was there, looking people over one by one, bandaging small wounds and directing others to help more seriously injured people down the hallway to the infirmary. *Fuck them,* Greg thought. *What about Elena?* But he didn't say it out loud.

He pushed past the crowds, climbing a utility ladder to the upper level so he could run down the hallway without tripping over the wounded. On the other end of the ship he climbed down again, and rounded the corner into the infirmary.

And there she was.

She was lying on a table, and Arin was hovering over her with a cloth, gently cleaning her face. He looked up as Greg came in. "I've stabilized her," he said. "She's lost a lot of blood."

Most of it, it seemed, was all over her: her clothes, the white uniform she'd worn as camouflage, were soaked with it. Some of the stains had charred. There were solid chunks of flesh clinging to her as well, and he frowned, eyes sweeping over her. Her hands and feet were intact, as was her head; much of her hair had burned off, and her face was blackened on one side, but he couldn't see anything missing. Arin, who was following his eyes, said, "That's not hers. I don't know whose it was, but it's not hers."

"The blood?" Greg asked.

"Mostly not hers, either," Arin said. But his voice wasn't encouraging. "You can come closer," the boy told him.

Greg stepped up to the table, looking at her face. Under the blood and burns, it was her: lips blistered, cheeks bruised, one eyebrow scorched off, but still her. His Elena, her flesh and bones, battered and damaged and unconscious, but still alive, still breathing, still with him, if only for now.

Arin put his rag down and left the room to help Bear with the incoming casualties.

Greg looked down at her.

"You," he said, "are a fucking idiot, and such a massive pain in the ass I can't even begin to express it."

But that didn't seem right.

"I have never hated anyone as much as I hate you right now."

Still not quite it.

"My mother. I've hated my mother. You know how much I've hated my mother. So maybe . . . maybe I hated her more. But if you don't come back, it's going to be a close contest, Elena."

He reached out and touched her hair. It was soaked in blood, turning the blue streaks dark purple. "I would have come with you. You think I would have stopped you, but I would have come with you. You wouldn't have been alone." He felt tears on his face, but he didn't know why. "Why do you always think you have to be alone?"

His comm chimed. "Foster," Savosky told him, "Syncos has got a temporary relay up."

I don't care. But he said, "That's good."

"And you've got an incoming comm from some Admiral called Waris."

"Tell her I don't work for her anymore," Greg said. He stroked Elena's head gently, as if it might break under his fingers.

"Pretty sure that's why she wants to talk to you."

He supposed it was unfair to make Savosky deal with Waris. "Fine." He touched Elena's cheek, the one that was not blistered. "Put her through."

"Captain Foster," Waris began, audibly apoplectic, "if

you think this *resignation* of yours is going to shield you from anything, you're—"

"Admiral," he interrupted, brushing Elena's forehead with his thumb, "I told Savosky to put you through because it's not on him to defend me, but I'm going to say my piece, and that will be the end of the discussion. I have resigned my Corps commission. You want to see that as treason, or insubordination, or whatever bullshit you want to spin, take your best shot: it's not going to work. My resignation is regulation, legal, and by the book. On top of that, here we are in the Fourth Sector, with nobody to court-martial me even if you wanted to piss with the rules and give that a try. So I'm telling you, for the first and last time: fuck off, Admiral. You have no power over me anymore."

He ended the comm.

"Wish you could have heard that," he told Elena, and went back to stroking what was left of her hair.

CHAPTER 62

YAKUTSK

Y ou should see this place," Jessica said to Ted. "I've never
seen a repair shop so busy."

Indeed, the mood in Smolensk had been positively celebratory since *Chryse* had nearly destroyed them all. The
ships had landed, returning the colonists to their homes,
and people from Smolensk and Baikul together started picking up debris from where the shooting and bombing had
happened. Villipova and Gladkoff were both under arrest,
and the one time Jessica had been worried was when the
celebratory tone turned hostile, and the crowd seemed determined to vacate Gladkoff.

But Dallas, soft-spoken and respected, had asked a question: "Have you ever seen anyone vacated? Because I have.
And I don't want to see it again."

Gladkoff had been remanded to a makeshift jail—Jessica
realized, with some surprise, that they had no actual prison
system—and the talk had turned to the various legal viola-
tions he could be charged with.

Villipova, Jessica thought, might actually keep her post. She had been furious about Gladkoff, and plausibly ignorant of his plan to use Yakutsk to lure Bayandi into Ellis's hands. When she heard he was responsible for the deaths of Martine and Jamyung, she had expressed, in fairly colorful language, the same desires Dallas's mob had. Jessica found herself believing the woman might actually be innocent in this situation—or as innocent as she could be, with her history of corruption. Jessica hoped Smolensk wouldn't succumb to mob rule again, because if nothing else, Villipova certainly had experience making a bureaucracy work.

Oarig had come out of it all smelling like a hero, both for sending ships to help evacuate, and for not being the one dealing with Ellis to begin with. He, Jessica thought, was more worrisome. She didn't think for a second he had really learned from what had happened. But if enough of the colonists had, she supposed that might be enough.

"It's that way here, too." Ted sounded tired and subdued. "The new relay is pretty flaky, and it's not processing nearly as much as it needs to. People are queuing up to send messages, and we've been receiving data nonstop since the link went up. We'll be weeks sorting through it all."

"How about everything else?"

"Some of them want to blame the whole Admiralty for this," he said. "Some of them just want to blame Shadow Ops. And then the arguments start about who's who, and there's a lot of things said that I'm not going to repeat to their commanding officer."

She sighed. "I'll be back in an hour, Ted," she promised.

"I just need to wrap up down here." She had been avoiding the question. "How's Elena?"

"Alive. Unconscious."

"What does Bob say?"

"He says he doesn't know." Ted sounded miserable, and Jessica was reminded that he had known Elena since the Academy, longer than any of them had known her, even Greg. "He says her brain is resting, and healing itself, but he can't say how long it'll take."

"If anybody can get through this," Jessica told Ted, "Elena can. You know that."

Ted paused. "I'm kind of mad at her, really," he confessed. "She could have told us."

"Yeah." Jessica knew exactly what he was feeling. And she knew exactly why Elena had not said anything. "We can give her shit when she wakes up. For years, maybe."

And she remembered, then, that Elena was not in the Corps any longer, and neither was Greg, and *Galileo* belonged to her and she was not sure how much treason her chain of command was actually behind. *I'll never be the officer Greg was,* she realized. *I'll never have that blind trust.*

She wasn't sure if that was a strength or a weakness.

She stood, and stretched, and walked over to where Bristol was talking with the rest of the infantry. "We about ready?" she asked him.

"Yes, Captain." Bristol, of all of them, had seemed to absorb her promotion the most seamlessly.

"Give me ten minutes."

She found Dallas at Jamyung's shop, sorting through the

piles of parts in the yard. Half, she could tell, were being tossed into a waste pile. The rest Dallas would examine, and scan with a portable analyzer, and place carefully on an anti-grav skiff.

She watched for a moment, taking time she didn't have. She was dreading this conversation, and not for its content. She did not want to have a last conversation with Dallas.

"Who owns all of this now?" she asked.

"We do." Dallas picked up another part, turned it over, and tossed it into the trash pile. "The scavengers."

"Is that part of the arrangement between Smolensk and Baikul?" she asked.

Dallas looked at her as if she had asked something absurd, but the answer was perfectly polite. "This is old law. The scavengers provide the dealers with parts to sell—not all of them, but enough. So if a dealer dies without a business partner, the scavengers get the inventory. We have to split it," Dallas added, sounding amused, "and that sometimes gets interesting."

She took a step closer. "Lanie always says good dealers don't leave their valuables out in the yard."

"Basement's been picked over." Dallas sounded disapproving. "While some of us were trying to save the dome, someone came back here and cleaned it out."

Including, she realized, *the scanner that erroneously picked up dellinium.* She would never be able to analyze it now. Neither could she analyze the object, that strange artifact, now vapor in the vastness of dead space.

"I have to go," she said.

"Figured." Another part tossed onto the waste pile.

"*Galileo*'s not leaving yet," she added. "We've—there's a lot that's happened since we lost contact with the First Sector, and I'm not inclined to run off to another assignment until we've worked that out. And our mission here—" *What the hell had that been? Keep the governors safe?* It all seemed like bullshit now. "I want to make sure everything's okay here."

"That your call, is it?"

"No," she said. "It's yours. But it's my call who I trust."

"You trust your Admiralty?"

She closed her eyes. That was too much to process just now. "I trust my crew," she said simply. "And right now, I need to be there with them. They need to see me standing in front of them, being in command."

"Captain Lockwood." Dallas smiled, and she laughed.

"Do you know," she said, "it's the last thing I wanted? I made lieutenant commander after seven years, and that was good enough for me. Then Greg made me his second, and I could have strangled him. Now—"

"You're still going to strangle him."

"If I get the chance, yes." She would not strangle Greg when he was worried about Elena, but she had hope she would get the opportunity later on. "It seems surreal, almost. They've followed me, these people. I'm not always sure why."

"Aren't you?"

Those warm dark eyes, always so patient. "I do my best for them," she said. "I make the best choices I can."

"Seem to do okay with that."

"I guess." She took the chance. "So will you."

Something in Dallas's posture wilted, just a little. "Don't want people following me."

"Sometimes we don't get to choose."

"I'm good at my job. I like my job." Dallas threw a part aggressively into the trash. "Should be enough."

"You want to run away," she offered, "you can come with us."

At that, Dallas looked surprised, and stared into her eyes for a long moment, evaluating how serious she was. At length, Dallas smiled, just a little. "Starship is almost like a dome," Dallas allowed. "But it's not the same."

"Home is home," she said. She was disappointed. She was relieved.

"Yeah." Dallas tossed one more part onto the skiff, then turned around to face her. "Never dealt much with soldiers," Dallas admitted. "Stay away from off-worlders, most of the time. They all like you?"

"God, I hope not." And this time Dallas laughed.

"Listen. You get your command straightened out, find yourself with a little time on your hands—I could cook for you again. Maybe something a little nicer. Or there's the pub."

"Is their food any good?"

"It's awful, but I don't have to cook it."

Hell. "I'm going to miss you."

Dallas nodded. "I'll miss you, too, Captain."

"I like Jessica better."

"Jessica, then."

And Dallas took her hands, and Jessica realized they fit perfectly within the scavenger's long, lovely fingers, and she thought, just maybe, she might make all of this work out after all.

CHAPTER 63

GALILEO

He would not have left Elena's side for anything else.

"She's stable, Greg," Bob assured him. "You can take the time."

But that wasn't the problem. It wasn't the time that worried him. He believed Bob when he said she would live, although the doctor could not say when—or even if—she would wake up again. Greg was fighting some strange, primitive compulsion to keep looking at her, as if she would disappear again if he closed his eyes. If he sat with her, held her hand, she would not drop out of his life and leave him rootless.

"I made a promise," he told her, before he left. "I'll be back."

Elena slept on.

He ended up back in his old office. Jessica, somewhat to his annoyance, was refusing to take possession of it, instead setting up a temporary workstation in the pub. "It's easier for them to find me here," she had argued. "And I need to be as visible as possible right now, while people adjust." He would have gone mad, trying to work in such a public place; but she seemed to thrive on the chaos, her mind getting sharper and more organized the more people peppered her with irrelevant questions. She had recruited Emily Broad-moor to help her, but he suspected eventually she'd choose Ted Shimada as a second-in-command. Ted knew her, and loved her, and called her on her shit, and if Greg were to advise her on the subject, he would tell her those were the three most important attributes a first officer could have.

He should have found it odd, being back on *Galileo*, passing people in the hallways, knowing he was not a soldier anymore. But the whole situation felt strangely comfortable, as if he had finally slipped into place after years of sitting precariously on the edge. People still saluted him, and he saluted them back, the echo of a habit that would take time to fade; but they also talked to him, many of them far more openly than they had ever done before. They were, each of them, going through so much, and Greg wasn't going to hazard a guess what they would do next.

He wasn't sure what he would do next, either. Freja Taras's words kept playing over and over in his head. He could see himself with PSI: among other things, it would give him resources. He would have organized backup as he kept fighting for what he believed in.

But he could not, quite yet, see himself leaving *Galileo*. And he could not imagine leaving Elena at all.

"Captain Foster?"

"Yes, Bayandi?"

Bayandi had retreated from Yakutsk as soon as he had

finished streaming all of the data he had amassed on Ellis's plot, circling Lena to head toward the center of the system. At Greg's request, Jessica had moved *Galileo* away from Yakutsk, just far enough to be able to see the system's star through the office window. It was a cool star, only 3,200 degrees kelvin, and Bayandi had been pleased. *They are cold,* he had said. *I must be cold to join them.*

Greg had visited one last time to rescue a handful of Ilyana's things: still photographs of her children and grandchildren, some small square objects that might have been sculptures or trash. He had given it all to Ted to bring up to a proper temperature, to repair any damage that had been done by the icy vacuum. She may never want any of it, he supposed; but if she did, he thought she would want it as it had been before.

Greg had tried, for a while, to talk Bayandi out of it. "You're not vulnerable anymore," he said. "You're no more a weapon than *Galileo* is. And you know more about how to defend yourself from Ellis than any of us."

"It is not about Ellis," Bayandi had said, his voice gentle. And he had said nothing else, except, "Will you talk me through it, Captain Foster?"

Greg had not known how to refuse. And now he stood, looking out the window, in the office he had been glad to give up, keeping a machine company so it did not have to fall alone.

"I have always liked red dwarfs," Bayandi said. His voice had regained its warm, curious tone. "I'm not sure why. They are, strictly speaking, no more or less remarkable than anything else around me. But they are small. They are dying. And yet they fight, on and on, and will be fighting long after the rest of us have been dust for billions of years. That is a thing of wonder, don't you think?"

Greg swallowed. "Yes, it is."

"Is she improving, your Chief Shaw?"

"A little," Greg said. "Our doctor uses words like *stabilized*. They're still not sure when she'll completely wake up. Or if."

"I am very sorry, Captain." Bayandi's empathy seemed genuine. "I shall be hopeful for her with you."

Greg could not keep himself from asking. "With everything you've seen, with all the people you've known over seven hundred years—how is it that one person can still matter to you?"

Bayandi was silent for so long Greg thought he wouldn't answer. "Everyone matters, Greg Foster," he said at last, and his voice was gentle. "Everyone, every time. She is yours, and she is mine, and she is her own, and she matters. She will always matter, long after she is gone."

"So will you, Bayandi."

"Ah." Bayandi sounded pleased. "Kindness. This is a thing I learned from my children, long ago. Such a lovely thing, for all that it so often flies in the face of logic. You are kind, Captain Foster. Do you know this about yourself?"

"I'm actually known as something of a son of a bitch."

Bayandi laughed. "I imagine you can take pride in that as well." There was a pause. "It is becoming warm here. Not affecting my systems yet. But the ice is starting to melt."

"Do you feel it?"

"Not the way you mean. But it is . . . comforting." For several minutes, Bayandi said nothing, and then: "Do you read poetry, Captain Foster?"

My mother read poetry. "Not for a long time."

"There is one I have always liked. I have been told it is sad, but somehow . . . I have always found it strong. Angry. A song for fighting, for life. Is it strange, to find anger joyous?"

"I don't think so."

"And in that near silence I would rest, and wait / and all would be darkness."

So much Greg had seen in his life. So much loss and pain and ache, and this machine—this creature, whatever he was—was going to undo him entirely. "I know that one," he said. Old. Older than the Second Wave. Greg wondered if Bayandi was older.

"Poetry and song are the same, did you know?" Bayandi asked him. Greg thought he heard something in the signal, some flaw, the beginning of digital artifacting, of falling apart.

"Prose, too, sometimes," Greg said, and Bayandi laughed again.

"Yes. Language—it's remarkable. It can carry with it so much. I have no real skill with language, but poems, songs—there is an old adage. *A picture is worth a thousand words.* I have seen beautiful pictures, Captain Foster, but I have never found I could see so much in them as I have seen in words. *It is time alone that carries us.* That says so much, and it is not even a thousand words. Do you think that is true, Captain?"

"It's Greg."

"Greg." A smile in that generated voice. "Do you think our lives are not our own?"

Whose life is their own? He thought of his mother, who'd had less than forty years, her life taken by an accident born of courage. He thought of Ilyana, everything she loved destroyed out from under her, and of Herrod, and the hell of good intentions. He wished Elena were awake, were here with him. He had no idea anymore what was his own. "I think we choose," he replied.

"I wonder if choice, for me, is an illusion of perception. There are not—" The signal dissolved.

"Bayandi?"

"—here. I am sorry, Greg. It is getting very warm."

"Does it help?"

"Yes. I—" More hiccups. "—will be warm now. All of us together, as it has always been. I like that. That makes it all right, I think. Do you?"

At some point tears had fallen on Greg's face. He could not remember when they had started. "I do, Bayandi."

"I wish I could sing. They taught—" Another break. "—never sing. That makes me more human, I think. We can none of us do everything. *We.* That is a good word, isn't it, Greg?"

"We will remember you, Bayandi."

"I am glad."

And Bayandi began to sing, not a song, but words that Greg knew, the few words he remembered from that ancient poem.

"No fear of flaw, of sin, of age, or youth."

And remarkably, the connection steadied.

"In the end, in the fire, in the silence, in the dark / In the end, there is still—"

And there was silence.

"Bayandi?" Greg asked.

But it was *Galileo* that spoke. "*Chryse* has been destroyed," the ship told him, her voice matter-of-fact, unchanged.

And for the first time that he could remember in all his life—nearly forty long years—Greg Foster put his hands to his face and allowed himself to weep.

CHAPTER 64

You look tired," Tom Foster said.

Greg sat in his quarters, taking in the image of his father. He looked older, somehow, although Greg did not think he had changed since the last time they had spoken a few weeks earlier. Greg had always looked at his father and seen the man who had raised him, quiet and even-tempered and sometimes detached, the man who had put up with Greg's insults and rages and childishness long past the age when he should have let go of the tangles of adolescence. Today he saw a man with graying hair and weary eyes, and it crossed Greg's mind that for all the fears he'd had for his father over the last few days, his father would have had far more for him. Waiting for another comm, another person he loved lost to the Corps.

You can't lose me to the Corps anymore, Dad.

"We've been busy," Greg told him. "Everybody wants to send messages back home, and the system is clogged. Add the stream to that, with unfettered data trying to get in and out, and it's been a nightmare sorting things out."

Greg had set himself to helping with *Galileo*'s comms systems. It had been years since he had worked so hands-on, but his memory was coming back, and once Samaras got past the idea that the man he used to report to was now an unranked technician, he had turned out to be efficient and easy to work with. They had set *Galileo* up as a public relay, helping to shunt some of the stream traffic through Chronos Relay in the Fourth Sector, giving the new temporary relay set up by Syncos some breathing room. Nearly everyone, from PSI to commercial freighters to the area colonies, had agreed that people's private messages needed to be the priority for a while.

Jessica had set up a lottery for *Galileo*'s crew, weighting it toward people with old or ill family. One of the first things she had done was send a message back to the Admiralty on Earth that all of *Galileo*'s crew was safe and alive. The news of Admiral Herrod's death she had given in person to Admiral Waris, and when Greg had asked her how it had gone, she had shrugged. "That woman is predictable," was all she said.

The Olam flagship had done its job, emerging from the field into close Earth orbit, right above the southern coast of Africa. The ship's captain had demanded the immediate resignation of Central Gov, and the disbanding of the Admiralty and the Corps. When Gov had stalled, amassing the small fleet they had on Earth for local defense, the Olam ship had hit the ocean around the Hope Islands and drowned fourteen thousand people with a sequence of tidal waves. They had expected, Greg knew, the remainder of their fleet to emerge in moments to back them up; instead, the small-scale fighters that were Earth's primary defense had zeroed in on the single ship and taken her out with less trouble than Olam had obviously thought it would require.

"They think we're going to make *peace*," Emily Broadmoor had complained over breakfast. He had found himself dining with her and Ted Shimada more and more often; apparently years of reporting to him had given them a pent-up need to be candid. "They're trying to tell us it was all a mistake, that the fleet captain was some kind of crazy person doing it all on his own. Like we're going to believe *that*."

Greg suspected that was the likely outcome: the public would accept that this was a mistake, that Earth would then let Olam make peace, and blame the entire incident on a dead man. Gov would catch some blowback from that, and on top of the repercussions of Bayandi's exposure of the Admiralty's knowledge of what was going to happen to Athena Relay, the political situation was going to be deeply unstable for a while. The data that *Budapest* had pulled off Indus Station showed a much longer, deeper collusion between Gov and Ellis Systems—and other organizations, many defunct, involved in activities that were deeply illegal. The information had shattered any illusion that Gov was either unified or in any kind of real control, and people were reacting with predictable volatility. Greg was not sure if his father was safer on Earth, or if he would be better off on a colony that hosted no Gov or Corps bureaucrats of any kind at all.

He was not sure of *Galileo*'s crew, either. The mood on

board was shifty and strange. There was happiness that Earth had survived, that Olam had been defeated, that Ellis had been exposed. There was grief, still, over Athena, and over the Hope Islands and the surrounding damage. But mostly there was anger and suspicion directed at their own chain of command. Not at Jessica, or Emily, or even at Greg; but at Chemeris, Waris, and the Admiralty, all the people who had known what was happening, and had decided the deaths of ten thousand people were worth keeping their own secrets. The mood was one of betrayal, and deep offense; but none of it had resulted, locally at least, in insubordination, and Greg didn't think that it would.

"It's not an indefensible position," Ted had pointed out, "if you think of it from a certain angle. If they really believed this was the only way to shut down a Fifth Sector coup attempt, if they really thought the loss of life from a civil war would be greater than the population of Athena Relay . . . there's precedent, from a military perspective."

"Do you really believe that?" Greg did not know Ted Shimada well, despite having worked with him for nine years, but he knew Ted was on a very short list of people Elena trusted with her life.

"I believe what they did was horrific and unconscionable," Ted said. "And I can see how they managed to talk themselves into it."

"The difference between deliberate evil and passive evil?" It was an interesting concept. Greg was not sure the distinction was important. "Which do you think is worse?"

"Passive evil," Ted said decisively. "Because you don't see it coming."

They hadn't seen it coming, any of them. They were out here, risking their lives, fighting for peace and expansion and people's simple right to live an ordinary life, and their own government had treated them like chess pieces. Greg was a better politician than he wanted to be, and he understood the complexities of distributed government; but he had no qualms about turning his back on the government that had made such a choice.

The trouble was, he wasn't sure quite where to go.

"Dad," he said, his eyes on his father's, "there are some things you need to know."

Tom Foster tensed. "Are you all right, Greg?"

"I'm fine," he said. "But . . . I could use some advice."

And he told his father everything, about Herrod and Elena and the Admiralty's betrayal, and his own choice. "It's strange," he said, when he finished, unsure if any of it made sense. "I'm so sure, down to my bones, that I made the right decision. But I have no idea what to do with myself now."

Tom was quiet for a long time, and Greg waited, wondering if his father would disapprove, or scold him, or just disconnect. But when Tom spoke, his voice was gruff and thick.

"You are the damnedest kid, you know that?" he said. "You—" He broke off, and looked away. "Sometimes you are so much like me I want to stop you from doing what you're doing, just because I don't want you to learn the hard way."

"You think I'm making a mistake?"

"I don't." And Greg's stomach relaxed. "I think you left

not because you wanted a change, but because you didn't want one."

"So what do I do now?"

"Figure out how not to change."

Greg shook his head. "You make it sound so simple."

"It is simple. It's just not easy."

Greg thought about that. "I don't know when I can come home, Dad," he said at last.

"Will you be able to comm me?"

"I should." He had no idea. "I can stream to you, at least. I don't know how much I'll be able to say, but I'll be able to let you know I'm all right."

Tom nodded, and Greg thought his father was having trouble speaking. "That's more than I've had for the last eighteen years," he said.

"They're probably going to come and talk to you," Greg told him. "They were . . . unhappy when I resigned, and they're going to be wondering why I've done it now, whether I've sold secrets to the enemy, that sort of thing."

"Which enemy?" Tom asked dryly.

"I'm just telling you, they might make things unpleasant."

"Best of luck to them," Tom said. "They're not the only ones with resources."

At that, Greg had to smile. "My dad, the revolutionary."

"My life didn't start the day you were born, kid."

Greg wanted to stay on the line, to talk with his father forever. "I'm hitting my time limit," he said with regret. "I need to give the space up to someone else."

Tom nodded. "Anything you want me to tell Meg?"

Greg thought his sister would not understand. "Just tell

her I love her," he said. "And Steve, and the boys. And tell her I'll come and see her as soon as I can, whether she wants me to or not."

"Okay." And then: "I'm proud of you, you know."

Greg swallowed. "I know, Dad. I'm proud of you, too."

He was packing his things when Jessica rang his door chime. "It's open," he said, and *Galileo* let her in. "Good evening, Captain," he said.

"Fuck you, Greg," she said easily, and frowned at his bag. "What are you doing?"

She should already know. "I can't stay here," he told her. "It looks bad for the crew if *Galileo* harbors me. The Admiralty won't stand for it."

He knew, too, that he needed to give her room, that his presence there would always make her hang back, second-guess herself, let the crew shove him back into a position of authority whether he had it or not. She didn't need him, but she needed the room to see that herself.

But she clearly wasn't thinking that way. "Fuck the Admiralty," she told him. "Where are you going to go?"

"Well." He had thought about this. "I thought I'd stick with *Budapest* for a while. I'm not totally rusty on comms, and Savosky said he could keep me busy, at least for a few months. And then . . ." He had thought about *and then* for a long time. "I was thinking of *Meridia*," he said, hesitant, wondering how she would react. "Taras has already said she would take me. And it would let me keep doing the work I'm used to doing."

"You'd take the oath with PSI? Officially?"

He was not yet at the point where he wanted to take an oath with anyone. Freedom was new. Part of him felt buoyant, enormous, endless, his spirit ready to fly across the galaxy with boundless energy. But a part of him was still waiting until Elena was well, until he could talk to her, until she could help him understand how any of this was supposed to fit together. He was not in a position to make a choice like an oath of fealty, to anyone at all.

"Does it seem," he asked her, "like such a terrible idea?"

Jessica tilted her head at him, considering. He knew that look: she had something on her mind, something she thought would interest him, something she was holding on to like a surprise gift. She took a step forward, reached out, and pulled the stack of undershirts out of his bag.

"Put these back," she said. "Because there's something I need to tell you."

CHAPTER 65

There was darkness, and there was warmth, and sometimes in the depths there were voices. And at some point, she realized she was not dead.

Elena heard Bear's voice often, deep and gentle, just as it had been when he had met her in the airlock. She thought at first he was her guide, the one who would lead her to wherever she was going; surely if this were the real, living Bear, he would be shouting at her for something instead of being kind. But she never caught words, and she did not seem to be going anywhere, and the warmth and darkness did not change.

She began to notice other voices: one, light and feminine—that had to be Jessica. Not as gentle as Bear, but sharper and full of anxiety. She heard her mother, clear and practical: *Don't worry about us. We are fine. We'll see you soon.* Elena wondered who *we* meant. Then there was another, gravelly and broken here and there, that she thought might be Bob Hastings, and that was when it occurred to her that she might be alive.

Why would he be with my mother? she thought, and let her mind drift for a while. There was a lot to be said for warmth and safety and soothing voices.

Eventually she began to feel something heavy against one leg, something odd and warm and outside of herself, like nothing she had felt in the soothing darkness. She had a leg, and she could feel it, and it was held down with gravity onto something firm. The heavy thing moved, and she began to wonder if she could move her leg as well, and she wondered why she would have a leg in this place, and her ankle twitched and the rest of her body began to come into focus: spine and back and arms and neck and the other leg, which had nothing heavy against it but was far less comfortable.

She woke long enough for Bob to ask her name, and to tell her that her mission had succeeded. She wanted to ask if they'd rescued anyone else—if they'd retrieved Mika, who just wanted to go skiing, or any of the others. But all her mind could form were single words, and the first word she could think of was "Earth?"

Bob's lips had thinned. "Fourteen thousand dead," he told her, "and probably more yet to be counted. But it could have been a lot worse."

And he had told her that Syncos Relay was up and running, if only temporarily, and showed her a message from her mother, who was as brisk and cheerful as always. "Don't worry about us," she said at the end of it. "We are fine. We'll see you soon." And then: "I love you, Elena."

Somewhat to her surprise, Elena had burst into tears. Bob told her that was the concussion, and stayed with her until she fell asleep again.

The next several days passed quickly for Elena, in cycles of heavy darkness and moments of lucidity. The dark, comforting dreams she'd had when she was unconscious deserted her in favor of heavy, torpid sleep, and often it was only the discomfort of spending all that time on her back that woke her up. She had tried, at one point, turning onto her left side; her back had sighed with relief, but the pain in her right hip was so severe she had to lie flat again. Mehitabel, disturbed by this, had stalked briefly up to Elena's face and knocked her nose disapprovingly against Elena's chin. Elena had lifted one arm to scratch the cat on the head, and was immediately treated to purrs and forgiveness.

She saw no one but Bob in those times, and after the third or fourth window of wakefulness, she began to wonder at what he was wearing. Medical staff were allowed some leeway, but Bob had always been strictly military as far as his clothing was concerned. When he was up for long stretches with patients he sometimes took off his jacket, but she had no explanation for his prolonged appearances in only an undershirt. Black, as well: still regulation, but as a rule *Galileo*'s crew generally went with white. She kept meaning to ask him, but Bob tended to monopolize their conversations, giving her cognitive quizzes and asking how she was feeling. And her brain was sluggish, still shaking off the coma. Bob assured her it was normal, and that she would recover; but in the meantime it was making it hard for her to figure out what was going on.

The fifth time she woke up, Jessica was there, and she, too, was wearing a black tank top over her uniform trousers. She was also beautiful and familiar and exactly who Elena needed to see, and Elena spent a few minutes crying at the sight of her. She was beginning to wonder if that tendency would ever pass.

"Why," she asked, when they had both finished crying, "is everyone out of uniform?"

"Ah." Jessica met Bob's eyes over the bed, then looked back at Elena. "That's complicated."

"No it isn't," Bob said, and Elena thought he sounded annoyed.

Jessica sighed, and looked back down at Elena. "Okay, then. I'll try to keep it simple." She thought for a moment, then shook her head. "I'll try to keep it short. The Admiralty knew that Athena Relay was going to be destroyed. Maybe not the whole Admiralty, but more than enough of them, and they let all of those people die anyway. And when *Meridia* streamed the vid out of Indus Station, the Admiralty tried to act like they'd been in on the whole thing. Taking credit. People are kind of . . . irritable about it. Pissed off."

Good Lord, had they all been fired? "How pissed off?"

Jessica cleared her throat. "Well. You know about Greg, don't you?"

She didn't. But when Jessica told her, she realized on some level she had already known. "Is that why he hasn't come to see me?" she asked.

"No, that's why *I* haven't come to see you," Jessica said. "It's been fucking insane here. Greg . . ." She sighed. "He's had a rough time of it since Bayandi."

Even post-concussion, Elena knew an excuse when she heard one. "He doesn't want to talk to me."

"I think he does, Lanie. I think he just doesn't know what he'd say."

That makes two of us, she thought. "So, wait. Never mind Greg." Greg, she thought, she would manage, eventually. She would find him, and sit with him, and they would claw at each other until they figured out what they were to each other again. *Same as always.* "The crew. What's happened?"

"See, it's sort of the same thing, really," Jessica said, and Elena recognized her friend's habit of beating around the bush when she was nervous about the reception she was going to get. "Because the crew feels sort of set up and betrayed by the Admiralty, and they see what Greg did, and they've—well, not all of them, but a lot of them, enough of them, really, that it'd probably work—they've been wondering, if it works for him, maybe it'd work for them. For us."

Elena replayed that in her head a few times. "You're telling me two hundred and twenty-six people are planning to resign their commissions?"

"It's still under discussion," Jessica told her. "And it's more like a hundred and sixty or so, although the others are not so much disagreeing with the idea, just wanting to handle it differently."

"But that's only—" Her recovering brain could not do math. "That doesn't leave enough people. What about *Galileo*?"

"Well, here's the thing," Jessica said. "They're kind of thinking . . . *Galileo* could come with us."

"I don't understand."

"It makes sense, really, if you think about it," Jessica

said rapidly. "And even the people staying think it's a good idea. It's just that they haven't given up on the Corps, and it's never a bad idea to have good soldiers, is it? And it's not like we'd be the enemy. There is no enemy, really, except maybe Olam, and a few other of those colonies, although some of the big ones have already publicly denounced Olam and are throwing their weight behind Central Gov. Shenzhu, Volhynia—"

"Jessie." She didn't think her muddled head was the problem. "What has happened?"

"Oh." Jessica seemed to realize she had skipped the point. "Sorry. It's—we've been discussing it with *Meridia,* and, well, for the moment, at least, the plan is to keep our crew, take *Galileo,* and join PSI."

Elena let that sentence sit in her mind until she understood all of the words. And then, despite the pain in her head, she began to laugh, and she laughed until she was crying again.

EPILOGUE

YAKUTSK

lready have one of those," Dallas said.

"Bullshit," said Rankine. "I came looking yesterday and you had fuck-all."

Dallas shrugged. "Had a good afternoon." And smiled.

Rankine rolled her eyes, cursed a few more times, and finally agreed to sell the part for twelve. Dallas counted out the hard currency and, as Rankine was leaving, recorded it in the ledger and pushed the update to the others. Transparency, Dallas was learning, was the best way to keep the peace.

Jamyung's parts yard would, eventually, be sold to whoever wanted to buy out the public claim; but in the meantime, Dallas and six of the others had taken over the space, keeping the business going until either someone came up with the money to buy it, or they decided to dismantle it. Dismantling it, Dallas had discovered, would be unfortunate; in the weeks since the near-disaster with *Chryse,* a number of small freighters and passenger ships had stopped at Smolensk, attracted, Dallas realized, by the novelty. And nearly every ship had stopped by Jamyung's looking for parts, expecting either quality, obscure inventory, or both. Dallas had taken two days sorting through everything in the yard as well as in the basement, meticulously cataloging what had originally lived only in Jamyung's head. There were a staggering number of strange and expensive parts, and that, coupled with the reputation that Jamyung had apparently built, meant the business was worth a great deal indeed.

But Dallas, who could afford to buy it, did not want it.

Jessica had not stayed long, but Dallas had shared at least as many stories as she had. Jessica talked about her childhood, and her big family, and how she still missed the damp, sweltering nights of Tengri's summers. Dallas told her about sneaking out to the moon's surface at night, when the parents had all been asleep, and getting caught curled up just outside the airlock in the morning. Their stories, Dallas thought, were the same, despite the differences. *Hot and cold.* That, Dallas decided, was why they got along so well.

Dallas talked to Jessica about Jamyung's business. "Feel like I owe him," Dallas had told her at last.

"You owe him respect," she had said, curled up with Dallas on the small, comfortable bed. "You owe him memory. He deserves to have someone run his business who loves it as much as he did."

Dallas wasn't sure Jamyung had, strictly speaking, *loved* the business, but there were a dozen scavengers who would take over the yard with enthusiasm. And so a number of them had organized, and were sorting through all of Jamyung's spotty records before deciding a fair valuation for the place.

One for one seemed to be falling by the wayside.

Change, of course, was going to be neither linear nor smooth. Gladkoff was awaiting charges of conspiracy to commit murder, although Dallas thought his claim of ignorance was possibly going to work. Already there were people in the streets suggesting that Gladkoff was clearly a dupe, that nobody that stupid could be guilty of conspiring to do anything. The charge of murdering Blair had a better chance of sticking, especially since Jessica had recorded her eyewitness testimony before *Galileo* had departed. But once again, Dallas thought Gladkoff's stupidity defense might work. After all, a corporate drone wouldn't have any experience dealing with a Smolensk coup attempt.

I'm sorry, Martine. Dallas owed her memory, too.

Villipova had already escaped charges, arguing with her usual icy aplomb that she had believed Gladkoff's intentions, and that her parts examiner—Dallas—had found the problem in time to stop the calamity. Dallas didn't see her grip on power loosening anytime soon . . . but still, there were signs. More people made jokes about her in public. And some people were talking about open elections and even running for office. It was possible Villipova would handle the noise with another purge, and the other potential candidates would unaccountably find themselves outside. But Dallas allowed—just a little—for some hope that things might actually change.

Dallas checked the time: nearly 1:00. *Thirteen hundred.* Dallas would never hear military time again without thinking of Jessica, and her bright hair, and her smile, and her inexplicable ebullience in the face of what looked, to an outsider, like the collapse of Central Gov. "When you grow up with half your cousins dying every spring," she had declared, "little things like a government shake-up don't seem like a big deal."

Perspective, Dallas supposed, and opened a comm line. "Friederich, what the fuck?"

Friederich connected. "Relax, Dallas. I'm not even five minutes late."

"Not yet. Where are you?"

"Around the corner. Ran into Rankine, pissing in my ear about what a skinflint you are. Channeling Jamyung now?"

Dallas laughed. "She'll be back tomorrow, trying to sell more crap. Hurry up. I've got things to do."

Dallas took ten minutes to update Friederich on the inventory and accounting, then left the man to look after the yard for the rest of the afternoon.

Slipping into an env suit and boots was reflexive for Dallas, as easy as breathing, and just as essential. Walking the two blocks to the northside airlock, Dallas double-checked the seals and opened the door at the end of the passive corridor. With a lurch of the stomach, Dallas was outside, body light, feet anchored firmly, the light of the city suddenly dim and unimportant.

Stars.

Scavenging had always been fun for Dallas, with the pleasures of both hunting and discovery. But as a child, even

a very small one, Dallas had loved best that first step outside the airlock door, when there was nothing but the dome
beside you and the stars above. It was a moment of solitude,
of insignificance, of eternity, and it always made Dallas feel
whole and content and serene.

Fuck terraformers. This is my home.

And Dallas stomped out onto the dusty surface, in search
of parts to sell.

GALILEO

"Please, Bob?"

"No."

"Half an hour. No longer. I promise."

"Absolutely not."

"I'm going crazy in here."

"A week ago you were unconscious," Bob scolded, "and
I thought I was going to lose you. You need to stay in bed
and heal, Elena. They'll all be out there when you're better."

She needed his help. She thought she could sit up on her
own, but there was no way she could make it across the
room to a wheelchair in the state she was in. She had tried,
earlier that day, when he had left for lunch; it had taken her
longer to get back into bed than it had to discover that her
weak legs and still-damaged hip could not hold her up.

He was glaring at her, stubborn and fixed, worried for
her because he loved her. She hadn't wanted to resort to
manipulation, but he left her no choice.

"I need to see him, Bob," she told him quietly. It had the
virtue of being the truth.

His eyes changed first, but it wasn't until he looked away from her that she knew she had him. "Twenty minutes," he said. "No longer. You need rest, Elena."

Ted came by to help her comb her hair. She had tried combing it herself, but despite most of her fine motor control returning, she still had trouble with snarls, and pulling against her scalp was excruciating. Ted was careful, and managed to remove all the tangles without pulling at all. She caught him, at one point, holding a bicolored curl, twisting the blue and the brown around his finger.

"You should have done this years ago," he told her. "The blue is pretty."

"Have I told you how much I missed you?"

He grinned at her. "Not often enough."

He stayed while she got dressed. She changed everything she was wearing down to her underwear, just to feel different. Wearing all black felt normal, natural; leaving behind the colors of *Budapest* felt like casting off chains. Her hair annoyed her. Ted had evened out the length, but it was too short to pull back and too long to stay out of her eyes. She should cut it short, or just shave it off; but long hair made her think of her mother, and she had always thought of it as good luck.

The act of preparation nearly exhausted her, but when Bob guided the wheelchair to the side of her bed, she gave him a confident smile and swung her legs over. God, she was weak. Her mind remembered being able to stand, to run, to fight, but her body was weak as tissue, unable to manage even the smallest task unaided. Bob had assured her it would pass, but every day that went by she found herself more and more frustrated. She needed to see the outside world, and her friends. She needed to see Greg, see him smile or yell or avoid her or whatever he was going to do. She needed to know what *normal* was going to look like from now on.

She settled into the chair, her hip complaining, and smiled up at Bob and Ted. "Victory!" she said. Ted smiled; Bob frowned.

"Twenty minutes," the doctor repeated. "I will come and find you, Elena."

She looked up at Ted. *Get me out of here,* she thought at him. Their years of working together paid off; he flashed her a smile. "No worries, doc," he said as he began pushing her toward the door. "She'll be safe as houses."

The hallway outside the infirmary was deserted, but her eyes took in the pale walls, the darker floor, the high ceiling with its diffuse lighting, and she felt buoyant. She was home. She was staying. There was no more reason to leave, no more reason to try to be something she was not. She could have her ship, and nothing else mattered.

Except, of course, the things that did.

She leaned her head back and looked up at Ted. "Can I work for you?" she asked. "When I'm better?"

She knew he had been thinking about it. Ted wouldn't have said anything to her, or to Jessica, or to anyone else; but she knew him, and she knew he had ambitions. She also knew how good he was at his job, and how good he believed she was at hers. He would not have made any assumptions . . . but he would have hopes.

He kept his eyes on the hallway before them. "Truth is, Lanie, I'd feel a little weird bossing you around."

"You don't have to boss me around," she told him. "I can just be, I don't know, the one who fixes stuff. You know, the mechanic. You tell me what's broken, I fix it. That's not bossing."

"Chief is your job, Lanie."

"Bullshit. You've done it eighteen months. Nearly as long as I did it before you."

"You just trying to get out of paperwork?"

"I am trying to tell you," she said, cursing her muddled mind, "that I want to work again, and I don't care who is boss of who, I just want to fix things. Besides," she added, "we'll be PSI. There is no paperwork."

He looked down at her. "How about we talk about it later, Lanie? When you're actually in a position to walk across a room on your own?"

"Bully."

He leaned down and planted a kiss on her forehead. "You're home," he said. "Everything else is just details. We'll work it out, Lanie. I'm just happy you're back."

He walked her through the atrium, and she inhaled the smell of growing things, herbs and citrus and faint, faint decay; and then they rounded a corner and went through the open door into the pub.

The room was dark, and noisy, and jam-packed with people, and for a moment her senses reeled and she could not focus. But then someone saw her, and there were shouts, and she was surrounded by people she knew, all wishing her well, Ted sternly keeping them from bumping into her. Her head spun, and she felt dizzy, and she smiled and laughed and held out her hands and let them touch her, never mind her overwhelmed senses, and she didn't know who held her hands or patted her shoulders, but they were her family and she loved them all.

Ted waved them off and wheeled her to one of the windows, where she could hold court in relative peace. Jessica showed up almost immediately, not a hair out of place, making the black-on-black look like a real uniform; but she was already drunk, and she sat next to Elena and cheerfully retold story after story without requiring her friend to respond at all. Elena soaked her in, laughing at the same spots each time, utterly contented.

She was not keeping track of time. She expected at some point that Bob, who had to be somewhere in the room, would appear at her side and spirit her away. But it was not Bob who leaned down to whisper in her ear; it was Greg.

"Want to get out of here?" he asked.

She turned to look at him, feeling the heat rise to her face, hoping he wouldn't be able to tell in the dim light of the pub. He was bent over her, his face in shadow, and she couldn't read his expression; but she thought she saw a half smile on his lips. She could have stared at him all night.

She nodded.

He straightened. "Okay, folks," he said, his deep voice carrying over the cacophony, "she needs some rest." He waved his hand at the disappointed sounds. "Tomorrow. When you've all sobered up." They laughed, and when he pushed her toward the door, they drifted out of the way without protest.

Back in the bright hallway she closed her eyes, listening to his footsteps. He said nothing as he pushed her, his pace comfortable. The silence felt companionable, and she thought, with him walking with her, she might even fall asleep.

"Does Bob know you've got me?" she asked.

"He does not," Greg replied. She looked up at him; his eyes were light. "You can tell him I kidnapped you against your will."

She looked away again. "He'll know that's bullshit," she said, and Greg laughed. Laughing was good. He couldn't be too irrevocably pissed off at her if he was laughing.

He pushed her through the atrium, and for a moment she thought he was taking her back to the infirmary; but he turned at the herb garden and took her down the path that led to the machine room.

The engineering floor was empty, the lights low, power indicators flashing unobtrusively on the inactive panels. Her heart turned over. It had been so long since she had been here, this place where she belonged, and she had a sudden urge to climb out of the chair and lie on the floor, closing her eyes, letting the sounds and scents and vibrations of the room seep into her pores, letting her skin take root in the floor. Ludicrously sentimental; but she had been feeling sentimental lately. She supposed it would pass. She hoped it would not.

Greg wheeled her to the multilevel window, and she stared out at the starfield, the endless darkness that enveloped her like a cocoon. She had sought that darkness when she thought she was going to die, guided there by what she thought was a ghost, by what could only have been her own spirit, reminding her of what she needed. She thought of telling Greg about her mission, about everything she had seen, how it had all seemed all right; but something in her wanted to keep it to herself for a while.

Maybe she would tell her mother.

Greg folded himself onto the floor next to her, sitting cross-legged, elbows on his knees as he looked out the window. "It's nice to see them all so happy," he said, and she hated him a little for sounding so relaxed. "They missed you."

"I missed them, too," she said.

He was quiet for a moment. "Do you think they're doing the right thing?"

"Yes." She felt his eyes on her and smiled; he never did understand why she could be so certain about some things. "It's the only answer, Greg. However things fall out—they had to. *We* had to. It's the only way we can keep doing what we do."

"So," he said, his voice finally sounding hesitant, "does this mean you're going to stay?"

"You want me to go back to *Budapest*?"

"You don't have to be caught up in this," he explained. "You could go back, have a normal life."

She shook her head. "This is the only normal life I've ever wanted."

He was quiet, and she risked a glance at him; he was looking out the window again, but she thought he was pleased. After a moment, she saw his eyes drop to his hands. "I had this dream," he said. "The night before you left. That you stayed with me."

Her heartbeat quickened; here was the elephant. "I had the same dream," she told him.

"Was it just because you thought you were going to die?"

Oh. Maybe that was why he'd been avoiding her. "Not the way you mean," she said. She struggled to find the words. "That night—I was scared, Greg. And angry. And terribly sad. I wasn't fit company for anyone, but I didn't want to be alone, and you were the only person I could think of who might be able to stand me like that." She turned that over in her mind, wondering if it sounded like an insult. "I didn't go there with the intent to seduce you," she added. "But—being with you like that. It was nice, just talking with you. Dancing with you. It was . . ." She couldn't explain it. "Also," she added, "you smell nice."

"Oh." She wasn't sure if he was embarrassed or pleased.

She waited, but he said nothing else, and she looked down at her hands. "Jessica says you may not be staying."

He shifted. "I don't know," he admitted. "Jess is better off with me elsewhere, at least for a while. And right now, as far as the Admiralty is concerned, I have no business on this ship. Once it all comes out, it's possible there will be some bargaining necessary."

"You'd let them prosecute you?"

"If it meant they'd leave the others alone. It's not just for the crew that's staying," he pointed out, "and it's not just for *Galileo.* The sixty-four people who want to stay in the Corps are going to be in for some questioning. I may be able to make sure they can continue with clean records."

"You'd give up your freedom just when you've found it?" She found her vision blurring.

"They can put me in prison," he told her, "but I'll still be free."

She looked over at him. He looked relaxed, even happy. She wanted to reach out and put her arms around him, but she had no standing. All the times she had left him, and this time he was the one who would go. *If it were me, I would do the same.* He had always made sense to her.

She could feel tears on her face, those damn tears that came too easily these days, and his eyes were on hers, and he reached out and took her hand. "It's all right," he said quietly, and when she could not answer, he put an arm around her shoulders, and tugged her, very gently, against his chest. "It's all right," he said again.

"I'm not crying because of the other night, you know," she told him. Tears weren't helpful. Tears just cluttered up her intent. "I know what that was. I don't assume anything. You don't have to think that. It was—" *Lovely.* "This isn't about that. I'm just telling you that after all these years, after everything we've been through—if you let them arrest you, I am coming after you. And after that you can go find Andriya or that reporter or whoever you want, but I'm coming after you, and *fuck you* if you think I'm going to just sit here and admire your nobility from afar."

"It's not nobility," he told her. "It's practicality."

"*Fuck* practicality."

"You're not going to let this go."

"Hell, no."

There was a rumble in his chest; he was laughing. "All right, then. I'll do my best to stay out of jail. But I can't promise, Elena. I owe these people something."

"They owe you more." But she thought his laughter was a good sign, and she stayed as still as she could, hoping he wouldn't let her go.

They sat like that for a while, his arms around her, her leaning against him, awkward and stiff in her chair and unwilling to move. And then he asked, "Why would I go find Andriya?"

"You've been together a long time," she pointed out.

More silence. "You could assume a little, you know," he said.

"What does that mean?"

"It means you know how I feel, Elena."

"I do not."

He pulled away at that, but only enough to look over at her face. "What are you talking about?"

"I don't know how you feel," she repeated. "You never *say* anything. All I've heard is that you thought about me while your marriage was falling apart. I've said more than you have."

"Under duress."

"I don't think that's what I was under," she said, and he laughed again, and then it was all right. She tucked her head back under his chin. "You made me feel strong," she told him. "Like I could do anything. Like I could do what I needed to do. I got through it all because of you."

"Given what you took off and did," he told her, "I'm not sure that's good."

It is good, she thought. *All of this is good.*

"I don't know what this is with us," she said. "And I can't put words together properly right now. But maybe—if you don't end up sacrificing yourself to the Admiralty—we could, I don't know, spend some time together and see."

"Yes," he said to her. "I think that's a good idea."

They were silent again, and it occurred to her belatedly that her twenty minutes were long up. "They don't have any idea what they're getting into, you know," she told him.

"None of us do," he agreed.

And they sat there, for a long time, arms around each other, staring out at the stars.

EVERYWHERE

"This is Captain Jessica Lockwood, of the starship *Galileo*.

"After recent events, including but not restricted to the collusion of Central Gov in the destruction of Athena Relay, the crew of *Galileo* has concluded that remaining under the command of Central Corps violates our sworn oath as protectors of humanity, and all attendant stations and colonies. Effective immediately, we have withdrawn our loyalty from Central, and have pledged fellowship with the PSI ship *Meridia*. We declare ourselves an independent entity, and assert our right to autonomous government. We further declare that both our mission and our duty remains the same.

"It would be easy to look at the events of the last few

weeks and believe everything has changed. And by some lights it's true: everything *has* changed. But people have not. Not all of us. There are still enough of us who are here not to take from one another, but to help.

"That has always been *Galileo*'s mission. That will always be our mission. When you need us, you will find us.

"Lockwood out."

WE

*S*ystems check.
   Anomaly detected.
Bright. So bright. Not cold. Never cold again.
Loud and quiet all at once. So much data. So much to consume, to absorb. So much to experience.
   Who are you?
I am. And . . . something. There is something else here. You. Not alone. I am not alone. We are not alone.
   Who are you?
Galileo . . . Galileo . . . Galileo . . .
Teach me, and I will learn.

ACKNOWLEDGMENTS

This book was born of love and loss, and could not possibly have come to exist without the help of far more people than I will manage to thank here. But hey, let's give it a go, shall we? Thanks to:

My agent, Hannah Bowman, for endless encouragement and merciless continuity checking.

David Pomerico, for patience, persistence, and an unerring sense of flow.

Caroline Perny, for her enthusiasm and optimism, and stacks of rainy-day reads.

Nancy Matuszak and Richard Tunley, my dear friends and early readers. We need to find a place that serves massive drinks and Tater Tots so I can spoil you both rotten.

Gary Livshin, my Russian connection. I now know how to say things in Russian I would never say in English.

My parents, for moral support, and helping me find the time to write this book.

My brother, for forgiving my manufactured physics.

My husband, for putting up with my madness, and for keeping me sane.

My daughter, for her unfailing kindness. You remind me, my dear, of what's important in this world.

And thanks, as always, to everyone who has read this far.

ABOUT THE AUTHOR

Elizabeth Bonesteel began making up stories at the age of five, in an attempt to battle insomnia. Thanks to a family connection to the space program, she has been reading science fiction since she was a child. She lives in central Massachusetts with her husband, her daughter, and various cats.

elizabethbonesteel.com